DEADLY FEAR

CYNTHIA EDEN

FOREVER

NEW YORK   BOSTON

Copyright © 2010 by Cindy Roussos
Excerpt from *Deadly Heat* copyright © 2010 by Cindy Roussos
All rights reserved. Except as permitted under the U.S. Copyright Act of 1976, no part of this publication may be reproduced, distributed, or transmitted in any form or by any means, or stored in a database or retrieval system, without the prior written permission of the publisher.

Cover design by Claire Brown
Cover photograph by George Kerriga
Book design by Giorgetta Bell McRee

Forever
Hachette Book Group
237 Park Avenue
New York, NY 10017
Visit our website at www.HachetteBookGroup.com.

Forever is an imprint of Grand Central Publishing.
The Forever name and logo is a trademark of Hachette Book Group, Inc.

Printed in the United States of America

First Printing: August 2010

10 9 8 7 6 5 4 3 2 1

*A special thanks to Alex—my fantastic editor.
Thanks for your insight!*

*For Dr. Laura . . . thanks for leading me
into the minds of monsters.*

*For Joan . . . Yes, you were right.
You were right, and you're an awesome friend.*

*For Saundra . . . Another fabulous friend.
You're always an inspiration to me.*

And, for my mom . . . I love you.

DEADLY
FEAR

Prologue

Is the girl still alive?" The question came from Special Agent Jonas McKall.

The guy had been with the unit for just over two years, tracking killers for a hell of a lot longer—and the man really should have known better.

Keith Hyde grunted and reached for his weapon. "It's day four. You know the perp's MO. Two days of fun and games." *Sick, twisted fuck.*

Would the girl still be alive? Doubtful. Five other bodies had already been found. Young girls, in their teens, slaughtered.

Katherine Daniels had disappeared from her bus stop on Monday. They'd finally tracked the killer to his hole today, but the knot in Hyde's gut told him they were too late.

Always too late.

"Go in slow," he ordered, aware of the sweat trickling down his back. His team was trained for this shit, but he gave the warning anyway. The guy inside that cabin—he was smart. He'd had the cops and the Bureau chasing shadows for the last year.

While he sliced his girls apart.

"If Katherine's alive, we can't take the chance of spooking him." Or of giving him the opportunity to finish her off.

The three agents around him gave quick nods.

"Sir, but what about—" Quiet, nasally, the voice grated in Hyde's ears.

But he halted and turned to face the profiler.

"What about Mary Jane Hill?"

The third girl who'd gone missing.

The profiler's gaze darted to the wooden cabin. "Her body wasn't found. . . ."

Hyde's back teeth locked. "Because the bastard dumped her in the woods, and the animals got to her first." They'd found the other bodies, ravaged and torn, just before the beasts had.

But not Mary Jane.

Hyde figured they'd never find that poor girl.

"But what if—"

"She's been gone for over three months, Brown. She's dead." The freak never broke his two-day rule.

The profiler should *know* that.

But, Brown, with his perfectly pressed suit and too-thick glasses, was a replacement. He'd signed on with the team just days before they'd gotten one lucky-ass lead.

The last profiler, Jasper Peters, had bailed on the case. Jasper had come to him with red cheeks and shaking hands. *I can't do this shit anymore. Can't stop the monsters—they'll never be stopped.*

"Just stay back," Hyde growled. Crickets chirped in

the distance and a faint light glowed from within the cabin. "*Stay back.*"

He lifted his hand. Motioned to the team.

And prepared to enter Hell.

Hyde picked the lock on the door—snuck in as softly as a whisper. As soon as he stepped inside, the stench slapped him in the face. Blood and decay. Rancid and thick in the air.

The girl wouldn't be found alive.

He swallowed the bile that rose in his throat and held his weapon steady. Somewhere in this pit, the killer hid.

They'd mapped the area. Even managed to find the builder who'd erected the cabin over twenty years before. There was a basement. A small, perfect-for-killing room down below.

That was where the man who'd been dubbed "Romeo" waited.

Hyde's heart slammed against his chest when he saw the metal door. Thick, with a padlock dangling loosely from a chain.

Keeps them locked in when he's gone. No way to escape.

But the lock was open now because the bastard was having his playtime below.

No more.

Hyde reached for the door, yanked back the handle.

The hard squeak of the metal grated in his ears like a scream.

Fuck.

Hyde flew through the doorway.

Still alive?

Doubtful. But maybe, maybe...

His boots pounded down the steps. Lights flickered overhead. Fluorescent bulbs that revealed, then concealed.

He tripped on the last step, but caught himself and shouted, "FBI! You need to—"

Laughter. Rich and dark. Shadows moved, and a man stepped forward. Young, in his mid-twenties, good-looking.

The profiler had been right about that.

He doesn't force them to come with him. He seduces them. Offers them a temptation they can't resist.

Romeo, tempting the girls to walk on the wild side.

"Put your hands up, asshole! Let me see 'em!" The other agents pounded down the stairs, then fanned the room.

Romeo just smiled, flashing a dimple. His hands were behind his back. A long white apron, stained red, covered his chest and legs. "Too late," he whispered.

And he stepped forward.

Hyde shook his head. "I will fucking put a bullet in your heart."

Another step. "Then you'll never find my sweet Kat. ..."

Like they hadn't found Mary Jane.

Hyde's finger tensed around the trigger. "And you'll never slice another girl. I'll be a happy man."

The smile faded as the lights flickered once more. "Playing the tough guy, Hyde?"

So the killer knew his name. Seeing as how his face had been splashed across the news for the last few months, that wasn't a real big surprise.

"Clear." From Jonas. "She's not here."

For just a moment, Hyde looked away from Romeo. His gaze flickered to the chains on the walls. The tray of surgical instruments.

Twisted ass playroom. But no girl.

"Cuff him." A snarl, barely human, because he wanted to fire. Wanted an excuse. Time to put the rabid animal out of his misery.

Jonas reached for his cuffs.

Romeo launched forward, his arms flying from behind his back as he pulled out a gun, one the perp had hidden under the back of his shirt.

My perfect excuse. A split-second thought that filled Hyde's mind as he squeezed the trigger—

"*No!*" A woman's scream, loud and wrenching.

He wavered. For one reckless moment, his attention diverted, and he searched for the victim.

Romeo laughed and fired just as a woman—no, a girl—slammed her body into the killer, and they crashed onto the floor.

A flash of a knife.

The blade sank deep into flesh.

Laughter.

Screams.

Hyde shook his head and surged forward. He grabbed the girl, hauling her back while his agents swarmed. She fought him, twisting, the knife shaking in her small fist.

Where the hell had she come from?

"It's all right," he murmured, trying to be soothing when he wasn't the soothing sort. "He's not going to hurt you anymore."

Romeo threw back his head. Two officers were on him. "I've *never* hurt her. I love her. She's mine!"

Hyde's right shoulder throbbed like a bitch. The bullet had caught him, but was luckily just a graze.

The girl lunged again. Hyde struggled, then held her tight, ignoring the pain. "Easy, Katherine. It's over." He bared his teeth at Romeo. "Get him the hell out of here."

Her body shook against his as Romeo was hauled away. Hyde's gaze darted to the left. A door had swung open. Hell, it looked like a damn piece of the *wall* had swung open. A closet waited inside. No, the space was not even big enough for a closet. Barely two feet.

He'd been keeping the girl in there?

"Let's go outside, Katherine." Because the team needed to come in and sweep that stinking pit from top to bottom.

Her fingers tightened on the knife.

"Uh, I'm gonna need you to drop the weapon." He didn't want to hurt her. She'd been hurt more than enough.

One minute. Two.

Very slowly, her fingers uncurled, and the knife hit the floor with a clatter.

"Good girl."

She flinched at that.

Her dark hair was a tangle around her face. A long black shirt covered her chest, and loose sweat pants seemed to swallow her legs.

Alive. Talk about a fucking miracle. Jonas would never let him hear the end of this one.

Hyde led her to the stairs, waiting silently when she faltered as she stared up at the door.

"Locked." The whisper was hoarse.

He blinked, and a fist squeezed his heart. "Not this time, baby."

She gave a nod and then crept up the stairs. One mincing step at a time.

For just a second, she hesitated near the door. Then she lifted her hands and touched the cold metal with fingers that shook.

He shoved open the door and pushed her gently over the threshold. "I'm gonna get you home, Katherine. Your parents are gonna be so glad—"

She froze beside him. The light shone bright and steady in this part of the cabin. She tilted back her head, and the bluest eyes he'd ever seen stared up at him.

Romeo had particular tastes. Girls between fifteen and eighteen. Brunettes, all with blue eyes.

The girl stared at him a moment, then she shook her head.

"It's okay, you're safe," he told her.

"I—I'm not Katherine." Same hoarse whisper. Those blue eyes, eerie in their intensity, held his.

Dirt covered her face. Dirt and grime and God knew what else. But as Hyde gazed at her, recognition kicked into place.

And he knew he was staring straight at—

A fucking miracle. An angel who'd survived hell.

CHAPTER *One*

Sixteen years later

*S*top! *FBI!*" But, of course, the words didn't make the perp slow down. No, they just made the punk in the black ski mask run faster—and Agent Luke Dante ground his back teeth as he pumped his legs and shoved through the crowd.

A woman screamed. Another one hit *him* with her purse.

Christ. So much for being the good guy.

He couldn't aim a weapon in this crowd. Too many people on the street. Too many kids—

Luke jumped over a boy on a bike and swore when he caught his ankle on the handlebars.

Fuck. This was so not his day.

All he'd wanted was a cup of coffee before hitting the office. Just—A—Cup—Of—Coffee.

He'd gotten an armed robbery instead.

The perp ran into traffic—*they always did that*. Horns blared as brakes squealed. Luke shook his head. Traffic was stopped now so he lunged after the guy.

Close, so close—he could hear the perp's ragged breaths—

Luke launched forward, grabbed the idiot, and they slammed onto the street.

Asphalt ripped away the flesh on his arm. He felt the wet flow of blood slide across his skin. The robber bucked beneath him, twisting, kicking, swearing, then turning with a gun—

Luke snapped the perp's wrist and heard the guy howl. The gun hit the pavement.

"FBI," he gritted. Drops of blood flew from Luke's wound and stained his shirt. "Man, you chose the *wrong* damn convenience store."

The scream of sirens reached his ears. Finally. In this age of cell phones, he really would have expected one of the shouting folks he'd passed on the street to have punched 911 sooner.

"Fucking bastard asshole, you let me go, you let—"

Luke shifted and pinned the perp beneath him. Glittering green eyes stared up at him from the slits in the ski mask. "Was the fifty bucks worth it, genius?" He ripped away the mask.

A kid stared back at him.

The perps just got younger every day.

Acne spotted the kid's face—his perfectly smooth face. Not even a hint of facial hair yet. The punk's blond hair was a dirty mop brushing against his round face.

Jesus, the kid still had baby fat. "What are you? Fifteen?"

"I'll fucking kill you!" Veins bulged in the kid's forehead.

Luke sighed. He knew that look. The glassy-eyed

stare. The trembling body. The kid was flying high—and wanted to keep flying—which explained the robbery.

The swirling police lights hit Luke's eyes. Doors slammed. Luke glanced up to see the cops charge at him.

"Stand up and step away!" An order given over a drawn gun.

"Easy." No sense in anyone getting trigger happy. "I'm with the FBI."

And this really was one bad morning.

Because Luke knew that before the questions were finished, he'd be late for his new assignment. Late the first day.

Hell of a way to make an impression on his new boss.

When Luke entered the J. Edgar Hoover Building two hours later, scratches covered his arms and blood stained his shirt. But he walked in with his head up and his shoulders back. This wasn't his first time in the building. Though he'd been stationed in Atlanta, he'd been to the D.C. office a handful of times for different cases. But this time, he wasn't just a visiting agent.

His palms were dry when he punched the button in the elevator. His gaze locked on the floor indicator lights. Three. Four. Five...

A soft ding, then the doors opened. A long hallway waited. Two branches at the end. One led toward the crime lab. One toward the SSD—Serial Services Division.

The division was still pretty new at the Bureau, and it was one that he knew a few dozen other agents would have killed to get in.

And they'd picked me. He'd busted his ass to get this

spot, and now that it was his—*try to pry it from my cold, dead hands*.

The weight of his gun and holster pressed against his side as he marched down the hallway, then branched to the left. *SSD*. Luke shoved open the perfectly clear glass door. Phones rang. Voices hummed. Luke took a breath and glanced around, wondering if he'd be able to sneak—

"About time, *partner*."

Luke's gaze shot to the right.

"I was beginning to think you'd bailed on me and—ah..." The guy, tall, lean, with close-cropped black hair, winced and his gray eyes narrowed. "Trouble at home, eh?" There was a hint of laughter beneath the question.

He grunted. "Armed robbery. Had to take a perp down."

"Showoff." The agent shook his head even as he extended his hand. "Trying to make the rest of us look bad on your first day? Real bad business, that..."

Luke took the hand, squeezed once, then dropped his hold. "Sorry," Luke said and cleared his throat. "Maybe next time I'll let the bad guy get away."

A smile broke the man's face. "Name's Kenton Lake. And Dante, I think it'll be...interesting having you here."

Here. The only unit in the Bureau solely dedicated to tracking and trapping serials. Rapists. Killers. Even the serial kidnappers who stalked the streets.

"I'd heard you were a bit...strong-willed when it comes to your work," Kenton said.

Yeah, and Luke could just imagine where the guy had heard that. But he was pretty sure "strong-willed" hadn't quite been the adjective used. "I believe in getting the job done."

One brow rose. "By any means necessary?"

"Damn close." He'd clashed with other agents before. So if the guy thought he was reckless for chasing down that perp, well, it wouldn't be the first time.

And it wouldn't be the last.

"We're a team here, Dante. No one-man show. Remember that, and you'll be fine."

Luke inclined his head. He wasn't about stealing glory. Just helping the victims. His eyes scanned the line of offices. "Everyone here is part of the team?"

"Part, but not the core. The core's waiting for you—" He jerked his thumb toward a closed conference room door. "Right inside."

And he got to meet them all covered in blood. Fair enough.

"Lead the way."

The smile widened. "You know, I can't decide, but I *think* I'm going to like you, Dante."

Then he turned and headed toward the conference room. Luke took a deep breath.

When he crossed the threshold into the room, the first person he saw was...

Her. *Oh, Jesus*.

Luke wasn't aware that he'd sucked in a sharp breath. He just knew his cock was twitching, and the temperature in the room had gotten very—

A snort from beside him. "Don't even think it, man. Not going to happen."

But Luke didn't take his eyes off her as he and Kenton slid into two empty chairs in the back.

The woman stood at the front of the room, her hands lightly gripping either side of a podium. Her midnight black hair teased her cheeks, the short blunt cut ending just under her slightly pointed chin. The woman's skin was smooth, perfect and pale, and her eyes—

So blue.

Monica Davenport. Already a legend in the department, and she was barely easing past thirty. One of the best profilers going. She had like, what? Three, four degrees?

And a hell of a lot of field experience. *An agent who didn't take shit.*

One who also had a reputation for being pure ice.

Pity, because from the outside, she sure was the stuff hot, wet dreams were made of.

His dreams, anyway.

Those brilliant eyes locked on him. His lips started to curl. But not even a flicker of recognition crossed her face.

Ice.

Her voice, smooth and easy, continued without so much as a hitch. "With assistance from our team, local authorities in Waylon, Virginia, apprehended the perpetrator last night, and the Midnight Strangler's latest victim, Julia Marcus, was returned *alive* to her family."

A round of applause. A whistle from the Lucy Liu lookalike up front.

"This is the ninth serial case closed by the SSD since its inception six months ago—"

"But our work is just getting started," a deep, could-be-the-voice-of-God rumble interrupted. Luke straightened. He knew that voice. Keith Hyde. Hell, the guy *was* the Serial Services Division. The group was his idea, his baby, and he'd handpicked every member of the team.

Luke had been passed over in that first hand-picking, but when Mark Lane had taken a leave of absence from the team, he'd fought and finally shoved his way inside the all but closed door. *This* was where he wanted to be. Needed to be.

The briefest hint of a smile lifted Monica's full lips as she ceded the floor to Hyde.

Hyde nodded to the assembled agents. The guy was huge, with thick shoulders and skin as dark as night. He smiled, a real smile, not like Monica's, and flashed his perfect, white teeth. "We're kicking ass, people, and I'm proud of every single one of you."

Some laughter there. Grins lightened the tense faces of some of the other agents in the room.

"But we're just gettin' started. Nine down, the fucking rest of the serials to go." Hyde's eyes zeroed in on him. "And...we've got a new member on our team. One who finally decided to show up."

Luke winced.

"Better late than never, huh, buddy?" Kenton murmured.

When Hyde's eyes narrowed, Luke shot to his feet. "Sir. Glad to be a part of the division—"

"You should be. We're the best in the business." He pointed to the lady beside him. Lucy Liu. Uh, no, she was—"This is Kim Donalds, and don't let her size fool you, she's one of the toughest agents I've ever seen."

Kim turned to face him fully. Almond shaped eyes—dark green—stared up at him, measuring him. Weighing.

A sprinkle of freckles covered her nose. Small, delicate, but—

Deadly.

He knew about Kim, too. Pretty package, one slyly concealing the perfect hunter inside.

"You've already met Kenton."

The guy saluted him.

"This is Jon Ramirez, he's an—"

"Ex-sniper." Luke gave the hard-eyed shooter a nod. "I've been doing my homework, sir." Jon Ramirez had fought like hell with the army in the Middle East, only to come home and join the Bureau.

"Then do you know me, too?" Another woman. A tall, thin redhead with wire-framed glasses. Her lips pursed as her gaze met his.

"Samantha Kennedy, computer genius extraordinaire." Yeah, he knew about her. She'd gotten her Ph.D. in computer sciences from MIT before she'd turned eighteen, and been drafted by the government within the year. She'd made a switch to the Bureau just a few months back.

Samantha flushed and dropped her gaze. "Ah...yeah. That's me."

"And you're Luke Dante..." Low, husky.

Monica.

"The bad-ass from the South who managed to bring down the Sorority Stalker all by yourself." One black brow rose. "Impressive."

Not really. He'd stumbled onto the asshole when he'd been tracking down witnesses. He'd gotten lucky— another two inches, and Carl Malone's knife would have driven into his heart, instead of just giving Luke his latest tough-guy scar.

He forced a smile. "I do what I can."

Hyde glanced between them. "So I'm guessing you also know our lead profiler, Monica Davenport."

Yeah, he did. "We've met."

Glacial blue eyes held his.

"Good." Hyde reached into his briefcase and yanked out a stack of manila files. He passed one to Luke and handed another to Monica. "You two are heading out on a plane to Jasper, Mississippi, in about…" A quick glance at the gold watch on his wrist. "Three hours." Two more folders were tossed to Kenton and Samantha. "You two are backup."

Luke's hold on the file tightened when Hyde added, "The sheriff down there thinks he's got himself a serial."

Monica cocked her head. "Does he?"

"Don't know—that's for you and Dante to figure out. The guy's got two dead bodies. Different CODs, but the sheriff thinks he's looking for the same killer."

Usually a serial used the same manner of death for his victims. Almost like performing a ritual again and again. Two different causes of death didn't seem to fit—

"Read the files," Hyde ordered. "Then get your asses on the plane." He clapped his hands once. "That's it, get back to work—*and damn good job.*"

Luke blinked and glanced down at the file. Kenton patted him on the shoulder. "Get ready to pop that cherry, man, looks like you're up—"

Luke cut him off, firing out, "Thought we were working together, *partner.*"

A wide grin. His dad would have called it a shit-eating grin. "Ah, man, that was just bullshit. Teams change here every week. You trust us all, or you don't trust anyone."

Good to know.

Kenton leaned toward him. "Good luck with Ice. You're going to need it."

Ice.

Monica shoved the file into her bag and walked toward him. The room had emptied, fast. Other than Kenton, he and Monica were the only agents left.

"You screw up, she'll eat you alive." Another slap on his shoulder. "Have fun down South."

He'd just come from the South. Hot as hell weather. Humidity that killed. And southern drawls that he loved.

Drawls like the one that whispered just beneath Monica's words.

Monica brushed by him, not even saying a word.

Well, damn. So much for a big, warm welcome.

He kinda would have expected a bit more from the woman who'd once given him the best sex of his life.

Ice… his ass.

Shit but she had bad luck.

Monica sucked in a deep breath. Then another one. And another. Her heart thudded against her ribs.

Here. Of all the divisions and teams in the Bureau, Luke Dante had come—

"What do you think of the hot guy?"

Her eyes snapped closed. Samantha.

"Did you *see* him?"

It would have been kind of hard not to see him, considering Luke had been *in* the meeting with them. Her lashes lifted.

A long sigh from Samantha, then she said, "When he turned those eyes on me—and did you *see* those eyes?—I swear I felt my skin burn."

Kicking with her right foot, Monica swiveled her chair away from the window and turned to face the agent. "May I help you with something, Sam?" She let more than a hint of impatience slip into her voice. She didn't have time to listen to Sam moon over Dante. She sounded bitchy. So what?

Being a cold bitch let her avoid conversations like this one. Usually.

This wasn't Gossip High. This was the FBI, for God's sake. But Samantha, who'd just celebrated her twenty-third birthday, had a hard time respecting boundaries.

Samantha's eyes widened behind her glasses.

Kid genius. Super smart, but not too socially savvy.

"Uh...I—I...was just..."

Great. Now Monica felt like she'd kicked a puppy. One with really big brown eyes.

"Hyde wanted you to have this."

Another file.

Monica reached for the file. "Thanks, Samantha." *Apologize?* She probably should, but the words stuck in her throat.

For someone who was supposed to be so adept at figuring people out, she pretty much sucked at the social scene, too.

Samantha whirled around and hurried for the door.

"Sam—"

She froze.

"Thanks for the file," Monica said softly.

A curt nod.

The door clicked closed behind the other woman. Didn't slam, just...closed.

Monica shook her head. Oh, yes, she knew how to make friends fast. It had always been a strength for her.

She glanced at the file, flipped it open—

And saw the ravaged body of a woman.

Blood and death—now *that* was what she understood.

Hyde stopped Monica just as she was leaving the office. His dark eyes were hooded as he stared at her. "You okay with this case?"

They were in the hallway, just beside her door. She glanced to the left, then the right, making sure they wouldn't be overheard. "I *told* you I didn't think bringing Dante on the team was the best plan." Oh, she'd told him more than a few times.

But Hyde shook his head. "Not talking about Dante, we need him." A long exhalation. "You work the killers, he works the victims. It's the perfect setup."

Perfect, maybe, but that didn't mean she had to like it.

"If you need me on this one, you call right away, got it?"

She nodded. Hyde was always there if she needed him. If any of the agents needed him. "I will." But she could handle the case—and Luke Dante.

CHAPTER *Two*

So...are we gonna talk about it?"

Monica froze at the deep voice. Her notes were spread in front of her, the shade on her window firmly closed—because she really hated to fly—and with only about ten minutes left on the private flight, it looked like Dante had decided to get chatty.

Great.

"I mean...we're gonna be working together, and we can't pretend the past didn't happen...."

Sure they could. She spent most of her days shoving the memories of her past away.

Carefully, Monica set down her pen. Then she lifted her gaze. Dante sat across from her, his long legs spread out, taking up too much room. He'd changed before they left, thankfully gotten rid of the blood, and now he wore loose khakis and a button-down shirt.

Over the years, she'd tried not to think about Dante. Tried to pretend the fling with him hadn't happened.

Tried and failed really, really well.

"Like what you see?" The words came out of his mouth sounding like some kind of sensual purr.

Asshole.

And, dammit, *yes*. Luke Dante was sex, he was power, and he was *temptation*.

A temptation she hadn't been able to resist when she was twenty-two. But one she *would* ignore now.

Tall, muscled, with bright emerald eyes and sun-streaked blond hair, Dante was a southern boy with charm and a dimple in his chin.

A long, thin scar marred his right cheek. She'd been there the day he got that scar. The mark didn't detract from Dante's looks. No, the scar just made him look all the more dangerous.

She stared at him, trying to be detached. A strong jaw, wide lips, slightly twisted nose—he *shouldn't* have been handsome.

But he was.

No, not handsome. Sexy.

Dammit.

Monica cleared her throat. "The past is over, Dante." They'd been over this before, when he'd made the mistake of tracking her down. *Serious mistake*. "We're professionals, we can—"

"Pretend we never had sex? Pretend we didn't nearly tear each other apart because we were so fucking hungry those nights?"

Her heart thumped hard enough to shake her chest.

He smiled at her, flashing his white teeth. "Don't know if I'm that good at pretending, *Ice*."

Her eyes narrowed. She *hated* that nickname. The

jerks she'd been in training with had tagged her with it. No one understood.

Control—control mattered. But she'd sure lost control with him.

Dante was her one mistake over the years. The one slip that had broken past the walls she'd worked so hard to erect.

Ice.

All the agents had been given names in their class.

Dante had been called Devil. The guy liked to take risks, to push boundaries. A devil who didn't care about being cautious. How were you supposed to resist the devil?

His name hadn't stuck, though. Hers had.

Monica sucked in a hard breath and deliberately relaxed her fingers. "Long time ago, Dante. And I don't deal in the past." *Wrong.* She'd spent years running from her past. "I focus on the present." As much as possible. She held his stare and knew that her face would be expressionless.

She'd practiced that. *Ice.*

So, okay, maybe she'd helped a little bit with that nickname. But being cold kept the others away, and it could be dangerous when someone got too close.

Straightening her shoulders, she said, "I'm the senior agent here, and I'm not looking to screw around." Too dangerous. "We're on a case. We work together because that's what we have to do in order to get the job done." Simple. Flat.

Dante didn't so much as blink.

"Now, are you going to have a problem with that? Because, if so, it won't be too hard to send your butt back to Atlanta." Total bullshit now. Like she had that kind of power.

Hyde wanted Dante on his team. He'd been adamant about him. He'd even overridden her objections, and the guy usually listened to her opinions about people. Not this time.

A muscle flexed along Dante's jaw. Perfectly shaven now, but she'd seen him at dawn, seen the rough stubble that—

"No problem, *ma'am*," the title was a sardonic taunt. "I can do my job just fine." A pause.

"Good."

"Can you?"

Monica ground her teeth together. "Trust me, Dante, it won't be an issue for me." *Liar, liar...*

She could still remember all too well what the man looked like naked.

And what he felt like.

She swallowed.

Leaving him before had nearly ripped her apart, but there hadn't been a choice. The man was a weakness, one she couldn't afford.

"Prepare for descent." A male voice broke over the intercom system. "Buckle your safety belts. We'll be arriving in Jasper..."

Monica caught the belt in her hands as the rest of the pilot's words washed right past her. *Snap.*

If Dante handled his first SSD case right, she'd be working with him, every day and all those nights, for a long time to come.

Shot down. Luke blew out a slow breath. He could handle it. A case waited. Victims. He could focus and get the job done.

They climbed down the small flight of stairs leading out of the plane. A private plane. His jaw had nearly dropped when he'd caught sight of it.

Hyde must know some serious dirt on the higher-ups in order to have swung a plane—just for the SSD. But the ride had been pretty close to torture. Trapped in the plane with her, he'd been able to do little more than drink in her scent and drink in...her.

Even after all these years, the woman was still too beautiful. Smooth, pale skin. Nose perfectly straight. Full, red lips. And those legs...

He could still feel them around him, digging into his back, clenching tight as he drove into her, as hard and as deep as he could go. *Those legs...*

On the plane ride from hell, she'd crossed them, then begun to kick one foot slowly while she made her notes. Watching that foot, then letting his gaze rise to follow the smooth lines of her legs up to the edge of her skirt...

Once, he'd licked his way up her body. Tasted the flavor of her skin. But that was the past.

In the present, the woman had frozen him out. She'd looked at him with those blank eyes and pretty much told him to go screw himself.

Hands off or your ass heads back to Atlanta.

So much for picking up where they'd left off.

Business only. He could do that.

Luke jerked his gaze off the sway of Monica's ass and caught sight of the two uniformed sheriff's deputies waiting for them.

Stick to the case. Forget the girl.

Her high heels clicked across the pavement. The two

cops shot up from their slouching positions and hurried toward her. Smart men.

"Agent Davenport?" The first guy to reach her asked, shoving out his hand. A fresh-faced kid, he looked like he'd just skated past twenty-one. He had black eyes, olive skin, and twitchy fingers.

Monica gave a firm nod. The wind on the runway caught her hair, tossing the dark locks and wrecking her smooth style. She ignored the wind and caught his hand, shaking once.

"I'm Deputy Lee Pope, and this here is Deputy Vance Monroe."

She nodded to the other deputy, then offered her hand.

He caught the slight widening of Vance's brown eyes. The second deputy was older than the other guy—tall, with ruddy cheeks, dark red hair, and a nose that looked as if it had been broken more than once. Vance seemed to hold Monica's hand a little bit longer than was really necessary.

"This is my associate." Her voice rose easily above the wind. "Special Agent Luke Dante."

He flashed a smile, and when the deputies blinked, he figured maybe he'd used too much teeth.

Reflex. He'd been trying to bite back a pissed-off snarl.

"Sheriff wants us to take you to see the bodies, ma'am." From Lee. He shifted from his right foot to the left. "You don't—you don't really think we got us a serial killer down here in Jasper?"

Luke positioned himself next to Monica. He caught a glimpse of the faint tightness around her mouth.

"I don't know what you've got, deputy." Monica stared down the guy. "I just know my boss told me to get on a plane." A little shrug. "So here I am."

Senior agent.

Hyde had given him a quiet warning before he'd left the office. "Don't screw up, hotshot. When in doubt, do whatever Davenport tells you."

They'd trained together. Studied together. Graduated together.

But from the beginning, he'd known Monica was being fast-tracked. *Everyone* had figured that out pretty much from day one.

The profiler who *knew* the killers. Whispers about her had floated through every area of Quantico. There wasn't a test the woman didn't ace. Wasn't a drill she didn't nail.

She'd graduated at the top of her class. Then been swooped up by Special Projects the next day.

He'd worked his cases over the years, busted ass and proven that he knew the victims better than pretty much any-damn-body. Yeah, he'd shown he could crack the cases, and he'd *gotten* the coveted interview with Hyde.

"True serial killers can be very rare," Monica said, voice cool and easy, with just a hint of her own southern drawl creeping through the words. "Your Sheriff Davis simply wanted us to come down and give our opinion on these cases."

"We got a twisted fuck out there." Deputy Vance shook his head and spat on the ground. "*Ma'am*, I saw what he done to that Moffett girl."

He'd seen, too. Thirty knife wounds. All on the face and chest. Pretty girl, at least in the *before* pictures. After...

Deputy Vance was right. *Twisted fuck.*

Though Luke doubted Monica would consider that a professional term.

"Her body's still at the morgue?" Luke asked. From the report he'd been given, he knew the victim had been found two days before, dumped like garbage in an abandoned house.

If the deputies hadn't raided that place, looking for a drug dealer...

"Yeah, she's still there." Lee stepped back. The sun glinted off his badge. "You folks need to get settled at the motel or you wanna—"

"Take us to the body," Monica ordered just as Luke said—

"The body."

The deputy yanked out his keys. "Sorry... but you two are gonna have to ride in the back..."

In the back of the squad car. Nice.

Monica climbed in first. Luke sucked in a breath, smelling *her*, warm woman and a hint of that light perfume she'd always worn, and he tried his level best not to touch the woman as he crowded in beside her.

His thigh brushed hers. *Focus.* He cleared his throat and managed to say, "The second body—I didn't see much about that victim in my files." He leaned toward the gray cage that separated him from the uniforms. *The better to get away from Monica's soft flesh.*

The engine kicked to life, and the car shot forward.

Vance, buckled in the passenger seat and with the radio at his mouth, glanced back at him. "That's cause there wasn't much left of Sally to see."

• • •

Morgues sucked. Luke hated 'em, always had.

And the dead—they were *everywhere*. Hell, he'd joined the Bureau to save lives. Not to sit with the dead.

But Monica, she sauntered around the room, those heels tapping, staring at the dead woman from every angle, her bright eyes narrowed and intense—and not the least bit hesitant as she fired question after question at the ME.

"Time of death?"

"What was the killing wound?"

"Any drugs in her system?"

"These marks on her face...that look like a pattern to you?"

Her white-gloved fingers pointed right above the woman's left cheek.

The ME, Doctor Charles Cotton, was a balding man with some of the palest skin Luke had ever seen. Cotton eyed her with a worried stare as she circled the table like a vulture coming to pick apart her prey. The two deputies were there, huddled at the back of the room. Lee kept glancing at the floor, and not the body, and old Vance had his lips pressed so tightly together Luke thought the guy might draw blood soon.

Not morgue guys. He didn't blame 'em, not one bit.

Luke swallowed and tried to ignore the scent of death that shoved up his nostrils.

"So our killer took his time and did all of this..." Monica motioned to the criss-cross of wounds on Patricia "Patty" Moffett's face and chest, "before he decided to kill her."

A prick who liked to play.

"That's what my report says." Cotton crossed his thick

arms over his chest. The guy's half-eaten pizza sat on a table behind him.

The guy *ate* in here with the bodies? Jesus.

Monica glanced over at Luke.

Ah, his cue. Luke took a step toward the body. The stiffs *really* weren't his specialty, and he hadn't thought they were Monica's either.

The killers—those guys were all *hers*.

But if one thing had been drilled into him in those profile classes at the Academy, it was that even dead victims could talk. You just had to know how to hear them.

He glanced at Patty's wrists. Saw the purple circles.

Restraints.

Luke stalked to the end of the table and lifted the sheet. The same circles mottled her ankles.

"No drugs." At least not when the slicing started. You didn't restrain someone who was out cold. "She was awake and aware while the asshole carved her up," he said, fury boiling through him. The woman had been small, petite, and she'd just turned twenty-nine.

Hell of a way to die.

"The wounds on her face are so precise," Monica whispered.

He heard the shuffle of feet behind him. A look over his shoulder showed the deputies craning their necks and inching closer.

"No hesitation." Monica inhaled sharply. "Pleasure cuts."

The ME's jaw dropped and so did both of his chins. "*What?*"

Luke nodded because he knew exactly what she

meant. Cuts to make the vic suffer and to give the perp his sick thrill.

The door of the morgue shoved open.

"Pope, Monroe—get your asses back out on the street!" Luke turned at the snarl and saw the sheriff, his uniform perfectly pressed, his hands balled into fists on his hips. "Billy Joe is drunk down at Taylor's again, and Ron needs backup."

The two deputies shot to attention. "*Sir!*"

"Now!"

They flew past him.

When the door slammed behind them, the sheriff marched forward and faced Luke. "You here to tell me what the hell is goin' on in my county?"

They were there to try.

"Guessing you're Dante," the sheriff muttered. The sun had tanned his skin a dark brown. Lines cracked the planes of his face and gray dotted the black hair near his temples. "And you..." His gray eyes drifted to Monica. "You must be Davenport."

Her head inclined toward him. "Sheriff." Monica's cool-as-you-please voice. A brief pause, then, "We're going to need to see the other body."

But the sheriff, Luke remembered his name was Hank Davis, shook his head. "Not gonna happen. Sally Jenkins was buried yesterday."

Luke clenched his back teeth. Exhuming bodies was a *bitch*. Especially in these small-ass southern towns. Folks didn't like it when their dead were jerked back out of the earth.

Not that he blamed them.

Monica's eyes narrowed, and she stepped away from

the slab. "She's been buried? You knew the FBI was coming; you're the one who called us! The body shouldn't have been released—"

"Wasn't a body to release." His jaw flexed. "Just pieces of little Sally..."

Emotion there, lurking in the eyes and in the voice.

The guy had known the victim.

"You didn't send a lot of information about Sally's death to our office," Luke said, trying to choose his words carefully now that he knew the connection was there for the sheriff. "I've got to tell you, I'm confused as hell. Why would you figure a woman who'd been stabbed to death..." *Pleasure cuts.* "And a woman who was killed in a car accident were linked?"

The sheriff and the ME shared a hard glance. Then Davis looked back over his shoulder, as if checking to make sure neither of the deputies had snuck back in to eavesdrop. "Didn't send the info, but I told Hyde." Davis's jaw flexed. "Told him, and he understood. *He sent you* because he understood."

Cotton shuffled over to a filing cabinet. The drawer groaned when he pulled it open. "I think you two should see these."

Luke grabbed the file from him and tried to keep his face blank as he flipped through the pictures.

Shit.

Wreckage. Twisted metal.

Pieces. Not of the car. Of...her. The wreck had torn her apart.

Monica eased beside him. Luke heard the hard breath she sucked in when she glimpsed Sally.

He studied the photos, examining and—"What the hell?"

Monica's fingers lifted and clamped around his shoulder.

"Guess you see why I was worried about Sally's death." A hard, biting blast from the sheriff. "Not every day you see an accident victim who was tied to the steering wheel."

No, not every day.

Christ. One hand and wrist were still attached to the wheel, hanging by the thick, knotted ropes.

"We found marks on the bumper—someone pushed Sally, hard and fast. That somebody drove her right into that ravine."

And Sally had been helpless.

But...

But the crimes were too different. With Sally, maybe someone had wanted to off her and claim insurance money that would have come from her "accident." Maybe the killer had thought the car would blow up on impact, and the bindings on her wrists would have been destroyed. Maybe.

The stabbing, well, stabbings were personal. Intimate.

"Does Sally have a husband, a lover—someone we can talk to?" Monica asked.

Silence.

They looked up at the Sheriff. He licked his lips. "Sally's husband Jake was killed in a car accident last year. A year to the day of Sally's death." He swallowed. "She was in the car with him, barely survived."

This time, she hadn't.

Someone had made absolutely certain of that.

"What makes you think these two crimes are related?" Luke asked. Bizarre, yeah, but to say the same perp was out there—

"In the last ten years, we've only had two murders here in Jasper." A heavy pause. "They both happened within the last two weeks." The sheriff held his stare. "You think we got two murdering SOBs all of a sudden in the area? Or just one fucked up asshole?" His right hand moved to rest on the slab, right near Patty. "I'm betting my money on one asshole."

CHAPTER *Three*

Walking through a dead woman's house, poking through her possessions and rifling through what was left of her life was not really Monica's favorite thing to do. It was a part of her job, though, a necessary one. Just one that she hated.

Every profiler knew, the first step was assimilation. She'd seen the body, seen the photos, read the autopsy reports, now she needed to work on victim profiles.

Luke flipped on the light as he stepped into Patty's bedroom. Monica hesitated, just for a moment, then followed him inside the small room.

"Just what do you think we're gonna find here?" he asked.

Hell if she knew. The locals had already been over the place. The sheriff had good instincts and good training, so she doubted the guy missed much.

But she always went to the victims' houses on her cases. The houses and then the crime scenes. That was her pattern.

She rubbed the back of her right shoulder. "We need to do a thorough scan of the house, just in case the deputies overlooked something." What that something was, well, she didn't know. Yet.

Her gaze darted to the nightstand. A framed picture. A smiling, beautiful Patty, hugging a man, a good-looking guy with glasses.

"Guess that's the boyfriend," Luke murmured.

"Kaziah Lone." He was on her list. Rule number one in these cases: Always talk to the lovers.

Especially on knife kills. An intimate crime, an intimate kill.

Luke yanked open Patty's dresser drawers, searching through the clothes. "What's your take on the case?"

Don't know. "Hyde sent us here, that means he thinks we've got a serial." Or a potential serial. Because sometimes, weeding through the cases and finding the *real* serials—that was another job he liked to give his team.

More photos lined the walls. Pictures just of Patty, always smiling. Posing with her dark hair framing her perfect face.

Hyde's report said the woman had done some modeling for an agency in New Orleans. She sure had the look for it.

He shoved the top dresser drawer closed. "But what's *your* take?"

His gaze held hers. God, Samantha had been right about his eyes. She'd never seen eyes like his before.

Never been able to forget those eyes.

Or him.

The one man who'd come too close. The one man who'd made her burn, made her desperate.

And he could do it again. One look, and the need had quickened in her. It would be so easy to go back, to let the lust ignite between them. So easy...

When they'd been on that plane and he'd been so close, his scent had surrounded her. She'd remembered the strength of his touch and she'd *wanted* him. She'd talked tough, but, dammit, she wanted him.

Luke Dante had always made her feel alive. In those precious hours with him, she'd felt wild and reckless.

No ice maiden. There'd been too much pleasure for that. Too much passion.

Temptation. He was still as dangerous as before. Monica licked her lips. The crimes. The kills. *Focus.* Now wasn't the time for any weakness.

Even if he was the one man who could make her weak. She exhaled on a long, hard breath. "The kill methods are off. They don't make sense to me." She turned away from him, worried those eyes would see too much.

Even when they'd been together, she'd always made him turn off the lights. *So he wouldn't see...*

Patty had a small desk in the corner of her bedroom. Monica pulled open the long, top drawer. Pens, paper clips, a worn romance novel.

She pushed the drawer closed—

But it stuck.

She froze.

"Monica? You got something?"

Dropping to her knees, she carefully pulled the drawer back and eased it out of the grooves that held it in place.

An envelope. It waited, smashed at the back of the desk, like it had gotten pushed up in the drawer and then caught.

Maybe when the police were searching?

Her gloved fingers reached for the envelope.

No return address. Just Patty's name, scribbled across the front.

Monica rose, turned—

And found Luke standing right in front of her.

Too close.

She didn't make the mistake of looking into his eyes. Not this time.

Monica straightened her shoulders and opened the envelope. The top had already been ripped apart, the ends tattered and loose.

A slip of paper hid inside. Carefully, she eased it out and read the same distinctive scrawl.

Pretty lady, what scares you?

An image of Patty's face flashed before her eyes. There had been so many brutal cuts and slashes on her face. Not her body, where the knife would have done more damage. But on her face.

What scares you?

Monica's gaze jerked to the photo above the bed. A big 11×14 of Patty laughing on a bridge.

"*What scares you?*" Luke read, the words a whisper.

A shiver skated down her body.

She had a good idea what would have frightened the beautiful Patty.

And, from the looks of things, the killer had known too.

Luke had just dropped onto the edge of his sagging motel room bed when the connecting door—the door he'd stared at a good three minutes after entering his room—flew open.

Unlocking it had been a very good idea.

His blood pumped, hard and fast. Screw exhaustion, he was more than ready to—

"We've got a problem."

For just an instant, her gaze dropped to his chest. He'd stripped down to his boxers, so the lady wasn't getting a full-on show. Not yet anyway.

Her mouth snapped closed then she spun around. "I didn't…think…" Her hands lifted, fell to her sides. "I should have knocked. Sorry."

But she didn't sound sorry. Not really.

And he damn sure wasn't sorry Monica had stormed into his motel room. If only she hadn't come about business.

"Get dressed." Her voice was flat. "We have to talk."

Shit.

Monica stepped forward, obviously heading back to her room. *No.*

"Stay." He bit out the command. Dammit. She glanced back at him—

Luke forced a careless grin. "Not like you haven't seen me before." The woman had touched every part of his body. With hands and mouth.

And he sure as hell didn't mind having her eyes on him.

But she shook her head. "We're working a case, I don't need to—"

His jaw clenched. *Ice.* He snatched up his jeans. Tugged them on in less than three seconds. "Didn't ask you to touch, now did I?"

Finally, her eyes met his and flashed blue fire, for just a second.

So hot, not cold. Not cold at all.

He stalked toward her. Monica turned fully to face him. Her breath came faster, her chest rising and falling too quickly.

Because she was pissed at him? Or because she felt the same hunger that he did?

The hunger that he could never fucking slake. No matter how many nights passed, no matter how many women he took.

Not enough.

Because no other woman was Monica.

"Luke..."

Ah, *Christ*, but the way she said his name. Husky, soft. Like she'd whisper it in bed, when her legs were wrapped around him, and he was driving deep and she was arching toward him, those nails of hers digging into his back.

His fingers lifted and curved around her chin. *Taste. Take.*

"You got scared," he charged, the words he'd wanted to throw at her for too long firing out. "I got too close, didn't I? And you had to fucking run."

Monica didn't flinch. Her eyes didn't waver. She just stared back at him. Cold. Like ice.

But he knew how she burned.

Christ, he needed to taste her.

The arousal had his muscles stiffening, his cock jerking. From the minute he'd walked into that meeting and seen her, he'd been fighting the lust.

The memories were too strong.

She was a temptation he didn't want to resist.

She had the prettiest pink nipples.

Luke swallowed. "We touch and you get wet for me, don't you?" He couldn't get much harder for her.

Monica's fingers rose, hovered over his shoulders.

To push him away or to pull him closer?

"Damn you, Dante," she muttered as her hands locked over him—then hauled him closer. Monica rose up on her toes and crushed her mouth to his.

Hell, yes.

The fire ripped through his blood at the touch of her mouth—just like before. Just. Like. Before.

Lips parted. Their tongues met. Took. A moan rose in her throat, the sound sexy and raw and wild.

His hands dropped to the curve of her ass. He'd always loved her ass. His fingers clenched as he pressed her hips flush against his arousal.

And, oh, yeah, no denying he was aroused. His cock was so swollen that he didn't know how long he'd last once he got her out of that torment-me skirt and—

Her nails dug into his shoulders. A sweet bite, one he'd missed.

The bed. Get to the bed.

He couldn't take his mouth from hers. Her taste had haunted him over the years. Sweet honey, rich wine. Fucking insane combination that was only...Monica.

His fingers began to hike up her skirt.

So he wouldn't last long the first time. The second, he'd make it up to her. The second, he'd have her screaming and twisting as she came against him. Around him.

The back of his hand brushed against her panties. Soft, silky panties. She'd always been so wet, so hot.

His index finger eased under the elastic. *Sweet fuck.* The woman could burn him alive with just a touch.

Her breath caught, went ragged. His hand climbed higher, pushed against creamy flesh, got ready to—

A hard knock rattled the door.

What?

Monica wrenched her mouth from his. His gaze fell to her red lips, glistening from his mouth.

He wanted to kiss her again.

But more annoying as hell rapping came again. Not from his front door.

Monica had left that thin-ass adjoining door open, and the knocking was coming from her room.

"Agent Davenport?" A loud voice demanded right before another hard knock. "It's Vance Monroe. I got them papers you wanted…"

Her eyes held his. As he watched, the fire faded, cooled.

No.

She shoved against his chest, hard, and Luke rocked back.

"Get dressed," Monica said, then she rubbed the back of her hand over her mouth.

Luke stiffened. No, she didn't just—

"The case…the deputy has something we need to see."

She swung away from him.

Luke grabbed her arm and swung her right back around to face him.

"What are you—"

He kissed her. Hard. Fast. When his head lifted, he glared at her. "Don't wipe me away again, baby."

Their eyes held.

So blue.

"Get dressed," she repeated, gritting the words. "And *let go* of my arm before I have to hurt you."

He dropped his hand.

The deputy pounded again and called for Monica.

She crossed the threshold, entering her room, and he couldn't help but say, "Baby, you weren't stopping me." No, he had the claw marks to prove she'd been enjoying the hell out of him.

And *she'd* kissed *him*. Luke didn't point that out. Yet.

She didn't even slow down at his words, but he was pretty sure he heard her mutter "asshole" beneath her breath.

He smiled and snagged his shirt off the side of the bed. Yanking it on, he slid into his shoes and slipped into her room just as the front door swung open to admit the deputy.

The guy was waving two pieces of paper, his hands shaking. "F-found it in Sally's garbage. Just like you said—"

Luke's brows shot up. Monica—and the deputy—had been busy.

"Davis has the original, but he said to bring you copies."

Monica took the material from him, a faint line forming between her brows. Then she looked back up at Luke. "We need to call Hyde."

Luke crossed to her side and took the papers from her.

The first was a grainy photo, as if from a newspaper. A picture of a smashed car, one turned into a pile of twisted metal. The headline above it read, "Local Fireman Victim of Drunk Driver, Wife Survives Crash."

The next page made a curse rise to his lips. *I know what scares you.*

"Looks like the same writing." She bit her lower lip, staring at the paper. "Same off-slanted looping on the 'l', same too-right angling on the 'w', same half-cut on the 'y' line."

That near photographic memory of hers was so handy.

"Messy scrawl," she muttered. "Like it's fast, hurried, but this guy *isn't* a disorganized killer. The writing is this way because he *wants* it to be." Her eyes lifted and met his stare. "We'll send the notes to SSD for a full handwriting analysis, but my gut says it's the same."

That hard fist in his stomach said the same thing. "We need to examine the papers." Check for fingerprints, fibers, hell, even check to see if they could figure out where the paper had come from. In this business, he'd learned to never overlook any avenue.

"We'll overnight them to Kenton. He can start the checks." Her shoulders seemed to fall, just a bit. *"This could go to hell, very fast."*

He knew what she meant. It looked like Davis had been right to call them in on the cases. Because if a serial were hunting in this sleepy southern town—and it seemed there was no denying that possibility now—more blood would flow.

The squeak of a door woke Monica hours later. She reached for her gun before her eyes even opened. Old habit.

The air conditioner had kicked off at some point and a light coating of sweat covered her body. Her tank top stuck to her as she climbed from the bed, her fingers tight around the butt of the gun.

Shadows. Silence.

She'd left the bathroom light on, another habit she'd yet to break, and the faint glow spilled onto the worn carpet.

No one's here. But her heart kicked like a racehorse.

A car door slammed. Close. *Out front.*

An engine purred to life. Headlights flashed on, shining through her lone curtain as—

Sonofabitch.

Monica ran for the door. She yanked it open and raced outside—

Just in time to see the fading taillights.

What in the hell?

"Monica?"

She whirled at the voice, her gun still ready, and found Luke slipping from his room. He froze, his arms poised in front of him. "Easy with the gun."

Her breath rushed out.

His gaze raked down as his eyebrows climbed up. "Nice outfit, Davenport."

Screw him. Shorts and a tank top were not femme fatale material, but—ah, hell, Luke could probably see her nipples through the thin top.

She lowered her weapon grudgingly. "Some jerkoff was out here, revving his engine and flashing his lights."

"Uh, huh." His hands fell to his sides. "And you thought that warranted, what, a bullet in the head?"

Ass. Monica shook her head and turned away. "Go back to bed."

"Come with me."

Temptation.

She swallowed. "My mistake earlier." She'd be woman enough to admit that. Dante—he was her weakness. One she'd have to guard against. "Won't be happening again." The case—*it* came first. The victims.

The killer.

"Get your beauty sleep, Dante." *You'll need it working with this unit.* "Six a.m. will be coming fast." She wanted to see the Moffett crime scene before she checked in with the Sheriff again and made another call to Hyde.

She pushed open her door and heard his whisper.

"Maybe it won't happen again, baby, but maybe it will...."

Maybe.

Monica hesitated, then said, "I can't give you what you want." Brutally honest. He deserved that. He'd deserved the truth before, but she'd been a coward. She'd wanted him, she'd taken him, and she'd wanted more.

But she wasn't the kind of woman who got the picket fence. A happily ever after wasn't in her future. No kids. No husband. She'd learned that long ago.

"You don't know what I want," he growled.

Goose bumps rose on her arms. His voice—that deep rumble. Her nipples tightened.

Sex. Sex was all she had to give him, and even then, she had to be so careful because Dante was a lover who took too much.

"Come with me," he said again. "Let me see if we were as good as I remember...or if I just made you a freaking fantasy in my head."

A fantasy. That's all she'd ever really been to him. He didn't know what waited under her skin. If he did...

Monica shook her head. "Get some sleep. We've got a crime scene to check tomorrow."

She entered her room. Shut the door.

Her knees started to shake.

Damn him. Couldn't the man just leave the past alone?

The killer carried his precious burden through the woods, the load banging against his back as he walked.

He hadn't planned to hunt that night, but then...he hadn't realized just who'd be coming to town so soon.

The FBI. Hell, when he'd seen those two agents, he'd almost laughed. The woman—yeah, he knew her. He'd seen her picture plenty enough in the paper.

The FBI knew about his kills. Shit, he'd been so excited by that, he'd had to go in close and see the agents' motel. Watch Monica's room.

Then he'd had to hunt. Had to prove to her that *he* was the one in charge of this game.

His prey had been so easy to find. Too fucking easy. He'd planned to take her next week, so really, moving up the hunt hadn't been hard.

He carried the bag easily, barely feeling the weight. She wasn't crying anymore. No more whimpers, no more shuddering.

Fucking finally. The drugs were working. About damn time. The bitch had been getting on his nerves.

Sucking in a sharp breath, he stopped. *This was it.* He slung her body onto the ground.

Thud.

Her eyes didn't open. *Would've thought she was dead.* But she wasn't. Hell, where would the fun be in such a quick death?

The hole waited for him. Deep and wide—perfect. He'd dug it with care, knowing this moment would come.

A smile lifted his lips. He wished he could see her face when—

No, no, he couldn't do that. Not with this one.

The last girl—oh, yeah, he'd watched her. Seen the fear choke her. The terror bulge her eyes.

Beautiful.

This time, he'd have to imagine the fear. For now, anyway.

The box was in position. He'd built it himself. Couldn't damn well buy one of the things—that would just be stupid.

He stared down at the bitch. Red hair tangled over her face and hung on her busted lip.

She'd tried to run from him. The whore hadn't realized that running wasn't an option.

His cock swelled as he stared at her. So weak. He could do anything he wanted to her. No one could stop him.

No one.

He bent and trailed his fingers over her breast. A little small for him. He liked bigger tits.

The bitch moaned, and her eyes cracked open.

Would she remember him? Didn't matter. She wouldn't live to tell anyone about him.

So he smiled and, crouching more, he eased his arms under her back. Then he lifted her, just a few inches, and tossed her into the hole.

Her body slammed into the box.

Face-first.

When the drugs wore off and she woke fully, she wouldn't even be able to turn over. He flattened his body over the earth and managed to slam the lid of the wooden box. His tongue snaked out, and he licked lips gone dry with excitement.

Too fucking easy.

The shovel waited for him, just a few feet away.

I want to see her face. Nothing like fear. No—damn—thing.

Guess he'd just have to catch a glimpse of her when the cops hauled her body out. *If* they found her.

He pushed up to his feet and went to get his shovel.

The house was really perfect for murder.

Situated near the edge of the woods, pretty much in the middle of nowhere. Accessible only by a long, twisted old road.

No neighbors close by. No one to hear the screams. No one to see the kill.

Monica had a feeling there'd been a lot of screams coming from the broken little house at the end of Pine Bend.

The windows were boarded up. Vines snaked across the house. Yellow police tape criss-crossed the sagging front porch.

"Big coincidence that the cops raided this place right after the bastard's kill," Luke said as he climbed from their rented SUV.

Yeah, big coincidence. Only Monica didn't really believe in coincidences. Never had. "The department got a tip about this place. It wasn't just a chance raid." That info had been in the notes Hyde gave her. She circled around the vehicle, her gun in its holster. Her gaze scanned the woods.

Secluded. *No eyes to see.*

A curse from Dante. "You thinking the *killer* called the cops?"

Her stare dropped to the ground. Studied the red dirt at the end of the worn road. *Tire tracks.* "I'm thinking what good is a kill if no one can appreciate it?"

Silence.

Monica's eyes narrowed as she said, "The way Patty was found, she was still…fresh. Bigger shock value. If she'd stayed here, decayed, police wouldn't have known what happened to her without one thorough autopsy—" She broke off and glanced behind her.

"Monica?"

The wind blew her hair, whispered in her ears. She motioned toward the house. "Let's do a sweep." Shouldn't be much to see, but then again, she hadn't really figured on finding that note before.

"I'll go around back," he said, "You take the front."

Fine by her. So what if his voice was clipped, and he'd barely glanced her way all morning? They had a job to do. No time for screwing around.

No matter how good the screw.

Monica gave a nod and drew her gun. It never paid to be too careful.

Luke disappeared around the side of the house. She climbed the porch steps. They creaked and sagged beneath her feet.

Her cell phone vibrated, shaking against her hip. Shit, the freaking thing had made her jump. So much for

Ms. Tough FBI agent. Sucking in a breath, she lifted it up to her ear. "Special Agent Davenport—"

"Another girl's gone missing."

She knew that slow drawling voice. Sheriff Davis.

"*What?*" Her fingers clenched around the phone. No, not this soon. Sweat slicked her palms.

"She didn't come back home this morning…not answering her cell…" His voice faded in and out. "Her boss said she left after her shift…Need you and your partner at the station…"

Monica's heart raced too fast.

"Her parents are here, got to tell 'em something—"

"We'll be there, Sheriff, but I want to check—"

A crackle of static. Loud enough to have her wincing. She should be grateful to even *get* a connection out here, but—

"Where are you, Davenport?"

"Moffett crime scene. Dante and I want to see—"

"*Where?*" Followed by another scream of static. "I need you—"

Monica spun around, instinct driving her as her gaze dropped to the tracks. "When was the last time your men were out here?"

"Wednesday." Static. "Come to the office… parents…missing…"

Her eyes rose. The tall pines around the house swayed back and forth. Oh, yeah, this connection would be dying soon. "Be there in thirty." Monica wasn't sure if he heard her.

Wednesday.

She clipped the phone back in place on her hip. She

always checked out the weather before one of Hyde's trips. She liked to know what she was getting herself into before she hit the road or the skies.

Thunderstorms had ripped through the area Wednesday night. A tornado had even touched down right outside the county lines.

In the days since, this part of Mississippi had been nothing but hot and dry.

And that meant the tracks were fresh.

So who the hell had been out here?

"Monica!"

She tensed at Luke's call, then took off in the direction of his shout. Her legs pumped as she rounded the edge of the house. She jumped over a fallen pine, ducked her head to avoid a slap from a branch.

There. The early sunlight filtered through the treetops in a hazy glow. Luke stood near a line of pines, his hands on his hips.

"Dante, what's going on? What'd you find?" The gun was up, her body on full alert.

He glanced back at her. "Something I think you should see."

She hurried to his side. His finger pointed through the brush. "I caught sight of it when I was doing a perimeter check."

Her eyes narrowed. Trees. More trees and—

Holy shit. Her breath caught.

A twig snapped beneath her foot when she stepped forward. *Watch the scene. Don't screw up any—*

Luke's hand pressed against her back. A warm, steady weight. Almost reassuring.

But she didn't need reassuring. Didn't need him.

"Looks like someone's been digging, huh?"

She managed a weak nod. Right in the middle of the clearing, there was a patch of dirt—not a patch, about a six foot span—higher than the rest.

Fresh dirt. Someone had definitely been digging.

No, not digging, *burying* something.

"You thinkin' what I am?"

Yes. She shoved her gun back into the holster. "We've got another girl missing."

Dante looked back at the mound of dirt. "Not anymore, we don't."

The punch in her gut told her that he was right.

What scares you?

"We don't know *what* is buried here," she said and was surprised by how cool her voice sounded. How calm.

Ice.

"One way to find out."

She couldn't take her eye off that mound. One hell of a way to die. Buried in the woods, shoved in the dirt.

Monica yanked out her phone. Quickly punched in the number she'd memorized that morning.

One ring. Two. Good thing she had a stronger signal this time.

"Davis."

Monica wet her lips. "Think I'm going to need you to come to me, Sheriff. We found...something out at the Moffett scene." Something. *A body*.

Right size.

She'd seen holes just like this before on her cases. Too many. She'd told Dante they didn't know, but, she did.

"Fuck." A snarl from Davis.

Yes, she felt the same way. She'd joined the FBI to stop the killers.

Not to keep finding the dead.

Would the scales never balance?

Her eyes closed as she said, "And, sheriff, when you come...you'd better bring some shovels with you."

CHAPTER *Four*

A half-dozen deputies were on the scene in less than ten minutes. Luke watched them running around like ants, hauling out yellow police tape and attaching it to the swaying pines.

Sheriff Davis stood in the middle of the chaos, a shovel gripped in his hands. He hadn't started digging yet. He just stared at the ground, his jaw clenched, his face white. Every few seconds, he'd mutter the same thing. "*Sonofabitch.*"

Over and over again.

Luke rolled his shoulders and glanced back at Monica. Her eyes were narrowed and locked on the freshly turned earth. He walked to her side. "You know they're screwing the evidence trail." All those bodies. Trampling over everything.

"She hasn't been missing long...." Monica's voice seemed distracted. She ran a hand through her hair. "He dumped her so fast."

The sheriff drove his shovel into the earth.

"He did it too fast," Monica whispered, stepping forward, and Luke knew she wasn't talking about the sheriff.

Luke grabbed her arm and tried hard not to notice the silky feel of her skin. "What are you thinking?"

But she still didn't look at him. "He likes to play too much for this." She shook her head. "*Too fast*," she said again.

Deputy Lee reached for a shovel. "Damn shame," he drawled, his voice carrying easily to them.

Monica wrenched her arm free and shoved past the deputy. "Sheriff! Sheriff, we need to talk."

Davis looked up at Monica. His face flamed beet red. "What we need to do is dig. Right damn now."

"But why dump her? And here? Why—"

The shovel drove deep again.

Lee hesitated behind her.

Her hands knotted into fists. "This isn't the way he plays."

He. Luke knew she was in the killer's head. No surprise. Monica always seemed to be in his head. She knelt and her fingers hovered over the dirt.

"Monica?" Maybe they should back off a bit, and let the locals claim their dead. At least the parents weren't here. They didn't need to see their baby girl get hauled out of the ground.

"*Sonofabitch.*" This time, the snarl came from Monica. She jumped to her feet and grabbed the shovel from Lee's hand. And started digging. Hard and fast.

Davis blinked.

"Dante, help me!"

In two seconds, he had a shovel in his hands. In three, the shovel dug into the dirt.

More deputies joined them. No one spoke, but they worked fast, seeming to catch the desperate energy vibrating through Monica. He glanced up once and caught Davis eyeing Monica with a hint of suspicion in his eyes.

No ice now for her. Her movements were fast, jerky, and—

"Stop!" Her voice broke on the word.

Every man—and the one female deputy there—froze.

Monica leaned in close. "Do you hear that?"

Oh, the hell no, she wasn't saying—

She fell to her knees and began shoving dirt away with her hands. He saw the wood then. A faded brown.

And he heard...

Something.

A whisper.

A moan.

No damn way.

Monica's fingers pressed against the wood. Then she aimed her shovel, catching the tip under the wood and wrenching it back.

Boards snapped. More dirt flew.

Luke caught a glimpse of flesh. Looked like the back of an arm lying so still.

"Take it!" Monica tossed her shovel at a slack-jawed Deputy Vance. She caught the broken boards with her hands, began to pull and wrench—

Luke crawled down beside her. The wood bit into his palms and groaned like an old man when he pulled it back.

Snap.

Blood dripped from Monica's palm but she kept working and then he saw . . .

Long red hair.

Monica shoved her hands into the makeshift coffin and locked her grip around the body. She jerked the woman up, turning her so that Luke could see—

A young, pretty face. Smooth and unlined. Eyes closed. Lips pale. Skin chalky.

Dead.

His jaw clenched. For a minute there, the way Monica had been acting, he'd sure thought—

The woman's eyes flew open, and she sucked in a sharp gasp of air. Then she screamed. A loud, broken screech of pain and fear. Her hands came up, nails broken, fingers bloody, and she clawed at Monica's hold.

Vance jumped back, swearing, and Davis rushed forward. "Get the EMTS—get 'em now, get 'em—"

Monica caught the woman's wrists and held tight. "It's okay. You're safe. It's—"

But the woman in the broken coffin kept screaming, and Luke knew she didn't believe them.

Not that he blamed her. Not one bit.

"I want to see my daughter!" Monica looked up at the fierce demand, her eyes locking on the woman who was all but crawling over the nurses' station.

"The mother's here," she told Dante and rose slowly to her feet. Her right hand had already been bandaged. No stitches, luckily. She hadn't realized how deeply the wood had cut her.

Too busy trying to get to the vic.

Knew she was alive.

No way would the perp have let his prey go that easily.

Where would the fun have been in a quick kill? There was no fear in a fast death. No time for the victim to realize what was coming.

A man with stooped shoulders grabbed the woman's arms and pulled her back.

"I want my daughter!" She fought his hold, not even seeming to realize she'd just elbowed the guy, probably her husband, in the eye.

Such was the way with fear.

Monica slanted a quick glance at Luke and found him watching her. Eyes steady. Seeing too much.

"How'd you know she was still alive?"

Monica swallowed. "I—I didn't." She hadn't known, not at first.

The fear, the hope, had slowly built within her as she studied the scene. *He'd attacked too fast.* Dread had tightened her body and squeezed her heart until she'd had to *dig*.

Get. Her. Out. The mantra had screamed in her head.

He rose, his body brushing hers. His fingers feathered over her cheek, pushing back her hair. "Yeah, you did." His gaze held hers. "I saw it in your eyes."

She'd have to watch that. No, watch him.

"He enjoys his game," she told him, and this was the truth. "The more I thought about him..." She forced a shrug and realized the heat from Luke's body surrounded her, and she could smell him. All these years, and the guy still wore the same cologne. "He likes for his victims to suffer."

His hand fell away from her. Stupid, but she missed the touch. "But why bury her? Why—"

She jerked her thumb toward the parents. The mother was crying now. No quiet tears there. Loud, shuddering sobs. "I'm betting they'll be able to tell us why."

Monica broke away from that green stare. She squared her shoulders and walked across the tiled floor. She felt Dante's stare on her, then heard the tap of his shoes as he followed her.

The mother looked up at her approach. Mary Billings, retired third-grade teacher. The guy patting her shoulder—definitely the husband Alan—looked scared to death.

Smart man.

Monica cleared her throat and flashed her ID. "Ma'am, I'm Monica Davenport with the FBI, and I need to—"

The sobs stopped. "You saved my girl."

She blinked. *Saved.* Laura Billings had been close to catatonic when they brought her in to the ER. Her eyes had been fixed on a nightmare vision only she could see. After they'd pulled her out of the grave, she'd stopped screaming and hadn't said another word. But at least the woman had still been breathing.

"I—I...ah...know this is a difficult time for you..." Not like she really ever got to talk with the families in a non-difficult time. Not with the cases she worked. "But I—"

Mary Billings threw her arms around Monica and squeezed hard enough to take her breath away. "Thank you." A whisper in her ear.

Monica froze. The woman smelled of peppermints.

"Mary..." Alan reached for her.

With a loud and wet-sounding sniffle, Mary pulled back.

Emotion. It always got her. She didn't know what to say. What to—

"Agent Davenport is happy she was able to help your daughter." Dante's smooth voice. "And she will be even happier once we manage to apprehend the person who took Laura."

Right. *Took*—was that the new euphemism for buried? But Luke was a charmer, and he always knew just what to say. She could connect with killers, but Luke had always been the one to link with the victims and the one to get the witnesses to talk. When he wasn't being an ass, he could be charming.

He'd charmed her right into bed.

Mary gave a weak nod.

Alan's face reddened. "Do you—do you know who the bastard is?"

"We're working on it," Dante said. "And we need your help."

Mary blinked. "O–our help? Wh—what can we—"

"This may sound odd, Mrs. Billings," Monica interrupted, "but can you tell me, does Laura have any phobias?"

The woman's brown eyes widened.

Monica licked her lips. Had to be careful now. "I mean, is she afraid of flying or heights or—"

"Laura's claustrophobic," Alan said softly.

Bingo.

Mary shuddered and, for a moment, it looked like she might hit the floor. Alan's hands tightened around her.

"Is there a reason for her fear?" Luke asked quietly. "Did something happen to cause Laura's—"

A tear tracked down Mary's cheek. "She got locked

in a closet when she was eight. Sh–she was playing hide and–and seek at a friend's. She got tr–trapped in—the knob broke on a closet. They couldn't find her, at first. It took two hours t–to get her out."

Plenty of time for fear to set in.

"Laura won't even ride in elevators," Alan said, "she's—"

Mary crumpled. Her legs gave way, and if it hadn't been for Alan, she would have hit the floor. Monica and Dante reached out, helping the older man to steady her.

"My baby," she whispered as the tears came faster. "My p–poor baby. All alone in–in the dark…"

Alone in her nightmare.

What scares you?

He'd known. Just like with the other victims.

Monica stared into Mary's grief-stricken eyes and knew there wouldn't be time for many more questions. The woman wouldn't be able to answer anything soon. "Mrs. Billings." Monica snapped her name out, hard and fast, in an effort to bring her back.

A dazed blink.

"Did Laura say anything to you about—"

The emergency room doors flew open. A doctor came out, a woman with bright red hair and pale skin. "Billings?"

And she lost them.

Monica and Dante stepped back, the better to avoid the trampling as the parents shot forward.

"The bastard knew," Dante muttered. "When we turn her place, we'll find a letter, won't we?"

"Yes." If the killer was staying to his course.

The doc was talking about Laura, saying she'd been given drugs to help her sleep.

There'd be no questioning the vic then. Hell, probably not for a while. "We're going to need guards stationed at her room," she said.

Dante stiffened. "You think he's coming after her?"

She glanced his way. This time, she was ready for the heat of that stare. Well, okay, maybe not. "Laura Billings is the only victim—that we know of—who has survived this guy's sick game." She took a breath. "I don't think he plays for survivors. He just plays for death."

A death Laura had cheated.

"Let's go find Davis. He can put some of his deputies to use." Then they'd have to call Hyde because he needed to know about Laura. And about the killer out there, playing games with people's lives.

"How does he do it?" Dante asked, rolling his shoulders. "How does he know what scares his victims?"

Monica held his gaze. "Wouldn't be too hard, not with so much information being a click away." Simple, really. "With the first two vics, he could pull up old newspaper reports, sneak access to police records, accident files." *Should be harder*. But information came easy now. "Then all he has to do is use the fear to get into their heads." With Laura, though, that info wouldn't have been found in a police file. He would have needed more intimate access to gain that knowledge.

"You *knew*, didn't you?" He lowered his voice and leaned in too close. "You knew it was another fear trap, didn't you?"

Fear trap. That's exactly what it had been. "Why bury a body? This guy wants us to see his work." The car crash had been shoved right in the faces of the local Sheriff's department and that phone tip—hell, yes, that had been deliberate. *Let me show you what I've done.* "There was no reason to hide the body, and every reason—"

"To suspect he'd just set up another game for his prey," Luke cut in. "Trapped in a coffin, sealed in the ground—it wouldn't get much worse for someone scared of tight spaces."

And the dark. Because she'd be willing to bet that closet had been dark that long ago day when Laura had been trapped inside. She'd probably screamed for help. Beat against the door with small hands.

No sense denying what they both knew. "More bodies are coming." At the rate this guy was escalating, blood would flow again too soon. "We need Samantha to do a state-by-state check. Our guy's killed before, but something—something's set him off here. He's killing too fast. This kind of escalation doesn't happen overnight." She exhaled slowly. "We find him and we stop him, soon, or else we'll be spending our days with the dead."

Dante gave a grim nod, and Monica tried to ignore the echoing sounds of Mary's sobs.

Fucking bitch.
Alive.
Not the way the game was supposed to end.
His hands shook, so he balled them into fists, and when the FBI assholes walked past him he ducked into the shadows of the parking lot.
The bitch should have been dead. No damn way should she have been breathing when those suits pulled her out of that hole.

He'd had fun with Laura. He'd sealed her up, but hadn't buried her. Not right away. He'd let her wait. Let her scream. Let her know what was happening.

Hearing the screams had been even better than seeing her face.

You could hear fear so clearly. Those high, desperate cries, those broken sobs. He'd drunk in the sounds.

Then, he'd dumped the earth on her. Nice and slow. Letting her *hear* it, letting her know exactly what was happening to her.

He'd timed things so perfectly. Laura Billings should have died in that ground. Died trying to gasp air that just wasn't there. And she'd been close to death...

So close.

But no, those assholes had wrecked his plan and now—*now* he'd have to change the rules.

Laura would still die. She'd been chosen, and her reprieve would be brief.

He glanced over at the hospital as an ambulance sped through the lot, its bright lights flashing and its siren wailing.

Maybe it would be better this way. Laura had feared the darkness and the confinement before. Now she'd fear him.

So when he came for her, the fear would be even sweeter.

"Hyde is sending backup." Monica tossed her cell phone onto her bed and put her hands on her hips. "He knows the killer's notes are coming and he'll have the techs and handwriting analysts work on them right away."

"Who's coming?" Luke asked. "Kenton or—"

"Kenton. Hyde wants him to handle the media fallout on this one. Kenton's good at that kind of thing." A pause. "And if there's trouble, he'll have our backs."

Absolute certainty in her voice. Huh. He'd always thought she wasn't the trusting sort. "Close to him, are you?"

Her hands dropped. "I've worked my share of cases with Kenton."

Oh, so that guy was *Kenton*, but she acted like it would kill her if she called him anything but Dante. "Sleeping with him?"

Her eyes snapped to his and froze him in his tracks.

Jealousy could be one major bitch. Luke licked his lips. "Ah, what I meant..."

She paced toward him, bright spots of color on her cheeks. Her eyes were glacial and narrowed to slits. "I don't need this crap from you," she gritted out and jabbed her index finger into his chest.

He caught her wrist and probably held too tight. "My mistake," he managed. The words seemed to stick in his throat. "Who you sleep with is your business." *Lie, lie, lie.*

Everything about her was his business. Had been, from the moment he'd taken her into his bed.

"You think because I had sex with you..." She paused, lifted that chin up another notch, "that I screw all the men I work with?"

Oh, she'd better not. Kenton's grinning face flashed through his mind.

"*Don't even think it, man. Not going to happen.*" Kenton's words. Had he meant...

She turned away from him. Straightened her shoulders. "I respect Kenton, do you understand that? We've been into Hell with some of our cases, and I have never—*not once*—seen him lose his control. He always does his job, and he does it damn well."

Control. Oh, yeah, that had always been important to her. Not so much to him.

"And I *don't* sleep with agents on my team, okay? I learned a lesson from you. Business and pleasure aren't meant to mix."

But they'd mixed so well.

Not sleeping with Kenton. Thank you, Jesus.

"The guy can have a bad sense of humor, but I trust Kenton to watch my back." The heat was gone, and the control she loved was firmly back. Pity. He'd liked that flare of steam. "I trust him to do his job, a job I've seen him do very, very well."

He gave a hard nod. "You trust everyone on your team, or you don't trust anyone." More words from Kenton.

"Exactly."

"But that trust only goes so far, doesn't it? Only as far as the job." *Shouldn't have said it.* But, he was the kind of guy who liked to push.

No, he liked to push *her*.

Monica froze. "Trusting someone with your life—you think that's easy?"

"No." The woman could twist and turn everything. She could trip a suspect up in two minutes, could get those confessions to spill so fast. "I think you trust them because it's your job, but when it comes to the secrets you carry," and he *knew* she had secrets because everyone had them, even him, "you don't trust anyone."

Now she did glance back. "Leave it alone, Dante."

"You mean, leave *you* alone?" He'd tried that. Gotten a lot of sleepless nights and hard-ons as a result. He sucked in a deep breath and caught more of her heady scent. *The case. Stick to the case.*

Her eyes held his. Dammit, no one should have eyes that blue.

When she came, those eyes had gone blind with pleasure. *Hell.*

"Sorry," he growled and eased back. The better to escape her scent. Her.

She didn't blink. "It's been a long day."

A day filled with crime scene analysis. Witness interviews. And a lot of jack shit. Because the killer was good.

Or he *had* been, until Miss Laura Billings had survived his attack.

"Get some sleep," she told him in that perfect, you-don't-bother-me voice. "The doctor said Laura will be up tomorrow. We'll find out what she knows then."

Laura had permanent protection now, courtesy of the Jasper County Sheriff's Department. A deputy would guard her door every minute.

He'd seen Laura before they left the hospital. She'd been out cold, her breathing so soft and slow she'd appeared to be near death. *'Cause she had been.*

When she woke, there was no telling what she'd say. Would she remember her attack? Remember the bastard who'd grabbed her and left her for dead?

Her face had been slack with terror when the ambulance hauled her away from the crime scene. A fear like that... "She's not going to want to talk with us."

"She *has* to talk."

"Vics always hate talking about the attack." One of the hardest parts of the job. Seeing those shattered stares and hearing the hollow echo of pain in their voices. "They just want to forget."

"Forgetting's not easy." Monica sounded certain. "Just because you don't talk about it, it doesn't mean you forget. She'll talk with us. She'll tell us everything she knows." More certainty. "Because she'll want the bastard stopped."

Vengeance. That he understood, and he knew the victims understood, too. Sometimes, the thirst for vengeance was all that kept them going.

"Go to bed, Dante," she said again, her voice softer, but still firm.

He turned away from her. Stared at the white connecting door. *Walk away.*

He could do it. She had.

He stalked forward and curled his fingers around the door knob. "I know it shouldn't matter." This was choking him. "Who you see. What you do." He wouldn't glance back because this time, he didn't want to see the ice staring back at him. "But it does. And after today, when death was so damn close I felt him breathing on my neck when we were digging up that girl's grave…"

He *knew* death. No mistaking that chill on his spine.

"Sometimes you want to feel alive. When you see death so much, you just…want to feel alive again." Being with her had always made him feel alive. Running fast and hot and free. He opened the door and the squeak of the hinges seemed way too loud. "If you wanna feel alive, you know where to find me."

And that was all there was to say.

• • •

When the door closed, Monica let out the breath that had filled her lungs. She slowly unballed her fists and saw that her fingers were shaking.

Weakness. At a time when she just couldn't afford anything less than full strength.

But the girl had gotten to her because Monica had recognized the terror in Laura's eyes. The fear so deep it ate your soul and stole your hope.

Dante had been right. Death had been with them that morning. Laura knew it. She'd felt him coming. Laura's chest had rattled as the woman fought to breathe—the rattle was proof that they'd been minutes away from finding a corpse instead of a live victim.

When you knew you were going to die, those last moments were the darkest and longest that terror could bring.

She'd seen those moments, seen the fear reflected in other eyes. Eyes that she couldn't forget, no matter how hard she tried.

Monica looked down at her hands. Those stupid shaking fingers. Another few seconds and Dante would have noticed.

She'd known bringing him on the team was a mistake. She'd tried telling Hyde, but once the boss made up his mind there was no changing it. And, hell, Hyde had been right. He almost always was.

The SSD *did* need Dante. The guy could get to victims like no other. She'd read through his files, all his supervisors' reports. He knew how to pry information out of the vics that they'd even forgotten themselves.

He slipped right past their guard, made them feel safe, and got them to tell him their nightmares.

They needed him.

So she'd spewed the tough talk on the plane. Hands off. Just work the case. Blah, blah.

But the truth of the matter was that he was tempting her again. Chipping the ice away and making her *feel*.

Alive.

And just how was she supposed to hold out against that? Against him?

Because she could spout bullshit with the best of them, but the reality was she wanted back in his bed. She'd missed him, dreamed about him, and just—

Wanted.

She wouldn't kid herself. An explosion was coming. If he hadn't left when he did—

Luke had always been so good at working past her defenses.

Monica pulled off her shirt and headed toward the shower. Goose bumps were on her flesh, and she was so tired of feeling cold. Just so tired.

She wanted to feel—

Lust. Heat. Need. Passion.

Alive.

She wrenched on the hot water.

Damn him.

CHAPTER *Five*

Monica woke with a scream on her lips. Her heart raced, the thud filling her ears, even as she reached for the gun she'd learned to keep close.

Closer than any lover.

Her fingers curled around the cold butt of the weapon. Her grip wasn't steady. No, her hand shook too much for that.

Nightmare. Memory?

Sometimes, she just couldn't tell.

The faint light from the bathroom spilled toward her. A beacon. She stared at that light, stared until the trembling stopped and she could breathe without feeling like a fist was pounding against her chest.

But she didn't lower the gun. Not yet.

Trapped in that coffin. No room to move. Darkness all around.

Monica knew to fear the dark, too.

Trapped.

That damn fist was back. Pounding, pounding...

A car door slammed.

Her head snapped to the right, toward the blinds that covered her only window.

Instinct had her moving from the bed. She spared the briefest of glances toward the clock. Three a.m.

She lowered her weapon and used her left hand to part the blinds, moving them just enough to see into the parking lot.

Probably some late night truck driver. A traveler who couldn't go any farther or—

A man stood in the darkness near her and Dante's SUV. The man wore a sweatshirt, one with a hood pulled up high to shield half his face.

She couldn't tell for certain, not with the darkness, but the guy seemed to be looking straight at her room.

No, straight at her.

The light from the bathroom—was it showing her silhouette? Oh, hell. She shifted a bit to the right and her bare feet brushed against something.

Monica glanced down and saw a small scrap of white paper. Her brows pulled together and she bent, reaching down. She hadn't noticed that before, but she'd been tired and—

What scares you?

Dammit! The note fell from her fingers, and she shot back up to her feet. Her hand slammed against the blinds, parting a big hole so she could see...*him.* Still there.

Her heart slammed into her ribs. He lifted his hand and yes, the guy pointed straight at her. Then he whirled away, and started moving fast, running, zigzagging through the parked cars.

Hell, *no.* Monica yanked on a pair of sweats, screwed

the shoes, clutched her gun tighter and wrenched open her door.

She knew how the games were played.

Into the minds of monsters.

The only place she could go.

Luke shot up in bed. The image of a dead woman still floated in his mind. What was—

A door. No, not *a* door, Monica's door.

Slamming shut.

"Damn, not again," he muttered even as his heart kick-started with a slam into his chest. He jumped from the bed, grabbed his weapon, wrenched the door knob, and was outside of his motel room in five seconds flat.

He saw her instantly. A pale flash of skin darting through the cars. Her gun was up. *In pursuit.*

Luke choked back the call on his lips. He wouldn't make a rookie mistake and alert any perp out there. His legs moved fast, as he ate up the distance between them. A light mist began to fall, coating his bare arms and chest.

His eyes scanned the lot, searching for—

Monica spun toward him, her gun up. "*Dante!*"

He froze. A smart man knew to do that when a woman aimed a gun at his heart.

She blew out a hard breath, and the gun barrel dropped. "He's here."

His eyes tracked to the right. Then the left. No star-light or moonlight tonight, not with those clouds sweeping over them. The lights in the lot were dim, and he could only see shadows and hear the fast beat of his own heart. "Where?"

She stepped back, the move jerky. "I–I saw him from my window. He was here. He *was*, but now—"

Now there were two armed agents standing in an empty lot. Dante cleared his throat. "It was a tough day. Finding the vic like that, hell, it would make anyone edgy."

Monica growled at him. Really growled. And, yeah, wrong place, wrong time, but that rumble had his blood heating.

Talk about being screwed.

"A man was here." Her eyes swept the lot as rain began to fall. Harder now, not just a light misting. "He left me one of his damn notes. I *saw him*. He stood right next to our SUV, and the guy pointed at me."

Luke's brows shot up. He headed toward the SUV. No broken windows. The alarm hadn't sounded. "How'd you know he was even out here?"

"I heard a car door slam."

But not their door. Not unless the guy had found some way of bypassing the alarm. He glanced back at her room. He could see the faint glow of light through her blinds.

The touch of the rain turned into a sting. He tucked the gun into the back of his sweats. "Let's get inside. Show me the note and—"

"That's it?" she demanded, voice low but fierce. "Someone's watching us, Dante. We can't just—"

He caught her arm and dragged her close, ignoring the gun. "He might still be here and standing out in the open isn't my idea of the best plan of action." Raindrops clung to her lashes. Trailed down her cheeks. Her breath rasped out.

Her t-shirt was wet, clinging to her and...

"Let's get inside," he said, his voice rumbling out. If that asshole was out there, watching them...

Monica gave a grim nod. Her hair curled slightly in the rain. Her eyes—he could still see them so well in the dark.

He kept his hold on her as they walked back to her room. His eyes searched the lot. The rain was going to screw them. If anyone had been at their SUV, well, no prints would be found on the outside of the vehicle now.

They went in silently. The air conditioner whirred with a soft purr, and the cold hit them. She shivered, a long shudder that worked over the length of her body. Luke slammed the door shut behind them, locked it, and tried real hard to keep his eyes on hers. "Tell me what's going on."

Her wet hair clung to her. "I already told you. He left me a note."

Temper spiked his blood, heating his body. "So you ran out there without backup? What the hell, Monica? You know better. You think there's some perp out there, you get me; you come and get—"

"There wasn't time," she spoke grimly. "He got away before. I–I think that was him last night, too. I didn't want him to get away again."

But he—whoever *he* was—had gotten away. "Where's the note?"

Her gaze shot to the floor. "There. I—shit, I didn't use gloves when I picked it up before."

He grabbed a tissue from the desk. Used it to hold the note carefully, just by the left edge. *Fuck.*

What scares you? Same messy scrawl. Dark ink.

No, that bastard was *not* coming after her.

She shoved back her hair. Water droplets littered the floor. "He's watching me," she said, and there was an odd, tense note in her voice.

She wrapped her arms around her middle. Rocked forward. "He's bringing me into the game."

Not gonna happen. Laura's desperate face flashed in his mind.

And Monica's blue eyes stared back at him.

No one can see into a killer's mind like Davenport.

She inched back and carefully put her gun down on the nightstand. "I think he was watching last night. I–I think he knows exactly who we—well, who *I* am."

And he thought he was going to play his sick-ass games with her? He opened her kit and sealed the note in an evidence bag. "We're getting this dusted. Maybe the bastard left a print."

"Maybe," she whispered, but he heard the doubt and understood. The killer they were after was too good for that. Too organized. Every move, planned in advance.

"We need to call Hyde. We can switch motels, we can—"

She laughed at that. "If the killer is watching us, he'll just follow wherever we go. Not like there are a lot of places to choose from in Jasper."

True, but...

"We stay on guard, Dante. That's what we do. We tell the sheriff and we get his deputies to patrol so that we have extra eyes outside. If I see the perp again, I'll get him."

"*We'll* get him." He shut the case with a snap and went back to her, closing the distance between them. "New rule. You see anyone—*anyone*—out there again, you come and get me before you go storming outside." Luke didn't want her facing the monsters alone. Not when he'd walk through fire to be by her side.

Monica licked her lips. Her hands came up, pressed against his chest. The touch seemed to burn his flesh. So hot, but her flesh felt so soft and silky. "You should...go get dressed," she told him, her voice dropping and getting that husky little edge that he'd never been able to forget.

The edge that told him she needed. Wanted. Lusted.

Just like he did.

And Luke realized he was half-dressed, wearing just a pair of jeans. The rain had made her shirt all but transparent. They were wet. Close.

Just as hungry for each other as they'd always been.

An inch, maybe two, separated their lips. He wanted to close that distance and take her mouth. To plunge his tongue deep inside and taste her.

But he'd already crossed the line with her once. His hands fisted. She'd made it clear what she wanted, and what she didn't want. No sex. No emotions. Just business.

He closed his eyes. Lust had his cock twitching, rising and swelling, and she was so close.

Too close.

He spun away from her. "Stay inside," he ordered, his eyes opening. "When I come back, we'll take that note in."

"You were right about me. Us. I didn't want to remember, but—" Her voice, so soft, froze him. He had to strain to make out the words.

He glanced back. Big mistake. Monica's head was tilted to the right. Her eyes were narrowed on him.

"Remember what?" Because he'd never had a problem remembering what it was like to be with her. To touch her and taste her and see the pleasure wash over her face.

No, that hadn't been a problem. Forgetting, though, had been pure hell.

"Sometimes..." She licked her lips. "I want *to feel*."

Oh, no, the woman could *not* be jerking him around like this.

She took a step forward. "When I'm with you, Luke, I've always felt so alive." Monica shook her head.

Luke. His name, finally rolling off her tongue with that nearly forgotten hint of a southern drawl. Oh, Christ. If he wasn't careful, she would drive him crazy. Or have him on his knees.

His cock throbbed behind the fly of his jeans. He tried to keep his voice firm when speech was nearly impossible. "What am I, then? Some kind of convenient screw?"

Deliberately, he pulled out his gun. Put it on the sagging chair next to the wall.

Her eyes held his as her chin tipped back. "You're many things, but convenient isn't one of them."

The woman had just made a joke. He was so stunned he almost laughed. Instead, he moved forward and caught her close.

Not getting away. Not now. "Just sex?" Yeah, he was losing the power of speech because those words were definitely more of a rumble than anything else.

Her lips parted. *Ah, screw it.* The hunger beat in his blood, the lust nearly blinded him.

Taste. Take. And he did.

She rose onto her bare toes and wrapped her fingers around him, clutching his shoulders and holding on tight.

His mouth crashed onto hers, and she met him with wet lips, open and eager. Her nipples stabbed at his chest. Hard from the cold? Or from the stark need between them?

Her tongue met his. A fast dart, then a slow stroke that had him shuddering. Monica had always known just how to use her mouth on him.

And just how to push him past control.

He caught her hips, yanking her closer. They stumbled a bit, and his leg bumped into her nightstand. A lamp hit the floor.

The bed waited. Two steps away. Monica, naked in bed beneath him. How long had that fantasy haunted him?

If she was willing, he wasn't gonna be fool enough to walk away.

Just sex.

She wanted to feel? He'd make her *feel*.

They hit the bed. The mattress groaned, sagging beneath their weight.

Her legs came up, locking around his hips. Not good enough. Too much clothing between them. Way too much.

He tore his mouth from hers and kissed a path down her neck. Monica moaned, arching beneath him. Oh, yeah, he remembered what she liked, and he knew what she needed.

Her nails bit into his shoulders. "Luke..."

Shit. His back teeth clenched, and he fought to hold onto his control. That husky voice could break him if he wasn't careful.

He lifted up, pushing his palms flat against the

mattress on either side of her. That shirt would have to go. He grabbed it and yanked up.

Sweet hell. The woman had perfect breasts. Tight, dark nipples, firm and round flesh. If she still tasted as sweet...

His mouth closed around a nipple. *She did.* He licked, sucked, and her hips rocked against him as her hold tightened around him.

"Lose the jeans!" She managed, her breath panting. "Ah...I can't—hurry!"

She'd always liked the sex fast. Fast and hard and in the dark.

But it wasn't dark now. She'd forgotten the light, and he could see that pale flesh.

He bit her. Light, not too hard.

Not yet.

She shivered beneath him, and her hands slipped down, sliding over his back. Lower, going down to the top of his jeans.

Okay, the first time would be fast. His hand pushed between their bodies. Jerked open the snap on his jeans.

But the second time, he'd savor her. Savor and taste until she screamed.

Or came. Again and again.

A high-pitched jingle of sound exploded from somewhere behind him.

Monica's breath caught. She stared up at him, eyes widening.

Ignore the damn phone. Ignore it.

He bent to kiss her again.

"No." A whisper. Soft but certain.

Because his luck could never, ever be good.

Another loud ripple. She swallowed, and he saw the hard motion of her throat. "This late...could be Hyde. Or—or the sheriff."

His hands fell away from her, and he rolled back onto the bed, clenching the covers in his fists. "Get it."

He smiled when he saw the shadows part.

Really, they should have known better than to leave the light on. But Agent Davenport had kept her light on all night long.

Interesting.

Those who used lights usually feared the darkness.

This was going to be so much fun.

The ringing in his ear stopped. There was a click, then, husky, soft, "Hello?"

So. Much. Fun.

Monica swallowed and her hold tightened around the thin cell phone. This time of night—it had to be the Bureau. "Hello?" She said again. "This is—"

"Agent Davenport."

A man's voice, grating and hard.

Static crackled.

"Who is this?"

Behind her, she heard the rustle of bed covers and then the creak of the floor as Luke edged toward her.

Laughter flowed over the line, and her shoulders stiffened. She knew what was coming next, even before the bastard said—

"Tell me...what scares you, Davenport?"

Her breath caught in her throat. A vision of blood and a swirl of darkness flashed through her mind.

Trapped, waiting for death, just like Laura.

The blade slicing deep, over and over. Just like before.

Victims screaming, begging for help. Help that wouldn't come.

"What scares you?" A whisper now, taunting.

Her teeth clenched. "Not a damn thing," she gritted. "Not a—"

Click.

The phone bit into her palm. She forced herself to ease her grip. It was either ease the grip or shatter the cell.

"Monica?"

Luke's deep voice, still tinged with the rough need that had burned so hard moments before.

Before.

She glanced back at Luke. "It was him." The note hadn't been enough. He'd wanted to make a personal connection. To taunt. Was that the way he always worked? They'd have to pull all the victims' phone records and see what they could find.

"The damn killer was just on your phone? He's got your *number?*"

She'd need to call in at headquarters. Get them to trace the call A-fucking-SAP. Ten to one, though, it would go back to a disposable cell. She glanced down at her caller ID.

No, it wouldn't be an easy trace. This guy wouldn't be so sloppy. He wouldn't get tripped up so fast.

"Monica?" Luke stood right in front of her. "What's happening?"

She swallowed. No more time for pleasure. Back to death. And wasn't that always the way for her? "We need to get that note down to the station. And we've got to talk to Hyde, right away."

"*Sonofabitch.*" He swung toward the blinds, his hands clenching.

Was he watching them now? Because this guy, she knew he liked to watch. But what he didn't know, not yet...was what scared her.

If she had her way, he never would.

No one would know.

He whistled while he walked down the long hospital corridor. He looked like he belonged, so no one even so much as questioned him as he strolled right through the place.

His boots squeaked on the tile. He glanced down, and his reflection shone back up at him.

Mighty fine.

He rounded the nurses' station, tossing up a wave. The guard was there, just as he'd known he would be since Miss Sissy Sue Hollings worked the night shift. Pretty little Sissy Sue with her corkscrew curls and slick red mouth.

The deputy barely glanced his way. The guy was too busy leaning over the counter and hitting on Sissy Sue.

So he whistled and strolled down the hall, then took a left. Ah...there. Room four-oh-eight.

Too easy, really.

He slipped into the room. Silence greeted him. No hiss and moan of machines. Perfect. He pushed back the green hospital curtain that enclosed her bed and saw his little survivor.

Laura's eyes were closed, the lashes casting shadows

on her cheeks. No cuts, no bruises—not on her face. He glanced down at her hands.

Ah, there we go.

Torn nails. Jagged and discolored flesh. She'd tried to get out on her own but failed.

He wanted to talk to her. To find out what it had been like. Those moments after she'd awoken and realized she was in her personal hell.

How terrifying. How perfect.

He reached for a pillow, but he...hesitated.

This seemed so wrong. To die like this, sleeping. So easy.

A smile lifted his lips. Really, this wasn't his way at all.

Laura Billings had feared the darkness, feared being trapped. He'd given her a taste of that hell.

But now, she'd fear him.

In seconds, he had his gloves on. Ready for work.

He let the back of his fingers skim down her cheek. The doctors had pumped her full of drugs. He knew it—that's what they did with the patients who wouldn't stop screaming. And after Laura had snapped from her silence, she'd screamed and screamed.

He'd heard some of the nurses talking about those sweet screams downstairs.

"That poor girl..."

"Can you imagine? Trapped in the ground..."

If only they knew.

He stroked her face again, and her eyelids flickered. Ah. Good.

No time to waste.

When her eyes opened, confusion appeared first. A

furrow etched a line between her brows. She licked her lips. "Where—"

"Shh..." He put his finger against her lips. Then he lifted the pillow. "Don't worry, I'll make it faster this time."

Then it came. The fear. Blossoming in her stare, growing, spreading, making those pretty eyes bulge as her mouth opened to scream.

Too late.

He shoved the pillow onto her face. Caught her wrists in his left hand and held her while she thrashed.

She fought more than he'd expected. Once, she almost got free from him.

Almost.

Then...she was still. So very still. No more fight left.

If she'd been hooked to the machines that were pushed in the corner, one of the nurses would have been racing to the room, wondering why the patient had flat-lined. A lucky break for him.

He touched her again. Couldn't help it. She was still warm. He could feel her warmth through the gloves. Not that the warmth would last long now.

When he lifted his hand, he saw the tremble that shook his fingers. Not from fear, never that.

Carefully, he arranged her pillows.

One last look, because death could be such a thing of beauty, then he slipped from the room.

When her cell phone rang again, Monica was ready. She answered even before the first ring was finished. "Davenport."

"We traced the cell," Sam's voice, high with excitement. "Are you armed?"

What? Her gaze met Luke's. He stood just across the room, arms crossed over his chest. "I have my weapon here."

At her words, he took out his own gun.

"The cell phone came up as registered to Laura Billings—"

Dammit.

"We used repeater triangulation to pick up the GPS chip in the phone...*Monica, the phone is right outside your room*...Whoever called you—"

"Laura Billings is still in the hospital." Her gun was in her hand, and she hurried for that door. "It's her attacker, playing a game."

"*Be careful! You don't know—*"

"Dante's here. I've got backup." She hung up the phone. Took a deep breath. "He called from right outside."

A muscle flexed in Luke's jaw.

They went out together. The light near her room flickered, sending out bursts of sickening yellow. Monica's gaze swept the lot. Left. Right. Left—

The SUV waited just a few feet away. The first place she would have gone to the next morning. The one thing she would have seen.

In seconds, she was at the vehicle. No broken windows. The doors were still locked. Luke covered her while she ran around to the rear.

The phone had been tossed beneath the back tire. It was still on; it had to be so that Sam could track it with the FBI's satellite.

Damn him. Her gaze swept the lot once more. *Long gone now.* But he'd wanted her to know. He'd wanted to make absolutely certain that she knew he'd been close enough to touch.

Or to kill.

CHAPTER *Six*

Monica stared at the body. The closed eyes, the parted lips. The raw and bruised fingertips.

Laura Billings had cheated death once. She hadn't been so lucky the second time he came calling.

The muffled sound of sobs reached her ears. The mother. Monica's hands clenched. Mary had thought she'd gotten her daughter back.

So very wrong.

She cleared her throat and forced her gaze to lift from the body and lock on Davis's hard stare. "What happened." Not a question. "You had a guard here. Why the hell am I looking at a dead woman?"

Their only witness. Killed when a deputy was less than fifteen feet away.

Unbelievable.

A muscle flexed along the sheriff's jaw. "If you're saying my man—"

"We've got a dead woman on your watch." Monica stepped back for the crime scene tech. "*That's* what I'm saying." She could have screamed right then. They'd needed Laura. *So close.* So close to ID'ing the killer and now—

Now he'd finished his job with Laura. Dammit.

A ripple of movement beside her. "I want to talk to the deputy," Luke snapped.

Yeah, so did she. She jerked her thumb toward the door. "Outside." The scent of death was just growing thicker in the room.

Thought I'd managed to save one. Finally.

But the killer had just been waiting. Biding his time— *and screwing with me.*

She eased around the techs at the door and caught sight of Laura's parents. Her gut clenched.

Mary's watery eyes found her. "You...I thought you...s-saved her."

Staring into those eyes, seeing the pain...Monica swallowed. "I'm sorry for your loss, ma'am." So cold and brittle. "We'll do everything in our power to apprehend—"

Mary blinked. She shook her head and seemed to fall apart. "I don't want him c-caught!" she cried. "I want my baby back!"

Monica turned away. "I need to talk to...that deputy," she spoke through gritted teeth as her temples throbbed. "And she...needs to be taken away from the crime scene." Mary didn't need to see them wheel out her daughter's body.

Luke pressed his hand against the base of her back, guiding her forward. They rounded the corner and saw more uniforms and nurses. One woman—fresh-faced, pretty, with thick curls—sat huddled behind the desk with her shoulders hunched and her chin down.

Deputy Pope stood next to her, his dark head bent, a trembling hand running over his face. Beside him, another deputy, tall, with a shaved head and a small brown goatee, stood with his hands clenched.

"Vickers!" The sheriff's voice barked behind her and the taller deputy flinched. "Son, you got one hell of a lot of explaining to do!"

His head whipped up. Pink stained his cheeks and his Adam's apple bobbed. "I-I swear, sir...I-I didn't leave my post all night—"

This was so not the place for an interrogation. Too many eyes. Too many ears.

Monica pointed to the small white door across from the nurses' station. "That the break room?"

Curly nodded.

"Good." Monica drew in a deep breath. Jesus, she hated the smell of hospitals. "Go in there, deputy." Once inside, he wasn't getting out until she figured out exactly what had happened.

He nodded and shuffled forward.

Curly reached for her bag. "I-I'm going home. I'll talk to you later, Lee," the nurse said.

Right. Like that was going to happen. Monica fired a glance at Luke.

He gave a slight nod and said, "Ah, miss, we're gonna need to talk to you."

Her baby blue eyes widened.

"So why don't you just stay put a bit." He flashed a smile. One with lots of teeth. "And we'll all have a real, nice talk soon."

Davis motioned and Melinda Jenkins, another deputy, stepped up beside the nurse. She'd been waiting for

Monica outside the hospital. Petite and soft-spoken, but with a no-nonsense attitude. Good thinking on Davis's part to bring Melinda in, especially with that dazed stare Lee was flashing at the nurse.

The nurse's hold on her bag tightened. "B-but I didn't do anything!"

"You were the nurse on duty, weren't you?" Monica asked quietly. She knew the answer. Davis had pointed out the blonde when he'd led her off the elevator.

A grim nod.

"Then you were here when the killer struck. You saw him." A pause. "And he saw you."

That pretty face paled.

"I'm afraid you're not going anywhere, ma'am," Luke said, his drawl deepening, deliberately, she was sure, to make the nurse feel like she was talking to another good ole boy. "We need to ask you a few questions because we sure need your help."

Melinda sidled close to the nurse. Real close. Monica met the deputy's dark eyes and knew that Curly wouldn't be getting away.

"Why don't you come with me, honey..." Melinda said in that gentle voice of hers.

"But—but I just wanna go home...."

"Ah, Sissy Sue, I'm afraid that's just not an option right now." Still soft, but no missing the steel.

Monica realized she could like Deputy Jones. If only *she'd* been on duty for the night, maybe Laura would still be breathing instead of being wheeled to the morgue.

She drew in a deep breath, then exhaled slowly. Davis stood by her side, his whole body tense. "One other thing you need to know about tonight, Sheriff."

His brows pulled low.

"The killer made contact."

Davis's jaw dropped. "Bullshit."

"Not quite. He called me," probably right before the bastard had gone after Laura, judging by the lividity of the body and the waxy color of the flesh. "He knows we're hunting him." Her gaze held his. "And I think he likes it."

Deputy Andrew "Andy" Vickers looked like he wanted to cry. Maybe he *was* crying. Luke narrowed his eyes and braced his legs as Monica began questioning the guy. Sheriff Davis stood to the right, shaking his head in disgust every few minutes.

"I didn't leave! I didn't!"

"Then who did you see?" Monica pressed. "This hallway was cleared. No other patients. Just Laura. Who did you see on her hallway? And why the hell didn't you step up and stop—"

"Nurses and doctors!" he said, still rubbing his hand over his face. "All night...I only saw nurses and doctors coming to check on her. No one else!"

"You were supposed to stay at her door," Luke said. "But you didn't, did you?" He could just guess why. A reason that was about five-foot-two, one hundred and twenty pounds...

Shame there, flashing on Andy's face. "I just went down to talk to Sissy. Ten minutes, I swear—and I could still make sure the hall was clear from the station. I could see the room!"

Bullshit. If he'd still been able to *make sure the hall was clear,* Laura wouldn't be dead.

"That's the only time you weren't right next to Laura's room?" Monica asked, pushing back her hair.

"Y-yeah…"

"Then who did you see? Who passed you when you were chumming it up with Sissy? *Who?*" When she got going, Monica could be fierce.

Hard. Smart. Sexy.

He cleared his throat.

Andy blinked a few times. "I-I…a doctor. Yeah, yeah—a doctor. He had on green scrubs and one of them little hats and—"

"Did you see his face?" Luke asked.

Andy's eyes met his and fell.

Luke knew the answer before the quiet response even came. "No."

Sissy Sue Hollings had enough nervous energy to fill up the whole room. Her body vibrated. Her curls bounced, and her eyes shifted from Monica to Luke to the Sheriff, then back. One really big circle, over and over again.

Monica crossed her arms. "When you were talking with Deputy Vickers—"

"At approximately 4:30 a.m.," Luke felt obliged to help.

"Did you see a man walk past the nurse's station?"

Sissy Sue's lips parted.

"Did you, Sissy?" Now Davis was stepping up. He'd suspended Vickers, told the deputy he'd be sitting on the sidelines, but Davis's anger still had his cheeks tinted red. "*Did you see him?*"

The faintest of nods. "But-but that was just a doctor—"

"Really?" Monica asked. "Which doctor was it? What was his name?"

Sissy's mouth closed. A furrow grew between her brows.

Come on! "Did you see his face, Ms. Hollings?" Luke demanded.

She shook her head.

"Right." Monica's hands dropped. "And I'm guessing the idea of stopping him and asking for ID never crossed your mind."

Or the deputy's. But then, Luke knew exactly where Andy's mind had been.

"He—he was a doctor..." Sissy's whisper.

"No," Monica told her. "He was a killer."

Monica waited until she was alone to make the call. She didn't bother calling the SSD. She used Hyde's private line, a number she'd had for years.

"What happened?" No grogginess, no confusion. Blunt and hard. Always the way he answered the phone, and, of course, he knew it was her. He would have seen the caller ID.

Monica took a deep breath. "Laura Billings is dead." She glanced down the long hospital corridor. Luke had gone back to talk to the family again. He'd come back with a list of names—friends, lovers. Luke had a way of working through the victims' grief and always getting the information he needed. "He got to her, Hyde. Came right in the hospital last night and killed Laura in her bed."

"*Dammit.* What about the guard? I know you stationed—"

"He walked right by him. Looks like our guy stole

some scrubs and just slipped in." Bold, but then, she'd already known that about the killer.

"This story is going to leak to the national media soon." He sighed. "Kenton will be there in a few hours. Let him take care of the reporters. You just stick to working this perp."

Her fingers tightened around the phone. "He made contact."

Silence. Thick. The tension hummed over the cell.

"Run that by me again." She could almost see him, pacing near that picture window in his den. He would have grabbed his cordless phone and gone in there immediately. He always thought better in his den.

"Earlier tonight…" Dawn was almost here now. "He slipped one of his notes under my motel room door and then he called." She kept her voice even. Good thing she'd practiced doing that over the years. But if anyone could look past the surface, it was Hyde.

"He called the motel room?"

"No." And this was worrying her. "My cell phone. I don't know how he got access—and we need to find out—but he called my private line. I've already talked to Sam. The bastard used Laura's phone, and he left it for me, right by our SUV."

"Any prints?"

"Doubt it." He wouldn't have made a mistake like that. "I gave it to the techs down here for dusting. We're also checking to see if any other calls were made by our guy." The phone records should be ready for her by the time she got back to the station.

"Where's Dante?"

"Talking with Laura's family." She turned, gazing

out the window, and knew he'd be doing the same. "He wanted me to know he was watching. Fair enough, because I'm sure after *him*."

"I don't like it. Dammit, I don't like *any* of this."

Neither did she. "It's not unexpected. Perps can often fixate on the agents assigned to track them. He knows the SSD is here. It's a pissing match, sir. He's trying to show he's not going to be scared." *That we should be scared.*

"Monica..." Not Davenport, not this time. "Are you okay?" Soft, quiet, and she knew it wasn't her boss who was asking. It was the man who'd seen her through the dark.

"He doesn't scare me." It took so much more than this guy.

"If you need me, I'm there."

He'd always been there.

Footsteps sounded in the hallway, tapping lightly on the tile. She glanced over her shoulder. Luke was headed toward her. "Yes, sir, if we see the need for additional backup, I'll make sure we contact you right away." Her gaze held Luke's.

"You do that," Hyde said into her ear. "And you send me everything you've got on this perp. I don't want him playing his games with you."

Too late.

The sheriff gave them a room to work in at the station. Not a big office. Maybe a ten-by-eight space with one window. But the size didn't matter. Luke was damn grateful they'd finally gotten some privacy and a solid door between them and the good folks of Jasper.

He and Vance had dragged one desk and two chairs inside. A war room. For him and Monica.

Luke waited until Deputy Pope walked out, then it was his turn for the interrogation. He closed the door, very softly. Leaning back against the wood, he got ready to work. "What did Hyde have to say?"

"He said he's got Samantha cross-referencing murders in the U.S. that fit our pattern." She pulled out a desk chair and when the wood slid across the tile, a long, painful squeak filled the air.

He paced toward her. "Our pattern? *Our* pattern is that the perp gets off on his kills. He tortures the victims, gives them their nightmares and—"

"Exactly." She sat, nice and prim, and opened up her laptop. "He does."

They hadn't managed to save her. He'd been so stunned to see Laura gulping down air when they'd dug her out of that hole. Then to see her so pale and still in that hospital bed...

I'll find you, bastard.

He could still hear the sound of her mother crying.

"The man we're looking for..." Monica glanced up at him. "And we do know it's a man, thanks to my call and the deputy's description..."

Yeah, Vickers had been adamant about the perp being a male. Tall. Thin.

And Monica said the voice she'd heard had been masculine, low, grating, but certainly not female.

It fit. Most serials were males.

"Our guy's kills are elaborate and designed for optimum fear." Her nail tapped on the computer. "His murders didn't just start here in Jasper. He's killed before.

For him, it's all about the fear. He needs his victims to be afraid. He sets the stage, he plays with them—"

Like he'd started playing with her last night?

"When Samantha runs her screen, she's not going to be looking for gunshot victims. She's going to look for fear crimes. Unusual kills. Those that fit our guy's signature."

"But the Jenkins death looked like an accident at first. And Laura—hell, if we hadn't found her grave, we wouldn't have even known she *was* one of his victims." So young, barely twenty-five. She could have just left town. Run off with a lover.

Or been buried alive.

"He's good," Monica said. "But Samantha is better. She'll find one of his kills. It's only a matter of time."

And the early kills, if they could find them, would be sloppier. He knew serials improved their craft, such as it was, over time. They learned not to make mistakes and became more careful.

That's why a lot of would-be serials were caught fast and sent down after only one kill.

But the others... they honed their craft. The more bodies, the harder they became to catch.

"No fingerprints are going to turn up on the notes he sent, and all the prints that were lifted from Laura's hospital room," she gave a little shrug, "they'll all be identified. Our killer is organized."

Yeah, he'd figured that, too. The "organized" killers always planned every move in advance, and their crime scenes were often meticulous.

"He's highly intelligent," Monica continued, "and for him, the crimes aren't so much about fear, as *controlling* the fear. Making the victims tremble and beg while he holds all the power."

He stared down at her.

"Odds are high our killer didn't have power when he was younger. He was afraid, and it broke him." Her gaze was on him, but he didn't think she saw him there.

Luke yanked out his chair. "You think he started killing when he was a kid?"

"It's definitely possible. But I *know* something set him off recently. Something made him start killing here, in this town. With these women. A trigger. We just have to find out what's driving him—then we can find *him*."

The sooner, the damn better.

"He knows them. By the time he kills them, he knows them better than any lover. He sees past the skin and into their hearts." Her voice softened. "He breaks them, and he watches the fear roll over them."

"Right before he kills them." Bastard.

"He doesn't rape them," Monica said. "But this—the way he kills is still just as intimate. To him, it's the most intimate he can be with anyone."

"I'll start working the victims and see if I can find any link between them." He'd take the vics any day over the killers.

Monica gave a slow nod. "Okay. Sounds good."

If he looked hard enough, there *would* be a link. Victims were rarely as random as people thought.

"Kenton will be down here in a few hours," she said, her attention back on the computer. "We'll use him to help question the friends and family."

"How do you do it?" he asked, because she was slipping away from him.

He'd held her in his arms, come so close to claiming her again. But right then, Monica might as well have been a thousand miles away.

Her fingers hesitated over the keys. "Do what?"

"Get into their heads so well." Because that's where she was heading. Right into the killer's mind. "It's so easy for you. Like breathing."

"Yes, it is." She didn't look at him.

"How?" Everybody had always wanted to know.

"I become the killer." Still not looking at him, but there was something in her voice. A tension.

Almost sounded like fear. *Almost*.

"If you become them, then profiling..." She gave a little shrug. "It gets easier."

Didn't sound easy. The last thing he ever wanted to become was a fucked-up killer.

She cleared her throat. "I've got a lot to do, okay? Are you going to finish interviewing the hospital staff and the family?"

Ah, dismissed. Right. "Yeah, yeah, I am."

That wall she'd surrounded herself with really pissed him off. He rose and sauntered around the old desk. She would *see* him. He skimmed his fingers down her cheek and Monica took a quick breath. But those eyes didn't meet his.

"Luke..."

His muscles clenched. The way she said his name. *Damn.* "We're working the case. We're catching this asshole." He had to say it because she needed to know what was coming. "But you and me, this thing between us...we're finishing it, too."

Finally, her bright gaze met his. "You don't really

know what you're getting into." A pause. "You can't handle me, Dante."

Now that sounded like a warning, and it sure didn't sound like the woman who'd caught fire in his arms hours before. "Let me be the judge of that," he said.

Their gazes held. His fingers pressed against the satin of her skin.

A knock rapped at the door. He didn't move. They were settling this first. "You backing away? Running?" He challenged, and he liked the way her eyes narrowed, just a bit, at that.

"I don't run."

The woman could be such a liar. She'd run from him but he'd finally caught her. Maybe.

The knock again. More of a pounding now.

Christ.

"I want you." The words came out, bold, a little fast, from her lips.

And those words—they made him hard. *Not the time.* He gave a nod. "I'll have you again."

A real smile. Just a flash. For just a moment. "No, Dante, I'll have *you*."

Well, damn.

Then, because it sounded like the door was about to be knocked down, he left her.

But he'd be back. For her, he'd always be back. He yanked open the door, ready to confront one of the deputies. Someone who obviously didn't understand that a closed door meant privacy, someone who—

"Hey there, Dante." Kenton flashed him a wide smile.

Shit. Monica had said he wouldn't be there until later.

"Good thing we got our own plane, huh?" Kenton craned his neck. "Nothing like flying first class. But, hell, is this our office? Figures...."

Luke gave Monica one last, hard look.

"Uh, is everything okay in here?" Kenton's gaze swept between them, lingered on Monica. "You okay, Monica?"

"Just fine."

"Right." That stare came back to Luke, seemed to weigh him. "So why don't you guys bring me up to speed and let me know just what's going on here?"

Two hours later, Luke and Kenton returned from their interviews. The door to their new office stood open, and Vance had paused outside. His head was cocked, his focus totally inside that small room.

"Always wanting what they can't have." Kenton said to Luke. "You had that same look on your face when you walked in and saw her."

Luke's jaw locked. He strode forward, and, blessedly, someone called out for Kenton. Luke could see through the doorway. Monica had pushed away from the desk. She'd worn a skirt today, and he caught a quick glimpse of her calves, then her smooth thighs as—

"Don't even think it." He muttered the words in the deputy's ear. "You don't want to mess with her." *But I so do.*

Vance jumped and his face flushed nearly as red as his hair. "No...no, I—ah, shit, uh, I gotta—"

"Go."

"Right." And he shoved past Luke.

Luke's eyes narrowed as he watched Vance hurry off. *Right. Keep moving, buddy.*

"Dante." The chair squeaked as she rose, shaking her head. She came toward him, a file in her hands. "I don't need you handling baby-faced deputies for me."

"I know." He should step back, and he would, soon. But that sweet scent—lavender—filled his nostrils—and he really liked lavender. Before her, he hadn't even known what the hell lavender smelled like.

After her... he'd never been able to forget.

"What we do, what we're gonna do, that's just between us." Her chin came up, and she stopped inches from him. "Same rules, remember?"

"Maybe it's time for the rules to change."

When her lips parted, he knew he'd caught her by surprise.

And, just for the hell of it, just because her lips were so red and soft, he thought about kissing her.

Her hand pushed against his chest. "Five deputies and a really pissy local sheriff are watching us right now." Her voice came slow and soft. "What you're thinking—*don't.*"

She brushed by him. "Sheriff! I've got something you need to see here." Just for an instant, Luke's gaze dropped to her ass.

Ah, damn.

Monica glanced back at him. "Ready for a road trip?"

"What?"

"We've got an early kill. Samantha did it. She found another of the perp's victims."

The ticking of the clock on the sheriff's desk was loud. Loud and annoying, and if Davis didn't hurry up and say *something*, Monica was pretty sure she might scream.

That'd blow her ice image to hell.

She cleared her throat. "Uh, Sheriff?" He'd been staring at the data she'd compiled for ten minutes.

His bushy brows rose. "What does this have to do with that asshole hurting women in my county?"

Kenton shifted beside her. Luke didn't move. He simply sat as steady as a rock in the chair to her left.

Monica leaned forward. "I had a special agent at the home office do a search, matching some specific criteria I'd set up." She tapped the grainy black-and-white photo of Saundra Swain. "The man we're looking for likes to attack women. Young women, in their twenties to early thirties. He sets them up to face their greatest nightmare." While he got off on their fear and pain.

She took a breath and shoved aside the mental image of Laura's still body.

His gaze dropped to the photo. "This . . . this here's just an animal attack. Snake bites—folks get bit all the time down here in the summer."

"Yeah, but most folks aren't tied to a tree when the snakes are biting them."

His eyes met hers.

"When the victim was discovered, she was still bound to the tree. Someone tied her up and left her there to die."

He shook his head. "You're sayin' this guy killed some girl in Louisiana—"

Monica gathered her patience as quickly as she could. She was explaining all this to him as a courtesy. Hyde had already given her the go-ahead here, but Davis—he'd lost three women. He'd known two of them. He knew their families. The way she figured it, the man deserved to know how they were hunting the killer.

So sure, she could have pulled Bureau rank, run right over him, and done whatever she wanted.

But then she'd find herself with zero backup from the sheriff's office.

She took a deep breath, then said, "Last summer, Saundra Swain was tied to a tree by an unknown assailant, and after she was bound, I believe the perpetrator wrangled the snakes and set up the attack on her. With the right prodding, he would've had them ready to bite—and she would have been kicking at them, fighting..."

"That's one painful way to go," Kenton murmured, and Monica was pretty sure she caught a shudder working through his body. Figured the city boy wouldn't be wild about snakes, not that she blamed him.

"Yes, it is." She waited a beat. "When she was six, Saundra was bitten by a snake while on a Girl Scout trip." Sam had tapped into the medical records for her. "The doctors gave her anti-venom, and she recovered."

"But I'm guessing she didn't go out on any more scouting trips," Luke said.

"No. She didn't." She eased back a bit.

What scares you?

Davis's fingers tightened around the handles of his chair. "That sick bastard—"

Using snakes for a kill was very tricky business. The guy would have needed to know an awful lot about the rattlers. Snake wrangling sure wasn't easy. But then, this guy seemed to have all sorts of knowledge at his fingertips.

"This is the earliest kill we've found." But it was not actually *the* earliest. She knew that in her gut. "Luke and I are going to take a little drive over to Gatlin, Louisiana."

Because there had to be an event that had sparked these crimes. Find that event, find the killer.

In Gatlin, it seemed Saundra was the only kill linked to the perp. But three victims were tied to him in Jasper. Why Jasper? She hadn't figured that out yet, but she would. He'd picked Jasper for a reason. The killer must have some connection to the city or to someone there. The connection *was* there.

But before she could put the puzzle pieces together, she had to go back to the past. *Louisiana.*

Goose bumps rose on her arms. Who said you couldn't go home again?

"What can I do?" Davis asked, his voice soft, tired. His eyes were bloodshot, and the lines on his face even deeper. "I gotta say something to the people. I got a damn call from CNN today—"

"I'll handle the media," Kenton said. "You just keep your patrols out there. Do your damnedest to keep your people safe."

"And we'll track this guy," Monica added, sounding way, way more confident than she felt.

Louisiana.

Home was where death waited.

CHAPTER *Seven*

*T*oo late.

She ran as fast as she could, but the tree branches hit her, snatching her back. But she had to get out, had to help—

A scream cut the air. High. Sharp.

Then, silence.

Monica froze. She shouldn't look back. She knew she shouldn't. If she looked back...

She spared a glance over her shoulder.

Saw the body. The blood.

The eyes staring sightlessly up at her.

Oh, God, no—

"Monica!" Hands gripped her hard, biting into her flesh.

Her eyes opened, and a scream built in her throat. Her hands scrambled, diving beneath her pillow as she twisted and tried to find her weapon.

"Wake up, baby, wake—"

She had the gun pointed right between his eyes.

Luke froze.

Pain squeezed her chest. *The damn dreams were back.* Four months. She'd slept like the dead for over four months, and now they were back.

"You gonna lower that anytime soon?"

Her hand wanted to shake so she tightened her fingers around the butt of the gun and then, slowly, carefully, put the weapon on the nightstand. "S-sorry." Her voice came out hoarse.

She'd screamed once. For so long. Until her voice broke and only a whisper remained.

No, no, Laura had been the one screaming. When they'd gotten her out of that grave and put her in the ambulance, she'd screamed and screamed—

Until her voice broke.

Like me.

"Wanna tell me what that was about?"

The shadows crept around them. The light on the nightstand was on. She'd left it on. Like she always did.

With that faint light, she could see him. Bare chest. Muscles gleaming. He wore a pair of dark faded jeans— Luke had always liked his jeans. As her gaze dropped over him, she saw his length swell beneath that rough fabric.

"Monica..." A warning edge there. One she chose to ignore.

The pounding of her heart filled her ears. Better that than the sound of screams.

Rain fell lightly onto the cabin. *The cabin.* The only place left for visitors in the dot on the map that was Gatlin, Louisiana. Made of old wood, the one-bedroom cabin probably was supposed to be cozy and quaint.

Maybe for someone else, it would have been. But not for her.

The old cabin, the dark swamp, the constant chirp of the crickets and God knew what else outside—*not* for her.

They'd arrived after midnight. He'd taken the couch, hadn't pressed her for sex—*and why not?* And she'd taken the bed.

Then the damn dreams had come back.

"Talk to me. What were you dreaming about?"

There he was. Caring, being a good guy. That was Luke's problem. Deep down, past that tough veneer, he was *nice*. Didn't he know that was dangerous?

"Talking is the last thing I want to do." She'd never spoken truer words to him. Her hand flattened over his chest. His heart drummed beneath her fingertips, racing just as fast as her own.

His jaw worked, and she could see the lust on his face, but he held back. Dammit, he held back. "You can't keep hiding forever."

Her breath caught. *He knows.* "The dreams don't matter." She wouldn't let them. "Tonight, I want you."

Her right hand swept out. Hit the lights. When she had him, she didn't need the light.

Her lips took his. A wet, open-mouthed kiss.

The fire hit her. Hard and fast. The need that shot through her blood and moistened her sex and made her want. *Made her want—*

Luke. The rough slide of his body against hers. The feel of him in her, and his voice, whispering to her.

She moaned into his mouth even as her nails bit into his skin.

He came down on her, the strong, hard length of his

body pushing against her. His lips were tight on hers, and she knew he was as hungry as she was. Six years.

But it seemed just like yesterday.

His mouth ripped from hers, and his lips took her throat. Kissing. Sucking. Licking. Her sex creamed as she arched her hips toward him. The man knew all of her weak spots.

After all this time, he should have forgotten, he should have—

"Luke..." Her turn to lick. A swipe of her tongue near his ear. Because she still remembered what *he* liked. "Ditch the jeans." There'd be no pulling back tonight. She needed him too much.

Silence the victims. Make the cries stop. Make me forget.

Her fingers eased their hold, then skated over his chest. Over the slight ridge, the new scar he'd added to his collection. A killer's mark.

A chill skated down her spine but she pushed her hands between their bodies. He had on jeans. Easy enough to get rid of those, but, ah, damn, he'd have to move his hand—

"Easy." His rough whisper in the darkness, rolling with his smooth drawl. That drawl always grew thicker when he was pissed or when he was aroused.

Easy?

"Not what I want," she whispered right back. He should know better. She wasn't the kind for cuddling and soft kisses. Not her.

Her fingers drifted away from the scar. Stroked over those abs. She found the snap of his jeans.

He slipped back. She pushed forward. A hiss, and his

zipper eased down. No boxers. He must have dressed fast when he came to her.

She wrapped her fingers around the straining length of his cock. "You know what I want," she told him as her fingers tightened. "And I know just what *you* want." Her left hand pushed against his shoulder, trying to ease him back.

He caught her wrist, curled his fingers tightly around her. "Not. This. Time." Gritted.

But what—

He stood up, fast. Luke fumbled in his back pocket, then ditched the jeans. "It's been too fucking long," he muttered.

Yes, it had been. But she'd been afraid...

And then her past had come calling.

Can't run. Won't run.

She shoved her panties down and kicked them away.

He caught her legs. Spread her wide and, even in the darkness, she felt the heat of his stare. "Too fucking long," he said again and then his fingers were on her. Sliding between the damp folds of her sex and finding her clit and rubbing, just the way she needed. Her head tipped back. A moan built in her throat. Her nipples were tight, aching, the soft fabric of the shirt rubbing against them as—

He shoved her shirt up to her neck, exposing her breasts. His mouth closed over her nipple. His tongue swirled over the hungry peak, his teeth scored her flesh.

And he drove two fingers into her.

She clenched around him and stiffened.

Not enough.

The fingers retreated. Plunged deep.

"Luke!" The bastard knew better than to tease. *He knew*.

His head jerked up. His eyes glittered down at her. "Ready?"

Not like she could get more ready. He had to feel the cream coating his fingers, the tremble of her sex around him.

"Hope to hell you are," he growled, then pushed up on his arms. A packet was in his hands. *Condom*.

He'd had that in his back pocket? The man was a freaking Boy Scout.

She loved that.

He ripped the packet open with his teeth. Sheathed his cock, that long, thick length that she'd really wanted to taste again, because Monica knew she could drive him to the edge and beyond with her mouth and she wanted—

He shoved her thighs apart wider and pushed between her legs.

"Missed you." He thrust deep. So deep she nearly bucked off the bed. So deep his name broke from her lips. So deep the bed sounded like it might break apart as the old boards groaned beneath them.

Just what she'd wanted.

He plunged into her, again and again, hard drives that she met with blind pleasure. Her legs wrapped around him, squeezed tight.

And the fury built.

Faster.

Faster.

His eyes were the only thing she could see in the darkness, glinting at her.

His arms were locked on either side of her head as he thrust, driving them both to that wild release.

Closer. *Closer*.

His cock slid over her clit, pushed into her core and—

She broke. A muffled scream slipped from her lips as her sex spasmed around his thick length. Pleasure and madness. A climax so strong she squeezed her eyes shut and held onto him as hard as she could.

Still he thrust. Deep, deeper, every hard movement of his body making the pleasure last and last.

Luke.

His name broke from her lips. She pushed up, wrapping her arms around his neck as she lifted against him.

Face to face. Sex to sex.

She kissed him. And rose. His cock slid over her sensitive flesh.

Monica pushed down. Rode him.

She rode him fast and deep. She took him, even as the heat of release whipped through her again.

Took him—took everything.

His cock swelled. Lodged tight within her.

He came.

So did she—a long, hot wave of release. Pleasure.

He'd always been able to give her exactly what she needed. Always.

He was so screwed.

Luke knew this for a fact. An absolute-damn-certainty. He woke up, alone in the bed. The scent of sex and Monica hovered in the air all around him. His cock was already up and twitching, and he knew he was in trouble.

Sex with her hadn't been as good as before.

It had been better. They'd barely touched, and he'd been about to explode in his jeans.

Then when he'd gotten inside her, and the tight creamy clasp of her sex gripped his cock—

Screwed.

The bathroom door opened with a soft groan. Monica stepped out. Her hair was perfect. Not a strand out of place. She'd applied her makeup, a light touch at the eyes and a sexy slicking at the lips. She wore khakis and a white blouse.

Perfect.

Then she saw him. Her eyes met his and for the briefest of moments, she paused.

She looked...uncertain. Then that chin rose. "You're up."

He glanced down at his cock. "Glad you noticed."

That sound could have been a choked laugh. But then her eyes fell to his flesh and she took a deep breath. "Luke..."

He could still feel the press of her fingers on him. "What time do we talk to the first witness?" He could play this game. *Business.*

She turned toward her suitcase. "Eight-thirty."

Ah, right. He glanced at his watch. "Gives us forty minutes." Time to hop his butt in the shower and get his game face on.

Time for pleasure too, but with those stay-away vibes Monica was tossing out...

The pleasure would have to wait.

Business, first.

That was okay. He'd had his taste. *Just as addictive as before.*

So much for being able to walk away after one more screw. They were just too combustible.

He yanked on his jeans and rose. Because he was watching her—what else was new?—he caught the swift glance she tossed him and he saw the way her gaze dropped to his chest. Luke couldn't help it. He had to flex, just a little.

A man had his pride.

"You…you came pretty close to death on that last one."

He blinked and stopped the flex. Not what he'd expected.

Then a thought hit him, an unbelievable one, and Luke paused. "Worried about me?" Because with her, he never knew where he stood.

The tight nod she gave had his eyes widening.

She turned away from him. "I heard about the stabbing. Right after—"

She'd heard, and she hadn't come rushing to his bedside. No big shocker. Not like it was his first injury. "Just another scar to join the others." He lifted his hand, rubbing his right cheek.

Monica's mark. Stupid, the way he'd gotten that. For her.

She glanced back at him. Her gaze darted to his hand. The mark. Then right back to his eyes. "You should've had backup."

Ah. Not gonna talk about her mark, not yet. "I was interviewing witnesses. Didn't need—"

"In the SSD, you do." She set her shoulders. "That's why we're going together. The perps we hunt here—you can't take chances with them."

So he'd learned with Carl Malone, aka the Sorority Stalker. An ex-psych professor who'd crossed the line into straight-up crazy. No longer content to just watch the pretty young girls, he'd had to touch them. Then kill them.

I stopped the bastard.

Luke set his shoulders. "Give me five minutes in the shower, and I'll be ready to go."

Stamping down hard on the lust—because yeah, it was there, was always there when she was near—he headed across the room. One bathroom. Great. The room would smell of her.

But then, *he* smelled of her too and...

"Thank you, Luke."

He stopped right beside her.

Her hand lifted, rising over his cheek. Her fingers trailed past the early morning stubble and up to the scar.

Was she thanking him for that long ago night, when they'd been in the alley and that bastard had come out of the bar swinging that knife?

He'd been kissing her then. Tasting her and feeling the weight of her breasts crush against his chest. They'd snuck outside, away from the others who were celebrating the end of a brutal training session.

Monica hadn't normally gone with them on the celebrations. But she'd gone that night, for him. He'd had to get her alone.

Luke just hadn't counted on the drunk idiot with the knife. The fool looking for money who hadn't realized he'd walked straight into trouble.

But then that idiot had made the mistake of turning his focus onto Monica. With her shirt slightly undone and the top of her breasts just peeking out—

Luke had taken the bastard down. So what if he'd gotten a little scratch? No one was hurting Monica on his watch.

"Last night…" Oh, hell but that voice of hers was like a stroke right to his groin. "I needed you."

His jaw dropped.

"Thank you." She cleared her throat. "When you're dressed, we'll go get the evidence file and see what we can turn up."

He caught her hand. Brought it to his lips. "There's no going back."

Her eyes met his. Held. "I've never wanted to go back."

No, Monica had always struck him as a living-for-the-moment kind of woman. No past. And no future.

"If Hyde finds out…" She exhaled. "He'll bust our asses."

Probably. But some things were worth the risk.

"You folks here about the Swain murder?"

Monica looked up at the deep voice. Her nails were flat on the counter of the sheriff's office. Luke stood beside her—

And a shiver worked through her body.

Her focus narrowed on the man strolling toward them. Tall, thin, with a mop of red-blond hair. His brown sheriff's uniform was perfectly straight, and his gold star glinted.

She pulled out her badge. Her fingers were rocky steady. "Yes, I'm Monica Davenport with the FBI." A flash of her ID, just to show him she wasn't bullshitting.

His golden eyes dipped to the badge, then met hers.

The briefest curl lifted his thin lips. "The FBI, huh? Don't get many Bureau folks down here."

Not surprising. Gatlin was a small speck on the map, lodged between the swamp and the woods. Not exactly a prime hotspot for crime.

Well, unless you were talking body dumping. Because the swamp would sure be great for that.

"I believe you were contacted by my supervising officer, Keith Hyde. We need to see the crime records for Saundra Swain's—uh, is everything all right?"

The guy's eyes had narrowed, and he crept forward, that intent gaze on his face. "I...know you."

She felt the ripple of movement beside her as Luke suddenly came to attention. Monica made herself blink. Once. Twice. Then she shook her head slowly. "I don't believe I've ever had the pleasure, Sheriff—"

"Martin. Jake Martin."

The name meant nothing to her now. Just as it had meant nothing when Hyde told her she'd be meeting up with the fellow.

"Huh. I don't usually forget faces...."

"Neither do I," she told him quietly.

That stare lingered a little longer, then Martin's gaze drifted to Luke. "You her partner?"

She caught his shark's smile. "Luke Dante."

A grim nod. "Got those files for you. Sherri will be bringing them along and—" His gaze came back to her. "I *know* you."

Monica forced a shrug, but sweat began to dampen the skin between her shoulder blades. *Because of the insane southern Louisiana humidity, of course.* One of the many reasons she preferred to spend her summers up north.

"I don't believe we've ever met personally before." Her words came out smooth and easy. "But I have worked several high profile cases with the SSD. Perhaps you've seen a photo of me in a newspaper or caught an interview on TV." Though that was really more Kenton's specialty with his pretty boy face. She shrugged and let her lips curl. "Or maybe I just have one of those faces."

"I'm good with faces," the sheriff murmured, shaking his head. "And I'm sure we've met."

Now the guy was starting to get under her skin.

"Sheriff, you said the files were ready?" Luke demanded, his tone a little sharp.

"Ah, yeah, they're—"

"Here you go, Sheriff!" A woman's high voice called out. A small lady with a mop of gray curls bustled from the back. She had an old, yellowed box in her hands with "Swain" written in black marker across the front. "Found it in the basement."

Martin turned his head toward the woman, just a small shift in angle, and Monica caught a strong view of his profile.

Oh, damn.

Her cheeks iced, then pinpricks of heat shot across her skin.

"Monica?" Luke's fingers curled around her arm, and she realized that she'd stumbled back.

Martin—she did know him. Take off about fifteen years, add more of that hair, and he'd be...

A young deputy, pulled into Hell. Reaching out a hand to help a victim in the darkness.

"You okay?" A soft rumble from Luke.

She pulled away from him. "Of course." Perfectly

calm. "Sheriff, is there a quiet office we can use to review this information?"

He glanced at her, smiling now. "Ah, ma'am, this whole place is quiet. I transferred over here about ten months ago, and I can tell you, not much happens in Gatlin."

Except an occasional murder. Once in a blue moon, a woman was tied to a tree and terrorized. Did that really count as "not much"?

Four hours later, they were in the woods.

Not her favorite place to be. Monica could completely sympathize with Saundra. Insects chirped all around them, and Monica was pretty sure the temperature had kicked up another twenty degrees out there.

Pine trees stood, still and tall, around them. She and Luke jumped over branches and headed deeper into the woods.

"Wanna tell me what all that was about back at the station?" Luke asked.

Monica glanced down at the map in her hands, then back up—the better to avoid tripping over a root and slamming into the ground. "All what?"

"The sheriff." He stopped and faced her, putting his hands on his hips. "You knew him, didn't you?"

Careful. "If I did, I don't remember him."

"But he remembers you." Too watchful. That gaze of his was way too watchful. "And Monica, let me just tell you, you *don't* have one of those faces."

What was that supposed to mean?

"No one else looks like you," he said. "No one."

Was that a compliment? He'd always given compliments so easily to the other women she'd seen him with. But he'd only complimented her in bed.

And why did she care? "Look, I don't know what the guy was talking about. Maybe we met at a convention or something. Maybe he heard me do a lecture." She paced ahead of him. Turned to the right. "I don't know. I'm not going to worry about it now and—*there.*"

His footsteps hurried up behind her.

Monica stared at the thick pine. Her eyes trekked from the base, up the thick trunk—had to be at least thirty inches in diameter—and on up to the top branches that seemed to touch the perfect blue sky.

Dead flowers, looked like roses, sat at the base of the tree. Someone had cared about Saundra's death out here.

Maybe her parents.

Maybe her killer. Wouldn't be the first time a serial had come back to the scene to pay respects to the victim.

"It's been a year," Luke said, "What do you really hope to find out here?"

She didn't know, but there had been damn little to help her in that case file. Black-and-white photos of the scene. Saundra's bloated body, sagging against the tree.

Inside the yellowed box, they'd found some recorded interviews with two of Saundra's co-workers at a dive called Gatorbait. They'd read a deputy's notes about Saundra's home and her family.

No fingerprints were recovered on the rope that had bound Saundra. The techs hadn't discovered any fibers or hairs from the person who'd left her tied to the tree. And though the ME ruled that the bites came from rattlers, none of the snakes were found at the scene.

Though two rattlesnakes were killed a week later outside of a church. That careful notation had been in the file.

But with all those bites on her body, there would have been more than two snakes. A lot more.

"Monica?"

She flinched at his voice and realized she'd been staring at the tree and those dead flowers for way too long. "I'm not sure what we'll find, but this *is* the earliest kill we know about—"

"How can you even be sure this is the same guy?"

"Because it's all about fear." Twenty-one-year-old Saundra had been dying to shake the dust of Gatlin from her boots. She'd been working, saving her cash, and planning to head out as soon as she saved five grand.

She'd never wanted to see the woods or the swamp again. She'd *hated* the woods, hated snakes. Pity she'd died there.

"It's too much of a coincidence," Monica said, and it was. "She was bound to the tree. The killer brought in the snakes." Easy enough to transport if he knew how to capture them. Then, once he'd been at the scene, he'd probably had a snake hook with him—he would have used that to herd the snakes, to get them exactly where he wanted. *Ready to attack Saundra.* After he was finished, he'd probably tossed the snakes and the gear into the swamp. "He wanted her to suffer." *To be afraid.*

"You know there was no mention of a note in the file."

What scares you?

"Doesn't mean there wasn't one." She knelt before the tree, her brows pulling together. "Or maybe he added that little touch as he went along."

"Developing his signature?"

"Something like that." She eased down beside the

flowers. Monica stretched her arms out as she tried to match that death pose, the one that was now seared into her memory.

"Sweetheart, what the hell are you doing?"

Her head jerked up. *That's a good girl... aren't you, my sweetheart?* "Don't call me that." Fired out—fast and angry.

He stared down at her.

Those damn crickets seemed way too loud right then.

"My mistake." Wooden. "How about this... Monica, what the hell are you doing?"

She managed not to wince. Barely. It was just being here in the woods, with those insects driving her crazy and with death hanging around her.

Why couldn't memories just stay dead?

Breathing slowly, evenly, Monica fought to hold onto her calm. "Sorry." The apology came out quietly. "I just... don't call me that, okay?"

He strode toward her, blocking the rays of the sun as they filtered through the tree branches. "Keeping it only business?"

"No, it's not that, it's just—" *How's my sweetheart? Pretty little sweetheart, I'm gonna break you....* She licked her lips. "I don't like it. Sweetheart. Not for me, okay?" Where was her control? It was because of that guy, Martin. He'd thrown her off. Made her start to remember.

"Um, okay, but the question remains... what the hell are you doing?"

She tipped her head back. Let her gaze sweep around them. "Could you step over? A little to the left?"

He moved.

"Thanks." She noted the trees, the thick grass, and the

bushes. Jumping up, she brushed off her hands and hurried away from the tree.

Saundra died there. Probably screaming for help.

And the bastard with her had probably laughed.

Why did the perp love the pain so much?

"There's a reason he picked this spot." She stopped, her eyes narrowing. "There's always a reason."

"Uh, yeah, because this place is freaking deserted and no one could hear her scream."

Monica swallowed then started walking. *There.* Toward the two twisted pines that grew about ten feet away. They looked like lovers embracing. "The car accident back in Jasper—Sally Jenkins died at the exact same spot her husband did. And that abandoned house? I got Sam to run a check for me. Turns out Patricia Moffett lived there when she was a kid."

A low whistle. "What was the connection for Laura? Why dump her at—"

"Don't know." She stopped in front of the embracing pines. "This place though, *it's important*." She could feel it. "The killer picked the spot. He tied her there, pointed her to the east, because I think he wanted her to see something."

What was the last thing Saundra had seen before she died?

These trees. Why these?

She walked around the trees, her gaze scanning the ground.

A stump. Looked like maybe another pine. The tree must have fallen years ago.

Her eyes narrowed as she crouched down. Her fingers lifted, hovering over the wood. "Lovers," she whispered.

"Yeah," he said. Monica turned toward Luke. His eyes were on the trees as he said, "I guess those pines do kinda look like—"

"Here." She tapped the side of the stump. "Initials. See them?" Her fingers traced the letters. S.S. + K.W.

Lovers no more. Not once death came calling.

The initials were barely noticeable from this angle. Time had faded them, making them blend with the ripples on the top of the stump. A deputy doing a run-through of the scene probably wouldn't have even noticed them.

But the killer had known they were there.

And Saundra had known.

"We've got to find K.W." Excitement had her blood pumping fast and hard through her veins. This crime had been intimate, far more personal than she'd expected. "We find him—"

A fast grin split Luke's face. "We might just find our killer."

Yes, they just might.

We're coming, asshole. Time for me to find out . . . what scares you?

CHAPTER *Eight*

With a name like Gatorbait, Luke really hadn't expected much from the bar in Gatlin. So he wasn't disappointed.

They waited for the night crowd to roll in, the better to find folks who might be willing to talk. Or just drunk enough to run their mouths to FBI agents.

He and Monica took a booth in the back—a booth with a table that liked to tilt, cushions that were split open, and the smell of sweat, cigarettes, and fried catfish hanging around it.

Luke didn't really get the catfish part. As far as he could tell, the place didn't serve food. Just really bad beer.

A waitress came over to them. Short white shorts, long, tan legs, low-cut black tank top. Big boobs. Boobs strategically placed very close to his eyes.

Nice. He'd bet they were real, too. Oh, yeah, those...

Monica's brow rose.

He pressed his lips together. The better to hold back

the *No way are they as good as yours* comment that
wanted to burst free. Like she'd appreciate that. Even if
it was the truth.

"Another round?" The waitress—she'd said her name
was Donna—asked with a big grin. A grin she shot his
way. Flirting for tips. He'd watched her and the other waitress. They leaned in close to the men, smiled a lot, and
flaunted cleavage.

Smart women.

But that could be a dangerous game if they tried to
play with the wrong men.

"Donna?" Monica called, cutting through the rumble
of voices in the bar. "We need to ask you a few questions." She pulled out her ID, flashing it nice and fast.

The tray in Donna's hands wobbled just a bit.
"Wh-what? Why's the FBI in Gatlin?"

"Just following up on an old case," he said smoothly,
trying to divert her attention. An old trick. Divide the
focus, get to the truth faster. A handy way of questioning
that had worked well for him in the past.

"What old case?" The tray steadied, but Luke was
willing to bet Donna's heartbeat hadn't climbed back
down yet.

"Investigating the murder of a friend of yours…"
Monica tucked away her ID. "Saundra Swain."

Donna fired a fast glance at the bar. "*Saundra.*" Her
face paled.

"Was Saundra seeing anyone?"

Hesitation, faint, but there. "No."

Luke smothered a sigh. Now why did people always
want to lie?

"Really?" Monica sounded surprised. The woman was

a pretty good actress. Actually, maybe she was too good. "That's not what we heard in town."

They'd actually heard jack shit outside of the bar. The folks of Gatlin were a tight-lipped bunch, at least when they were sober. Maybe once they started knocking back drinks...

Donna's lips, painted a dark pink, tightened. "I'm tellin' you, when Saundra d-died, she wasn't seein' nobody. *No. Body.*"

"But what about before she died?" A quick press from Monica. "What did I hear?" Laser blue eyes turned on him. "I'll have to pull out my notes, but I think it was Kevin; no, Kenny—"

"*Kyle.*" The woman looked like she'd pass out any minute. Because talking about her dead friend hurt? Or was it something more? "She and Kyle weren't seeing each other, okay? That was long over. Saundra knew she could do better. She ditched him, told his ass to hit the road."

"Right." Luke drummed his fingers on the sticky table top. *Got the first name, just need the last.* "And where can we find old Kyle? We need to clear up a few things with him."

A toss of her hair. Really blond hair. So blond it kind of hurt the eyes. "Hell if I know. Bastard split town right after..." Her lips trembled. The crack showed in her shell then. *Pain.* "He cut out a few weeks after we buried Saundra."

"Kyle—right." Luke gave a nod. "His last name was—"

"West," Donna snapped out. "And if he knows what's good for him, he ain't never comin' back."

"Guess you didn't like him much." Luke figured that was a big understatement. "Wanna tell us why?"

One shoulder lifted in a hard shrug. "He screwed around on Saundra. She caught the jerk with his pants down...."

Now he had a feeling she meant that literally.

"That man was her *life*. She stayed in this shithole for him..."

So Donna wasn't exactly loving Gatlin, either.

"—and when she found out what he was really like, she planned to split as soon as she could. She was almost there." A sad shake of her head. "Two more weeks, and she would have been long gone."

Instead she was just dead.

"She didn't get out, he did." Monica tilted her head back and studied Donna with steady blue eyes. "Doesn't really sound fair, does it?"

"Hell, no, it—"

"Donna!" The bartender's voice roared across the room. "Table six needs a refill!"

She jerked her head. "On it." Her tongue swiped over those too pink lips. "You think—you think Kyle had anything to do with Saundra's death?"

"Is there anyone else who might have wanted to hurt her?" Luke asked softly, not really answering.

"No. Saundra—she was good. Class, you know? Never said a bad thing about anybody. She didn't deserve what she got."

"Most people don't," Monica murmured.

Donna stared down at her. "Find the bastard who hurt her, would you? Maybe I'll sleep better then." She spun away, blond hair fluttering.

"I doubt you will." Monica pushed away the beer she'd never tasted. "It doesn't usually help."

But Donna was already at the bar getting more drinks, flashing a big smile at the bald bartender, and acting like she didn't have a care in the world.

But Luke had heard the quaver in her voice. Donna *did* care.

Luke leaned toward Monica. "There wasn't a mention of this ex-boyfriend in the file."

"There should have been. The guy would have been at the top of my suspect list."

His, too. Sometimes, the people you loved the most could be the ones who hurt you. Very, very badly.

He sure as hell knew that lesson.

"I'm going to step outside and call Sam," Monica said as she rose, brushing back the midnight hair that skimmed her cheeks. "Let's see what she can find out about this Kyle West."

If anyone could find the guy's deep dark secrets online, Luke figured it would be Samantha.

"Try to keep your eyes off Donna's chest while I'm gone, okay?"

He blinked. Wow. What was that? Jealousy? "Baby, you don't have to worry." Donna wasn't the one he wanted. Only Monica.

Her lips parted, and he saw a flash of surprise in her eyes. *She hadn't meant to say that.* Ah, maybe that façade was falling away. His lips rose in a half-smile as she spun away from him and hurried away.

Damn, but he loved to watch her leave. Well, loved to watch that ass anyway. That sway was so nice. He'd take that view over *any* view of Donna every day of the week.

Monica pulled out her cell phone and tilted her head down. *Probably already briefing Hyde.* She always seemed to be checking in with him. After a moment, she vanished in the huddle of bodies.

He reached for his beer. Long day. Shit-tasting alcohol, but really, a beggar couldn't choose.

The lip of the beer bottle touched his mouth, and he heard the shatter of breaking glass. The thud of flesh hitting flesh.

Monica.

He was on his feet in an instant, charging through the crowd. Another night flashed through his mind. Another bar. Another...

A woman screamed. Not Monica.

He shoved through a swarm of bodies and saw a redhead on the floor, her skirt twisted under her. Blood trickled from her lip.

"Fuckin' cheatin' whore!" A guy staggered, slipped, then lunged for her. "I'll make you so..."

Luke tackled him. He slammed the drunk into the nearest table and felt the wood splinter and crash beneath them.

The man's elbow clipped Luke hard, right under the eye, and the bastard roared as he twisted and rolled.

He was a big one. Tall, thick with fat and muscle, and the guy was a fighter.

Big and Meaty swung a ham-sized fist at Luke's face. *Definitely a fighter.*

Luke dodged, then kicked out of the tangle of wood and limbs. He jumped to his feet and raised his arms. "Look, buddy, you don't want to do this, I'm a—"

A snarl. A long, low, barely human snarl, then the drunk attacked.

Luke struck out, catching the guy in the jaw. His turn. Hard and fast. The dude staggered a bit, but didn't go down.

The woman started sobbing, then she lunged for Luke. "Leave him alone!"

Leave him alone?

Christ.

He tried to shake her off, even as the bull got ready for another attack.

The guy came at him, slamming his fist into Luke's gut while the woman held on with all her strength. *Doesn't pay to be a boy scout.*

He kicked the bastard right in the groin.

"*Fuck!*" The guy's high scream. The bigger they are, the harder they—

The woman dug her nails into Luke's back. "Dammit, I'm with the FBI, you can't—"

The bull was back on his feet. Breathing hard and balling his hands into fists. Not standing fully, probably couldn't.

Catcalls came from the crowd. Some cheers.

No help. Of course not.

"Shouldn't have got between Charlie and Lynn...."

"Poor bastard."

Luke figured *he* was the poor bastard in question. Great. He shook off the redhead and tried one more time to reach for his ID.

But *Charlie* took a swing at him.

Luke swung right back. His fist connected, Charlie's didn't, and the guy staggered.

What does it take to get this guy down?

"*Aahhhh!*" Great. Now the woman was screaming and charging him and—

"Freeze!" Monica's shout, full of icy rage. "FBI. Don't even *think* of taking another step."

And for her, both Charlie and Lynn stilled. Their eyes widened. Their shoulders sagged.

Luke brushed off the bits of broken glass that clung to his arms. *Not real sure where the glass came from.*

He took his time crossing to her side. She was armed, her gun out and aimed.

"Call the sheriff," she barked at the bartender. "These two have just assaulted a federal agent."

"Wh-what?" Charlie shoved a hand through his thinning hair. "He ain't no—he didn't say—"

Oh, for fuck's sake. Luke bent down and scooped up the ID that had been knocked from his fingers. "FBI, asshole."

Monica looked at him. Shook her head. "Two minutes," she muttered when he drew close, and she didn't lower her gun. "I was gone for two minutes."

He licked his lip, tasted blood, and said, "Helluva lot can go down in two minutes."

That eye would be black soon. Monica stood at the bar, watching as Luke lifted a rag filled with ice and pressed it to his already darkening left eye.

Her gaze skated across the room, to the redhead with the torn shirt that the sheriff was leading out of the bar. Monica sighed. "You're always trying to save the ladies." His M.O. As long as she'd known him, the guy had carried this rescue complex.

He turned toward her, sending droplets of water flying from his makeshift icepack. "What's that supposed to mean?"

She lifted her brows. "It means every time you see a woman that you think is in trouble, you jump in—"

"He *hit* her."

"She's not going to press charges against him." The woman kept calling good old Charlie's name and saying everything had been a mistake. Maybe her face had mistakenly gotten in the way of Charlie's fist.

Luke's Adam's apple clicked as he swallowed. "She damn well should. If she doesn't get away from him, he'll kill her one day." Grim certainty.

And something else. Pain. An old echo. *Personal.* Her head tilted. "Luke? There something going on here?"

He lowered the ice. "Fucking makes me sick. Every time I see a guy punching a woman."

She touched him and felt the steel of his muscles beneath the flesh. This wasn't about Charlie Donalds and Lynn Front. This was personal.

"They don't leave." His fingers clenched around the sodden rag. "Why the hell don't they ever just leave 'em?"

She forgot the sheriff, the crowd, and the country music that made her temples ache. "Who are you talking about?"

He'd never told her about his family. Okay, she'd never asked. Because she hadn't wanted to share her own screwed up past. When you were just hooking up for sex, you didn't have to share. And you weren't supposed to care.

Why did he make her break the rules?

"No one. I'm not talking about any damn one." He tossed the rag onto the counter. "Come on, let's get out of here."

She took a breath and hesitated. More was there, boiling beneath the surface, about to break right through that razor-thin control.

"We've got to head back to Jasper." His hand pressed lightly against his stomach, and she was pretty sure he muttered "*Sonofabitch.*"

Getting hit by Charlie had to be like getting hit by a bus. If Luke was hurt like this, Lynn wouldn't survive many more "mistakes."

They left the bar. There wasn't any more information to be had there, anyway. While Luke had iced his eye, she'd talked to the bartender and another waitress. Both had given her the same story about Saundra. A great lady. Lots of friends, but with a dick of an ex-boyfriend.

Outside, gravel crunched as a deputy's cruiser pulled away.

"You sent them off together?" Luke demanded. Headlights cut across the bar's parking lot.

Martin spun toward him. "She's not gonna press charges. She never does."

"Screw that. The whole bar saw what happened. There is no way..."

"The witnesses say you didn't identify yourself, Agent Dante. That you attacked first."

What? Monica's gaze shot toward the star-dotted sky. Great. Just great.

"She was on the floor, bleeding, and he was getting ready to go at her again. So, hell, yes, I went in to stop him."

Just like Luke. She glanced at him. Saving the world, one woman at a time.

"I can't find anyone who actually *saw* Charlie hit

her." Martin crossed his arms and stared down Luke. "And they both say she slipped and hit her chin on the table."

"Bullshit."

"Ah, Luke..." They could use a bit of tact with the local authorities.

"No, no—he *knows* this is bullshit, and he's not doing a damn thing about it! That woman is his punching bag—"

"From what I hear, that woman jumped you, Dante."

Yeah, she had. Monica's jaw had dropped when she'd walked back inside and seen the woman going for Luke's back.

"He's got her brainwashed," Luke said. "She thinks she deserves the crap he's giving her, and she's staying with him because he's her *man*, and—"

"Luke." Monica put her hand on his chest and felt the tension tightening his body. "Take a breath." They hadn't come to Gatlin for this. He had to stay focused.

"I don't need a breath."

"Box it up," she told him, making her own voice clipped. "We're working a case here, Dante."

His eyes flashed at her. Fire there.

"I thought ya'll already got the information on the Swain girl." The sheriff's voice came on a slow roll. "What you doin' out here at Gatorbait?"

Monica kept her hand on Luke's chest. The fire in his eyes was contained. For now. "We were talking to friends of the victim."

"Huh."

Her eyes narrowed. "Sheriff, why didn't the name Kyle West come up in the reports?"

"Don't know, ma'am. That was before—"

"Before you transferred here. Right." She licked her lips. "And the former sheriff? Patterson had a heart attack, didn't he?"

"Yes, ma'am. Henry, bless him, passed away in September." Not long after Saundra's death and real close to Kyle's disappearance from the county.

Things could never be easy.

"Well, thanks for your help, Sheriff." She dropped her hand. "Looks like we'll be heading out of Gatlin."

His eyes were on her, studying way too closely. "And did you find what you were looking for?"

"I think we did." But she'd found more. Memories that she didn't want. "Let's get out of here," she said to Luke. He was all but vibrating against her. That rage might kick free soon, and she'd hate for him to be close to the sheriff when it did.

She headed for their vehicle. Heard the thud of his steps behind her. This little trip hadn't been...

"Now I remember." Martin called out, and her blood froze.

She stilled at his words, and the darkness that always surrounded her seemed to grow thicker. Monica took a quick breath before glancing back at him. Deliberately, she didn't let her eyes stray to Luke.

"Remember what?" Clear and cold.

He gave a nod. "Kyle West. Seems I recall hearing about him...he was the sheriff's nephew."

Now she did risk a glance at Luke and saw the understanding in his eyes. Sometimes, even law enforcement looked the other way when it was family.

"Something else you should know, Dante." The

sheriff's words were thicker now. "I don't like this shit with Lynn any more than you do."

She caught the tightening of Luke's jaw. "Oh, really?"

"Hell, yeah. Lynn—she's my sister." He stalked toward them. His voice lowered when he said, "And I'll be damned if I let her wind up in a grave."

Family.

Yeah, sheriffs, agents, the cops on the beat—they could all break the rules for family. Especially when death came calling.

"Then you better make sure she stays the hell away from Charlie," Luke ordered, "because that's where he's gonna put her."

The two men's stares locked. Then the sheriff gave a hard nod. "I'm workin' on it."

Family. Just how far would you go to protect family?

How far had Sheriff Patterson gone? "Tell me, Sheriff," Monica said. "Are there any other members of Kyle's family in town?"

He spat on the ground. "Just one. May Walker. Lives up on Grimes, past the fork that leads to the right."

"Somebody lives here? We're sure about that?" Luke asked, eyeing the dilapidated house on Grimes Street.

She could understand his disbelief. The house didn't exactly look inviting. Darkness from within, two windows boarded up, and an overgrown lawn with thick, twisting trees that seemed to surround the rundown house.

"Don't you take so much as another step or I'll shoot you!"

Monica stiffened at the yell. A woman's voice, coming

thickly from the darkness of the porch. And, ah, yes, she could see the barrel of a shotgun. "We don't mean you any harm."

"Get off my property! Been robbed twice this week. Fool sheriff won't help me; I'm helping myself! You're not takin' anything, so—"

"We're not here to rob you," Luke told her, his voice carrying easily. "We're FBI agents, ma'am. We need to ask you some questions about your nephew, Kyle West."

Silence.

Then, "What the hell you doin' comin' out here so late? Tryin' to give an old woman a heart attack?"

"Uh, no—"

"Show me your ID!"

Carefully, Monica reached for her badge. Luke's movements mirrored hers. Wood creaked, and a small figure of a woman with a bun of gray-streaked black hair eased down the steps. She still had a tight grip on her shotgun.

She squinted. "Can't see shit."

Good to know when that shotgun was so close.

After a moment, she dropped her gun. "If you're robbers, you're the loudest damn robbers I ever heard."

"We're not robbers," Luke began.

She grunted. "Agents from the FBI." She whistled. "And you lookin' for Kyle, huh? You not gonna find him here."

"We heard he left town," Monica said.

"Yeah, yeah." She rocked forward a little bit. "After Saundra—sweet little Saundra—he took off." Her head turned a little bit to the right.

"And do you know where he went?"

May turned away. "Ya'll come inside. I want to see them IDs in the light."

They followed her in, and the steps creaked beneath them, a rough groan of sound.

The inside of May's house was packed with old boxes, piled high, nearly touching the ceiling. There were old newspapers and dolls—lots of porcelain dolls with wide, black eyes.

Not any room to sit on the couch. It was covered with books.

But there was plenty of light, and May took her time looking at their IDs. Finally, she said, "Don't know where Kyle went."

"No idea at all?" Luke pressed.

"You get in a fight? What the hell happened to your eye?"

His shoulders lifted in a small shrug. "A fist that didn't agree with me." His gaze held hers, an intent look. "Ma'am, do you have any idea where Kyle is right now?"

She hesitated, and then her already narrow lips thinned even more. "Maybe out West. Used to talk about goin' to California to try and find his dad."

Luke pulled out a notebook and scribbled down the information. "And his dad is?"

"Hell if I know." May shoved aside some books and sat down on the end of the sofa. "My sister Margaret— she didn't know, either. Some guy she met one night. Idiot who promised her a new life, but screwed her and left her to rot with a kid."

Ah, not the most warm family moment there. "So Kyle never knew his dad?"

"Nobody ever knew him. My brother said he was gonna hunt him down when he found out that Margaret was pregnant, but Henry never did. Couldn't find the bastard. Hell, maybe Henry didn't even look."

Right. Henry. That would have been Sheriff Henry Patterson. Monica began to walk casually around the house. The papers were at least ten years old. And most of the books were covered with dust. May wasn't reading the books, just keeping them.

And, apparently, almost everything else. "What about Kyle's mother?"

As she turned back to watch her, Monica saw the other woman flinch. "Dead."

"I'm sorry," Luke said smoothly. "It must have been hard for you, losing your sister."

A jerky nod.

"And how did you lose her?" he asked, as he stepped closer to May. A slow, easy move. No threat. Just compassion there, on his face, in his eyes.

May frowned at him. "A f-fire. She died over fifteen years ago in a fire on Brantley. Hey, don't go messin' with my stuff!" A hard bark toward Monica.

Monica eased away from the papers. "May, do you happen to have any letters from Kyle? Maybe, I don't know…even some of his old school work?" Highly likely, given the state of the house. May seemed to keep everything. And maybe they could get their hands on a sample of Kyle's handwriting for comparison.

May blinked and rubbed her head. "What? Why'd you be wanting that?"

So I can see if he's a killer. "It relates to an investigation we're pursuing," she told her.

"You investigatin' Kyle?" Her head shook, back and forth. "No, *no*, he ain't done nothin'!"

"Easy, May, it's all right," Luke said.

But she backed away, ramming her elbow into a stack of newspapers and sending them crashing to the floor. "M-my head...startin' to hurt again. Need my medicine..." Her lips twisted and she muttered, "*Be mine, Valentine.*"

What? Monica cleared her throat.

"Um, where is your medicine, May?" Luke edged closer to her "Tell me and I can get it for you."

"No! No! I don't need you. I don't—"

"All right." He tossed her a light smile. Still so easy. "Was Kyle with Margaret when the fire started?" Luke asked.

The color bleached from May's face. Fear flared in her light green eyes. "I want you to leave, you hear me? *Leave.* I'm a sick old woman. You shouldn't be here, messin' with me."

"Sorry, May," Luke said immediately, "we didn't mean—"

"*Leave!*" She jumped to her feet, and her hands fisted.

Monica met Luke's stare and inclined her head. "Thanks for your time." Soft. "And if we could just get those old letters of Kyle's..." Because she needed them.

May's thin lips twisted. "No. I *know* my rights. You can't take anything from me!"

Not without a warrant. But if that was the way they needed to play, so be it.

They headed for the door. Luke stopped and offered May his card. "Just in case you hear from Kyle, give me a call, would you?"

She snatched the card. "Won't hear from him. Haven't heard from him in a year, ungrateful little bastard."

Right. A "little bastard" that the woman sure seemed to be protecting. "Thanks for your time," he told her.

But Monica hesitated. *Be mine, Valentine.* Where had that come from? And why? May's voice had softened, saddened when she said it. "When was the fire—I mean, what date?"

"Val—Valentine's Day."

Monica managed to keep her eyes steady on May. "I'm sorry for your loss."

"Leave." A whisper now, holding the edge of desperation.

Monica knew they wouldn't be getting any more help from May. She crossed the threshold, with Luke walking out into the night ahead of her.

May slammed the door shut behind her. Almost got her foot.

"Not a lot of Southern hospitality there," Luke murmured.

No, and Monica sure would have liked to learn just what "medicine" May was taking.

"Think she's telling us the truth?" He headed toward the car.

Monica glanced back at the closed door. "Probably not." But her fear—that stark flash when she'd asked about Kyle and the fire—*that* had been real.

"Don't go back to the motel, not yet."

Luke had thought Monica slept beside him as he drove. The SUV had eaten up the interstate, leaving the cypress trees and the heavy moss behind.

She had lain back beside him and closed her eyes, leaving him. For sleep?

No, he should have realized her mind was still working. Always working.

"Did you hear me?" She stirred a bit, straightening. "Don't go back to the motel yet. Take us to the Moffett crime scene."

"What?" His gaze slipped toward her, just for a second, then back to the road. But he could still see her from the corner of his eye. She pulled at her seatbelt, then rubbed her forehead, the back of her hand pushing back that silky soft hair.

"It doesn't make sense. I mean, the tree, I get. Saundra's kill was personal; he wanted her to die seeing what she'd lost." A quick sigh. "And the car wreck—it was the exact same place. He was forcing the vic to relive the worst night of her life."

Monica had been working the case during the drive. He'd thought she was dead on her feet, and she'd been mulling over the case.

Monica's nails drummed on the armrest. "That's what he was doing—forcing them all into the past. With Saundra, with Patty, with Sally—he took them to a place from their pasts. And he made them *fear*."

His hold on the wheel tightened. "Then why'd he bury Laura behind that house? How was that important to her?"

He steered off on the exit ramp, turning north and heading for the house of death.

"We missed something out there," she said. "I know we did."

"You really think we're gonna be able to find anything

tonight?" They should just go back in the morning, with plenty of light, and maybe she'd be able to do her voodoo and figure out what message that twisted creep was trying to send them.

No, not to them. The message was to the victims.

"This guy does everything for a reason. The people he picks, the way he kills them. The places he chooses—and *when* he kills," Monica said. "I want to see the scene the way he saw it."

She'd come to play his game. He watched the lights of the agents' SUV cut through the darkness.

Back so soon.

She hadn't even been in Gatlin a full twenty-four hours. Not time to learn any good secrets. Disappointing. He'd expected more from her. She was supposed to be the best.

But she'd hardly presented any challenge so far.

He pulled onto the road behind them and kept his lights off. They'd never know he was there, getting so close.

Tonight wasn't a kill night, not for her—because he didn't know yet what Monica Davenport feared. So many things could chill. So many things could wake her up in the night, screaming. But what was the *one* thing that scared her the most?

He had to know. He *would* know. It was his mission. Find out, break her.

They didn't turn toward the motel. He tensed a bit at that. He'd expected them to go back. Maybe to screw. Because he'd seen the way the man, Dante, looked at her.

Lover's eyes filled with possession, heat, and lust.

It would be too easy to figure out Dante's fears.

But Dante wasn't his prey.

They turned up ahead, taking Peter's Junction, and his foot eased a bit on the accelerator.

That way—it led to the Moffett house. *Why go there? Why tonight?*

He pulled off the road, taking a deep breath. No, that wasn't the taste of fear on his tongue. He wasn't afraid. Never afraid.

But maybe Agent Davenport had learned more than he thought in Gatlin. If she'd stumbled onto his secret, someone would pay. Someone would scream and beg and bleed—and *pay*.

Behind him, a muffled groan broke the silence.

He smiled. *Pay.*

They took the flashlights from the back of the SUV. Big, thick Mags that were like mini-spotlights, cutting through the darkness that surrounded them.

"The woods," she said, jogging ahead and pretty much seeming to talk to herself. "Why these woods?" The woman always hurried ahead of him.

He pulled out his weapon. He wasn't about to take any chances on a killer's hunting grounds.

His light swept the perimeter and caught the glittering stare of a possum.

Luke kept close to Monica, his gun ready. Branches bit and tore at him. An owl hooted somewhere far in the distance, and crickets chirped from the cover of darkness.

And Luke couldn't shake the feeling that this was a very, very bad idea.

Monica halted just outside of the secured yellow police tape. Stars glittered overhead, and the moon was out, thick and full, giving them more light. She circled the grave. Her flashlight flickered over the ground.

Piss poor idea. He should have told her that, but no, he'd been drawn along with her. Always had been. Like a fucking moth to the flame.

Her light rose to the trees. He smothered a sigh. "You're not going to see anything."

She didn't seem to hear him. She crouched on her knees. The light swung some more.

"Monica?" The back of his neck was tingling. Time to get to the motel. There were too many places for someone to hide in the darkness. Being in the open like this didn't sit well. Not a damn bit.

She turned off her light.

Oh, that was just brilliant. He inched closer to her. Someone had to watch her ass. That was what a partner was for, right?

Her head tipped back. "I think—I think I can see a window from the house."

What? The trees were too thick. The pines too tall. No way could she see—

He cocked his head—*well, damn*. It looked like lightning had struck a pine about ten feet away, knocking down the top section of the tree.

And giving a dead-on view of what was left of the house's second story. The attic maybe? Or was that a window glinting—

"Laura's parents said she got locked in a closet playing hide and seek." She rose to her feet and brushed off her knees. "I think you need to talk to them again...and find out just where that closet was." Her light flashed on. "Give you ten-to-one odds that Laura knew Patricia Moffett, and that they were playing at the Moffetts' when that closet got locked."

Well, shit. "You're good."

One shoulder lifted. "Maybe I just know killers too well."

Maybe. But knowing killers could help her save victims and that was what mattered.

"Let's get the hell out of here."

"Right." She fell into step beside him. It was easier getting out, but Luke kept his weapon close just in case. The sooner they left this death house the better.

No, the sooner they caught the perp, *the better.*

Monica paused near the house and glanced up at it. "Probably was a happy place once." She shook her head, then kept walking. "I'll call Hyde. Let him know what we've found and adjust the profile. Maybe we can get a warrant for May's place and find some of Kyle's letters for a handwriting comparison. That'd be damn lucky if we could."

Luke stilled. His eyes swept toward the SUV. Something was wrong. That tightening knot in his gut told him things were about to go to shit.

The scene was off. He couldn't see how yet, but…"That's wrong." A few cautious steps forward then, "*Sonofabitch.*" The tires were slashed. All fucking four of them.

No wonder the SUV had looked odd; it was sitting too low to the ground.

"He's out here," a whisper of sound from his lips. But Monica didn't need to be told. He knew she understood.

He's watching us. Hiding in the dark and watching.

"Might not be him." Monica's voice. Unruffled. Soft. "This is a known drug area. It could be anyone."

Glass glittered on the ground near the passenger window. He inched forward. Maybe she was right. Maybe he'd find the radio jacked or the GPS gone or...

An envelope lay on the driver's seat.

And, yeah, the radio was still there. So was the GPS.

"It's him." That had damn well better not be one of his twisted little scare notes. Oh, hell, no. First the calls to Monica, now this—

She brushed past him.

"Wait—what are you..."

She had her gloves on. Luke kept his gun up while she opened the door and snagged the envelope. He closed the distance between them, letting his shoulder brush hers. The light from the SUV spilled out, and he saw the familiar black scrawl.

Bastard.

But the name on the envelope—it wasn't Monica's.

No, she wasn't the killer's next fear puppet. The name on the envelope was his.

Agent Luke Dante.

Sweat slid down his back. *Bring it, bastard. Bring it.* "Let's play," he whispered. *But you don't know, do you, freak? You don't know what scares me.* "Open it," he demanded, and his eyes rose to sweep the area.

"We need to call for backup. He's got us trapped here and—"

"Open the damn envelope."

Paper tore beneath her fingers. Something fluttered to the ground. He bent but she was there before him. Luke twisted, keeping his back to the vehicle, trying to keep her covered, keep them safe.

"Does he think he can scare me?" he snarled.

Silence.

He shot a glance back at her. There wasn't a handwritten note. No, her fingers were curled around some kind of old newspaper clipping. One that had been folded and creased. She'd just opened it, and he could see the big, black headline:

Romeo Killer Captured. One Victim Survives.

There was a photo under the block words. A grainy shot of a man—good-looking, grinning—as he was shoved into the back of a patrol car.

"What the hell?"

She shoved the clipping back into the envelope. "We can't stay out here." Her voice trembled and so did her hands. "Let's get closer to the house, get better cover. With that bastard watching, we can't take chances."

And they were sitting ducks right then. Yeah, they needed cover, so they could spot *him* and attack.

But going for a long shot with a gun wasn't really the guy's style. He was more the up-close-and-personal type. A man who enjoyed getting his hands dirty or covered in blood.

The Romeo Killer? He shook his head. That didn't make a damn bit of sense. What the hell did that bastard have to do with anything?

"Let's go," she said, and spun away. She ran through the darkness, her light extinguished now, and her steps nearly silent.

And he was right behind her.

Because he didn't know what kind of sick message the killer was trying to send, but he wasn't taking any chances. The guy wanted to play, that was certain, and the game could begin anytime.

Or maybe it already had. *Because he's watching us. Waiting.*

Game on.

CHAPTER *Nine*

*T*he Romeo Killer.

Bile rose in Monica's throat. She rocked back on her heels as her stomach knotted.

How had he known? No one should know. Especially not some sick, twisted bastard who...

"Yeah, we're out at the Moffett scene. Tires are slashed. He's here, Sheriff. What, how do I know? Because the freak left us a message. No—just get us some transportation out here, got it?" Luke barked into his cell phone.

He didn't understand the message because that clipping wasn't meant for him. It was for her. Her nightmare, coming true.

Looked like the killer knew how to get to her. But *how had he known?*

Not Hyde. Hyde wouldn't leak that information to anyone.

"What's he doing, Monica?" Luke demanded.

She swung toward him. "I haven't seen—"

"No—why's he leaving me crap about Romeo? I remember that bastard. He got off on carving up girls."

Yes, he had.

"What is it? Is he trying to tell us he's another Romeo? Because as far as I can tell, this creep isn't charming his victims; he's attacking—cold, hard and quick."

Charming? Yes, that had been Romeo's style. At first. "I don't—I don't know what he meant with the clipping." *Lie. Lie.* Sometimes, it was way too easy to lie.

She rolled her right shoulder. Caught herself.

"The sheriff's coming," Luke said, running a hand through his hair. "Fifteen minutes, maybe twenty with these back roads from Hell. He wants us to sit tight."

"I don't think he's coming after us tonight." No, he'd just wanted to leave his little message. Screw with her head, and let her know that he knew. And what would she do when Luke started putting the pieces together? Hell, was that what the killer wanted? For Luke to learn the truth about Romeo? "He's just playing with us tonight."

Building the fear. He wouldn't kill them, not yet.

Luke crept past her, his gun in his hand. "Sitting back isn't my style. Let's see what we can—" His breath whistled out. "Sonofabitch. *He's coming.*"

She crouched, bringing her gun up. No streetlights, but the moonlight trickled down, showing them.

"The bastard's walking in the middle of the road. And *he's coming right for us.*"

Her fingers tightened around the gun. She could see him. The thick bulk of a man stalking toward them. But that didn't fit. The killer wouldn't come right at them. Not his style.

She glanced at Luke. Too much darkness to see his face. "This is wrong."

He was already heading for the steps, keeping his back close to the house. "Cover me."

"Luke!"

He was gone. "FBI!" he yelled out. "Identify yourself!"

Sweat slickened her palms. She went after him, keeping cover, staying low. Her weapon was aimed and ready. But...

This isn't right. It's not his way.

The man didn't stop walking. The shuffle of his feet traveled easily in the night.

"I said, identify yourself!" Luke's order shook the porch.

But the guy didn't speak. And he was getting closer.

Not right.

Then the guy's hand lifted.

And Monica saw the glint of a gun. "Luke, he's armed!"

Even as she screamed her warning, a bullet exploded, firing at the house, chipping wood just inches from Luke's head.

"*Sonofabitch.*"

The man ran now, full-out ran, toward them. Yelling something as he fired, over and over.

Luke fired back.

So did she. Not aiming for the head. Or the heart. She should have, she knew, but...

Her bullet clipped him in the shoulder, and he staggered. Luke's caught him in the chest. Blood burst from his wounds, spraying around him.

But still, somehow, he fired.

"Drop the gun!" Luke roared. "Drop it! Drop—"

"*On…me!*" The gunman screamed. "*It's on me!*"

Monica's finger froze on the trigger. *Not our guy.* "Luke, hold! Do you hear me? *Hold—*"

The guy fired again, and the bullet blasted right across her left arm. *Oh, shit.* Fire ripped the flesh away.

"*Monica!*" Luke shot again. The bullet thudded into flesh.

The gunman fell back.

"No." She shook her head and raced across the overgrown grass.

"*Monica! Stop, he's not dead. It wasn't a heart shot!*"

The guy raised his head and somehow managed to lift his gun. Under the moonlight, she saw his eyes. So much fear there, and anger. *Rage.*

"B-bitch…not gonna…get me…" Blood dripped from his mouth.

"Drop your weapon," she told him, never wavering with her own gun as she ignored the throb of fire racing up her arm. "Do it, just drop—"

But he shook his head. "N-not…like…him…"

She saw the tremble of his hand. *Squeezing the trigger.*

He wouldn't miss her heart this close. Couldn't miss. "Don't make me shoot you," she whispered.

"*Monica! Get out of the fucking way! Give me the shot!*" Luke's furious shout.

The man, young, thin hair, thin face, tried to smile. "F-fuck y-you." The gun shook. "F-fuck him."

"Your last chance," she told him and heard the distant

wail of sirens. It had to be the sheriff, coming fast. "Just put down the—"

"*M-my*...way." He jerked up the gun.

"*Monica! Get out of the way, get out—*"

The guy fired.

The red lights from the ambulance flew in a sickening blur, lighting then concealing the crime scene.

Another scene. Another body.

"*Damn straight.*" The sheriff slapped Luke on the back, hard enough to make him nearly stagger. "Bringing you two in was the right choice. You got him. Stopped that freak cold—"

Davis was sure the dead man, the bastard lying in his own blood just steps away, was the serial they'd been seeking.

Luke lifted his eyes to Monica. She sat in the back of the ambulance. Her shirt was torn, her left sleeve completely gone. A guy in an EMT uniform pressed a white bandage against her flesh. She didn't move. Didn't blink. Just kept her eyes locked on the body.

The guy had blown his brains out right in front of her.

"Guess some killers just can't stand the thought of being taken in." Another slap by Davis. The guy wore one big, face-splitting grin.

People didn't normally get so excited over suicide. But then, this wasn't your average case.

"He kept the control by shooting himself," Luke said. A lesson he'd learned about serials long ago.

Control. For them, it was key. Lose the control, lose the game. Without control, the serials became sloppy. A sloppy murderer was one that could get caught. Or killed.

"Folks in this town will sure sleep better tonight, I tell you."

Tires squealed. Luke glanced over and saw a news van braking to a hard stop just beyond the red, swirling lights.

A news van? Christ, that was the last thing they needed right now.

"Don't worry, I've got 'em," Kenton said. He'd arrived on the scene, riding shotgun with the sheriff, just in time to find Monica leaning over the body.

Shaking the man who'd tried to kill her. Tried to kill *them*.

She'd yelled at him, demanded, "Tell me! No, don't do this! Tell me!"

But the guy hadn't been able to tell her a thing. Kinda hard for the dead to talk.

"Hold on there, son." Sheriff Davis straightened his shoulders. "This is *my* town. *My* people. They look to me for protection, and I'm gonna be letting them know they can sleep good again tonight."

Monica blinked, like she was waking up from some kind of dream. Then she pushed away from the ambulance attendant. Her forehead wrinkled as she hurried across to him.

"The killer tried to set you both up, but he was the one to end up dying." Davis shook his head. "Jasper is *safe* again. Our second brush with these bastards, but we came through. *We came through.*"

"*Sheriff.*" Monica's clipped voice. "We have no concrete proof this is the killer we are after. There's no evidence here to suggest…"

Davis's jaw dropped. "What the hell? Davenport— this here bastard slashed your tires. Left you one of them love letters of his, then he came at you with a *gun*." He pointed to the bandage on her arm. "You think he was just firin' warning shots there? He came to *kill* you."

"And he wound up killing himself." She shook her head and lowered her voice. "That's not the way this guy would go out."

Luke stirred a bit at that. "I don't know, maybe he would." She looked tired and far too pale.

The bastard had shot her. *Grazed her arm. A few more inches, just a few more…*

His body stiffened as a wave of fury seared through him.

She'd been in front of the killer, staring down his gun. What if the perp hadn't shot himself? What if he'd aimed for her?

Luke's stomach churned with fury and fear. Yeah, he knew she was just doing her job. Just like he was.

But he couldn't stand to see her hurt.

Good thing that bastard is dead. 'Cause I could send him to Hell myself right now.

Brain matter and blood littered the ground. The perp had done one hell of a number on himself. Half of his face was gone, blown to bits, and the eye that was left still stared, wide open.

A camera flashed as the crime scene guy snapped his images.

"Jeremy Jones has been nothin' but trouble his whole damn life," Davis said. "A real shame."

Jeremy Jones. Yeah, that was the name they'd found in the wallet. But Davis had ID'd the guy even before they'd put on the gloves and gone searching for proof.

"He was in and out of juvie. Had two arrests last

year." The sheriff shook his head, and his lips tightened. Luke realized the guy wasn't looking at the body. Hadn't looked directly at it, not since he'd run toward them, glanced down and identified the body. "*Jeremy, shit.*"

"So this guy was a career criminal?" Kenton asked, rubbing the back of his head. "What was he in for as a kid? Animal mutilations? Break-ins?"

"Drugs."

Monica's gaze didn't rise from the body. The sheriff wouldn't look, but she couldn't seem to look away. "What kind of drugs?"

"Any kind. Jeremy was what we call one equal opportunity boy."

Doors slammed. The news crew, coming closer.

"Showtime for me." Davis straightened his shirt and adjusted his star. "You two did a fine job on this one. I'll be sure to tell Hyde how impressed I am. Real good work."

"Don't tell Hyde anything," Monica said. "And don't talk to the media. This case isn't over."

But the sheriff shook his head and stood his ground as he frowned at her. "*It's over.* Everybody in this county knew Jones was trouble. Just like his old man. His dad died on the streets, and Jeremy did, too." He turned away, headed toward the news team and muttered, "Some folks just can't be saved."

Monica shook her head. "No, sometimes, we just can't save them."

Hell. Luke had to go to her. He closed the distance between them. Let his fingers brush her arm. Not too hard, not too intimate, but he *needed* to touch her. "You okay?" Because she'd scared a good ten years off his life. Maybe more.

Her lips pressed together, and she gave a small nod.

Not good enough. He caught her other arm, the uninjured one, and spun her toward him. "Stop looking at him. He's dead. He tried to kill *us*. Nothing we could do."

Her eyes looked so cold. Shards of ice. "There's always something we could do."

He really wanted to shake her. Or kiss her, hard. But too many eyes were around. "He was a killer. We closed the case." The sheriff sure thought so. "End of story."

"No, it's not."

Kenton cleared his throat. "Um, look, excuse me and all but..."

Luke glanced over at the other agent.

"You guys need like a moment or something? And, damn, man, what happened to your eye? I thought it was a gun fight."

A rumble rose in his throat.

But Monica snapped first. "What I need is for you to get over there and stop Davis from screwing up my case."

Kenton blinked.

"Don't let him tell the good folks of Jasper that they're safe. They're not."

One brow rose. "The dead body on the ground says otherwise," Kenton told her.

"Oh, it says something, all right." And she crouched down, right next to the blood and the pieces he really didn't want to think about too hard. "Right here." She pointed to his wrist. The wrist that had slumped over Jeremy's chest after he'd fired that last bullet. "Right here it says that he has rope burns." A pause. "They're on both wrists."

What?

"Ma'am, don't touch the—" The tech began in a high, nervous voice.

"I'm not touching the damn body!" Monica surged to her feet. Kept those shards of ice on Kenton. "Strange, wouldn't you say?"

Yeah, Luke would say that. Monica gave a hard *hmmm* like a revving motor then asked, voice tight, "Why was our killer tied up—pretty recently, by the look of those marks?"

"Maybe the asshole was into S&M," Kenton said, shaking his head. "Maybe his girlfriend got a little rough with him tonight."

"Maybe he's just not our guy," she fired back at him. Her delicate jaw worked a minute, then she called out, "Hey, deputy!"

Vance stumbled to a halt at Monica's call. He cast a fast glance down at the body, swallowed, then met her stare. "You—you don't want me to touch 'im, do ya?" He'd just arrived on the scene, and he already looked like he might pass out.

"You can't touch—" The tech said again.

Oh, Christ. Luke ground his back teeth together.

"No." Monica clipped out. She swiped back a lock of her hair and said, "You knew him, right, deputy? Davis said he was a local and—oh, hell! Kenton, Davis is going live with some shit over there. Go stop him!"

Sure enough, Davis had a mike in front of him and a shining spotlight covered him as the camera lens zoomed in.

"Fuck." Kenton took off at a lope. "Special Agent, coming through!"

Not that his announcement cleared his path. But it did get the attention of the reporter. Reporters always responded to Kenton.

"He's not blowing my case." Monica's spine straightened.

Vance began to inch away.

"You knew him." Monica pointed her finger at Vance's chest.

A quick nod. "W-we all knew Jeremy. He was ... always around. I-I think Lee went to school with him at Jasper High."

"Davis said the guy's dad died on the street. What was he talking about?" she asked.

Vance's muddy eyes darted toward Davis. A no-longer-talking Davis because Kenton had the mike firmly in *his* hands. "About seven years ago, the sheriff shot him," he whispered.

"How did it go down?" she pressed.

"H-he was dealin'."

Luke wanted to be clear on this. "Dealing what?" he asked.

"Meth. Jason Jones—he was...I mean, I wasn't here but I heard...he was making it, in his house. Word was...um, when the sheriff busted in, the whole place was near to exploding."

Yeah, he didn't doubt that.

"Jason, he ran. Sheriff and his deputies chased him." Another quick glance at the sheriff. "The guy ran into the street. They told him to stop. Everybody said they told him to stop."

"But he didn't." If the guy had been high on meth, no chance he would have backed down.

Vance scooted away from the body. "Is it—is it supposed to smell like that?"

"He defecated." From the crime scene guy. What was his name? Gerry? He'd been around a lot lately. Probably more work than the guy'd had in years.

"Def—oh, *shit*."

"Yeah." The tech stood and held his camera tight. "It happens." He strolled away, dark head bent.

Vance's face flushed beat red. "I'm gonna be sick." Standing over a body that had been blown to hell would do that to you.

"Come on." Monica grabbed the guy's arm and led him a few feet away. "Sit on the ground. Put your head between your knees."

But his head flew up. "Everybody will see me."

"Yeah, but at least they won't see you puking all over the place."

He sat and shoved his head between his knees.

"Breathe." Luke advised him.

He did. Luke heard the deep, shuddering breaths.

Gerry came back and put a sheet over the body. Finally.

Monica's shoulders had relaxed a bit, but a faint furrow lined her forehead. He could feel the energy rolling off her.

A bullet wound hadn't slowed her down. But then, he'd never known anything to slow down Monica. She was tough, fierce, and even in the midst of a nightmare, sexy.

He was *so screwed*. Luke sighed and glanced at the deputy. "Gonna keep the cookies down?" Luke asked the guy.

Vance managed a nod.

"Good."

"What happened after the sheriff told Jason Jones to stop?" Monica's quiet voice. Not threatening or demanding in the least. Smooth and easy.

Ah, she'd changed her style. Probably because good old Vance was close to a breakdown.

"I-I told you, I w-wasn't there, I'd just started workin' in Mobile back then—"

He saw her jaw clench. "I realize you weren't there, Vance. But what did you *hear*?"

"I—he—Jason pulled a weapon and fired on Davis." He licked his lips.

Luke looked up and saw the sheriff stalking toward them. Moving at a pretty fast clip.

"Sheriff Davis fired back," Vance's words came faster, too. Probably because he'd just seen the sheriff closing in on them. "So did two deputies. They took him down—"

"Right in the street," Monica finished.

Like father, like son. One hell of a coincidence.

"F-felt bad when I heard." Vance rubbed his hand over his face. "Shame, ya know? Watchin' your old man go out like that."

In a hail of gunshots and blood.

"*Watching?*" Monica leaned in close. Blood had appeared on her white bandage. Shit. She needed to get that checked again. She probably needed stitches.

"Jeremy was there." His Adam's apple bobbed. "His ma died when he was a baby. His dad—he took care of him. That night, word was that he ran after his old man—"

And watched him die.

"*Vance!*" Davis thundered. "Why the hell are you sitting on your ass? We got a perimeter to secure. Move, man, move!"

Vance scrambled.

"I spoke to the mayor," Davis said, giving a hard nod. "We're holding a press conference at 7 a.m. tomorrow."

Attendants loaded Jeremy's body onto a gurney. Zipped him up and rolled him away.

So much blood was left behind.

Not an easy death. *But he'd chosen to go out like that. Chosen the bullet.*

By his own hand.

"We're closing this case." Fierce voice. Blazing eyes. The sheriff's voice thundered with an authority Luke hadn't heard before. "Jones is the killer, and that's what I'm saying on the news. Jasper is a safe town. I won't have folks worrying anymore."

With that, he spun around and strode away.

"I think they do need to worry, Sheriff." Monica's voice came, quiet but clear, and stopped the guy in his tracks. "Actually, I think they should worry one hell of a lot."

The sheriff had frozen, but he didn't glance back at her. "My town is safe now," he said again, and Luke wondered if he was trying to convince Monica of that fact—or himself.

Then an EMT raced up to her, muttering about the blood dripping on her arm. And the sheriff kept walking.

"Sheriff—" Monica called.

Luke stepped in front of her. "Stitch her up," he ordered, shoving his hands into his pockets. The better not to touch. Hold.

Not now. Because that message was plain in her eyes. *Her rules. Her game.* Not for much longer.

Monica could hear the ticking of the bedside clock, counting off the seconds. So slowly and way too loud.

No, not too loud. The room was just too quiet.

Monica grabbed the clock. Yanked the batteries out and threw the damn thing across the floor. Her hands were shaking, her entire body trembling.

Fury rode her. It tightened her gut and pounded through her head. She jumped out of the bed. *Can't stay there.* Pressing her palms against her eyes, she began to pace. Fast, desperate strides.

F-fuck . . . you.

Her hands dropped. A dead man's voice, playing like a broken record in her head.

And even when she closed her eyes, she could see him.

His eyes—angry and afraid.

F-fuck . . . him.

Had he been afraid of her? Of Luke? Or of something more?

M-my . . . way. His way, all right. A shot to the head.

"Dammit," she whispered. "Just . . . dammit."

"*Monica!*" She froze. A fist pounded on the connecting door, hard enough to shake the wood. "Open the door—or it's coming down!"

Her heart thudded in her chest. *Luke.* Oh, Christ but she needed him, needed him so much she'd intended to stay away. Because she knew that the moment she was alone with him, she'd break. Shatter.

Covered in a dead man's blood.

That was how she'd left the crime scene. She'd stayed

in the shower for an hour, let the hot water scald her skin, but she still didn't feel clean.

"Open. The. Door!" Another hard thud with his fist.

I need him.

Too much. One touch, and the need, the hunger, would be too strong. In the past, she'd always had control with her lovers. Even with him.

"Fuck!" Wood splintered. The door flew open and banged against the wall. Her eyes widened.

He'd just kicked her door down. Well, damn.

Something hard slammed against the wall on the far left. A fist? "Keep that crap down!" A man's voice, snarled and sleepy.

Monica licked her lips. Her heart drummed in her ears, fast, faster, so—

"You could have died today."

He'd showered too. His blond mane was still wet. He had on his boxers but his chest glistened.

"He could have shot *you* instead of himself." The low words rumbled as Luke took a step inside. "You took a risk—you should have shot him."

She would have. Her finger had been squeezing the trigger. Then she'd realized he wasn't aiming for her.

No, the gun had been rising, turning, but not at her. At himself.

She'd just been too slow to save Jeremy Jones. A tremble ran the length of her body. "Luke, don't—" *Don't come any closer. Touch me, and I'll break.*

Touch me, and I'll feel.

Feeling, that was the dangerous part for her.

He stiffened. A muscle flexed in his jaw. "Don't what?" Another step. "Don't tell you how scared I was?

Don't tell you that I wanted to shoot the bastard, kill him cold the minute he pulled that gun on you?"

On us. Because he'd been trying to take Luke out, too, and when the shots had started, fear for Luke had nearly choked her. *Can't do this.* She could smell Luke. Could all but taste him. "Don't make me need you more."

His eyes narrowed. It seemed to take her words a minute to sink in, then he was on her. Grabbing her, jerking her close and crushing his mouth down on hers.

She clutched at him. Her fingers were greedy, desperate. Her mouth locked on his. Her tongue drove past his lips. She stroked him, tasted and craved more.

Her nails bit into his skin. She didn't care. Right then, the only thing she cared about was the way he made her feel.

No, *that* he made her feel. Even if the feelings were about to rip her apart.

His hands clenched around her hips. His cock—hard and long and ready—pushed against her sex.

Luke's mouth tore from hers and he started licking her neck. His teeth raked over her flesh, and he muttered. "Christ, Monica, don't scare me again, don't—"

She pulled back. "I don't want to talk." Not now. The beast inside her was alive. Hungry.

For him. For every damn thing she'd always wanted and couldn't have.

But for now, she'd take—

Pleasure.

She dropped to her knees before him.

"What? No, you don't—"

She caught the waistband of his open jeans and shoved them down. Took his cock in her hands. His length was swollen and heavy, reaching toward her with moisture glistening on the broad head.

Her hands pumped him. Primed him.

His groan filled her ears even as his hands fisted in her hair.

He wanted this. So did she. Time to take what she wanted.

Her lips closed over the rounded tip of his erection. She took that salty drop onto her tongue and swallowed.

"*Monica...*"

Deeper now. He tried to control her with his hand, but she didn't want control. Not from him.

Not from anyone.

Her mouth widened, and she took him deeper, faster. Monica used her tongue as she sucked and licked.

And he swelled even more inside her mouth.

Her panties were wet. The fabric rubbed against her, and her hips rocked in time with each move of her mouth. Arching forward, wanting his touch, the thrust of his length *in* her—

"*Enough!*" He caught her wrists and jerked her up. Luke didn't touch her wound; he didn't even come close. Because he wouldn't forget; *he* wouldn't hurt her. Not him.

She raked her nails down his chest, scoring the flesh. "Don't go easy on me."

The smile he flashed was one that the devil would wear. "I won't." At that rumble, she knew his lust matched hers.

He moved fast and pinned her against the wall as he took her mouth again in a hot, wet, open-mouthed kiss.

Luke ripped her panties away, and he tossed them to

the floor. She just wore a t-shirt now, an old, thin FBI Academy t-shirt.

His fingers pushed between her thighs, parting her folds and shoving deep into her sex.

Monica rose onto her tiptoes, choking back a moan. *More.*

Luke's head lowered. He laved her nipples through the shirt, and now she was the one to sink her fingers into his hair, to hold him tighter, to press him closer.

His fingers plunged, in and out, and his thumb pressed over her clit. Her muscles tightened, the wild rush of pleasure tempting her. So close. She could come if—

Her elbows jabbed against the wall behind her. Pain shot through her arm. Not enough pain to stop her, hell no, nothing would stop her now. Noth—

She came, exploded with a burst of pleasure so sharp her body shook.

"*Fuck.*" Luke slid on a condom and positioned his cock at her entrance. The thick head pushed inside, just a bit, lodging at the mouth of her sex. His eyes held hers, his pupils so big and dark, and then he shoved inside.

And the climax continued. Harder. Pleasure lashed her as Luke thrust into her. Over and over. *Oh, sweet hell.*

His fingers bit into her flesh, and he plunged, so deep. He lifted her—damn the man was strong, she had almost forgotten—and Monica wrapped her legs around his waist. Her heels dug into his hips, and she tightened and held him as her sex rippled around his cock and the contractions continued.

So good. *Living. Feeling.*

He stiffened against her.

Her eyes were still on his. So much heat in that green gaze. Need. Pleasure. The same fire that he would see in her eyes.

His mouth crashed onto hers as his hips jerked.

Pleasure.

Monica's knees trembled when she tried to stand on her own. *Good sex would do that to a woman.*

Luke wrapped his arm around her waist and braced her against him. Monica was so tempted to lean against him, just for a little bit longer.

But the vicious lust had been satisfied. A lust she knew they'd both felt. They'd been riding adrenaline from the shooting. Both skirting the fine edge of control. That wild rush happened all the time to cops, to firefighters. To FBI agents.

But the need was slaked. Her limbs seemed heavy now from the wild rush of release that had left her hollowed out.

She licked her lips and realized she didn't know what to say. "Thank you" just seemed awkward. Like he'd done her a favor by screwing her. "More" seemed too needy, and she wasn't one hundred percent sure she could go another round right then.

Her gaze slid over, drifted down.

He might be able to go again, though.

"Get in bed." The gruff order surprised her and had her head whipping back up.

Since when did Luke—

Forget it. Monica cleared her throat. "I-I'll see you in the morning." Because in the past, she'd always left after sex, or she'd sent him away. She'd stayed at the cabin, but that had been a one-time deal. The wrong place, too much need.

Monica had sex with her lovers. She didn't sleep with them. In sleep, her walls came down. She didn't want them to see her when she was weak.

Because sometimes, the monsters crept up on her in the darkness. That's why she had to stay on guard. Always.

Her gaze darted to the broken door. Ah...explaining that could be a bit tricky, but she'd get Hyde to toss in some cash to smooth things over with the owner.

"I'm not going anyplace tonight."

Her gaze snapped right back to him. Luke watched her, his jaw clenched. "Kicking me out isn't gonna work now, baby."

He headed into the bathroom.

Her brows shot up. Kicking him out *had* been the plan and now...

Now he came back, closing the distance between them quickly, minus the condom. Yeah, he was aroused again. Or still aroused, and she knew he'd climaxed. No way to miss that hard jerk of his cock inside her.

"I'm sleeping with you tonight." He caught her chin. "We're breaking the rules."

Of course he *knew* about her rules.

"Lay with me." A whisper now. Not an order but a soft entreaty from a lover. "Let me hold you." His jaw tightened. "And let me forget that you could have died today."

Let him. The whisper from her own mind.

Luke Dante. Her temptation.

Because she'd always wanted to be held in the darkness. To know she wasn't alone.

But what if the nightmares came again?

His fingers drifted down her throat. Goose bumps rose on her flesh.

If I wake up screaming, I can say the dreams are from the Jones shooting. Just a flashback. That's all. He'd believe the lie. He'd believed the others she'd told him.

"Come to bed with me."

What would it hurt? One night. The door was broken anyway. Might as well be in the same room because the door would be open all night.

She didn't realize that Luke had been maneuvering her to the bed until her knees bumped against the mattress.

"Let me have tonight," he said, and his eyes never wavered from hers.

She nodded. Hesitant, a bit afraid, but...

Too tempted.

A man died right in front of me today. His blood coated my skin. I'm taking this. Taking him. Holding on, for as long as I can.

She crawled under the covers, pausing only long enough to toss away her shirt. He was naked. She'd sleep that way, too.

Luke bent toward the bed.

"Ah, wait—"

He froze, and she saw the tightening near his eyes. The flash of—what was that? Pain? Anger?

She reached under the pillow near him and felt the hard butt of her weapon. Grimacing, she pulled out her gun. "Maybe we should move this." Tonight, she'd be safe.

He took the gun and stared at it. At her. Then asked, "Should I leave the light on?"

And he nearly broke her heart.

Because he *knew*.

She wasn't controlled. She wasn't Ice. She was weak. Afraid. She needed a light when she slept, like a damn child. The big, bad agent, needing a shield against the night.

But that light had let her survive through the darkest hours.

"I'll leave it on," he said as his knee pushed onto the top of the mattress.

"No." Dammit, she could *do* this. "Turn it off. There's no need for the light tonight." She had him. The demons could go screw off.

Luke left her. He turned off the light and plunged them into darkness. The covers rustled when he climbed into bed beside her, then she felt the hot brush of his flesh against her. His muscled, hair-covered legs. His steely arms.

He pulled her close. Held her against his heart.

Beating so fast.

"You scared me." The words drifted in the dark room. A stark admission from him. "I wanted to shoot the bastard. I was so afraid he'd kill you—"

He broke off and his arms tightened. His heart thudded against her. "Don't do that to me again, baby. Just *don't*."

Emotion there. Real and painful. Once again, she didn't know what to say, but she turned her head and kissed him. Not on his mouth but right on that strong jaw. "I'm here." It was all she could think to tell him. "I'm safe." Until the next time.

In their line of work, there was always a next time. He knew that, just as she did.

His breath expelled on a rush but he didn't ease his hold.

Silence. Then, "A long time ago, I watched someone I cared about die in front of me."

Monica tensed against him.

"I tried to help her, but there wasn't a damn thing I could do. She died—*there wasn't a damn thing I could do.*"

So much pain there, and fury. A rage that cut to the bone. She was well-acquainted with a rage like that.

"I'm not going through that ever again." His hold tightened, became painful. "Get used to it. We're a team now, and nothing's gonna happen to you again, not while I'm there to save you."

Save you. She rolled a bit, shifting against him. "Don't you know you can't save everyone?" A lesson she'd faced a lifetime ago. *Sometimes, you can't even save yourself.*

"I'm not like you," he told her. "I didn't join the FBI to stop the killers. I joined for the victims."

To save them.

She put her head on his chest. Listened to his heartbeat. "Who was she?" Monica knew she shouldn't ask. She didn't want to hear about the lover he'd lost, the one that had pain echoing in his voice. The one that had made him the man he was. She didn't—

"My mother."

Her eyes squeezed shut. "I-I'm sorry." *I'm sorry for your loss.* Wasn't that what she always had to say? But, God, she was sorry—for all the victims and families she'd seen, and for Luke.

Her Luke. The Boy Scout with the hard edge, trying to protect the world.

She stared at the darkness, listened to the steady beat against her ear, and didn't speak again. He didn't want to know that he'd lose his fight, and right then, she didn't have the heart to tell him.

She lay stiffly within his arms. So unsure. Nervous. But the exhaustion pulled at her. Heavy and deep and after a time, she slowly drifted away.

Her head on his chest. Her legs tangled with his. Bodies close.

Together, in the darkness.

No light tonight.

He stared at Agent Davenport's room, frowning. She'd broken her pattern. Why? Because she thought she'd taken him down? Foolish. Such a bad mistake.

One he hadn't expected from her.

So disappointing.

But she didn't have her light on, and Monica Davenport shouldn't have been so comfortable in the dark. Not her.

He stared at that small room. What was different?

What do you fear?

He'd watched her for so long now. Studied her.

Tonight, he'd learned that she didn't fear death. She'd stared down the barrel of a smoking gun and hadn't flinched.

Brave? Crazy? Maybe she was both.

But there had been one chink in her armor. One thing he'd noticed. She'd covered the other agent, jumped to his defense so quickly. Too quickly.

Shadows moving together. He'd seen them before.

Did Davenport care about the man? Probably not. Because Davenport was broken.

Just like me.

Yet she'd still defended her partner and he figured she'd fucked him.

Hmmm...perhaps an experiment was in order. And experiments—they were just so much fun.

He began to whistle as he pulled his hood closer to his face and walked back into the night.

The darkness was such a sweet lover. Maybe Monica was starting to understand that.

She slept in his arms, nestled against him. Soft, warm, almost trusting. As trusting as he'd ever seen her.

But Luke couldn't sleep. Every time he closed his eyes, he saw Monica, and he saw Jeremy Jones with that gun raised.

The game could have ended so differently. Jones could have shot her, instead of taking his own life.

Monica had hesitated on the kill. Why?

And why had he felt like he was shattering as he screamed for her to *move*?

The sweet, lavender scent of her shampoo teased his nose. She breathed, slow and easy, comfortable now against him.

She'd never let him stay before. But then, he'd known better than to ask. Because in the past, the answer, the *get the hell out* had been clear in her eyes.

From now on, he had no intention of getting the hell out.

His fingers brushed over her shoulder. He felt the faint rise on her skin, a scar. She'd had it before they met. He'd touched it the first time they'd made love, and she'd flinched.

Like he gave a damn about any scar she carried. He sure carried enough of his own. The life they'd chosen wasn't an easy one. Often, it was a deadly one.

But he'd made a point never to touch that scar again because he didn't want her going cold on him.

He wanted her hot, wild, *needing* him. Just as she'd been before.

Telling her about his mother...had that been a mistake? Probably. But the fear had been too thick in his throat, the fury bubbling and the truth was—

I'll be damned if I lose her, too.

He stared into the darkness, and he kept holding her. Luke knew that sleep wouldn't come any time soon for him.

She jerked against him. A fast, hard jerk.

He froze. What the—

Another jerk. Another. Like she was having spasms or seizing or—

"No!" A whisper, desperate and weak. "Let me go, let me—"

He dropped his hold. "Monica? Monica, baby—"

"I'll kill you..." A shudder. No, she was—

Her hand dove under the pillow. His pillow.

Looking for the gun?

"Monica!" Loud. Probably too loud. He grabbed her shoulders. Tried to keep her from jerking so hard.

But then she stilled, and her breath slipped out again. Nice and easy. Easy breaths. Deep.

Just sleeping. *Now.*

He stared down at her, confused, worried and—

"I'll kill you...." The words had been so clear. So fierce.

So different from that first fearful whisper. The threat of death—it had been very, very certain.

He'd shared a secret from his past with her tonight. And now, in the darkness, he began to wonder about the secrets Monica kept.

Secrets that he'd long suspected were deadly.

The call came in just after 2 a.m. Keith Hyde woke instantly, his hand flying for the phone he always kept close by his bed. "Hyde."

A crackle of static, then, "It's Hank. They did it, man, *they did it.*" The excitement carried over the line.

Hyde sat up slowly, rubbing his fingers over his eyes. These days, there just didn't seem to be much point in sleeping. "Just what is it that my agents have done?"

"They bagged the killer. He's dead, Keith. My town's clear."

His fingers tightened around the phone. Monica hadn't called him. If the case were over, she would have called. "You sure about that?"

"I'm in his apartment, bagging and tagging computer equipment. His body's on the way to the morgue. So, yeah, I'm sure."

But Monica wasn't. *Or she would have called.* He knew how she operated. She always called him when she closed the case, to let him know that the killer had been apprehended and to tell him she was safe. *All these years . . . she knows I still worry.*

Hyde sucked in a slow breath. If she hadn't called to give the all-clear, then she wasn't convinced they had taken the killer down. "You said you have some computer equipment there?"

"We're takin' it down to the station—"

"I've got an agent who specializes in electronic information retrieval." Samantha Kennedy had a handful of degrees from MIT, and a knowledge of computer technology that amazed him. "If you've really got the killer..."

"*We do.*" Such confidence there.

"Then let her take a run at that equipment. She's the best, Hank." Hank knew he wouldn't steer him wrong. They'd survived 'Nam together because of trust. He'd trusted Hank to watch his ass in that godforsaken bush, just as Hank had trusted him. They'd made it out, when so many hadn't. "I can have her down there tomorrow. She'll tie up any loose ends for you." *And for me.*

"All right, man." His drawl deepened. "I just...*thank you*, okay? I knew you'd come through for me. You always do."

Hank cared about his town, about the people. And Hyde knew that when the guy had first called, he'd been desperate. No mistaking that tone in a man's voice. "I owed you." For the two bullets that should have gone into Keith's chest. Instead, they'd ripped into Hank's shoulder.

"Consider that debt paid."

A few moments later, Hyde ended the call. He stared into the darkness for a moment.

They *had* to be sure of their killer.

He punched in Sam's number. Four rings, and then she answered, her voice groggy. "S-Sam..."

"You're flying out at dawn, Sam."

Silence. Then, "Hyde?"

He almost smiled. Almost. His name had come out fast and high. "Set your alarm, Sam. I need you to go down to Mississippi and hack into some computers for me."

"Sir! Yes, sir, I will, I—"

"Word is that Monica and Dante might have brought down the killer in Jasper." He rubbed still grainy eyes. "Go and find me some proof."

If they were marking this case closed, they damn well needed to be certain they had their killer in his grave.

CHAPTER *Ten*

The sound of the shower woke him. The groaning of the pipes broke through the layers of sleep.

Luke opened his eyes, squinting a bit at the sunlight creeping through the blinds

An image came to him. Monica. Wet and naked. Just a few feet away.

How was a guy supposed to resist?

Especially since he'd woken, cock up and ready for her. Because he'd been dreaming. Her mouth. On him.

Some dreams were good. Some...weren't.

But this time, his dreams had been fantastic.

He rose slowly, stretched, then headed for the only woman he wanted.

Luke opened the bathroom door and the heat hit him. Steam drifted in the air, light and lazy. He could see Monica through the shower's glass door. He had one fine view of the shapely outline of her body as she stood beneath the spray.

Luke cleared his throat. Then did it again, louder.

Soft laughter floated to him with the steam. "Perv, I was wondering if you were just gonna stand there all day." She shoved open the glass door. Smiled at him. Actually *smiled*.

A real smile. Not that brittle little grin she liked to toss off. A free smile. Happy and sexy.

"Are you coming?"

Almost. A few more seconds of staring at her naked flesh and watching the way the water trickled down her breasts and slid over her stomach, then, down, down to the dark hair that shielded her sex and—

Now she cleared *her* throat.

Luke managed to snap out of his trance. He walked forward and climbed into the shower with her. It took two seconds for him to realize that the space wasn't meant to accommodate two. Not that he really cared.

He soaped his hands, then reached for her breasts. "Thought I'd help clean you." Not so smooth. His voice came out like a bear growl but her soft flesh was beneath his hands and her nipples were pebble hard and he *wanted*.

Her hands skated down his chest. "Come on, don't think you're having all the fun." She took the soap from the cracked tray and lathered her own hands.

Then she started with his nipples. *Started* there, but made a swift trip down his abs and lower to the cock that stretched eagerly toward her.

One tight pump of her hands. Another. The soap had made her hold slick and his length slid easily in her grasp as she stroked again and again. Base to tip, base to tip.

Two could play. The water beat over him, washing away the soap from his hands. The spray fell, not stinging his flesh, but warming him. Heating flesh already hot.

Slowly, his fingers caressed down her body, and searched out her core.

She widened her stance. Let him in with a quick gasp. Her folds were slick from the shower and her own arousal. It would be so easy to lift her up. To take her against the shower wall with the water pounding down around them. As easy as taking her last night, but they were going slow now. The touches were soft. Tender. Their mouths touched. No voracious hunger this time. The lust was still there, but *easy*. Gentle.

He should have been gentle with her before but the fury of need had always swept through him, and his control was shot to hell. Now—*this* was different.

He'd fucking keep his control. This time, for her.

For her.

He kissed her, and swept his tongue against hers, enjoying her moans and most definitely loving the firm grip of her hands. The need built. The pleasure grew, and he touched her. Everywhere.

His fingers swept over her. Luke found the button of her need. He stroked the way she liked. Pushed inside of her. Not too fast. Not too deep. Just enough to make the hunger sharpen.

The base of his spine tightened. His climax was coming, but he wanted to be *in* her. Needed her flesh surrounding him, clenching and holding so tight.

He lifted her hands away. *Careful.* Luke positioned his cock against her. Pushed through those wet curls so he could feel her slick heat. *There.* Right there. What he needed. So close. Bare, sweet—

Bare.

His back teeth clenched. "Condom."

Monica laughed. *Laughed.* Then slipped from his hands and eased from the shower. He saw her ass. That perfect, heart-shaped ass that liked to torment his dreams and give him hard-ons. *Fuck.* His gaze followed the smooth line of her spine, leading up to her wet mane of—

What was that?

The mark below her left shoulder blade. Her scar. This was the first time he'd ever seen it in the light, and it looked *wrong*. Raised flesh, in perfect circles. Hard to see completely in the steam but—

In a flash, Monica spun around to face him, and the laughter was gone from her eyes. Fear flashed in her blue gaze. Stark and sudden.

What? Why was she—

She reached for him, grabbing his arm and hauling him from the shower. She kissed him. No more tenderness. No more sweet licks.

Hard. Deep. Craving. Lusting.

If this is what she wants...

He'd always give her what she wanted.

His cock pushed against her. His arms locked around her, and he lifted her up, carrying her back to the bedroom.

To the condom.

They made it to the bed, barely. She was biting, sucking his lower lip and driving him insane.

She tore open the condom. Slid it over his cock with gripping hands and make-me-come touches.

Then she straddled him. "*Now.*"

Took him.

A swift downward thrust of her hips. Her eyes locked on his. Blind with need. Just as he knew his must be.

No more fear. *Fear—why—*

Her sex squeezed him. She rose, going up on her knees, and the head of his cock thrust against the opening of her sex.

Then down. Fast. Balls-deep in a move that had her muscles rippling around him. So tight. Perfect.

Luke stopped thinking and just felt.

Her. Flesh on flesh. Sweet cream. Warm woman.

Moving fast, the rhythm wild and driving as they fought for release. The mattress squeaked, louder than her moans, and her breasts rose, bouncing lightly, and he had to have a nipple in his mouth.

His lips closed over her breast just as her climax ripped through her. Her sex contracted, milking his length as she came—

And he came, erupting, within her. "*Monica!*" A roar that burst from him.

So long. The pleasure wrung through him. Every muscle, every cell. So. Fucking. Good.

Their breaths panted out. His heart pounded like a freaking drum. And he could taste her.

Her sex trembled around him. *So good.*

But when the waves of release began to slowly ebb, he was left with a memory. Not of wild heat, or of a lust that couldn't be sated.

One of fear in desperate blue eyes.

"You know, some folks like to sleep at night," Kenton said, his voice gruff as he held a steaming cup of coffee real close to his face. "I mean, damn, you know—*sleep*, sometime, right?"

Monica blinked and vaguely remembered a sleepy voice shouting, "*Keep that crap down.*"

Oh, she was screwed. "Just where's your motel room located, Kenton?"

One brow rose and he stared back at her. "I'm Room 103."

And she was 102. Perfect.

He took a quick sip of the coffee. "Freaking rabbits."

"Don't." Luke's voice. Vibrating with fury. He'd come up silently behind Kenton, and yeah, he'd heard everything. *Just like Kenton had last night.* "You don't even want to go there," Luke warned.

"I did." Kenton's gaze cut to her. Monica held perfectly still. She kept her eyes open, and her expression clear. "Lucky bastard." His lips thinned. "How's that arm, Davenport? You didn't...ah, do any more damage to it last night?"

She'd all but forgotten her arm. "It's fine." She needed to breathe. *How could I have forgotten about him?* Those walls were paper-thin. Of course, Kenton had heard them. He'd go back to Hyde and tell him about her and Luke.

She sucked in a deep breath. *Didn't matter.* She'd planned to tell Hyde as soon as she got back to D.C. Luke was right; she had a lot of rules in her life. Rule number one—the only one that she always followed—she didn't keep secrets from Hyde. Never had. Never would. Luke was on his team. Hyde *would* know.

"Get a different room tonight," Luke advised him, as a muscle flexed along his jaw.

"Aw, come on, that is just—"

Her cell phone rang. She glanced down, not recognizing the number but immediately identifying the Jasper County area code. *Oh, hell.* In that instant, Kenton was forgotten. "Hello?"

A whisper of breath. Soft laughter. "Did you really think I'd eaten my gun?"

Same distorted voice. She waved her hand in a cutting motion, and Luke and Kenton shut up. "No, I didn't think that at all." *It's him,* she mouthed.

Luke immediately pulled out his phone and started dialing. She knew he'd be calling Sam at the SSD and trying to get a lock on the call.

"Good." A sigh. "I don't want to be disappointed in you."

Luke's gaze scanned the motel parking lot as he murmured into his phone.

"He still doesn't know yet, does he?"

Monica stiffened.

"Really, after all that fucking, I would think he knew you better."

"I don't want to play your stupid games!" she snapped. "Innocent people are dying so you can—"

"Is anyone ever really innocent? Jones wasn't, but I still offered him a chance. Maybe I'm getting soft."

What?

Laughter. "Maybe I'm not."

"Listen, you—"

"I guess you were innocent once though, weren't you, Davenport? But that was so long ago..."

Bastard. How did he know? *How?*

"You're like me, aren't you? Deep down, underneath the skin?" And she could almost hear pleasure in that grated voice.

"No, I'm *not.*"

"We'll see. I'm watching you, Davenport. Learning all about you." Softer now. "And I think I know—"

"What?" Her fingers were about to break the phone. "What is it that you *know*?"

"What scares you."

Click.

Silence a moment, thick and hard. Monica pulled in a slow breath.

"What did he say?" Luke asked her.

He still doesn't know yet, does he? That bastard's voice. Playing his game.

She would have to tell Luke sooner or later. Because she wasn't going to let this freak jerk her around.

You think you know what scares me, asshole? Come on—let's find out.

"Is Sam on the line?" she questioned instead.

"She's gone. Kim's running the check."

Monica took the phone and rambled off the number on her cell. *Bastard.*

The moments ticked by in silence, then Kim's voice came across the line. "It's coming up as registered to a Sally Jenkins." A pause. "That was...she was one of his victims, right?"

Yes. The bastard had taken her cell, just like he'd taken Laura's, and probably Patty's, too. Why? Had he really been planning this all along? Planning to call the cops and taunt them? Or planning to call *her?* Had he known the SSD would get involved when the murders were connected? Her unit had been in the papers so much recently with their other cases....

"I'm getting the techs to use the satellites to try and track the GPS in the phone now."

He'd trash the phone. She had no doubt of that. "I want to know every call this number has made." There'd been no hits on Laura's cell. The bastard had just called *her*, no one else.

"They can't find a link..." Kim's tight voice. "It's not online. No echoes, no triangulation...the damn thing is *gone.*"

And the FBI's tracking equipment was state of the art. They could use their satellites to track a cell within fifty feet of its location in just moments. She exhaled slowly. Dammit. "Keep trying, and if you find anything, let me know." She ended the call and glanced down at her watch. Time was running out. "We've got to hurry."

"Why, Monica, what's happening?" Luke demanded. "What did Sam say?"

"Our killer took some souvenirs from his crimes." She knew her smile wouldn't be pretty. "He's using the vics' phones to taunt us." Asshole. But he'd just had to make sure she knew...

He was still hunting.

Samantha Kennedy stepped off the plane. Not the fancy, private one usually reserved for the SSD. Ramirez had taken it because there was a serial rapist on the hunt in Bloomington, Indiana.

The FBI had pull, though, and she'd gotten a seat on the first flight down to Mississippi. She hadn't been able to fly in straight to Jasper. She'd had to go via Gulfport, one of the bigger airports in the state. Now she'd have a long drive ahead of her.

She hefted her carry-on over her shoulder, glancing around. Okay, Hyde had woken her up with his order to fly down here. He'd assured her that someone would be there to meet her at the airport. Maybe it would be Monica or that sexy new agent who made her blush way too much and—

"Ms. Kennedy?"

She pushed her glasses back a bit on her nose and turned to the right. A crowd was in her way, folks milling past as they hurried to get their luggage. But behind the bodies, she caught sight of a deputy's brown uniform with a gleaming silver star. *Ah, my ride.* She hadn't seen the guy's face yet, not with all those people blocking her. *If only I had about four more inches.* But being short— well, she'd learned to deal with it.

"Samantha Kennedy?" he called again.

Sam hurried toward him. "Yep, that's me." She didn't get out on many field assignments. Hyde liked to keep her chained to her computer. But since Sheriff Davis believed their serial killer had been eliminated, Hyde thought it was safe to send her out. *Finally.* She'd been trained for this job, and for months, she'd wanted to prove that she could handle herself. She *was* an FBI agent, just like Monica and Kenton. She could do the job. Time to show her boss that fact.

The deputy bent down, his hat shielding his face, and reached for her bag.

"Aw, thanks, I really appreciate—"

He stumbled against her, apparently tripping on the luggage. "You okay?" His arms wrapped around her. Too tight.

Something pricked her. A sharp jab, right near her neck. Sam blinked and then staggered a bit.

"It's okay," he murmured, pulling her close. "I've got you."

She tried to open her sagging eyelids. Tried to *see* him. "Something…wrong…" The words came out slurred because her tongue was thick and awkward in her mouth.

"No, Samantha." A whisper in her ear. "Everything's just fine."

They were walking. His arms were around her. Heavy and hard. She couldn't speak. Couldn't see. Was something wrong with her glasses? No, no, her glasses were gone, and everything seemed too blurry.

"Yeah, baby, I missed you, too…" His voice. Too loud. Why would he say that? What—

Her knees buckled. He lifted her. Put her—*what?* When had they gotten to the parking lot? Because she could feel a car seat under her legs. A door slammed.

She fumbled, trying to find the door handle. She needed to get out. Something was wrong. She was sick.

He hit her. Actually punched her in the face. "Stay with me, bitch." And fear bloomed beneath the enveloping fog that had started to numb her mind and body.

She caught the flash of teeth. A big grin. "You're gonna help me," he said.

She tried to shake her head. *Weapon*…she needed to find—

"Poor little Sam." An engine cranked. No, no, he was taking her away! And her eyes wouldn't stay open.

"L-let…g-go…" was all she could manage. The words should have been a scream. But her whisper came out as a tangle of words.

He was whistling now. The tune was so clear and loud, echoing in her head.

Then, right before the darkness claimed her, she heard

him say, "Tell me, agent, is there anything that scares you?"

You do.

"Davis, you can't go on the air now!" Monica paced in front of the dead body, her hands clenched. "The serial is still out there! This guy," she pointed toward the sheet. "He's another victim."

The ME's lair was quickly filling up with victims. And Luke hated coming in there with the dead.

"Jeremy Jones has never been a victim a day in his life." The sheriff's foot tapped on the tile. "Not one day."

What about the day he saw you shoot his father?

"Well, now, Sheriff, hold on..." Dr. Charles Cotton scratched his lower chin. "I did find some bruising around the ankles and wrists that would suggest—"

"He was tied up," Monica finished. "Our killer tied him up and—"

"And what? Gave him a gun and said, '*Son, do me a favor and go shoot those two agents for me now, ya hear*?'"

Luke blinked. Okay, maybe the good sheriff needed to dial things back a bit. Davis was dressed in his finest. Freshly shaved. Obviously the guy was ready for his moment in the sun. A moment that just wasn't coming.

"Tell me," Monica's voice came softly, "if you saw your father get gunned down on the street in front of you, what would you fear?"

Some of the heat faded from Davis's face. "That was a clean shooting. We told him, over and over, to drop his weapon. *He* tried to shoot *us*. He—"

"What would you fear?"

Davis's jaw worked. "You can't know for sure."

"Let me tell you what I think." She stood near the side of the gurney. "I think our killer took Jeremy Jones. I think he knew all about Jeremy's past. He held him and he gave him a choice."

"Why would he do that?" Luke asked. Why change the rules with Jones?

"Because he's a sick fuck." She barely missed a beat.

"A sick dead man." Davis raked shaking fingers through his hair. So much for his perfect news appearance.

"He's not dead," Monica assured him. "He's *not*. The bastard called me again today."

Davis paled. He knew about the first call; they'd briefed him right away. He inhaled deeply. "You *sure* it was him?"

"Same voice distortion. Same threats. It was him. He's using his vics' phones because he wants to make sure we *know* who he is and what he's done." Dead certain. "He couldn't let the last kill stand. He wanted us to know..."

Her, Luke thought. The killer had called Monica because he'd wanted *her* to know what he'd done. And that fucking pissed him off. *Stop going after her. Come after me, bastard.*

"...he's still out there," Monica finished. "And he's enjoying this. Every moment, he loves it."

Davis exhaled heavily. "I just...wanted people to be safe. I wanted this to be over."

"It's not."

Kenton burst through the metal doors. "You were right." His face was flushed, chest heaving. "I found a spot, about twenty feet away, at the edge of the woods."

"What?" Davis's brow lined. "What are you talkin' about—"

"The killer *was* there last night," Monica said. "He just wasn't the man who died."

And now that he knew the score, Luke wished things had been different. They could have saved Jones. But when the bullets started flying, he'd just seen a killer locking sights on him.

Monica, though, she'd known. That was why she'd held back.

"The killer had a gun on Jones." Kenton took a deep breath. "At the scene, I found grass bent, twigs snapped. The perfect place to watch, but not be seen."

The ex-sniper, Ramirez, would have scoped out the joint in less than three seconds. It had taken Kenton a bit longer, but Luke hadn't doubted Kenton would find the killer's sweet spot.

"When the killer called, he *said* that he gave Jones a chance. But I don't think he did, not really." She rubbed her forehead. "I think he sent Jones out with the gun and told him to kill me and Agent Dante."

Asshole.

"*Why?*" Davis was shocked, and behind him, the ME just stood there, his mouth hanging open as Cotton's eyes flew back and forth between them. "Going up against two armed FBI agents would be suicide—"

Death by cop. Or agent.

"You see your old man get gunned down in the street," Luke said. "Finding yourself on the *same* street, facing armed agents. Wouldn't that be a bitch?"

"What you fear most." From Kenton.

Davis swallowed. "I-I didn't…"

"He said something to me. Right at the end." Monica licked her lips. "*Fuck you. Fuck him. My way.*"

Luke saw Kenton's brows shoot up.

Monica glanced at Luke. "When he said 'him,' I thought he meant *you*, but now I realize he was talking about the killer. Jeremy didn't want to go out with us shooting him. He chose *his* way to end things. Not us. Not the killer's choice. Jeremy's."

Kenton nodded. "From the looks of things, I'd say the serial had a gun on Jeremy the entire time. Where I found the marks, that position would have given him a perfect view of the house." He gave a grim nod. "I've got a crime scene unit out there now."

Luke felt his heart spike. "Did you find something?"

"Ashes, could be from a cigarette." A faint shrug. "Saw 'em on the bent grass. No cigarette butts, that would have been too easy."

Because they possibly could have gotten DNA from those.

"No way did this guy just start killing," Luke said. No way. With this level of violence? No. People didn't just wake up one day and decide to become serials. The instinct to kill was there, often showing first when the perp was just a kid. When he decided to see what the family pet's insides looked like.

"No, he's been leading up to this for a long time." Monica rubbed her temple. "But he might have been too organized to get caught when he started his games."

Games. Interesting word for murder.

"I just don't get it...." Davis swiped a hand over his sweaty brow. "Why didn't Jones say somethin'? Why did he—"

"I'm betting the killer probably told him that if he hesitated, or if Jones tried to warn the agents, he'd put a bullet in the back of his head. With that position just north of the house, if you had a scope on a rifle, it would have been like shooting fish in a damn barrel."

Davis swallowed and seemed to pale.

"And because we're dealing with a sadistic bastard who likes to play," Luke's eyes narrowed, "I bet he also told him that if he took us out, he'd live." *He gave Jones a chance.* Kill the agents, get to live.

"That was a lie, though," Monica said. "Because this perp doesn't let his victims live."

No, he didn't. Poor Laura Billings was proof of that. She was in the room with them, locked up in the cold, just a few feet away.

He tied her to the chair, nice and tight. Then he watched as Special Agent Samantha Kennedy's head sagged forward. She'd be out for a while.

No playtime. Not yet. But soon.

Would she cry like the others? Break as easily? Beg? He'd bet she would.

They always broke.

Always.

How to break his prey—that had been his first lesson. The first of many he'd learned. And he'd been a very fast learner.

"*Samantha,*" he whispered her name. He already knew everything about her, everything that mattered. She wasn't the only one who knew how to hack into a computer system.

Learn the prey to break the prey.

Some people—their fears were right there, on the surface. Just begging to be seen, exploited.

Others...like Davenport...they hid their fears. Pretended to be strong when really they were weak and scared inside.

He could make anyone afraid. He could make anyone beg.

For fucking years, he'd tried to be normal. Tried to fit into the perfect mold that people wanted, then he'd realized there was no point to being normal.

And he was *better* than normal.

He picked up the knife, spun it around in his hand, letting the blade just brush his fingertips. She was kinda pretty. He lifted the knife, let the blade ease down her cheek.

Patty had been pretty, too. At first. When he'd finished working on sweet Patty, she'd been fucking beautiful.

The blade nicked Sam's cheek, and a drop of blood slid down her face. "I'll make you beautiful, too," he promised her. Death had a way of doing that. When she was swollen and the vessels in her eyes burst and her lips turned blue...Samantha Kennedy would be just as damn gorgeous as Patty.

Just as lovely as all the others.

The bloody tip of the knife slipped down her neck, smearing blood. Then down lower, right between her breasts.

His jaw locked. Just wasn't any damn fun when they were asleep. She couldn't *beg* when she was out cold.

His gaze lifted, and he stared out the window. The knife wasn't for her, anyway, even if he liked the feel of the blade in his hand.

No, Sam didn't fear the knife. A smile lifted his lips. But he knew what she *did* fear.

"Hank!" A woman bustled inside, small with curly red hair. The Sheriff's assistant, Lily, the woman who also happened to be his wife. "I, uh," a quick look at the covered sheet, then away. "We've got a problem."

Oh, hell. Luke really didn't like the sound of that. From the look on Monica's face, neither did she.

"Tell the press no story today." Davis crossed his arms. "I don't care how pissy that SOB from Channel 5 gets, you just tell him—"

"The..." Now a nervous look Luke's way. He tried to look harmless as he stared back at her. She cleared her throat. "The agent's missing."

Davis's eyes narrowed. "Lee's gone to get her. He'll be bringing her in from Gulfport in about half an hour."

"Excuse me." Luke lifted a brow and waited for the sheriff to glance his way. "Mind telling me just who's coming in?" Yeah, another agent, he got that part. But why hadn't he known?

The sheriff frowned. "Didn't you get the message I left at the motel?"

"No." And he'd be checking in with that desk clerk the minute he got back to the motel.

"I talked to Hyde last night. We found some computers at Jeremy's place. Hyde wanted to send down an agent, Kennedy, to work on the equipment."

"Samantha," Monica said.

"Yeah, yeah, Samantha Kennedy. She was due to come in this morning. Her flight was arriving at—" He shot a quick glance at Lily.

"Seven," she whispered.

"Seven," he said with a nod. "I sent Lee out there to get her." A brief pause. "Told Hyde I'd let you know. I thought you'd get the message about the agent—"

"And she's not there, Hank," Lily told him, voice tight. Her hands twisted in front of her. "Lee's on the phone. The plane landed. Some folks saw her get off, but she's *gone* now."

"Gone where?" Kenton barked.

Because they were talking about one of their own. Missing.

"How the hell do I know?" Davis's hair was crap now as his fingers ran through it once more. "She must've gotten a taxi or a rental or—"

Monica whipped out her phone. Punched in the numbers. Fast. Silence filled the room. Her eyes met Luke's. "She's not answering."

Could be nothing, though. Bad service. If Samantha were driving on her own through the twisting back roads, she could have lost her cell service any number of turns. Could be nothing.

But if it was nothing, why did Monica look so worried?

And why was the knot in his gut getting tighter?

The cell phone rang. Again and again. Some chirpy, happy beat that a federal agent really shouldn't have programmed on her phone.

He glanced at the phone's display. *Monica Davenport.* Ah, so she was calling already. Trying to find her friend.

But she wouldn't find her. Not yet.

He counted eight rings then the too cheery ring and the annoying vibration stopped.

He wouldn't answer yet. The time wasn't right. Monica needed to sweat it out as she wondered about her lost friend. The longer he waited, the more distraught Monica would become.

No, he wouldn't answer her yet. But maybe next time.

Monica thought she was profiling him, but he'd been watching her so closely. He was almost sure he knew her break point now. Almost certain.

One more test would show him. One more.

It had been so easy to take Sam from that airport. No one had even glanced twice at him. And for an FBI agent, she'd been almost ridiculously easy to take.

Davenport would be more of a challenge. He'd researched her, spent the last four months learning about her. He'd hoped the kills in Jasper would bring her in. She was supposed to be the best the SSD had—he'd counted on them sending in their best.

He'd even chosen this town just for her, then set his bait with the kills.

And she hadn't even made the connection yet.

CHAPTER *Eleven*

Romeo Killer Captured. One Victim Survives. Luke frowned down at the clear evidence bag, his eyes on the old newspaper clipping. "Did you get any prints off this?" he asked Gerry.

"Nah. Wiped clean."

Figured. He shook his head and stared at the clipping. "Why'd he give us this? Why not one of his notes? Why *this?*"

"Maybe he wants one of those killer names," Vance offered. He'd come into the lab about an hour before to do nothing more, Luke was pretty sure, than to make his life hell.

"I mean, nobody calls him nothin'," Vance said. "Maybe it's pissin' him off."

And the deputy was pissing him off.

"Maybe the Watchman," Vance mused and rubbed his chin. "Maybe that's what we should call him. 'Cause it seems, you know, like he's always watchin' people. He has to, right? I mean, to figure out what scares 'em."

Luke stared at the man, hard.

"Or maybe he just wants fame...maybe he wants to be like that other bastard who ruined Jasper's name." The sheriff shook his head in disgust.

The other bastard? "Which bastard are you talking about?" Luke demanded.

The sheriff's squinting gaze zeroed in on the deputy. "Get out of here, Monroe," he snapped. "Get the hell out and go find some drunk causing trouble and throw his ass in jail."

"Uh, right, Sheriff." A bob of the deputy's head. "I'm goin', sorry." He tripped, twice, then made it to the door.

Luke kept his attention on Davis. He waited for the deputy to leave, then said, "Romeo didn't kill in Jasper." He was absolutely certain of that fact. Romeo had attacked girls in Louisiana.

"Didn't kill here; he lived here." Davis exhaled. "Until he was ten years old, that boy lived in my town. Hell, I still remember the first time I was ever called over to his ma's place. I'd just started as a deputy...never will forget that day."

"What happened?"

"That boy had sliced open his cat."

Shit.

"Damn, sheriff..." Gerry exhaled on a hard breath.

"The mother was sure the neighbor had done it, said he was mad 'cause the cat kept gettin' in his garden. But I saw her boy when we were haulin' the carcass away."

Silence hung in the room.

"He was smilin'." Davis crossed the room and picked up the sealed clippings. "They moved away a few months later, and I forgot about the kid until I saw him on the TV fifteen years later." His shoulders hunched a bit and his eyes rose to meet Luke's. "I saw the evil in him that day, but I didn't have any proof he'd sliced that animal. I didn't do *anything*, even though I *saw*. When I learned about those girls..."

Raped. Tortured. Yeah, he'd seen the pictures.

"I wondered if I could've saved them, if I'd just paid more attention, followed that boy, or just contacted the sheriff in Louisiana to let him know what I suspected."

Christ. "Where did Romeo live?" The killer had sent these damn clips for a reason. "Are there any relatives here? Anyone linked to his case?" Bad blood—maybe literally.

"House was torn down years ago. Highway goes over it now. As for relatives...no, it was just the boy and his ma. The father died when the boy was young, in some kind of car accident."

But there was *something* there, connecting the cases. The perp out there hunting in Jasper wanted them to know about that link.

Something or *someone* connected the cases.

"Luke," Monica's sharp cry.

He glanced over to see her and Kenton hurry inside. "Lee interviewed all the rental agents at the airport. No one rented Sam a car," she told him.

"And no taxi drivers reported picking up her fare either." Kenton said, a muscle flexing along his jaw. "She's just...disappeared."

The sheriff's Adam's apple bobbed. "I told Hyde the county was secure. I told him it was *safe* down here."

Not even close.

"*Why?*" He glanced up, and his face flushed dark red. "Why would he go after that agent? He's been pickin' local women."

Monica shook her head. "Sheriff, I've told you, I believe this man has killed before, outside of your county. Killed women like Saundra Swain."

His tongue swiped over his lips. "You found something in Gatlin?"

They hadn't briefed the sheriff on Gatlin because, well, hell had broken loose last night.

"Maybe. I had Sam working to get some background info for me. The victim in Gatlin, Saundra, had a boyfriend who disappeared just after her death."

"You think it's him?" The sheriff asked. "What's his name? We can put an APB out for him!"

"We don't have any proof that he's guilty. We don't even know where he is right now. We're pulling up his driver's license photo now from the DMV, and we're waiting on a warrant to search a house belonging to the guy's aunt."

Her phone rang. Monica broke off and snatched her cell phone up from her hip. Luke caught the rasp of her breath right before she said, "Local number. It-it's the number Sally had."

Fuck. They'd gotten all the numbers for the vics because they'd known this call would be coming.

Her eyes were on Luke when she pushed the button to answer the call.

"I'm getting bored with you, Agent Davenport," he told her, brushing his fingers against the pane of the window. "You're supposed to be so good. I thought you'd be better at this game."

"Killing people isn't a game!"

Ah, she seemed angry. Good. "To me it is."

She sucked in a sharp breath.

He smiled. "And to your pretty little friend, it's a game, too."

"You have Samantha?"

Did she really need to ask? *Disappointing*. And he'd been told she was such good prey. "She's rather too trusting, don't you think? Supposed to be so smart, and she never even saw me coming until it was too late."

Because no one was smarter than he was. He didn't need those fucking fancy degrees.

"Let her go," Monica said, voice tight. "You haven't killed her yet so just—"

"Are you sure?"

Silence. Then, voice quiet, "Yes."

"*How* are you sure?" Not much time. He wouldn't talk much longer. The agents with her would have already started tracking his signal. He'd have to make the dump fast. He turned away from the window, headed for the back door. Really, they should pay better attention around these parts. Just anyone could walk in.

"I'm sure." He could almost see her. Dark hair straight and perfect around her delicate features. Face expressionless. His agent liked her control.

He wanted to shatter that control into a million pieces, and he would, when he shattered her.

"You haven't played with her yet," the agent who thought she was so smart told him. "You don't *know* her, don't know her fears."

He laughed. He couldn't help it. "Ah, but I do know. I told you, I've been *watching*." A quick glance at his watch. "I'll give you twenty-four hours." He kept the voice distorter, a handy device he'd picked up down in a New Orleans novelty shop, over the phone. "Twenty-four hours to save her." *Plenty of time for me to play.*

"What do you mean?"

"Find her." That was all he'd say. "Find her, save her. Twenty-four hours." And he'd be watching. Because Samantha Kennedy didn't matter. Monica did. This was *her* test.

What do you fear, agent? "Find her...or you'll bury her." Perhaps Monica would bury her either way because twenty-four hours might just be too long. It was so easy to get bored, and he really doubted that Samantha Kennedy would be able to last that long.

Monica stared at her phone. Her face felt cold. Icy pinpricks shot through her skin. "We've got twenty-four hours to find Sam."

"Fuck!" Kenton whirled around. "That bastard had better not hurt her!"

"He said if we don't find her in twenty-four hours," she found Luke watching her, his gaze steady and strong, "then we'll bury her."

I'll find you, Sam. Don't worry. I will find you.

Because she knew what it was like to be a killer's plaything. To know that he could hurt you, use you, break you—and that help wouldn't get there in time.

No, this time, I'll get there. Hold on, Sam.

Monica drew in a quick breath. *Can't panic. Work the case. Think like him.*

"Kenton, get me that picture of Kyle West. See what you can find out about his whereabouts. I want all deputies to know his face—everyone needs to keep their eyes open for him." One step at a time. "Luke, notify Hyde. He's gonna want to come down here." She hesitated, just for an instant. "I've got to talk to Sam's family."

Luke's eyes widened. "You're telling them? Already?"

"Yes." The grief would rip them apart, but she wouldn't lie to a fellow agent's family. "I have to talk to them. They're the only ones who can tell me—"

"What? What are they gonna tell you?" Davis demanded. "How are you gonna find her? This bastard is jerkin' us all around by the balls!" His voice rose to a yell as sweat beaded his upper lip.

"Yes, he is." Monica kept her voice quiet and firm. She understood the sheriff's fury. His people were dying. Now one of hers was, too. "But we *are* going to stop him."

"*How?*" The sheriff's faith was gone.

"Leave that to me." She tossed her cell phone to the tech who'd stood watching them, mouth open. "You were connected with the SSD, right?" They'd set the link up on Gerry's computer beforehand because she'd *known* this call would come. "Have they sent you the GPS data?" The SSD would have been notified the moment her phone rang. Kim had been standing by, just waiting. "I want him. I *need* to know where he called from."

"I-I think from right outside." A woman's voice said.

Monica spun around. Deputy Melinda Jenkins stood in the doorway, her face tense. She lifted her hand and raised a cell phone wrapped in a clear plastic bag. "I was getting a smoke. I-I found this out back."

Oh, damn. Every muscle in her body tightened. *There.*

So close to them…the bastard wasn't scared. "Gerry, I want that phone torn apart." *Find something. Anything.*

"Get your men out there, sheriff." The order was Luke's. "If that asshole was outside, *someone* saw him."

The killer was bold. And he was laughing right in their faces. Too confident. He knew the area too well. Knew the sheriff's station *too well*.

Every move they made, he seemed to be right there.

"If the bastard was here…" Kenton's voice came slowly. "Then where the hell is Sam? Christ, is she—is she even still alive?"

Monica swung toward him. "She's alive."

His gaze held hers. Kenton and Sam had dated briefly, and though they might not have made it as a couple, Monica knew they were friends. She could see the worry and fear on Kenton's face.

"He would have drugged her and left her tied up someplace," she said. "He wouldn't have made the call close to her. He knew we'd track him." Because he knew every move they made. *Every move.*

Sam opened her eyes and saw only darkness. Thick, pitch black. Her head pounded and nausea rolled in her belly. She tried to move but her hands were bound, tied behind her back. She sat in a wooden chair that was hard, with a high back. Her ankles were tied to the chair legs. The ropes were so tight that she could feel the dampness of her blood.

"H-hello?" Her voice came out as a rasp. Weak. No, she would *not* be weak. "Who's there?" He had to be there. Watching her. Getting off on her fear.

Don't show fear.

Monica had said that once. She'd been talking to the agents about what to do in a worst-case situation.

Oh, God, this is worst case. Trapped. Isolated. *He's going to kill me.*

Monica knew killers. She knew how to handle them. If she were here, she wouldn't be panicking, with terror nearly choking her. She'd be calling out to the killer, taunting him.

Staying in control.

Sam took another breath. A stale taste filled her mouth and that nausea was still rising in her throat. "Come out, bastard!" Yelling made her head hurt more. Dammit, what had he injected her with? How long had she been out?

Her eyes jerked to the left. The right. *Can't see anything.* The familiar weight of her glasses was missing. Shit. Even if the lights were on, she wouldn't be able to see much.

Why had he taken her? What did the guy want? She'd read the profile Monica faxed to Hyde. The guy tortured his victims by making them face their worst fears.

But there wasn't any way for him to know what scared her. *He* didn't know her.

And then she heard it. Sam froze. The faintest of sounds. Not too close, but it was . . .

The gentle lapping of water.

Oh, Jesus. No, no, he couldn't know . . .

"Are you there? *Are you there?*" Sam shouted.

That lapping filled her ears, and Sam choked back a scream.

"Mrs. Kennedy, this is Monica Davenport with the SSD." Her fingers curled lightly over the phone. Behind her, the sheriff's office buzzed with activity. "I'm calling about your daughter Samantha."

A faint hum over the line, then, "Monica, did you say? Ah, Sam's friend. You two work together." A flowing, cultured voice. Sam's parents were wealthy, old money. Not that Sam appeared to ever touch their money. Why had Sam joined the Bureau? Monica had been given no choice—once the monsters got inside, she couldn't get them out. But Sam—why had she traded the glitter for the grit?

Had she joined to save lives? Only to lose her own?

Monica swallowed. "Mrs. Kennedy, this is going to seem like an odd question, but I need to know, has Sam ever been involved in any sort of serious accident?"

"Wh-what?"

"Does she have any phobias?" *Just tell me no. Tell me Sam is perfectly normal. No, better than normal. Nothing scares her.*

"Sam doesn't like the water."

Monica's heart slammed into her ribs. "Why?" Cold, brittle.

Silence. Then, "Why are you calling me, Ms. Davenport?" Distant now, when there'd been warmth in her voice moments before. "Where's Sam?"

Monica glanced over at Luke. He'd just put a picture of Sam up on their crime board. Right next to the bloody image of Patricia Moffett and the still features of Laura Billings.

"Please tell me why she doesn't like the water." *Find out first. The parents break when they hear the news about their kids.*

A quick gasp. "S-something's happened to my baby?"

No lies. Not about another agent. "She's missing. We're working a case and…she's missing."

Some people thought you couldn't hear pain, but you could. Monica heard it loud and clear in the stark silence that came across that phone line. She cleared her throat. "This is very important. I need to know why she's scared of water."

"Sh-she was…eight. At our cabin. S-summer v-vacation…"

Keep talking. The grief was there. Whispering through the words. *Hold together, just a few more moments.* A patrol car was on the way to the Kennedy home. Hyde wanted a guard with the family because he wasn't sure what the killer might do.

Monica knew the family wasn't in danger, but she didn't want the mother left alone. Not with this kind of grief.

"W-walking on the-the pier. The wood was old, gave way—" And her words gave way to sobs. "We couldn't get her out. My baby—my baby wasn't breathing when we finally pulled her from the—the water."

Darkness. Water. All around. Closing in. No air. No light.

What scares you?

Monica swallowed over the lump in her throat. A lump that threatened to choke her. "Has anything else ever happened to Sam? Any car accidents? Any other—"

"Just…the water. She doesn't swim now…"

A bell pealed in the background.

"S-someone's here…." Confusion. A numbed voice.

"It should be a police officer. He's there to explain." *What? That a twisted freak had her daughter?* "He'll tell you what you need to know."

"F-find my baby...."

"I will." But would she find her alive?

Hold on, Sam.

Monica ended the call. Luke stood in front of her. "Are you okay?"

"I'm fine." Her control *would* hold.

He crept closer. "You look like you're about to break apart." His fingers smoothed down her arm, a hot touch that warmed her cold flesh.

For just a moment, she wanted to lean in to him. To steal some of his strength. That tempting warmth.

She always felt so cold. Like the bodies she found so often. Ice cold.

If she could just hold on to Luke for a few moments and take that warmth for herself....

But then she'd be weak. The ice would break, chip away, and what if he saw that underneath the protective cover, she was weak? Weak and scared.

Her gaze scanned the room. If she broke here, with him, they'd all see.

And no, she *wouldn't* be weak.

"Monica." His eyes were so intent. "We're going to find her."

I was such a bitch to her, Luke. Such a bitch. She wanted to be my friend. She was always talking to me, asking me to lunch, but I froze her out.

Just like I froze you out.

But she didn't say anything. Sometimes she felt like her damn secrets were suffocating her.

Always wondering, worrying. *What will he think if he knows the truth? What would he see when he looked at me?*

What would they all see?

She didn't want to be a victim, and she'd be damned if she accepted anyone's pity.

"You need to take a break. Get some coffee, get—"

"No." Her shoulders snapped back. They didn't have time to piss away, and she was *not* going to break. "We don't have time to waste. We have to find her, and fast."

His blond brows pulled low. "Twenty-four hours isn't a lot of time."

Monica laughed at that. She couldn't help it. "Do you really think he's giving us that long?"

Luke blinked.

"She'll be dead in six. He's fucking with us." And that pissed her off. "He wants to have his fun with Sam, but he wants to watch us scramble. So he'll play with her, kill her, then sit back and watch us struggle. And he'll be watching from a safe distance. A safe, *un-catchable* distance." Monica realized her voice was too loud. Her hands shook, and everyone was watching her.

Watching me break down.

Sam would break, too. The innocence that had been in Sam's brown eyes would be gone soon. If it wasn't already. She was an agent, yeah, but she'd been protected, kept safe. Hell, she'd probably only been in the field a handful of times.

There'd be no safety now.

Why did everyone have to stare? They needed to *move*. "Sheriff, I want a listing of every cabin or house that's got lake access in this area. Every one—and I want it yesterday."

He wiped his handkerchief across his sweaty brow. "Yes, ma'am."

Her chin lifted. "We're finding her, and we're finding her *now*."

The floorboard squeaked.

Every muscle in Sam's body tightened. She didn't know how long she'd been in that damn room, listening to the water, but she wasn't alone now.

Maybe she'd never been.

A scent teased her nose. Strong and thick. Not cigarette smoke. Deeper. *Smells like Uncle Jeremiah...*

But this wasn't her sweet old uncle. This was a sick freak who wanted to hurt her.

Then he whistled. A stupid, light tune. What was that? Something—

"I know." A whisper. One that came right next to her ear. Close enough for her to feel his breath against her skin.

To catch that smell—stronger now. Cigar smoke.

She jerked away. He laughed.

Don't show your fear. Her fingers curled down behind her. "You've made a mistake." Her voice came out sounding calm. Monica would have approved. "I'm a federal agent, and my team will be tracking me. You don't want—"

"That's *exactly* what I want." And he shoved something over her head. Something thick, heavy. A bag? Oh, God, he was suffocating her; he was going to kill her.

"Hold on, bitch, this might hurt." He sliced the ropes away. Cut her skin. "Hope it does." Ankles. Wrists. The blade pierced her skin every time.

But she didn't scream.

She did attack. The minute the ropes fell away, she shot to her feet, spun around—

And fell, taking the chair down, slamming her elbows and knees onto the floor. *Legs won't work. No circulation. Can't—*

He had her tied again in seconds. Just her hands this time. Thick knots of rope that scraped away her skin.

He hauled her up and dragged her because her legs wouldn't work. From the ropes or the drug? What had he done to her?

A door squeaked. Light flickered through the bag he'd shoved over her head. The lapping of the water teased her ears—louder—

"I know." Damn whisper, grating in her ears. "I know all about you, sweet Samantha Kennedy." His steps echoed, as if he were walking on something hollow.

Something hollow.

Fuck. A dock. They were walking on a dock. She could feel the slight shift in the wood beneath her.

"You really think you're the only one who knows how to dig and pick apart a person's life? A computer can show you so much these days. If you know just where to look, you can find anything."

Water lapped, so close.

"I know your father has spent his life screwing around on your mother. I know she spent her days and nights with the bottle to make it all better."

No, her mom didn't drink. Not anymore. Not since—

"And I know you, poor little Samantha. You were alone so much. Alone that day when you fell."

Please, God—

"And no one heard your scream."

She screamed now, as loud as she could. The bag didn't stop her; it was loose around her head. She could—

"No one but me can hear you now, and I don't give a shit." He threw her onto the dock, grabbing her arms and twisting another rope on her hands. She was tied enough. *Enough!* Sam tried to kick out at him. Pinpricks shot through her feet and up her calves. Feeling was coming back, painful and burning.

Her feet hit something. Not him. Something hard and heavy. Something that made her bare feet throb.

His laughter filled her ears, and her heart slammed into her chest. Sam shook her head, trying to get out of that bag. "What are you doing? What are—"

Splash. She jerked forward, moving hard to the right. *What the hell?*

Goose bumps covered her arms. "I haven't done anything to you!" A scream broke from her. *Splash.* "Why are you—"

"Because I can." *Splash.* "Guess what? You're next—"

He grabbed her, spinning her around. No, he wasn't pulling her, something else was. The rope he'd just tied to her; it was pulling her—

Sam slammed into the water. Hit it hard and sank fast because something was pulling her, pulling her down to the bottom of the lake.

The bag drifted away from her twisting head and fluttered up in the murky water. Bubbles flew past her face. Because she was still screaming. Swallowing water and choking.

She couldn't get free. The rope wouldn't break, and he'd tied her to blocks. Looked like cinder blocks. *Fucking splashes. That's what the sound had been.*

The blocks were dragging her down, straight to that sandy bottom. *Swimming with the fishes . . .*

Down...

God! Her lungs burned. The water stung her eyes, filled her nose, and poured down her throat.

Help me!

"Gatlin County Sheriff's department," a rumbling voice flowed over the phone line.

Monica inhaled a deep breath. "This is Monica Davenport with the FBI, and I need to speak with Sheriff Martin." *Now*.

"Ah, sorry, ma'am, I mean, agent, but Sheriff Martin ain't in the office today."

"Who is this?" Monica demanded.

"Peter Fillerman, Deputy Peter Fillerman."

"Listen to me, deputy, in just a few moments, your office is going to receive a fax from me. It's a search warrant I want you to take and immediately execute at May Walker's residence." She needed those papers. If she could compare the signatures and get a match—*got you.*

"M-May Walker's place?"

"She's got papers there, going back for years. You need to find—"

"If it's at May Walker's, ma'am, I won't be finding anything."

More deputies piled into the room. Monica turned away, lifting a hand to her left ear to muffle their voices. "Why not? The warrant is perfectly legal, there's no reason you can't execute it."

"There ain't nothin' left *to* search out at May Walker's place. There was a fire there late last night."

Her fingers tightened around the phone.

"Told Sheriff Martin for months that the place was a firetrap, but I couldn't ever get him to go out there."

"What about May?"

"She-she didn't make it out of the fire."

Monica's eyes closed. *God, what a terrible way to die.*

"Real shame. May didn't have any close neighbors and the fire was out of control before anyone knew what was happening."

And May Walker was dead. Another lost life. She swallowed and forced her eyes to open. "Thank you for the information."

"You want—you want Sheriff Martin to call you?"

She turned around and studied the gathered deputies. Luke was talking to them, his hands on his hips as he went over search procedures. "Where did you say Martin had gone?"

"I didn't."

No, she knew that.

"He's gone up to Angola. He goes up there every few months."

A chill skated down her spine. "Why?" Thousands of inmates were in Angola, but she knew one of those inmates very, very well.

A soft sigh. "Can't really say for sure, ma'am, just know he drives up to visit for a few hours now and then. Guess he's got someone up there he needs to see."

And she had someone she never wanted to see.

"You want him to call you?"

"I'll call him." After she did some checking to see just who the sheriff was visiting at Angola. Had to be just a coincidence, but...

But she wasn't taking chances. Monica ended the call with a push of her fingertip and stared down at the phone. Lost, remembering.

No one could hear you scream.

"Monica?"

She jumped when Luke called her name. Her head lifted, and she found his gaze on her. *All* of their gazes were on her as the deputies and the sheriff stood at attention. Waiting on her. She was supposed to tell them all what to do. She was the one they looked to. Right then, she couldn't afford another trip down Freak Memory Lane.

No time. Focus.

Her shoulders straightened and she pointed behind the sheriff. "That a map of the county?"

He gave a quick nod.

She strode forward and yanked the map off the wall. She spread the map out on the conference room desk. Her gaze followed the criss-cross of lines that were the roads in and out of town.

No one could hear you scream.

The perp would have taken Sam someplace secluded, so he'd have time for his fun and games. Someplace close enough for the bastard to quickly come in and make his call, then ease away before anyone noticed. "He knows the area," she muttered. A local, or someone who had been to Jasper often enough to learn every secret hollow and twist of land out there.

She bent forward, and her hand settled on the lake near the edge of the town. *Had to be near water.* And if he was going to do it right, make the torture the perfect match, he'd use a lake. He'd want to set the same scene for Sam. A nightmare come true.

"Are there cabins around this lake, Sheriff?"

"On the west." His fingers joined hers. "Three there, then two on the east side."

The east side was closer to town. The west more isolated. What choice had the killer made?

"They're rentals," he said, "but nobody ever goes up there these days."

"Kenton, get me warrants to search every cabin there."

"But I—"

"I know a judge," Davis said. "Consider them gotten."

Good. "Davis, I want you and your men to take the three cabins on the west side." She looked up, letting her gaze touch on Luke and Kenton. "We'll take the east side." *Hold on, Sam.* She exhaled and pinned Davis with her stare. "Not one whisper of a siren, got it? I don't want him to know we're there."

The female deputy, Melinda, stood behind the sheriff. From what Monica could tell, she was the one he trusted the most. But fear flickered in her dark eyes. Fear and excitement.

Monica knew that was one dangerous combination.

"We'll be as silent as a whisper," Melinda promised.

"Everyone, watch your ass." The butt of her gun pressed into her side. "He's playing with us, and taking Sam…" Too easy to follow the breadcrumbs and find those cabins on the map. "It could be a lure to pull us in."

Because the guy had been planning everything so carefully. The victims, their phones—he'd known he would be contacting her. Because he'd known the SSD would become involved? "He knew Sam's fear long before she got off the plane," she whispered and knew it was true. He'd known about Sam. *And he knows about me.*

"The bastard set one trap already with Jones," Luke's voice came, strong and steady. "Stay on guard. We need to be ready for any damn thing."

Including a guy using his victims as killers. "He's done his homework," Monica said. "He'll be ready, and we have to be ready, too."

The faces before her were tense. Grim nods met her words; a few offered, "Yes, ma'am" responses. She licked her lips. "Then let's get the hell out of here," Monica said, "because Agent Kennedy is *not* dying on my watch."

She vomited water. Dirty brown water that shot from her mouth and nose. Wood bit into her palms as Sam tried to shove off the dock.

Too weak.

More water poured from her mouth. Her eyes burned. She couldn't see anything. Too blurry.

And she *hurt*. Every part of her.

Laughter.

Her arms gave way, and she fell onto the dock.

"That was fun. For a minute there, I was afraid you wouldn't be able to get free of those ropes." His voice. Taunting her.

She'd kill him.

A violent coughing fit had her body jerking.

"Looks like that hurts," he murmured, and the dock creaked beneath his feet.

She swung out at him. She caught his legs and shoved. He fell back, slamming his head into the wood.

Move.

Sam lurched to her feet. Water dripped down her body as she stumbled. *Get away from him.*

From the water.

She'd clawed her way out of that watery grave. No way was she going back. *He'd* be dying.

He slammed into her just as she jumped off the dock and reached the sandy shoreline. They fell together, and sand flew into her mouth. He pinned her, holding both wrists against the ground and trapping her legs with his.

"Aw, sweet Sam…" His breath feathered over her ear. "You really didn't think I'd end things this soon, now did you? Playtime's just gettin' started."

She bucked against him and rammed the back of her head into his.

"Bitch!"

"Asshole," a hoarse croak. "L-let me—"

He spun her around. For an instant, he was a hazy mass above her. Some kind of cap over his hair. Dark shirt. She couldn't see his face—just a blur and then—his fist came at her.

Driving into her jaw. Once. Twice.

"Think you're so damn smart, don't you?" He taunted and her head sagged back. "You're weak, just like all the others. Weak and scared. A sad little girl, screaming for help that won't come."

He stood, kept her wrists pinned together, and began hauling her back toward the water. "This time, I'll hold you under. Let's see how long it takes for you to stop breathing. And maybe, maybe I'll bring you back and do it again."

Her legs kicked, and she twisted, and the sand flew around her.

"I'll feel you die."

Water sloshed against her. A shudder worked through her body. "No, *no,* you bastard!" It should have been a scream but her throat was too ravaged. "L-let me go! Let me—"

"Scream. I like it when they scream." Talking to himself more than to her.

He shoved her down into the water face first. His hands tangled in her hair, and he forced her down. Her mouth was open, and water pumped down her throat.

She clawed at his hands. Desperate. *No, not like this—*

He hauled her up. "Take a breath. Let's see how long you can last."

Sam gagged. Fought for her breath.

Then the water came at her again.

The search party headed out, and the damn reporters pounced the minute they left the station. Luke went out first, and they got him. Cameras, bright lights, and microphones were shoved right at his face. Dammit, this was *not* his scene.

"Is it true the Watchman has a federal agent in custody?" A perky blonde demanded.

"Do citizens need to worry?" A tall man with one really tacky hairpiece asked, his voice oozing fake concern. "Can you keep us safe from the Watchman?"

Luke's body tightened.

"*No statements!*" Kenton's booming voice. "Back off and give the team room to move here, or I swear to God, I'll make sure none of you get a peep about this until *after* the national news carries the story."

The reporters stepped back.

"Cut," the blonde muttered, while the man adjusted his toupee.

Monica shoved past the throng. Luke kept pace right with her. There had to be about ten more reporters there, all hungry for blood.

"Damn idiot Vance," the sheriff grumbled behind him. "Found him talking to Charlotte Peters earlier." A jerk of his thumb toward the blonde. "I sent his ass out on recon. I don't want him near those reporters again. *Watchman*, my ass."

The sheriff stormed toward his cruiser. "Melinda, radio Vance and Pope, tell them to meet us on Vernon, got it?"

Luke jumped in the SUV, and Monica gunned the engine. Kenton would follow behind them. And he'd follow fast.

She slammed her foot on the accelerator, and the SUV shot out of the lot, narrowly missing a news van.

"Monica! Christ, it's okay, be—"

"It's not okay." Her knuckles whitened on the steering wheel. "He's playing with her now, Luke. Hurting her. Making her scream and beg."

"We're *going* to find her." Monica had her sights on the killer, only him. The profiler was turned on, locked in. *Too locked in.* "Don't think about what he's doing. Focus on Sam. Finding her."

"I can't." Whispered. Desperate. A tear leaked down her cheek. "I can't ever turn it off. It's always there. I'm *always* thinking like them. Knowing what they'd do. What they'd like. How they'd hunt." She didn't look at him, just kept her eyes on the road.

He kept his eyes on her. "You're not like them." Her job was to profile; that was it. She wasn't evil, not like those freaks they hunted.

"Yes, I am." Still so soft. "More than you can know."

He touched her arm. Had to. She needed him.

She flinched away.

Too damn bad. His jaw locked, and his fingers curled around her. "You're not like them."

Another turn. Pine trees surrounded them now. Tall, twisting pines, their top branches stretching toward the clouds.

"You don't know me." Now she did spare him the briefest of glances, and her blue eyes stared blankly at him. Hollow. "You don't know me at all."

His fingers tightened around her arm, and he took the hit right to the gut. "Isn't that what you want?" No one got close to her. Not him, and he'd be willing to bet not any of the others at SSD.

She didn't answer.

"Why?" The demand slipped out. The GPS tracker indicated they had five more minutes before reaching the cabins. Not much time, but Monica's shields were down, and he had to know. "Why do you shove the walls between us?" He deserved an answer.

Another turn. Onto a red dirt road. Toward the sun.

"I'm afraid you'll see who I really am. What I am."

Luke almost didn't hear the whispered confession. Maybe he didn't. Maybe he'd just imagined it. Because that didn't make a bit of sense to him—and fuck, time to call it like he was damn well seeing it. "Bullshit."

She braked. A cloud of dirt rose around them. Monica spared him a glance. "Trust me, Dante—"

Dante? Oh, hell, no, she—

"You don't want to know what's inside me. Even you couldn't handle it." She shoved on her cap and reached into the backseat and snagged her bulletproof vest.

Clenching his teeth, he did the same. But this wasn't over. "We're saving Sam," he told her, "and then you and me, we're tearing down the walls between us, ripping 'em all down."

She blanched.

"I'll know you, inside and out, and you'll damn well know me," Luke promised.

CHAPTER *Twelve*

The place was too familiar. Monica froze beside the SUV, her eyes flickering toward the treetops. Sunlight drifted down to her, fading in tendrils toward the ground. The chirp of birds and insects filled her ears.

The dirt road. So similar.

Her heart thudded into her ribs.

Kenton's car pulled up behind her. Monica swallowed and took a quick breath.

Hold on, Sam.

She turned around and found Luke watching her. *I'll know you and you'll damn well know me.* Yeah, the promise was in his gaze. But there was more. When it came to her, the guy always saw so much more than others did.

"What's going on?" he asked, a quiet demand.

"We're stopping a killer, that's what's going on." They'd parked a safe distance away from the cabins. If the guy was there he wouldn't be able to hear the sound of their vehicles, not from here. "Kenton, don't forget your vest." Because she had a bad feeling about this one. *He's ready for us.*

Kenton jerked on his vest and jogged toward them. "You think—you think Sam's still alive?"

Since Sam had disappeared at the airport, she'd been missing for a little over four hours.

Plenty of time to die. "Yes." Sometimes, it didn't really matter what you thought. You had to say what was best for the others.

He let out a hard expulsion of air. "Then let's go find this bastard."

Luke didn't say anything. Just watched her.

He knows I'm lying. And since when could he see past her lies?

He brushed by her. "When this is over, you're telling me everything."

She grabbed his arm. "When this is over, I'm locking up a killer, and I'm making sure he never sees daylight again." This wasn't getting personal. Not now. They were staying focused on the killer.

Monica pulled her weapon. "We go on my count." She allowed herself a deep breath. "Stay to cover, no risks, understood?"

"Understood." From Luke.

"Kenton? Understood?" He always seemed so controlled, *like me*, but she knew there was a dangerous core to the agent. She'd glimpsed it on a few field missions before.

Like to like.

"Got you."

"Then let's go bring Sam back."

They ran, heading for the first cabin on Briars Lane.

So isolated. The two cabins on the east side were the only homes within a fifteen-mile radius. The guy was sure good at picking his kill spots.

The smell of sap had her nose twitching. So many pines here. The ground was hard, uneven, but she moved easily, leading the others.

They found the first cabin almost immediately. Small, one story, with big picture windows along the front. Not on the water, but nestled farther back in the trees. In less than four minutes, they'd gone in and searched every inch of that place, barely making a whisper of sound.

No Sam.

They went back into the woods, moving quietly, quickly. And then she saw the second cabin. Wooden, with an old-fashioned wraparound porch. A small chimney jutted from the top of the second-story's slanting roof. A picturesque place. The lake glittered behind the cabin, dark waves moving in the sun.

Luke and Kenton stilled beside her.

"Don't see anyone," Kenton murmured.

Neither did she, and that didn't mean a thing. "Go in slow," she whispered. Maybe Sam was in the cabin, alive.

Hiding in a closet. Waiting for that one weak moment to escape. The stench of death surrounding—

Monica shook her head. "You two take the house. I'll take the lake." Because this place *would* be the perfect kill spot. Isolated, with that second-story view giving the perfect vantage point for a lookout. And the lake, so close by . . . Sam's worst fear just a few feet away. If she'd awakened in the house, she would have been able to hear the water. *The better to stir her fear.*

Monica motioned with her hand, giving the signal to advance. Then they were moving quickly, cutting a trail through the brush and keeping their weapons up.

The men slowed near the cabin and crept up the porch. No groan of the wood. Sweet, sweet silence.

Monica circled around the back of the cabin. That water was Sam's fear, it would—

"*Sam!*" The scream tore from her lips even as she broke into a run. "*Dammit, no!*"

Sand flew from beneath Monica's feet as she charged for the lake, and for the still figure, floating face down in that murky water.

She jumped up on the dock. Ran over the wood. The *thump thump thump* of her shoes on the dock perfectly matched her heart.

Monica dove into the water. Sam wasn't out far, just drifting there, face down, so close to the dock. So close.

She grabbed Sam and spun her around. "Sam!" Pale face. Bruised. Closed eyes. Wet hair clinging to her cheeks. "Sam, breathe!"

But she wasn't breathing. Her body was heavy and cold.

"Give her to me!" Luke's yell. Monica kicked, turned around, and found him jumping from the dock. She pulled Sam, holding her tight.

Then Luke was there, taking Sam from her arms. Lifting her still body onto the dock and jumping up after her. Kenton laid Sam across the wood and bent over her, checking for a pulse.

Find one. Monica climbed back onto the dock. *Find one.* They needed a pulse. A beat—

He shook his head.

Water trickled from Sam's mouth and nose.

"You're not dying," Kenton's fierce order. He turned her head to the side and forced her mouth open wider. More water poured from her lips.

Luke pressed his hands over her chest, pumping. More water.

Monica grabbed Kenton's phone. Her fingers were shaking, trembling hard, but she managed to punch the numbers for the sheriff's office. Lily would be there, manning the phones while the sheriff and his deputies conducted their search. Lily would be able to contact him; she'd contact everyone on the task force and the woman would be able to make damn sure an ambulance got there ASAP.

Kenton closed his mouth over Sam's, breathing for her.

Lily answered immediately. "Jasper County Sheriff's Office."

"It's Davenport. We're at Briars, cabin two. We found her!"

Another breath.

"Get an ambulance out here, Lily, ASAP! Now, *now!*"

Luke's hands were on Sam's chest. Her chest was just lifting with Kenton's breaths.

Monica caught Sam's hand and squeezed. "You fight, you hear me? *Fight!*"

Giving up and dying was easy. She knew that. She'd thought about it often enough.

But easy wasn't her way, and it wasn't Sam's either.

"You do this," she told her, the words rasping out, "he wins. You don't want him to win. You want him to pay, to suffer, just like he made you suffer! You don't do this! *Fight!*"

And Sam jerked.

Kenton pulled back.

Sam rolled over, coughing, shaking, trying to suck in desperate gulps of air. *Breathing.*

Thank you, God. Monica caught Sam's shoulders. Held tight. "Get it out, get all the water out."

The woman seemed to have swallowed half the damn lake.

How long had she been in the water?

"It's okay, Sam, you're safe now, you're—"

"*No!*" An ear-splitting shriek of terror. "L-let…me die! L-let…m-me…" Shaking, shuddering, Sam struck out with her fists and feet.

Her elbow slammed into Monica's chest.

She punched Kenton in the face.

"S-stop…bringing…m-me…b-back—"

Luke caught her arms, pinning her to the dock. "Samantha! Stop! You're okay, you're safe! We got you out of the water, you're—"

Bloodshot eyes locked on him. "D-don't…p-put me…back." The words came out husky and broken.

And Monica knew what he'd done. Sick fuck. She *knew* how he'd tortured Sam. Into the water, again and again.

Luke stopped holding Sam down and wrapped his arms around her instead. "You're not going back in." A muscle flexed along his jaw. "*You're not going back in.*"

Monica's gaze slipped past his and went to the line of trees on the other side of the lake. "We have to check the cabin." But the killer wouldn't be there. No, he was somewhere else, watching. Because she knew he loved to watch.

I'm coming for you. Time for him to see what it felt like to be the prey.

His wet clothes clung to him, the same way Monica Davenport's held tight to her curvy body.

She'd jumped right in for the other woman. He'd wondered if she'd hesitate, just for a moment.

But no, not her. A full run, then straight into the water. But then she didn't fear the water.

He'd heard her scream, though. Monica's sweet, desperate scream had rang in his ears when she'd first spied the floating angel.

Fear. Now he knew the sound of it in Monica's voice, and he knew exactly how to rouse that fear. An attack on her wouldn't do the trick because Monica wouldn't break that way. She hadn't broken before. She wouldn't do it now.

He eased back and stripped off his wet shirt. He'd have to hurry. The deputies would be swarming soon. They'd search the area.

He didn't take his gaze off Monica. She was looking his way now, as if she could see him. If only.

The last piece of the puzzle had fallen in place. Finally, a way to break her.

He'd make her fear, all right. But not by hurting her. By taking the others.

He shoved down his pants. Yanked on fresh clothes. Then he watched as the other agent, Dante, put his hand on Monica's shoulder.

Got you.

The bastard had shown his attachment to her from the beginning, but now Monica...

She wrapped her hand around his. Held too tight.

Monica had just sealed the deal.

The sun had almost dried his hair. He'd slip away, blend with the others in Jasper. No one would ever know.

No one ever did.

Not until it was too late.

Chaos. That was the scene as soon as the sheriff arrived with backup. An ambulance followed fifteen minutes later. Deputies swarmed, seemingly from all directions. Some scattered into the woods, searching for the perp. Others went to the house. The EMTs surrounded Sam, a damn good thing because her pupils were huge and she couldn't seem to stop shuddering.

"Sam, tell me who did this." Monica stayed as close as she could. Pretty easy to do because Sam still had a death grip on her left hand.

But the other woman just shook her head. Tears leaked from her eyes.

"We've got to get her to the hospital," the EMT said, a tall, muscled blond. Lance. He'd patched Monica up last night. "They have to check her. Make sure there's no—" He broke off, glancing down at Sam.

Brain damage. Because they didn't know how long she'd been in that water.

And she could suffer heart failure, so common after a near drowning. Though not so near in Sam's case because the perp *had* drowned her. Again and again. He'd killed her for a few precious seconds, then brought her back.

Lance and his partner lifted her up and pushed the gurney into the back of the ambulance. Monica stepped forward. Sam wasn't heading out alone. She'd have protection, every moment, until this sadistic SOB was captured.

But Kenton shook his head. "I've got her." His shoulders were straight, and his hands clenched into fists. "I'll stay with her. They need you here, Davenport. Go see what the bastard left behind and stop him."

She gave a hard nod. "Don't leave her, not for a minute." Monica lowered her voice. She didn't want Sam to hear this part. "He's already gotten through to a survivor before. He could make a try for her." Because he didn't like for his prey to get away. "Don't leave her." She wasn't going to trust Sam's safety to the deputies.

"I'll be there every second," he said and jumped into the back of the ambulance. The siren screamed on.

Sam's head flew up.

More sirens blared to life. Monica watched as two cruisers spun out, heading behind the ambulance.

"I'm sending some deputies to Jasper Memorial Hospital." The sheriff strode toward her. "They'll make sure she's safe."

Like they did for Laura? But Monica bit the words back because Laura's death hadn't been his fault. It had been hers. *I should have protected her.*

Davis shook his head and eyed the house. "This place hasn't been rented out in over six months. After the last storm hit, we haven't had a whole lot of tourists."

"He knew it was empty." Just like he knew everything else. All the signs were indicating the perp was local, but Kyle West had been from Gatlin. If the perp was Kyle

West…was he in the town? A good old boy, hiding in plain sight and trying to disguise the monster inside?

If so, he was doing one fine job.

"Ma'am." Deputy Vance's voice. She glanced at him. The guy was sweating, but he seemed to be doing better at this crime scene. But then, there hadn't been a body shot to hell to shake him. "I—uh, we found something inside you're gonna want to see."

"Show me," she said. Monica followed Vance into the house, with Luke close at her heels and the sheriff bringing up the rear. They filed down the small hallway, took a left and entered what was probably the master bedroom.

Lee Pope glanced back at them. Sweat slickened the hair near his temples, and his face had a white cast. "It—it's blood, isn't it?"

Monica's eyes went to the only window in the room, the window that looked out over the water. Over what would have been Sam's grave.

The curtain had been pulled away from that window, and just below the glass, someone—their killer—had painted on the wall. In blood.

"What the hell?" Luke's gruff voice. "Whose blood?"

Good question. Monica crept forward.

"Guess we got us a damn artist," Davis muttered, and he pressed close to get a better look.

"No one's touched this?" Monica asked through numb lips.

"I pushed back the curtains, that was all," Lee said. "When we saw it, Vance went for you." His head cocked to the right. "Does that look like a flower to ya'll?"

Not just any flower. She rolled her shoulders. "It's a

rose." *Hyde.* She needed to talk to him and find out what the hell he wanted her to do.

The jackass was taunting her.

The other kills had been staged so that a final message was sent to the victims. Saundra saw her lost love. Laura saw the house that started her nightmare. Patty died in her childhood home. Sally was forced to re-experience the horror of her husband's car crash. Jeremy died on the same street that his father's blood had stained.

But this time, the final message wasn't for the victim. *Not for Sam.*

For me. Monica's gaze lifted to the lake. If she'd come inside the house first, she would have looked through the window and seen Sam's body floating on those glittering waves.

"I've seen this before," Luke muttered. "Dammit, I *know* I've seen this."

Her heart slammed into her ribs. "Get the techs to dust *everything.*" No killer was perfect. Something would be left behind. Some hair, some fiber, something. "And sheriff, I'm betting you've got some damn fine hunting dogs in this area."

A grim nod. "The best."

"Get them because we're combing these woods." They didn't need to worry about being quiet now. Time to bring out the dogs.

Luke crouched down, his eyes narrowed as he studied the blood. "Doesn't make sense."

She whirled away. *Yes, it does.*

"Maybe he's leaving a mark to claim his kills."

Monica froze near the doorway and glanced back at Luke.

"The more they kill, the more serials perfect their methods." His gaze was on that flower. "Maybe our guy is evolving."

"No." The word shot from her. The bastard wasn't evolving. He was playing a fucking game.

Luke rose, staring out the window. "Planned every damned bit, didn't he?"

Her eyes strayed to the deputies. "Vance, Lee, why don't you go join the search outside?"

"Yes, ma'am." Vance's gaze darted to the sheriff. He and Lee nodded quickly, and they hurried outside.

When she was sure they were gone, she asked the question she *had* to voice. "Sheriff, how many people knew that Sam was flying in from D.C.?"

He shrugged. "Don't know. Lily got the call. Left me a note and—" His bushy brows snapped up as understanding seemed to sink in, but he still asked, "What are you sayin'?"

She stared back at him, sure he knew exactly what she was saying.

The sheriff edged toward her. His eyes glittered. "You're not thinkin'—"

"I'm thinking I have an agent who was nearly killed," her voice lowered, "and the killer shouldn't have even known she was in the county, but somehow, he managed to be in the right place to grab her. Interesting, isn't it?"

His jaw dropped. "You're sayin'—"

"I'm saying I want to know the name of every person who knew about Sam's arrival."

"Anybody at the station could have—"

"That's right." He knew where she was going with this. At the station, she'd counted at least a dozen deputies and three assistants. All of them would have been given access to the sheriff's message board. Any of them could have learned about Sam.

And that damn phone had been dumped right there, at the sheriff's office.

Could be that they needed to search harder for the killer.

Or it could be that he was standing right beside them and they didn't even know it.

Luke stepped forward. "I'll organize the team in the woods."

And she'd take the house, in case there were any more messages. They went into the hall, the sheriff's curses following them.

Luke caught her hand. "You saved her."

"No, you and Kenton, you—"

He yanked her close and kissed her. Hard, fast, not enough. His tongue plunged into her mouth, and her fingers dug into his arms, holding on tight as she kissed him back with a stark hunger, the hunger and need that was always there. Even in the midst of hell.

Luke tore his mouth from hers and stepped back. "Christ, sorry. I shouldn't have touched you."

But she'd needed him. Monica eased away from Luke. No one had seen them. They were safe. But the game they were playing was so dangerous.

"You just looked broken when you found her," he muttered. "I can't see you that way."

She swallowed over the lump in her throat. "He's not going to break me."

"No, he isn't." His gaze lingered on hers. Then he turned and strode down the hall.

He nearly collided with Deputy Pope. "Sorry, ah, special agent," the deputy said.

Luke muttered something back and kept walking. Her eyes narrowed. The deputy was supposed to be outside, helping with the search.

Lee's gaze darted to her, and a flush stained his cheeks. Oh, shit, had he seen—

"Agent Davenport." Lee nodded, but his eyes were hooded. Too watchful.

Monica lifted a brow. "Something you need, deputy?"

His shoulders hunched a bit. "You—you like what you do?"

"Some days." But today... "Other days, when I have to get deep into a profile, those days are harder." Couldn't turn off the killers. No matter how hard she tried.

"How do you know..." he inched closer to her, "what he's thinking? I mean, you found the woman here so fast. How'd you know?"

"Because this perp works on fear. I found out what his victim feared, and I used her fear to track him."

A drop of sweat slid down his right temple. "You had school for that, right? Where they taught you how to tune in?"

Not exactly. "I've got a doctorate in psychology, but I also studied in the behavioral sciences division at Quantico." Then there had been the hands-on training she'd gotten from a sociopathic killer.

He licked his lips and glanced back over his shoulder. "I-I heard what you said to the sheriff."

She lifted a brow.

"I-I got to that airport on time, I swear I did, but the

flight was early. Agent Kennedy had already left." His thin shoulders straightened. "I didn't screw up this time, ma'am. I was there."

Just too late.

"I checked everywhere for her, *everywhere*. But she was long gone." His gaze bored into hers. "*I tried to find her.*"

She believed he had. "Pope, how long have you been working in law enforcement?"

He swallowed and wiped his palms on the front of his pants. "Four years."

Longer than she'd thought. "You worked a lot of crime scenes?"

"Not 'til lately."

Yeah. Not until their killer started terrorizing the town.

"With Jones...that was...bad." A stark whisper. Monica remembered that he'd known Jones. Gone to school with him.

"My old man died like that." His shoulders were so stiff. "Ate his gun." A fierce shake of his head. "You got to be desperate to do that."

Jones had been. As for Lee's father..."I'm sorry." Would the words always seem hollow?

He shook his head, seeming to shake off her sympathy. "I'm not like him. *I'm not.* I can help. I can do—"

"Pope! Get movin'! Dante needs more men!"

He flushed. "I can help," he said once more, then hurried out at the sheriff's command.

Monica watched him leave. "Sheriff, how long has Pope been on your team?"

"About six months." He took his time coming to her

side. "Got me some new recruits when Barnes and Lakely retired."

Interesting.

"He worked over in Gatlin County for a few years." His voice lowered a bit. "Word was that he'd had him a bad break-up so he got out of Jasper." Of course the sheriff would know the gossip. He shrugged. "But then he finally transferred back home early this year."

Home. Jasper County. The not-so-safe place to live. And he'd been in Gatlin, where Saundra had been killed.

Could be coincidence, or it could be one hell of a lot more.

"Sam? Sam, everything's all right."

She heard the voice from a distance. A man's voice, muted. Drifting to her so slowly.

She tried to open her eyes, but it was hard, and just when she'd get her lids up a bit, they'd fall again.

Where am I? What's happening?

Someone grabbed her fingers and held tight. "We're taking you to the hospital."

Hospital. Why?

Because she'd been in the water, drowning, over and over and—

Sam shot up, screaming. Wrenching cries that hurt her throat.

Strong hands clamped around her shoulders. "Hold her, we need—"

"*Sam.*"

A voice she knew. Blinking, she turned her head and

saw Kenton. His clothes were wet. His handsome face tense.

Safe. Kenton wouldn't hurt her. He was on her team. *Trust the team or trust no one.*

She sucked in a sharp breath. Another, but still tasted only the bitter water on her tongue. "Did you...get h-him?"

A slow shake of his head.

Fear squeezed her heart, a tight grasp that had her gasping.

"We *will*," he told her, his voice intense. "We're going to get him. Monica's after him. She's going to track him and stop him. He won't hurt you or anyone else."

Her body sagged, and he eased her back onto the stretcher. "She found you," he said, "and she'll find him."

Her heartbeat thudded in her ears. *Monica.* Sam remembered seeing her. Black hair, soaking wet. Monica had been there, holding her on the dock. "S-saved...me."

"Yeah, Monica pulled you out. Damn, you scared the hell out of us, Sam. You weren't breathing."

No, because that last time, he'd held her under too long. He'd grown tired of his game.

How many times had she been in that water? "He...knew," she managed. The man had known just how to break her.

Kenton just stared back at her. She saw the lines of worry near his eyes.

The killer knew her fears. This case wasn't just about random vics in a southern town. Had it ever been?

If he knew her fears, he could have targeted the other SSD agents, too. He could have set up the original kills to lure them in to his game.

"It's going to be okay," Kenton told her, but right then, she didn't believe him.

She wondered if even he believed the words.

CHAPTER *Thirteen*

Music blared from an old jukebox, a slow country beat with someone doing someone else wrong. Folks packed the inside of Pete's Bar. Smoke filled the air, curling lazily over the pool tables, and glass beer bottles clinked.

The people of Jasper were out having a good time. Relaxing, dancing, flirting. Acting like there wasn't a killer preying on their streets.

Luke had a cold beer in front of him, a fellow agent who was *alive,* and he knew he should have been celebrating like the deputies seated in the corner booth, but he couldn't.

Because something wasn't right. One thing kept nagging at his mind, and he just couldn't get past it.

That rose. That damn bloody rose. What kind of message had that been?

When Monica had seen the rose, all the color had blanched from her face. He'd been reaching for her, to hold her, to keep her on her feet, when her spine had straightened and she'd shoved back her shoulders. Whenever she felt threatened, she did that. Stood tall, straightened those shoulders and acted like she wasn't scared.

When he knew she was. He was surprised the woman still thought he bought that act.

The fear that had flickered in her eyes had vanished almost instantly, but he'd been left thinking…

That message is for her.

But Monica wasn't sharing anything with him. She was working on her profile, talking to the crime scene guys, huddling with Gerry the tech, and not telling him a thing.

"What's got you looking so angry, Agent Dante?" Gravelly, rough, and, of-piss-course, his boss's voice.

He lowered the beer and turned slowly to face Keith Hyde. What had him angry? *Take your pick.* "The asshole dicking around with us."

Hyde's lips quirked. "Yeah, it's time for the bastard to go down." He pulled up a stool and motioned to the bartender. "Water." Hyde didn't drink alcohol. Ever.

Or at least, he hadn't in over fifteen years.

A.A. If the stories were true.

"Sam can't identify him." Hyde's fingers rapped on the bartop. "I saw her right after I flew in. She doesn't even remember being at the airport." He exhaled a rough sigh.

"What does she remember?" Had to be *something*. Something they could use…

"Just being at the cabin, being in the water." Hyde paused when the bartender slid a glass of water his way. "She lost her glasses, so she couldn't see her attacker clearly. She could only say he was tall, over six-foot-two.

Probably weighed about one eighty to two hundred." A shrug. "More info than we had before, a whole lot less than we need."

Yeah, it was better than nothing, but still close to jack-shit. "What about his voice? Did she say—"

"He whispered to her." Hyde took a long swallow of water. "No accent."

"How is she?" Christ, to have gone through that guy's sick games....

"She doesn't know how many times he put her in the water. The guy got off on keeping Sam in the water until she nearly drowned. Then he'd let her out, let her think she'd survived—but every time, he just kept throwing her back in."

Sick fuck.

"Monica..." Hyde rubbed a hand over his face. "She told me that he probably only stopped when Sam gave up trying to survive. There wasn't any fear anymore, so he let her go."

He let her drown.

Luke raised his bottle. The beer looked like piss and tasted like water. Loud laughter broke out from one of the pool tables. He glanced over and saw Deputy Vance Monroe. Vance had one of the waitresses up on the table. His mouth was locked tight to the blonde's.

Huh. At least someone was having a good night.

"Monica lives for the job, you know." Hyde's attention hadn't wavered. Not for an instant.

Luke lowered the bottle and turned back to his boss. "Yeah, I figured that one out a long time ago." When it came to Monica's priorities, he knew exactly where he fell on her list.

Hyde smiled. It wasn't a pretty sight. The guy really had a shark's grin. "Such a smartass. Do you really think I don't know about you?"

Uh, what—

"I know about her past. I know about Quantico, and I know about *you*."

Luke's eyes narrowed. "*Sir,* I think you need to watch your step." He might respect the man, but Hyde wasn't about to get between him and Monica. No one was. "If you want me off this team because of an involvement I—"

Laughter. Not from the pool table group this time, but from Hyde. "Dante, I knew you'd slept with Monica before I brought you on the team. Hell, that was one of the reasons she gave me for *not* bringing you on."

What?

"Monica told me if you came on board, it might just happen again." Hyde shook his head, and a wry smile curved his lips. "Guess she knew what she was talking about."

Holy hell. Luke tried to shut his gaping mouth, but he had to ask, "And you approved the transfer anyway?"

Carefully, Hyde sat his empty glass down on the table. "I don't care what you do with your dick."

Yeah, good to know.

"I do care about how you do your job. My division isn't like others. We have our own rules. And rule one—your team members, all of them, have to be able to count on you."

"They can." He'd always done his job and done it well.

"If you let your feelings for Monica blind you, then

you're no good to me." Blunt. "Keep your control, keep your cool, and keep your job."

"You giving this same sweet talk to Monica?"

Hyde shoved away from the bar and took a moment to straighten his suit. "Don't have to. Monica doesn't lose control."

"Then you don't know Monica," the words came out too fast. But he was tired of everyone thinking she was some kind of ice queen. She had the same needs and hungers and *feelings* that everyone else did. And her control was starting to crack. He'd seen the fissures today. Maybe it had been cracking for a while.

"Ah, let me guess. You think *you* know her, right?" A shake of his head. "Son, I thought you were smarter than that." Hyde turned and pushed his way through the crowd.

He kept his eyes on Hyde's retreating back and watched him head for the door. Just when he reached the double doors, Monica stepped inside. Luke saw her say something to the boss, then her eyes rose and met his.

The woman might as well have punched him in the gut.

I am so screwed.

Keeping his distance today had been torture, and, yeah, he'd broken. That kiss in the hall ranked as a moment of idiocy. But he'd had to touch her.

Keeping control—not possible. He'd never had control with her, and he doubted he ever would.

"*Meet me tonight.*" A man's gruff demand.

Luke's brows shot up, and he glanced over to see Vance stroking the arm of the blond waitress. "When you get off work, come meet me."

She laughed and stood on tiptoe to whisper in his ear.

From the looks of things, the lady had to be whispering a "yes" before she eased back and hurried behind the bar.

His brows rose. *Seriously*? That guy was scoring? Luke's fingers closed around the cold neck of his beer as Vance sauntered toward him. Luke shook his head and said, "Didn't take you for a Romeo, deputy—"

Romeo. Not likely. Not that sick, twisted sonofabitch killer who'd carved up his girls and marked them. *Marked them.*

An image of the bloody flower flashed through his mind.

Luke stilled, a memory from an old crime scene photo pushing through his thoughts. *That flower.* Romeo had marked his victims with a flower. He'd branded the mark onto their flesh within hours of taking the girls. A mark to last forever.

A mark on the back of their shoulders, a raised, rigid rose.

Oh, shit. The beer glass shattered beneath his fingers.

"Whoa, man!" Vance's eyes bulged. "You all right?"

Hell, no. He threw a wad of bills onto the bar. Didn't bother answering Vance. Red coated his vision. His body vibrated with fury.

Monica came toward him, slowly easing her way through the crowd.

He just shoved the drunks out of his way. *I touched her body, every inch. Should have known.*

Then she was there. "Luke, I wanted to—"

"Come with me." He could barely get the words out as he locked his fingers around her wrist and pulled her back toward the front door. They had to talk, fast, and not here, with all the eyes and ears surrounding them.

Fuck. Fuck. Fuck.

His fist slammed into the front door, and he thrust it open. Lee Pope jumped and spun around, a cigar dangling from his fingers. "What's the—"

Luke glared at him and pulled Monica around the side of the building. No audience. Not for this. No damn way.

Voices were muted, drifting in the air and through the thin walls of the bar. He had to go farther, get her away and—

"Stop it, Luke!" Monica jerked her hand free. "Just—*stop!*"

He whirled on her, his body tight. "I can't believe I didn't fucking see it. All the signs were there, staring me right in the face!" He caged her between him and the wooden wall of the bar. "*He* knew, he knows everything."

Her face seemed to pale in the moonlight. "What are you talking about? What did Hyde say?"

"That we can fuck, but I can't lose control." Control? Yeah, what was that? He slammed his fist into the building behind her. "*Why didn't you tell me?*" Rage. Pain.

For her.

Christ, *her.* "*Why?*" he snarled.

Her eyes were so wide. So deep. They looked black in the moonlight, but they were blue. Such a beautiful blue. *That's right, because he'd had a type and Romeo liked—*

"I don't know what you're talking about, but you need to calm down."

He kissed her. Crushed his mouth to hers and just took.

Because nothing was going to change between them. He still wanted her more than breath. It didn't matter what had come before or what would come after him. He still wanted her.

Always.

At first, she seemed to freeze beneath his touch. *No, no, just—*

Then she kissed him back with a fury to match his. Her lips sucked his tongue. She tasted. She took. Her hips rocked against his. His cock was up, swollen and ready, for her.

Monica.

His hands closed over her shoulders. Squeezed. Held tight.

How many times had he seen her roll her shoulders? When she was working a case, when she was pressured at the Academy—

Her shirt had a long, V-necked collar, one that dipped to reveal sweet cleavage. His fingers slipped under the collar, found her soft skin.

His mouth hardened on hers. *All these years.*

His fingers curved around her right shoulder, pushed the fabric down, yanked it. Heard it rip.

Her mouth tore from his. "Luke, you can't—"

He'd bared her shoulder. Creamy skin. Soft flesh. Choking back the lust, he spun her around and saw the mark on her right shoulder blade.

Just enough light to see. The raised skin. White. An old scar. In the rough shape of a rose.

The mark of the Romeo Killer. The same fucking rose that had been in that godforsaken cabin.

His hands were shaking. *He* was shaking, about to

splinter apart. He touched the mark—no, not a mark, a brand—because Romeo had used a homemade brand on his girls. Burned their flesh as they screamed.

As she'd screamed.

"Baby…" His head fell toward her. His lips hovered over the mark. He'd touched the brand in the darkness before. Skimmed his fingers right over it and never realized.

She whirled around and shoved him back a good two feet. "Get your hands off me!" A voice he'd never heard from her. No control. Just fury.

He shook his head and stepped toward her, closing that distance. "Why didn't you tell me?"

Her chin came up fast. "Tell you what? That I have a scar on my back? Big deal, you've got—"

Oh, she wasn't going to bullshit him. Not anymore. "That's Romeo's mark." That bit hadn't ever made it to the press. The cops and agents had held the detail about the branding out of the briefings to the media. They always held something back in a case like that, something to try and trip up the killer later.

Luke had learned about the brand at Quantico. A profiler, Dr. Mark Brown, had been doing a talk on serials for the Atlanta office.

He'd said some of those killers liked to collect souvenirs from their kills. They'd take out the tokens and relive the murders, over and over.

But some serials preferred to mark their prey. A way of forever claiming the victims.

"Romeo believed he owned his victims. Their bodies were his to do with what he wanted. He cut them, he carved them, but first, he marked them with a brand. A rose on their flesh, a gift from their lover."

"Get away from me," Monica told him, her voice shaking.

But he didn't move back an inch. "That newspaper clipping—the one this freak left—it was about you, wasn't it?" Sole survivor. Oh, Jesus, *how* had she survived? He knew what Romeo had done to his girls. The torture that would last for days. "I thought it was about the town, but it was about *you*."

She exhaled on a hard breath. "I'm not talking to you here, I'm not—"

"*You've never fucking talked to me*!" Too loud, he knew it, but he couldn't help it. "This bastard out there knew. He's been using this against you all this time." *What scares you?* The bastard had been tormenting her. "Monica, he's coming for you! You needed to tell me. Shit, this is your life!"

Her lips seemed to tremble. "You're wrong, this mark isn't what you think."

"You've got his brand." And he remembered Romeo's type: Young girls between fifteen and seventeen, dark hair, blue eyes.

Monica. Years ago, she would have been Romeo's perfect prey. "You were the girl who got away from Romeo." The girl he'd kept with him for months. While he slaughtered the others.

A tear slid down her cheek.

Fuck. Luke yanked her into his arms, ignoring the push of her hands, and held her close.

But her tears were wetting his shirt, and her body shuddered against him. The unbreakable, broken.

She froze against him. Not fighting now, but not holding him. "I didn't want you to know," she whispered. "Not you."

He raised his head. She wasn't looking at him. He caught her chin and forced her head back so she *had* to see him. "You should have told me years ago."

"Told you what?" Her lips twisted, but it wasn't a pretty sight. Too sad. "That I'm so good at my job because I'm just like them? Exactly like the killers we hunt?"

What? No, she wasn't—

She shook her head. "Luke, how do you think I got him to keep me alive?"

His heart stopped, then started drumming way too fast. "You didn't—"

"I learned something from Romeo. No, I learned a hell of a lot from him." A deep breath. "The first lesson...people will do anything to stay alive."

How long had she been with Romeo? He couldn't remember, but he'd find out. He'd find out everything. But there was one thing she needed to know, *now.* "It doesn't matter, baby. Whatever happened, *doesn't matter.*" What mattered was that he had her in his arms, he could feel her flesh and—

"Yes, it does. He turned me into a monster, but you can't see that, can you?" Anger began to boil in her voice. "You look at me, and you can't see it!"

No, he couldn't. He just saw her. The woman he'd always wanted and needed far too much.

She shook her head again, then broke free of his arms.

"Monica—"

She shoved past him.

"Monica, shit, wait!" His hands balled into fists. Monica wasn't waiting. She was running now.

"She's not for you...." The whisper came from behind him. A man's voice. Luke whirled back around—

Too late.

Something slammed into the side of his head. Something heavy and strong and Luke went down, fast, with the taste of blood on his tongue and Monica's name on his lips.

The last thing he heard was that whisper. Grating in his ears, saying, *"I* see the monster in her, even if you don't...."

She left him. Monica jumped in the SUV and floored the gas and she didn't look back. Luke had his own car now, courtesy of Hyde. It wasn't like she was leaving him stranded, she was just—

Running. Yeah, that was what she was doing. So what? She couldn't handle him right then. Couldn't deal with his questions.

Because she didn't want to face her past.

Or him.

Her trembling fingers tightened around the steering wheel. All the years of keeping her dirty little secret, and the killer out there knew about her past.

What did she fear?

The truth coming out.

But he'd taken care of that for her.

So what else was the bastard going to do?

She drove to the hospital, skating fast through yellow lights and coming to a screeching stop near the back entrance.

What does he think of me? If Luke knew what she'd done, what she'd seen...

What Romeo had done to her.

That fucking brand! She should have gotten the thing removed years before. But she hadn't wanted anyone else cutting her. She'd had enough of that with Romeo.

Her eyes squeezed shut. She'd been fifteen. Fifteen freaking years old, and she'd missed her bus that morning. Just missed the damn bus...

It was gone. She jerked to a stop at the corner, a stitch in her side, and stared at the disappearing back of that yellow bus.

Her mom would kill her. If she had to call her home from the hospital so that she could get a ride to school...

No, she'd just walk it. It wasn't that far, not really. So she'd miss first period. Big deal. Mr. Matthew sucked as a science teacher. She'd make second. She had to make it; she had her English exam today—

A sleek black Corvette eased to the curve beside her. She glanced over, saw the tinted windows. Too dark to see inside. Her hand tightened around the strap of her backpack.

A soft whir of sound and the passenger side window began to ease down. She walked faster.

"Aren't you...Mary Jane?" A man's voice. Strong, sure, friendly.

She shot him a glance from the corner of her eye. The Corvette crept down the road, keeping perfect pace with her. No one else was around. Gone to work. Taking the kids to school.

All alone.

She swallowed when she saw his face, startled. Hot.

Seriously hot. Twinkling blue eyes, hard jaw, full lips, and dimples! Dimples...because he was smiling at her. His hair was dark, thick, just brushing the collar of his black leather jacket.

He couldn't have been more than a few years older than her. Probably in college or something and—

And he knew her name.

She stumbled to a stop. "H-How do you—"

That smile widened. "You don't know me, do you?"

No. Like she would have forgotten him. She shook her head, hard.

"I'm Ryan's older brother."

Ryan? Ryan who? There was a Ryan Thompson in her grade, real class-A jerk who tried to look up her skirt all the time. And then there was Ryan Jennings, but he talked to no one and—

The guy laughed. "I remember seeing you at some of the ball games. Mary Jane, you sure have grown up."

She hunched her shoulders a bit at that, all too aware that parts of her were still, um, growing.

"You missed the bus, didn't you?" Knowing.

Well, of course he knew. There she was, walking past the bus stop with no bus in sight.

"I can give you a ride, if you want. I've got to head over to Williams High anyway. My idiot brother forgot his lunch. Again."

Her lips wanted to curl because that sounded like Ryan Thompson. He was forever bumming off people. She turned fully toward him and hesitated.

The car braked. He leaned toward her, that smile stretching ever more. "Come on, Mary Jane. It's like, five miles to the school. You don't want to walk that."

No, she didn't. But she didn't know him. And if her mom found out she'd taken a ride with this guy she'd be so pissed.

Mary Jane licked her lips.

His eyes narrowed a bit, and his smile seemed to tighten. "Come on..." *he said again.* "Why should a pretty girl like you walk when you can ride?"

He thinks I'm pretty? Her skin flushed. "Thanks, but—" *But she didn't know the guy. Good-looking or not, she didn't know him, and her mom would freak.* "But I'm okay." *She tried a smile.* "It's really not that far."

The smile definitely dimmed. "You should get in the car."

A chill rose on her arms. He didn't seem quite so friendly now, and the longer she stared at him, the less good-looking he appeared. There was something about his eyes. They were so...

Cold. Mean.

She eased back a bit from the car. "Actually, my mom's on her way. She's gonna meet me here and take me the rest of the way." *Her chest shook because her heart was pounding so hard right then.*

His fingers drummed on the steering wheel. "Right. Well, you take care, Mary Jane. I'll be seeing you...." *The car squealed away, and the scent of burnt rubber filled her nostrils.*

She realized that her hands were sweating, her breath coming too fast. All because a cute boy had wanted to give her a ride.

No, something was wrong with him. *The thought slipped through her mind.* His eyes. *Something had been wrong.*

And she realized she was very, very glad she hadn't gotten into his car.

She started walking faster. She turned on Maple Street, and heard the frantic barking of Ms. Milly's two terriers and saw the back of a black Corvette. Parked just down from Ms. Milly's sidewalk.

Her feet stumbled. Wh—

"Your mother's not coming to pick you up."

From right behind her.

She spun around and saw that dimpled smile. "In fact, she's never fucking seeing you again." His hand lifted. She opened her mouth to scream—

He slapped his right hand over her mouth and stabbed her in the neck with a needle. He leaned in close and caught her when her body went limp.

"Shh . . . don't worry, sweetheart, I'm gonna take good care of you."

She'd known he was lying. But she hadn't been able to scream or fight, and her eyes had closed even as he'd thrown her into the back seat of his Corvette. And when she'd opened her eyes again—

No!

Monica sucked in a deep breath. She shoved open the car door. Her face burned as she hurried toward the hospital.

Control. Focus.

She gave a hard nod to the security guard on duty. Keeping her head up, she walked quickly past the receptionist and into the elevator. Her index finger stabbed the button for the sixth floor. She waited. Breathed slow and easy. *Slow and easy.*

She'd learned that trick long ago. When she realized

that she wouldn't be getting out of that two-by-three-foot closet anytime soon. She'd known she could let the panic take her or she could take control.

She'd taken control and fought to never let go.

Wish I'd killed him. Her one regret, after all these years. *If only Hyde hadn't stopped me.*

The elevator chimed, and the doors slid open. She saw the two deputies first. Not flirting with the nurses at the station, but standing guard in the hallway. A red-haired guy with a goatee, Paul, and Melinda.

She inclined her head as she passed them. Then she saw Kenton, sitting right outside Sam's door. His arms were crossed over his chest, his brows drawn low as he watched her approach.

"She doesn't want to talk," he said the minute she drew closer. "Kicked my ass out." A shake of his head. "But I told her I wouldn't go far."

She swiped her tongue over her lower lip. "I'm going in."

His hand came out, blocking the door. "I know you're the shrink, *Doc.*" Nobody ever called her that, least of all Kenton, so she knew he was trying to make a point.

Screw that. She didn't have time for—

"But I think she needs to be alone. Let her cry. Let her heal, let her—"

"You don't know what the hell it's like." The words slipped out because Luke had frayed her control. Or maybe that precious control had been slowly breaking and she hadn't even noticed. "You don't know what it feels like when a killer screws with your head, fucks with your body, and makes you wish for death." *Over and over. Until you begged to die.*

She'd seen it happen.

But I never begged. That had been another trick she'd learned. Not to beg. Not to give the killer what he needed.

Keep him wanting. Keep yourself alive.

His eyes narrowed a bit at the corners. "You're sounding awful personal there, Davenport."

"Move your hand." Or the way she was feeling right then, she'd be more than happy to move it for him.

He gazed at her, then after a moment slowly moved his hand. "Make her better."

"I'll do more than that." She slapped her hand against the hospital door. "I'll take away her monster."

And that was a promise.

"What the hell? Agent Dante? *Agent Dante!*"

The voice sounded hollow. Raspy.

Luke cracked opened his eyes, realized he was laying in—yeah, that smelled like garbage. He pushed up, wincing when pain rocked through his skull.

Sonofabitch.

"Are you all right?" A hand reached out for him. The scent of cigars teased his nose.

He looked up and met Lee's wide-eyed stare. "Someone jumped me." His fingers pushed through his hair, found a freaking goose egg and the sticky wetness of blood. *Shit.*

"You got attacked? You—"

Luke was on his feet. His hand pressed against the

side of the building as the world weaved a bit. "Where's Monica?"

"I-I saw her drive out about thirty minutes ago. When I came out again, your car was still here but I knew you hadn't come back in." He leaned in close. "So I came looking for you. Man—you sure you're all right?"

He took a step. Staggered. "No."

Fuck.

Luke sucked in a sharp breath. Another. Another. Waves of darkness flickered around him, but he fought them. "You see anybody?"

"Uh, when?"

God save him from the deputies. "Did you...ah...see anybody when you came in the," a deep breath, "alley?"

A quick shake of Lee's head. "Just you, man. You were lying there, facedown in the—"

Shit. Garbage. Whatever the hell it was.

"Did you see anyone else?" Like the person who'd slammed him?

"Y-You think the Watchman hit you?" Fear. Excitement. The guy really needed a life.

"I fucking know it." He'd been there, listening and watching.

Bastard.

Where was Monica?

"*Shit*—I'll call the sheriff!"

Right. For all the good it would do. The killer was long gone by now. *And why did he leave me alive?*

Because Luke wasn't his target. The game wasn't about him.

She's not for you. If the bastard touched her, Luke

would rip him apart. "Get on your radio and find out if anyone has seen Monica." He ran toward the lot, his head throbbing.

"Agent Davenport? Why is she—"

"Get on the damn radio!" Because he didn't have time to waste.

Neither did she.

CHAPTER *Fourteen*

I told you, Kenton...I don't want to talk." Sam's voice was a croak, so strangled and weak. She'd turned toward the wall, hunching her shoulders and pulling the covers high over her.

How many times had she been in the water? Monica cleared her throat. "I'm not Kenton."

Sam stiffened. "Not talking...to you...now."

"Yes, you are." Monica walked closer. She could only see darkness outside the window. "But first, I'm going to talk to you." And it didn't matter if Sam turned to look at her or not, she was talking.

Monica straightened her shoulders. "You need to know, he's *not* getting you. Kenton is staying with you, Hyde is coming, we're all taking shifts, and we're going to make damn sure you're not alone."

"So he doesn't...kill me...like he did L-Laura?"

"He's not getting you," she said again. "But we're getting him."

Nothing. Silence.

"You survived, Sam. You made it through his hell and survived." Did she understand how rare that was? "You made it through when—"

"I wanted to die! At the end...I just wanted it...over."

She was talking because, deep inside, Monica knew she wanted to talk. Needed to. "That's—"

"I wanted to be...like you. You're strong...you would have...told him to...fuck off...and fought."

A two-by-three-foot closet. No light. The only sounds— the screams. And they came too often.

"N-no one will...look at me the same...they'll all think...I'm—"

"Strong." Because she was. "You lived. You made it through. You fought him, and you stayed alive, even when you didn't want to."

Sam glanced back at her. "I...hurt so much."

"I know." She did. "And you just wanted the pain to stop." A small pause. "Tell me the truth though. More than that, didn't you want to stop him? To hurt him? To make him pay?" *Kill him.* The two-word mantra that had kept her going for all those months.

A grim nod. "But he was...so strong. I was...tired, weak—"

"He'd drugged you." Hyde had found that out from her tox screen. "He wanted you slowed down because it was the only way he could control you."

Because it was all about control. Something else she'd learned so long ago.

She stared into Sam's eyes and walked to the bed. "You're going to get past this."

"No." So sure.

But she'd been certain once too. "The nightmares will come; they might even always come." Hers still came. "But you're going to keep living. Keep doing your job. Keep taking lovers, keep letting the days roll right by." She stared down at Sam. "Because your life didn't end in that water. You *will* keep going."

A tear slipped from Sam's left eye. "How do you know...for sure?"

She caught her hand. Squeezed tight. "Because I did."

Sam's lips trembled, and a sob shook her chest.

"Don't make my mistakes," Monica whispered. "Don't close out life because you're afraid—" *Of living. Because you think you should have died, and you don't deserve any second chances. Christ. Don't miss out on life.*

Because you were afraid.

"I see that water...every time I close my eyes." Sam's eyes squeezed shut. "Stop him."

"I will." She'd find the bastard. One way or another. Even if she had to be the bait to lure him in....

Come and get me, asshole. Come and get me.

Monica slammed the SUV's door, pressed the lock button automatically, and heard the *blip-blip* as the vehicle secured. The light above her flickered, flashing too bright, then too dim.

New lodgings. Hyde had been insistent on a location transfer for her, Luke, and Kenton after Sam's attack. They were staying in a worn-down hotel, this one situated far off the main highway. Another dump.

But this dump only allowed access to the rooms from the lobby. One elevator. One flight of stairs, and, thanks to Hyde's quick work, one video camera set up to monitor the entrance area at all times.

Lights glowed from half of the rooms in the three-floor hotel. The humming of an air conditioner reached her ears. Monica hurried her steps. She wanted to get inside, download the info that she'd requested from SSD, and see what she could track down through the database of—

Monica froze. She'd heard something. A whisper of sound. A rustle.

Not the wind. There was no wind on this hot southern night. *No wind.*

Something else. *Someone* else.

Her gun was in her hands in less than two seconds. She turned slowly, sweeping the lot with her eyes. Too many trees near the edges of the pavement. Too many places to hide.

Was this place really supposed to be safer?

"Is someone there?" She kept her voice loud and even, because she would not give the prick the satisfaction of thinking she was afraid.

Silence.

Then lights, bright lights came, shining right at her. Monica squinted, but didn't lower her gun.

Darkness. She blinked, trying to adjust her eyes.

A door slammed.

"*Monica!*" Luke's fierce voice. Then he was there, running for her, catching her in his arms and holding her tight. "Christ, I was worried he'd get to you first. I went to the hospital, you were already gone, and I thought—"

She couldn't help but stay stiff in his arms. *Too much between them now.* "He?" She interrupted.

"The asshole Watchman or whatever the hell they're calling him." His fingers tightened. "Let's get inside. *Now*."

"Luke, are you all right?"

"No," he snapped. He let her go, just a bit, and took out his own weapon. "He jumped me. Right after you left Pete's, he caught me in the alley—"

What? Her heart slammed into her throat. "He attacked you?" And Luke had gotten away? "Luke, what did—"

"Inside."

Right. They shoved open the doors of the hotel and lowered their guns just as the night clerk glanced up.

Monica nodded to him and hurried past. He already knew who they were, and he also knew that the SSD agents were the only ones allowed on the third floor. That whole floor had been reserved for them as another of Hyde's security measures.

Luke flashed his ID as they passed the clerk. The guy's Adam's apple bobbed.

They didn't speak during the elevator ride. Monica glanced at Luke from the corner of her eye. He'd been attacked. She'd left him, and he'd been hurt.

Could have been killed. Then what would I have done?

She pressed her lips together to control the tremble that threatened to shake her mouth. He looked pale, the lines bracketing his mouth deeper, his jaw too tense. Her hand rose, her fingers feathering over the hard planes of his face.

The elevator chimed, and the doors slid open on their floor.

Monica dropped her hand and hurried out. She fished

in her pocket for her room key. The thud of Luke's steps told her he was following her.

She shoved her keycard in the hole. The light flashed green. When the lock snicked open, she twisted the handle and went inside.

Luke crowded in right behind her.

"Luke, tell me what happened."

"Bastard hit me with something." His hand lifted, his fingertips touched the back of his head. "Knocked me out."

Could have killed him. Her knees shook.

He kicked the door closed. Turned the dead bolt. "It's not me he wants. The asshole was just dicking around with me."

"We need to take you to a doctor, get you checked out—"

"*He's fucking coming after you.*"

She blinked. "Then let him." Better her than Luke.

He grabbed her, locking his fingers over her arms and pulling her against him. "Hell, no." Then his mouth crashed onto hers. Need, lust, hunger, and fury.

She tasted it all in his kiss, knew he tasted the same on her lips. Oh, God, she wanted him.

Monica tore her mouth from his. "No, you're hurt. We need a doctor—"

"Forget it…I'm fine." His eyes blazed. "No one, nothing, is making me leave you." Then he took her mouth again. Harder.

Her nails scraped down his arms. He growled and drove his tongue past her lips.

Not pity. Not revulsion.

No room for that here. He wanted her. Man to woman.

So she'd damn well take him. Take and take and take until the burning need was gone, and the pleasure was hers.

She grabbed at his shirt, sending buttons flying. They hit the floor, and she didn't care. Didn't care about anything right then but having him. His kiss—*he still wants me.*

A lover who knew her deepest secrets. A man who knew and didn't turn away.

Or treat her like she was some kind of broken doll.

Rough, wild—that's the way his hands were. The way she needed them to be.

The way she needed *him* to be.

"Strip." Guttural. "*Now.*" His demand. Might as well have been hers.

Monica shuddered, needing, her sex clenching and moistening as the lust quaked through her and fired her blood.

"Ah, fuck it...can't wait." His hands yanked up her shirt. Tossed it on the floor. He shoved aside her bra and took her breast into his mouth, sucking deeply, swirling his tongue over her flesh and making her moan for him.

He lifted her, still with his mouth sealed tight to her flesh, and carried her to the bed with a steel grip.

Luke took her down on the mattress, raising his head so that he could lick his way to her other nipple. Strong swipes. So much hunger...

She kicked off her shoes. Raised her hips and tried to shimmy out of her pants, but—no good.

The arch of her hips just put her against the thick bulge of his cock, and his mouth became rougher. The stubble on his jaw scraped her flesh.

And she liked it.

Liked the way he took her.

Wanted more.

Her nails scratched down his chest. No good girl here. No girl who'd lay still and spread her legs and wait for the pleasure.

She wasn't weak.

She wasn't damaged, dammit.

She was a woman, and she wanted.

Monica's hands found his waist. Unsnapped the button, pulled down his zipper. She took his cock into her hands, hot and strong. Already wet along the tip.

Only fair—she was more than wet for him.

They rolled, and she took the position on top. Perfect. She worked his cock, squeezing from base to tip, pumping him, feeling the tightening of his flesh beneath her palms.

He stroked her through her pants. "I'm tasting you tonight." Her nipples stabbed into the air. He licked her areola, swiping with his tongue, and her breath caught. "All of you."

She pushed up on to her knees.

The lights were on. She hadn't really realized until then; he must have hit the lights when she came in and she hadn't seen—

"*All of you*," he said again, the words gravel rough.

He can see me. No hiding. Uncertainty had her slowing, her body tensing.

"Fuck, no." He rose up and kissed her. "Stay with me."

She was right there with him. Not going anywhere.

"*Stay with me.*" His lips took hers again. Tongue driving deep.

He had her pants off, not sure how. Her panties gone. Tossed onto the lamp.

She was on her back again. He was between her legs. She'd spread her thighs wide, open for him.

His gaze raked her, so hot she burned. His fingers touched her sex first. Trailing over the straining flesh. Pressing against her clit. Then one finger, two, worked inside.

And his mouth took her. His lips feathered over her. Caressed, kissed, sent just the right pressure to her core. *More.*

His tongue swiped over her clit.

She moaned, her heels digging into the mattress.

Again. Again. His tongue worked her, stroking that aching flesh, licking, tasting, taking. His fingers plunged, his tongue took.

Yes.

Her fingers fisted in his hair, and her hips arched toward him. The pleasure built, flushing her body, tightening her muscles, so close she could feel the quiver of her climax coming.

So close.

His fingers pulled out.

"No!" Dammit, no, not when she—

His tongue thrust inside.

She came against his mouth.

The first time.

Because the tremors hadn't even ended before he was rising up to cover her body. Her breath choked out, and she realized she'd screamed his name.

"This way." His demand.

He pushed her into the middle of the bed. Rolled her onto her stomach.

Monica froze, understanding burning like acid in her veins.

No, no, he can see—

She pushed up immediately, rising onto her knees, shoving her hands flat against the mattress.

"Perfect." His growl.

His cock brushed between her legs.

Slick, open, and greedy, her sex took him right away, and they both groaned at the pleasure from that first deep thrust.

She was swollen, tender from her climax, and the slide of his thick length had her muscles clenching desperately around him.

His mouth feathered over her back.

No...

"You're the...most—ah, damn that's *good*—beautiful thing...I've ever...seen...." No hint of the smooth southern charm. Just raw need. His flesh pounded into her. And she loved it. Monica rolled her hips, taking more, taking him in as deep as she could as his arms curled around her body and his fingers stroked her clit.

He kissed her shoulder.

She should stop him, tell him not to—

His mouth pressed over the ragged flesh....

No!

"The...strongest...the sexiest..." Thrust. Slow glide out...driving thrust. One that shook the bed, and her. "I'd fucking...kill for you."

Monica threw back her head. Her climax slammed through her. Pleasure so intense it hurt.

He came in her, a long hot splash, as her sex contracted around him.

Her fingers dug into the mattress. She closed her eyes and tried to suck in as much air as she could.

He held her tight. His legs trembled against her. *Not the only one who's weak.*

She licked her lips and tried to swallow.

Luke's still firm length slid out of her.

Flesh to flesh.

"I'm..." A long expulsion of air. "I'm safe, Monica, you don't have to worry about—"

No condom. Her eyes flew right back open as reality reared its head.

But she wouldn't lie to herself. At that first hot touch of his cock, she'd wanted him. Bare. In her, just as he was. "I'm safe too. There's no...risk." She'd been on the pill for years. A backup. Just in case.

"Monica, we have to talk." Gruff.

But she didn't want to. She wanted to fuck, and she wanted to forget. The last thing she wanted was to talk.

She rolled away from him. "I-I have to clean up." She walked to the bathroom on legs that weren't quite steady. The door closed behind her with a click, and she stared into the mirror at the glassy-eyed woman with the flushed cheeks.

A woman who looked alive now, when she'd once looked like a ghost.

Monica turned her shoulder and saw the raised skin that marked her. Anger coiled in her belly. "Screw you, asshole," she whispered. He wasn't going to hurt her, not anymore.

Luke had taken her in the darkness, and in the light. He'd treated her like *his* woman, not some freak.

She stared into the mirror and let her shoulders drop.

Not a victim.

Just a woman.

And Luke was just a man. One who'd stood by her for so long, without knowing the darkness she carried.

That bastard attacked him. She'd left Luke alone in that alley, run because she was afraid of him knowing the truth about her past, and she'd left him for the killer.

Her fingers curved around the sharp edges of the sink. *What would I have done if he'd killed Luke?*

Her heart seemed to stop. Fear. For so long, it had been her companion. Awake. Asleep. So afraid... *what if others find out? What will they think of me? How will they look at me?*

She looked at herself in the mirror. Saw the same image she'd always seen. And the fear was still there, inside, lodged above her heart. But it was different now. Because now, she wondered... *What will I do if something happens to him?*

Luke.

He'd broken through the ice.

He'd screwed up. Luke lay on the bed, his forearm thrown over his eyes, and realized that he was one serious jackass.

The woman had needed tenderness. Care.

She'd gotten hard, fast, and desperate.

He'd taken her with the raw lust that always rode him when she was near. *Always.*

But just once, dammit, just once, he wished he'd been able to show her more than lust and fury.

He raised his arm and glared down at the cock that was still aroused for her. "Idiot." The throb in his head was back. When he'd been with Monica, he hadn't even noticed the dull ache. But then, he hadn't noticed anything but her.

Oh, Christ, what she must have gone through all those years ago. When she'd gone into the shower, he'd used her computer to log onto the FBI's site and access the Romeo files. He'd hit the files after he first found that clipping, but now, knowing Monica was the victim, he had to read everything again. Had to know every single detail.

Five minutes later, sweat beaded his forehead. He'd seen the pictures of the other vics. Seen that pit Romeo had kept her in.

Fuck. His hands were shaking.

The shower shut off. He sucked in a breath so hard his chest hurt. After he'd finished checking the files, he'd turned the lights off, for her, because he knew she'd want it that way. So now he lay still and quiet, waiting for Monica to come to him.

When the door opened, steam drifted lazily into the room. The light spilled onto the floor. She'd leave that on, just a hint of—

Monica turned off the light.

He could only see the faint outline of her body when she came to him. The carpet swallowed the sound of her slow footsteps.

Then she was at the edge of the bed. After the briefest hesitation, she slid in next to him. Warm flesh, smelling sweet and clean. Wet hair. Mouth—

Kissing his neck.

His greedy cock jerked.

Down boy.

"Thank you, Luke. You gave me just what I needed," she whispered.

He turned toward her. He caught her hand and held it tight over his heart. She had to feel the hard thunder. "And what did you need?" Sex? Anyone could have given her that, and he wasn't going to be *anyone* to her.

Not when she was everything.

"You treated me like I was a woman. Someone you wanted—" Like hell on fire.

"—not some victim, not some freak—"

His jaw clenched. "Who the fuck said that?"

"I did."

The echo of pain was in her voice, and he didn't know what to do. How was he supposed to make things better for her?

"I'm sorry I left you in that alley." So quiet.

"You don't have to apologize to me, baby." She was tearing his heart out.

"You scared me." Stark. "You knew too much about me."

And he'd felt like he knew nothing.

"I didn't want you to know what I was—"

"A victim?" She had to *know* that nothing was her fault. Whatever that freak had done to her, she was just a *victim.* Someone to be cared for, protected.

A part of him had always wanted to protect her. He still wanted to protect her, wanted to make sure no one hurt her.

"If only it were that simple." So much sadness. "You and I, we've always been so different." Her soft fingers pressed lightly against his chest. "At the Academy, you'd go for the victims first. You wanted to hear their sides, to help them get justice."

And she'd gone for the killers. Hunting into their pasts, tearing apart their crime scenes.

"I know you look at crimes and you see victims, but—but with me," the soft click of her swallow seemed too loud, "after a while, I wasn't Romeo's victim. After so much blood and so much death, I was just—just like him."

"*No.*" Did she really believe that bullshit?

Her breath whispered out on a sigh. "I shouldn't have left you," she said again. "My fear almost got you killed."

"No, some crazy asshole attacked me. You didn't do anything." He'd be damned if he let her blame herself.

"I'm not going to be afraid of my past anymore. I want to tell you everything. I *want* you to know the truth about me. After everything we've been through, I owe you the truth."

He'd wanted to know her secrets for so long, but he'd never wanted to cause her pain. Luke knew that right then she hurt, and he just wanted to make her pain stop. If he could, he'd take away all her pain. But there, in the darkness, with Monica in his arms, he just felt…helpless. And it fucking pissed him off. *She shouldn't have suffered.* If he had Romeo in front of him then—he'd rip the bastard apart.

A small tremble shook her body, and she said, "When my mom found out that the Romeo killer had taken me, she killed herself." Flat, brittle.

His fingers tightened around hers. "I-I know." He remembered that part. The nurse. The single mom who'd blamed herself when her daughter never came home. After a month, when the cops had given up, when the news had continued running the stories about Romeo's kills, Jennifer Hill had taken a bottle of pills and never woke up.

"I never knew my dad. He—he took off right before my mom had me. Said he couldn't handle things. Well, that's what she told me. And mom never lied to me."

She was talking to him about her past, and he wouldn't have moved right then even if Hyde had burst into the room. *Nothing* would have moved him.

"I got away, and I had no one to go home to."

Shit, he hadn't thought—

"I spent all those days fighting to stay alive, but there was no one waiting for me." A brittle laugh. "There wasn't even anyone looking for me. Do you know, when Hyde found me—"

Hyde? *Oh, Christ, that's right.* His name had been in the Romeo file.

"He thought I was one of the other girls, Katherine Daniels. *Katherine.*" His eyes had adjusted again to the dark, and he saw the sad shake of her head against the pillow. "But Katherine never lived past her second day."

What happened? He bit the words back because he wasn't going to push her. Not now. He'd pushed enough.

"He was breaking by then. He'd always been breaking. The rage was too much. He couldn't hurt them fast enough, when they screamed—it just made him angrier."

So quiet. No emotion there.

"Romeo wanted his girls to love him. He wanted them to *need* him."

Them, not *me.* "What did he want from you?"

Silence.

Shouldn't have pushed. *Why did I—*

"The first thing he did, the thing he always did..."
Her hand tugged free of his and rubbed behind her right
shoulder. "He marked us. He shoved the iron against my
skin—"

My now, not them. Because she wasn't talking as
Agent Davenport anymore. She was talking as the girl
she'd been.

Mary Jane. He'd learned that name in his search.

"He said, 'You're mine.' That's all he said, and I could
smell my flesh burning. But I didn't scream, and I didn't
cry. Not then." A swallow that he could hear in the darkness. "And I saw that he liked that. In his eyes, he-he was
excited."

Because he'd found someone strong enough to play
his games.

"If you broke too soon, he killed you. I learned that,
fast. He liked to hurt his girls. He said he was testing us.
That we had to be worthy of him. Able to stand the pain."

Luke kept his fingers light as they skimmed down her
bare arm. Light, when he wanted to grab her and hold
tight. But if he held too tight...

"I'd always been pretty good at reading people," she
told him. "Just one of those things. I'd pick up on body
language, voice—don't know how or why really—I just
always did. And I-I started reading him."

More than that. She'd gotten into his head.

"The first night I was there, he cut away my clothes.
Branded me." She took a ragged breath. "Then he beat
me. Not with his fists—he didn't like to touch us, not
directly anyway. He had a pipe he liked to use." Silence.
"He broke my right arm with his first hit. After that..." A
shudder. "Doesn't really matter."

Oh, shit, he shouldn't ask, he shouldn't, but he *had* to know. "Did he rape you?" Romeo had raped the other girls. But Mary Jane—that part hadn't been in the file he'd accessed.

Her breath caught. "He strapped me to his table. An operating table. Pulled my legs apart—"

Christ, no, he didn't want to hear this. Why had he asked? *Why?*

"He tied rope around my wrists and ankles so tight I bled."

His fingers dug into her arms. *Kill him.*

"But then he found out I was a virgin." She exhaled and he felt the soft shudder of air against his throat. "And he liked that. Said it made me more his." A humorless laugh.

"*You're not his.*" Never were. Never would be. That bastard should have gotten the death penalty for this twisted shit, and Louisiana usually wasn't a state to hesitate. But Romeo had a way of working women, even women on juries.

"He didn't break my hymen." Said clinically, coldly, as if she were distancing herself again. "When he realized—he pulled back and he *smiled* at me. He told me I was his good girl. His sweetheart."

Luke always knew what to say to the victims. Knew how to comfort them, how to help them step away from the darkness, but he didn't know what to say to her. And he sure didn't know how to channel the rage boiling his blood. *Helpless.* Not her, him.

"After that night, he didn't try to rape me again. He kept me locked in a freaking two-by-three-foot room, like I was some kind of dog. No windows, no light. He took me out to screw with my head, to show me what he'd done to the others so he could watch my reaction. Then he'd put me back." The words came fast, tumbling out. "Every time he put me in there, I felt like he was *burying* me."

Luke swallowed the lump that rose in his throat.

"I survived. I played his game, and he kept me alive."

"And the others?" Had he made her watch as they died? Watched as he carved up their bodies?

"When he brought them down, I-I heard them. He kept them chained in his playroom." Her head moved in a slow shake. "I told them not to scream when he hurt them. I pounded on the door and I *told them*."

Christ.

"I told them not to show fear because that was what he wanted." She trembled a bit in his arms. "*I told them* but they couldn't stop screaming. He'd slice them, and I could hear their screams for hours, and I couldn't get out to help them. *I couldn't get out*, not unless Romeo came for me."

He kissed her. Kissed her with the tenderness he should have shown her before. Her breath slipped into his mouth, and he stole it, giving her back his own with a sigh. His lips lingered on hers. Tasted the salt of tears.

Slowly, his head lifted. Silence then, thick and heavy in the air. He didn't think she'd say anymore, didn't think—

"After a while, he started letting me out of the closet. When no one else was there, he'd let me out and allow me to stay in his playroom. That's what he called it."

Her voice came stronger now, with anger boiling beneath the words. "There was a metal door at the top of the stairs. I tried to break that door down so many times.

I couldn't. He'd leave me down there for days, and I couldn't get out. I was trapped there, and I knew I'd die there, just like the others."

No. "You *got out*."

"He left a knife behind." Her hair was drying. The light lavender scent deepening. "I think it was a test. He'd been getting angrier and angrier with me. Telling me he knew what was inside of me. '*Time for it to come out.*' I found that knife, I kept it, and I knew that the next time he turned his back on me, I'd kill him." A brittle laugh. "Maybe that was the test. I think it was what he really wanted. To show that I was just like him."

"You're *nothing* like him."

"I tried to kill him. I *would* have killed him, if Hyde hadn't stopped me."

Yeah, and maybe Hyde should have been a little slower on that pullback. Because if anyone deserved a chance for payback, it was Monica. "The bastard deserved to die."

"He wanted me to be a killer. *Just like him.* He was pushing me, always pushing me, because he wanted me to cross that edge and be like him." Her hand pressed against his chest. "And I became one."

"No! You were a kid! Tortured by a sick freak—"

"I stopped being a kid the minute the door of his Corvette closed behind me. And when I left those woods, I was a killer. Even Hyde knew it."

Aw, fuck. Her skin seemed so cold now. He pressed a kiss to her shoulder and dragged her closer, trying to warm her with his own flesh.

"Everyone but Hyde wanted to throw me in a psych ward and toss away the key."

Luke squeezed his eyes shut.

"He wouldn't let them."

So he owed Hyde. Big time.

"Because he looked at me, and he knew what I was. And he knew he could use me." Her voice held a brittle edge.

Luke hesitated. "You sure about that?" Maybe there'd been more to the story. Hyde seemed to really care about her, as much as he could care about anyone.

"He only asked me one question in the ambulance. Everyone else was shouting constantly at me, but he just wanted to know one thing."

Luke waited. She'd tell him, just like she'd told him everything else.

"'How did you get him to keep you alive?'" she murmured.

It would have been the million-dollar question. "And what did you say?"

"'I got in his head. I became what he wanted, and I lived'."

The profiler who knew the killers. The whispers that had always followed her were so dead on.

"The state put me into a group home, but Hyde—he wouldn't let me go. He made sure I saw a shrink he'd picked out for me. Hyde had me in therapy for a couple of years. He visited me almost every day, and then he gave me a reason to keep living."

Because she'd needed one.

"Hyde gave me a new name. He told me if I could pass the classes, pass all the tests, I could hunt monsters. I *needed* that. I needed to take control. To stop the killers and not let them screw with my head. This time, I'd be screwing with their minds."

Get into a monster's mind like no other.

"I thought the psych tests would be harder," she said. "But by then, I knew all the answers. Knew exactly what to say. I wasn't different anymore. I'd trained myself to fit in and to be whatever I needed to be."

And she'd become cold. Untrusting. She'd locked herself away from the world because she was afraid someone would look past her perfect surface and see the monster inside.

But she didn't understand—there wasn't a monster inside.

He kissed her again. Deep this time. Harder, letting her feel his hunger and need because, yeah, he still craved her.

He wanted her just as badly as before, needed her just as much. Because Monica had a core of steel that had been forged from hellfire.

Monster? Not damn likely.

"Who knows?" he asked against her mouth.

"Hyde. You. A handful of higher-ups at the Bureau."

But no one close to her. No friends. No lovers. A heavy burden for her to carry. "This why you cut tail and left me before?"

"It's why I was going to leave you again."

Damn.

"I'm not an easy person to be with, Luke. I—"

"Keep your gun under your pillow because you're afraid of an attack. Keep the bathroom light on because you don't want the darkness. Keep control with men because you don't want to be weak with anyone ever again." All the signs of a victim had been there. He'd seen them, but had never guessed just how terrible the crimes against her had been.

A little hum from her, then, "Yeah, that about covers it."

A question nagged at his mind. "What was the first thing you did when you got clear of Hyde and those shrinks?"

"I got laid."

He couldn't have been more surprised if she'd slammed her fist into his jaw.

"Romeo wanted his good girl to kill, but he didn't want her to fuck. So I fucked. I found a man who wanted me, and I had sex because I wasn't *his*." Her fingers were still on Luke's chest, curling over his heart. And he didn't want to hear about her lovers, didn't want to hear her say—

"I did that for a while, until I realized I was still cold inside. The sex didn't matter. The men didn't."

Had he been one of those men? A shadow in the night?

"Then I met you."

She had to feel the sudden hard racing of his heart.

"And you tempted me to want more. I went with you when I'd *always* kept my work and sex separate. I went with you because I wanted *you*, and I wasn't going to let anything stop me from having you."

The same way he felt.

"Even though you scared the hell out of me."

Been there.

"Still do." Her voice was husky.

Done that.

Luke cleared his throat. "Some things you should know."

He felt her stiffen. His back teeth clenched. Did the woman really think he was about to turn away? Did he look like a fool?

"You don't have to—" Oh, yeah, that was her already withdrawing.

"I *hate* what he did to you—and I'd love to tear the bastard apart." *Let's see you scream, asshole.* "But knowing about your past doesn't change the way I feel about you, baby."

"And...how do you feel?" Did he imagine it or did her breath seem to catch?

Confession time. If she could bare her soul and reveal her past, then, it was way past time for him to show some trust, too. "You're it for me, Monica. I've known it from the first time I kissed you." His fucking world.

"*Luke...*"

He had to get this out. "I know you don't love me," he said gruffly. Bluntly. Better for him to say it than her. Hell, after what she'd been through, she might never be able to trust or love anyone completely—and that pissed him off. She should have had more. They should have. *Damn Romeo to hell.* "But give me a chance. That's all I'm asking. When this case is over, even if I have to leave SSD for us to be together, just give me a chance." He brushed back her hair. Smoothed his hand down her cheek. His cock was up, she was near—what was new? But he choked back the lust. This was the time for something else. "Give me a chance to show you what we can have."

She pushed up, and he knew she was trying to see his eyes in the darkness. "And what can we have? Luke, you don't know what I'm—"

"I know you. I want you. Always have, always will." Felt good to say it. Maybe he should have said it years ago. Wonder what difference it would have made?

"Knowing about your past doesn't change a damn thing about the way I feel."

A part of him wanted to hold her close, keep her safe, but Monica wasn't the type to stand back and let others protect her. Not her.

They'd both kept secrets, but no more.

This time, he'd get things right with her.

"What if I hurt you?" she whispered.

She already had. He'd survived. "You said I tempted you then...do I tempt you now?" She tempted him. Eve couldn't have tempted him more.

"Yes...."

"Don't worry about the pain." He kissed the soft column of her neck. "Let me tempt you, and we'll worry about the darkness later." Because with her, he knew there would always be darkness. It was in her soul, and she was in his.

And he'd fight like hell to keep her by his side, even if he had to fight the nightmares from her past.

And the killer waiting at the door.

CHAPTER *Fifteen*

A pounding at the door woke Monica hours later. She shoved her hand under the pillow automatically as her heart raced in her chest.

"Not there, baby," Luke's gruff voice, coming from the dark beside her. Because there was no bathroom light on—

Her memory came flooding back.

No shame. No horror.

Just relief. *He knows... and he still wants me.*

A fist thudded against the door. "Monica! Open up! Or tell Dante to drag his sorry ass out of your bed and open the door!" Kenton's thundering voice.

But he should have been at the hospital. They couldn't leave Sam alone!

She flew out of the bed. Raced to the door. Her eye pressed against the peephole. *Had to be sure, someone could be forcing him—*

No, just Kenton, looking pissed as he stood there with narrowed eyes and faint lines bracketing his mouth.

She yanked open the door.

His gaze raked her, and his eyes widened. "Wow, didn't expect to see you—"

"What? In a shirt?" Her hand caught the front of his shirt, and she pulled him inside. "Why aren't you at the hospital? What's—"

"I'd advise you to keep those eyes up, *partner*," Luke ordered as he walked toward them.

So she didn't have on shorts or pants. The shirt was long. She had on panties and now really wasn't the time for modesty.

But then, she hadn't cared about modesty in years. Not really. She'd stopped caring after Romeo.

"Hyde's working this shift. He sent me after you." Kenton kept his eyes on Monica's face. "He saw the surveillance footage from the airport. Got one of the techs at SSD to monitor every second of that video. *He saw Sam.*"

Monica rocked forward. "Did he see the killer? Did he—"

"Oh, yeah." His lips pursed. "And get this shit. The bastard was wearing a deputy's uniform. Hyde thinks he knew where the cameras were located, and he had his hat on, pulled low so we couldn't see his face."

A deputy's uniform. She shoved back her hair. "He could have stolen that uniform. He took a doctor's scrubs when he went after Laura." They *thought* he had. Maybe... "This guy is *good* at blending in." The cell phone had been at the sheriff's station, right there in the midst of all those deputies.

And who was working every crime scene? *Deputies.*

Davis worked hard at keeping his men and Melinda

apprised of every development in the case. There wasn't a move they'd taken that the deputies didn't know about.

"Something else you should know." Kenton's eyes bored into her. "Kyle West is a dead man."

Monica shook her head. "No, we talked to his aunt, she—"

"Jon called from the SSD. According to the records he's found, Kyle West was killed in a one-car accident six months ago."

"His aunt didn't know, and the sheriff didn't say anything about his death when we asked about Kyle." *Didn't make sense.*

A shrug. "What can I tell you? The man is *dead.*"

Then that put her back with her growing suspicion that the killer was very close indeed.

"Hyde said you'd know what to do. Seems to me we either got us a bastard dressing up like a cop—"

Not a cop. A deputy. "Or…" Monica said quietly, "one of Jasper's finest is killing and making us all look like fools."

A killer who'd been right there with them, for every step of the hunt. Watching…

Watchman.

Monica shoved open the glass door at the sheriff's station. Four a.m. Who'd be there?

"Agent Davenport?" The sheriff came out of his office, rubbing his eyes, looking dead on his feet, with a red mark on his cheek and a long, thin wrinkle on his forehead. "What are you doin' here?"

She glanced over at the fax machine. A pile of papers lay scattered on the floor near them.

Luke crossed the room and started gathering up the papers.

"Oh, shit, he hasn't taken another one, has he? Not another—"

Luke whistled. "Damn. It says here that May Walker was institutionalized twice in the past ten years." His eyes met hers. "She was schizophrenic."

That would explain her medications. And the woman's affect had been off, her responses too slow, and her anger had stirred too suddenly.

He rose, reading the pages. "May was told about Kyle's death a week after it happened." He shook his head. "She told the officer to keep the body and, 'bury it wherever the hell you want. Just don't make me see it.'"

And she'd forgotten to tell them? Or just hadn't remembered the guy's death? With a diagnosis of schizophrenia, there was no telling. If May had been having hallucinations, well, maybe she actually believed that Kyle *was* still alive.

"Kyle West?" Davis muttered. "Wait—ain't he our suspect?"

Luke held up a grainy photo for Monica. The same grainy license photo they'd accessed through the Department of Motor Vehicles before and given to the deputies. The image showed a guy with glasses. Too-long hair. An angular nose and weak chin.

"Not anymore," she muttered. But if it wasn't Kyle… "Why didn't Sheriff Martin tell us this?" Yes, okay, she could see May not being fully aware if she'd been off her meds, but Sheriff Martin should have known about Kyle's death. Informing local authorities was standard procedure. He *had* to have known.

And Martin had to know that they'd find out the truth. The guy knew the system. A search would turn up Kyle's death certificate.

But he'd held back that information about Kyle. And that part, well, it was damn interesting.

She'd remembered that dark night with Jake Martin... had he been just pretending? Had he really remembered her, too?

He'd gone to Angola, the prison that housed Romeo. A prison he visited every month. And the killer kept throwing Romeo up in the case. "It's all about Romeo," she muttered. Damn him, why couldn't he stay buried?

"Romeo?" Davis straightened. "Dammit, I'm tired of hearing about him. My fuck-up, coming back to haunt me."

Monica stiffened. Her gaze lifted, slowly, and locked on the sheriff. "Run that by me again." *His* fuck-up?

"You don't know?" Luke's rough whisper.

But she didn't look his way. Monica was too focused on the Sheriff. His lips pressed together, and for a minute, she wasn't sure he'd answer her. Then Davis said, "The Romeo Killer grew up here in Jasper. I met him when he was just a kid, when he was mutilating pets, and I—"

The Romeo Killer grew up here in Jasper. That was all she heard. Her face flashed ice cold, then pin prickles of heat shot beneath the skin.

"You didn't know." Luke spoke slowly.

Monica managed to shake her head. She hadn't wanted to know. Not a damn thing. She'd made a point of staying away from all the Romeo case files. She hadn't wanted to learn what made that asshole into the freak he'd become. After she'd gotten away from him, she'd never wanted to see him or hear about him again.

At the Academy, she'd even dodged a few profiling classes because she hadn't wanted to sit there and hear Romeo's crimes re-told to everyone.

Buried my head in the sand. Pretended he didn't matter.

"Are you..." A hand brushed her shoulder. Sheriff Davis. "Are you all right, agent?" Real concern rumbled beneath the words.

No, no she wasn't all right. She'd been so focused on protecting herself and hiding her past that she'd been blind. *So blind.* "That's the link." She spun away from him and his comforting hand. Her gaze shot to the victim board. Sally. Patty. Laura. Jeremy. She hurried forward, read their profiles again. All born in Jasper. Just like Romeo.

"Monica?" Luke paced to her side.

She shook her head and pitched her voice low. "The messages weren't about me." *Blind.* A rough laugh escaped her lips. "The killer's been telling us, but I didn't listen." Her head turned and she found Luke watching her, eyes so intent. "The newspaper clippings, the bloody flower—*it's all pointing to Romeo.*" Not her.

Hell, maybe she was some kind of sick side benefit. But all the other kills... "Like a damn tribute to him."

He used fear to break them. Romeo hadn't just killed his prey, he'd broken them first.

Just like the Watchman.

"What's happenin'?" Davis asked, standing hesitantly behind them, the lines on his face thick. "Who's gettin' a tribute?"

"Romeo." The name left a bad taste in her mouth and she swallowed quickly. "Sheriff, I want you to get the warden from Angola Prison on the line."

His brows rose. "*Now?*"

"Now." Her temples began to throb. Someone would be there, someone was always in the Angola office. "We need a log of every visitor that Romeo has had in the last two years." That would be a start. They might have to go back even further.

But if she was right and the Watchman was in Jasper, killing here because of some sick homage to Romeo, then she'd bet the bastard had paid Romeo a visit.

He'd gone to hell, and he'd learned from the devil.

The victims were different, the kill methods so different, but that damn rose had been left for a reason. That clipping had been about Romeo.

And he knows me. The killer knew her secret, a secret Romeo could have shared with him.

Too many damn links to overlook—especially since they were playing this deadly game in Romeo's old backyard.

A light rapping shook her door. Monica glanced up, expecting to see Luke. But the door opened and Davis was there.

"Uh, we need to talk…." He glanced back over his shoulder.

Okay. Monica eased back in her chair, her eyes narrowing when Davis shut the door and took a hesitant step forward. Not really the sheriff's usual style. "Did you contact Angola?"

"Yeah, yeah." His head bobbed up and down. "Me and the warden there, we go way back. Huntin' buddies."

Why wasn't that surprising?

"I called him at home. He's goin' in, and he said he'd personally fax the logs to us."

"Excellent." Once they got a look at the names on that list, they might just get a handle on the bastard.

Would Jake Martin's name be on that list? She was already planning another call to his office. She had questions that the sheriff *would* answer for her.

"There's something you should know." Davis's shoulders straightened, and he met her stare directly. "My name's gonna be on that log."

What? But she didn't say that. Instead she asked, "Why?"

"You know what he did, don't you?" Not an answer. "To those girls, *you* know."

"I do." She knew better than anyone else.

"I had him in my town. I looked at him, and I swear..." He licked his lips. "I saw the evil in him. Just a kid, but I saw it."

She pressed her hands flat against the desk top. "You had no idea what he'd grow up and become."

A fast glance over his shoulder at the still closed door. "I've read all those fancy studies, too, you know. Animal mutilations in childhood—that's how it always starts, right?"

Not always.

"The boy sliced his cat open. I knew he did it, but when the sheriff told me the case was over, I just let it go." His jaw tightened. "The boy needed help then. Help I didn't get him. If someone had just stepped in, if *I* had just stepped in, those girls might be alive today. They might have *families*."

Her breath came a little too fast. "And what about Romeo? You think he would've had a family, too?" *Can't see him that way. Only see him covered in blood.*

"Too late to know now. When I saw the pictures of those girls and I found out what he'd done, it made me *sick*. And trust me, ma'am, I've seen a lot of bad things in my life, but Romeo was in a class by himself."

Yes. "Why did you go see him?" she asked again.

Another slow step toward her. "Because I had to know why. Why he did it. Why he took those girls. Was he crazy? Did he just not know what he was doing? Was he so far gone he didn't understand it was wrong?"

Or had he done it just because he liked the sound of screams? She forced her hands to lift when her nails bit too deeply into the desk. "And what did he say?"

He inhaled on a hard rasp. "'Because the bitches begged for it.'"

No, they begged him to stop, begged to go back home, but he just laughed. "He *is* sick, Sheriff. He's a psychopath. He cares nothing for anyone else. He *can't* care. He's never felt guilt over his actions, and he won't." The words were clipped, cold, but the fury in her heart burned red hot. "He's incapable of feeling guilt, just as he's incapable of feeling empathy. When his victims screamed and pleaded with him, it did nothing. He just didn't care." She suspected that seeing the pain had been as close as he'd ever gotten to feeling anything.

Davis turned back toward the door. "Just wanted you to know. I needed to explain before you saw the file."

"Sheriff!"

He froze with his hand on the door.

"*You* didn't hurt those girls." *Me.* "He did."

He didn't look back at her. "You ever wish you could change the past?"

"No point in it." Why waste the time? "But I make sure I don't repeat my mistakes. I make sure the future's different."

Davis looked over his shoulder.

"That's all we can do," she told him, and knew it was the truth.

The end game was coming. He paced around the cabin, the scent of pine filling his nose. It had been such a fun match, but the end was coming.

The end always had to come.

Romeo had told him that. *In the end, the prey dies. Never leave a survivor, never.*

Romeo's mistake. He'd been weak. Left little Mary Jane because he'd thought she was special. Thought she was like him.

But Mary Jane couldn't even come close to touching Romeo's greatness. A pretender, that's what she was. And he'd prove it. He'd finish what Romeo started.

He'd break the bitch.

His steps were silent as he left the cabin. He had the perfect place in mind for his next attack. So perfect.

Mary Jane would appreciate it, he was sure. He'd talked with Romeo, spent hours getting the information so he could make everything just right.

A fitting ending. A *final* end.

Break her, then kill her. That had been the plan from the beginning. The moment Romeo had learned of the SSD and seen a picture of Mary Jane in the paper, he'd given the kill order.

Lure her to you. She was Hyde's right hand at the SSD—it had been a safe bet that she'd come to profile the serial in Jasper. And if she hadn't come, he would have just kept killing until she *did* show.

But she'd been the one to come first. Getting her into the game and out of her safe, D.C. office had been so easy.

Prove that you're smarter than she is.

He had. He'd killed, he'd taken her agent, and, soon, he'd be taking Monica.

In the end, she wouldn't be able to save herself.

Time to make her worst fears come true.

CHAPTER *Sixteen*

R omeo gets regular visits from his lawyer, a guy named Bryan Tate who lives in Gatlin," Luke said, the faxed log in his hands.

Monica's eyes narrowed at that. *Gatlin? We keep going back there.* "Run a check on him. Get Kenton to rip the guy's life apart." She wasn't taking any chances.

"Romeo had a few sporadic visitors, too. A woman named Kristy Lee. She...ah..."

Monica glanced back at him.

"The warden said she was one of those women who get off on being with serials."

The taste in her mouth just got worse. "Who else?"

His gaze darted to Davis. "Guess he already told you."

"How many visits?"

"Just one."

Can't take chances. "Anyone else that sticks out?"

"Yeah. Jake Martin. He's been to visit Romeo three times in the last year."

Dammit. Martin's voice drifted through her mind, that slight hesitation the first time they'd met. "*I...know you.*"

Sure looked like he did.

"*I don't usually forget faces....*" The Watchman knew all about her past. What a coincidence; it was a past she shared with Jake Martin. "I'll call Martin." She'd rather talk to him in person, and she'd be doing that real soon. But she wasn't going to let another minute pass without questioning him.

But she also wasn't going, to blindly focus on just one suspect, even though right then, Martin was looking suspicious as hell. *Why'd he lie about West?* The only answer that sprang to mind was a damning one. *To throw suspicion onto someone else.* Martin would know that she'd followed up on West, but maybe he'd just been hoping to buy a few days' time. Killing time.

"Those were all the visitors he had in the last two years." His lips tightened. "While you run down Martin, I'll get started checking everyone at the station."

Because they wouldn't overlook the obvious signs. A deputy's uniform. Someone who knew the area. Someone who knew the case.

"Do it," she told him, and knew they'd make some enemies real soon. Too bad. They had a killer to catch. "And you need to start with Lee. He's got a history in Gatlin." The sheriff's words were locked in her mind. *He worked over in Gatlin County for a few years. Word was that he'd had him a bad break-up so he got out of Jasper.*

Then he'd come back home, and people had started dying.

Luke walked away from her and cleared his throat as he approached the sheriff. "Davis, I'm gonna need to ask you a few questions about your staff here at the station."

And Davis wasn't slow on the draw; he knew this had been coming. "What do you need?" His shoulders stooped a bit.

Monica went back into her makeshift office and closed the door. A few moments later, she had the phone pressed against her ear and a slow ring drifted across the line as she waited to connect with the Gatlin County Sheriff's office. One more ring. Another. *Come on*—

"Sheriff's office." The woman's voice was slow, a bit sluggish. Seven a.m. must be too early in Gatlin.

"This is FBI Special Agent Monica Davenport. I need you to connect me with Jake Martin immediately." If he was at home, sleeping in his bed, they could just drag his ass out.

"Sp-special agent—"

"Agent Davenport, FBI," she said again and knew the words were clipped. "I need him on the phone, *now*. If he's not there, then give me his home number because I need to talk to him ASAP."

"H-he's out of the office today…family emergency…"

Out of the office again? Big coincidence. Hyde had taught her not to believe in coincidences.

An image of Martin's shiny star and perfectly pressed brown uniform flashed before her eyes.

The same uniform that Sheriff Davis wore. Standard issue—dark brown pants and shirt. Wide-brimmed brown hat. Yellow emblem high on the left arm.

I need to see that surveillance video. Kenton said

Hyde had gotten a copy transferred over on his laptop. It was with him at the hospital.

"What's your name?" She demanded and realized the silence on the phone had hummed too long.

"K-Kathy. Kathy Grant."

"Kathy, give me his cell." Did her voice tremble? Because she was trying real hard to hold back the rage.

The now-awake clerk rattled off the number, and Monica scribbled it down even as Kathy said, "H-he ain't gonna answer. I told you, it's a family emergency."

Sometimes the job trumped family. If he was a good sheriff, Martin knew that. "Tell me, Kathy, did your office get a report of Kyle West's death a few months back?"

"*What? Kyle's dead?*"

Okay. Guess that answered one question, but it just raised more. "You're telling me you never received official notification of his death?" Didn't make sense. *Someone* from highway patrol had gone and seen May Walker. That person would have stopped by the sheriff's office, too. Procedure would have dictated notification there.

For Jon to find the death notice in the system, someone had filed the paperwork. If not the Gatlin office, then who'd done it?

"No! I never—Kyle's dead?"

"You really don't know?" If only she could see her face. Sounded like truth, but some lies did.

"I swear, ma'am, *no*."

So maybe someone had screwed up the notification. Or maybe someone hadn't wanted the folks at the Gatlin County Sheriff's office to know that West had died.

"Thanks for the info, Kathy." She disconnected the call. In seconds, she'd punched in Martin's cell phone number, but when the call connected, it just went straight to voicemail. Damn. "Martin, this is Monica Davenport. I need to speak with you immediately. And guess what? I've remembered where we met." She rattled off her number.

She'd get a trace on his phone. If he turned the phone on, the SSD would find him. She put in a call to the main office, giving them instructions to monitor Martin's cell. If he turned his phone on, if he used it to make one call, the SSD could use the FBI's satellite technology to pinpoint his location.

It was the same technique they were using to find the Watchman. If he used another victim's phone... if he so much as turned on Patty's cell...

Monica sucked in a hard breath and hurried out of the office. She almost slammed into Luke and the Sheriff. "I need those personnel files." Monica met the Sheriff's glinting stare head on. "We're also going to need to talk to every deputy you have on staff—*immediately.*"

The sheriff shook his head even as he sagged back against the wall. "My men." Not a question, not anymore. The red heat had faded from his cheeks, leaving him looking pale.

"Every possibility has to be explored right now." But it was time for her to lay her cards on the table. "And the signs here are pointing to a law enforcement connection." She'd called Hyde right after seeing the bodies of the victims in the morgue. No DNA evidence had been left behind at all—*nothing.* "Everything's been too neat, Sheriff. Too tidy. No fingerprints. No hair. Nothing is left behind." The guy had too much crime scene knowledge.

Davis ran a hand over his face and didn't speak.

Luke stood at her side, aligning himself with her. Backing her up as she told the sheriff more news he wouldn't want to hear.

"This person has far more than a civilian's knowledge of crime scenes," she said, "and he knows your area, knows all the back roads and the empty houses. He knows how to use a gun." And how to keep it locked on prey from a perfect shooting distance.

"You tell us," Luke invited softly. "Wouldn't one of your deputies have all this knowledge?"

He flinched. "I work with them every damn day."

"And it might not even be one of them," she said. Because her other suspect was in the wind somewhere. "But we have to start ruling them out and narrowing down the field. Our killer's upping the stakes, making it personal by going after one of our own. We've got to stop him before we have another body on our hands. He knows Sam's alive. This guy—he doesn't like for his prey to live. He's going to attack again, soon." He'd have to. His strikes were coming far too frequently. He'd taken Sam less than thirty-six hours after Jeremy Jones's death. That kind of escalation…No, there was no way he'd just back off for a long cooling down period. He'd strike again, soon. Who would be his target this time? Another civilian? A deputy? An agent?

They didn't have time to waste.

He gave a weak nod.

"Only the folks in your office knew Sam was at that airport." And that fact pointed most heavily against Martin and right back at the good deputies of Jasper County.

"*You think it's one of us?*" The shocked whisper came from behind her.

Monica glanced back, turning her attention to Lee Pope. He stood a few feet back, eyes wide in his pale face. "Somebody on our team?" He shook his head. "Doing that twisted crap?"

"Deputy, I'm going to need you to keep this conversation absolutely confidential." Right. Like that was gonna happen. But she didn't really mind. She wanted word to spread that the SSD was turning the focus on the sheriff's office. It would help her stir the pot.

He spun away and slammed the door shut behind him hard enough to shake the glass in the window.

"You're gonna make a lot of enemies, Davenport," Davis warned her.

Yes, but what else was new? Making enemies, losing friends. Her way. Might as well go ahead and say it all. "I'm going to need to know your whereabouts for all the crimes, too, Sheriff."

He gave a grim nod.

Making enemies…

"So how'd that work for you?" Luke asked as they headed out of the sheriff's office. The personnel files were locked in her briefcase. She'd review them when they were secure and away from all the prying—and glaring—eyes.

"About like I anticipated." There wouldn't be a whole lot more cooperation coming from the Jasper County Sheriff's Office.

"*We aren't killers.*" Lee came around the corner of the building, a cigar dangling between his fingers.

Her nostrils flared even as she tensed. "I didn't say *you* were, deputy."

He shook his head, and ash drifted in the wind. "I know these people—we go to the same church. I dated Melinda in high school. *I know them.*"

"Sometimes you don't really know people like you think you do," Luke said softly, and Monica's gaze flew to him. "Sometimes, you never see past their surface until it's too late," he finished.

She'd never wanted to let him see past the surface. No, but she was trying so hard now because she didn't want to lose him.

Luke was worth fighting for. She'd known that years ago. She knew it now.

The difference? This time, she wouldn't be afraid to fight.

Lee raised the cigar to his lips and took a long pull. When he exhaled, cigar smoke plumed in the air, and he growled. "The things he's done, *it ain't one of us.*"

"I really hope it isn't," she said and meant it.

"I'd know it! If a killer were working with me, I'd know!"

She felt a bit sad as she told him, "No, Lee, you wouldn't." Because the guy they were looking for was perfect at blending in and hiding right in front of everyone's eyes.

That was why he was so dangerous.

Sam jerked awake, gasping for air, the water choking her as she struggled to kick up and away from—

"It's okay, Samantha." Someone took her hand and held tight.

She jumped at the touch, and her gaze shot to the left. Hyde was there, staring down at her from the shadows.

"You just had a bad dream," he told her. "You're safe."

No, she'd never be safe again.

She pulled her hand from his. *I can't be weak in front of him.* He'd kick her off the SSD, and she couldn't leave the team. It was all she'd ever had. Something that mattered.

Something that had almost gotten her killed.

A chair screeched as he pulled it closer to the bed. "There's no shame in being scared."

"And what do you know...about being scared?" Shit, had she just said that? To him? But, yeah, that croaking voice was hers.

His brows climbed up high. "More than you might think." He glanced at the machines that hummed and beeped on the other side of the bed. "If you make it through the rest of the night without any problems, you'll be able to get out of here tomorrow."

Her eyes skated around the room. "I want my gun." She had no idea where her gun was, but she needed a weapon, any weapon.

"When you get out," he said softly.

"I have to be ready, if he comes again—"

"You will be." That dark stare was so steady on her. *I won't break.*

"I telephoned your mother. Told her what happened."

Oh, no, not her mother. She would freak out. She'd—

Reach for the bottle.

No, no, she's past that. Mom's strong. She won't.

"She said for me to tell you she was calling Chris and that she loved you."

Sam took a deep breath. Chris was her mom's sponsor. Good.

"If you want to talk to her, I can get you a phone in here."

She shook her head. "No, not yet." She just couldn't handle that right then. If she heard her mother's voice, she'd cry, and she just might not stop. "She—she didn't want me to join the FBI." Mom had always thought working with the FBI was too dangerous. *What are you going to do when you get shot at? When you're on the streets and a killer comes at you? Come on, Samantha, this isn't for you.*

But it had been, until a killer *had* come for her.

"Glad you didn't listen to her." He leaned back in the chair and crossed his arms. "I would've missed out on one damn fine agent."

Her eyes widened. "You think I'm good?" She'd always felt like she didn't fit in with the others. They had an edge, a sharpness to their personalities, and they weren't afraid, not of anything.

There was a reason the killer had come after her. She knew it.

He'd realized she was the weak link. And he'd been right.

"I do." Hyde's head cocked to the right. "And I know you're going to get past this, and you *will be* even better."

Her lips pressed together so he wouldn't see the tremble. He said he knew about being scared. Maybe she'd been wrong about him. "What are you afraid of, Hyde?"

His eyes bored into hers.

"Fine, don't tell me." Her voice was raspier now. "I'm going back to sleep."

"I've seen a lot of death. Seen bodies mutilated, killers covered in blood..." He took a deep breath. "I know Hell's real because I've seen it. Not once, but many times."

"You keep working the cases." Her fingers tightened around the sheets. "Why?" Why didn't he ever give in and just give up?

"Because I will be damned if I let the killers win." Flat. "That's why I started the SSD. Why I go to work every single day. Someone has to stop those assholes."

He watched her silently for a time, then said, "Once, I thought there wasn't any reason to keep trying. Those twisted bastards out there were winning the battle. The body count just kept rising, and the killers kept slaughtering. I was ready to turn away from everything. *Everything*."

Now there was an intensity in his voice that she'd never heard before. "What happened to change your mind?"

"I saw a miracle."

She blinked, not understanding. "What do you—"

"We can stop the killers, Samantha. We can track them, we can catch them, we can put the bastards in cages so that they never hurt anyone else, and *we can save lives*."

Like Monica had saved her life. *Pulled me out of that water. A few moments more...*

"I'm in this business because I'm scared of what the world would be like if no one fought the killers. Someone has to do it." His shoulders lifted. "Might as damn well be me." A pause, then, "And you."

If only things were that easy for her.

Hyde reached into his pocket and pulled out a peppermint. She almost smiled. Her uncle Jeremiah had carried those, too. When he'd given up his precious cigars, he'd gotten hooked on them—

Her fingers dug into the sheets as her heartbeat monitor beeped, loud and fast. Too fast to match her racing heart. "I remember something," she whispered. The smell that had been so familiar to her. He'd leaned in close—*Jeremiah*.

"*Samantha!*" Monica's voice.

Her head jerked as Monica ran into the room. "What's happening?" Monica demanded, eyes bright. "Luke, get a nurse—"

Dante. She'd almost forgotten about him. "No, no...I'm okay."

Monica and Dante shared a long look.

"What are you doing here?" Hyde demanded. "I said I'd stay through the night."

"I need to get access to that security video," Monica told him. Sam had no idea what video she was talking about. "I've got files on the deputies, but there are more suspects than you know, and I need to see—"

"He smelled like cigars," Sam told them, blurting across Monica's words. Goose bumps rose on her arms. "I-I remember...when he untied me from the chair, he leaned in close, and he smelled like...cigars."

She saw Dante's gaze shoot to Monica. "Fuck," the guy swore and he spun around, heading right back for the door.

But Monica didn't move. "Are you sure about this?"

She could smell the scent even now. "Yes."

"And you didn't see his face?"

"H-he was behind me...then he..." Her hand circled in front of her face. "He put some kind of cloth bag over me so I couldn't see him."

Monica stared at her, and Sam could almost see the wheels turning in her head. Finally, Monica said, her voice so cool, "Then I've got a deputy I need to question."

Lee Pope heard the shuffle of footsteps behind him. He spun around, his hands clenched into tight fists. "You're not gonna believe this shit." Rage and fear pumped through him. *Keep this quiet? Hell, no.* "The Feds are looking at us for these kills."

"Really?" Vance asked, blinking. "Us?"

He could still see Monica Davenport's face. Perfect face, ice-cold eyes, staring too hard at him.

"They're running our records. Checking us all out." Lee shifted from his left foot to his right. "Ain't right." She had no business digging into his life. He'd already spilled his guts about his father. She didn't need to know anything else. His past—it was *his*.

"Man, what are you worried that she'll find?"

He stared into Vance's eyes. Confusion was there. No worry. Because what would Vance have to be worried about? As far as he knew, Vance only worried about who his next screw would be.

Get control.

Lee blew out a hard breath. "Nothin'." There'd be nothing for Agent Davenport to find. She could look all she wanted.

He'd be clean.

He brushed by Vance.

"Hey, hold up, where you goin'? I thought you had a mornin' shift."

Lee didn't glance back.

Something more important had come up.

Luke's eyes were grainy. Stubble coated his jaw, and if he didn't get a cup of coffee in the next five seconds, he might just go postal on someone's ass.

"Where is Deputy Lee Pope?" Monica demanded, leaning over Sheriff Davis's desk. "I need to see your deputy *now*."

"You think it's him?" Davis's chin sagged. "Him, me, maybe Jake Martin in Gatlin?" Animosity there. While they'd been gone, the fact that they were investigating his deputies, investigating him, must have really sunk in deep.

Luke saw her shoulders tense. "What do you know about Jake Martin?"

"I know he called my office five minutes after you left. He's at the hospital in New Orleans with his poor sister. The woman was beat damn near to death by some crazy boyfriend—"

"Sheriff, I want you to listen to me." She leaned forward and her voice—yeah, it would make a grown man shudder. "Either you get on your radio, and you get Lee Pope into this office *right now,* or I make the call for you because I am not dicking around here."

The sheriff whirled his chair around and grabbed for the radio he kept in his office. He punched in the buttons, tuned it, then said, "This is Sheriff Davis. I need Lee Pope to report to the station, repeat, I need Deputy Pope to return to the station. Over."

He raised his brows at Monica. "Satisfied?"

"No." She lifted the phone and offered it to him. "Call on his cell. Get him in this office."

His cheeks reddened. "You're wrong. It's not Lee, I'm tellin' you, not him. I'd know—"

"You can never know killers. You only know what they show you, and believe me, Sheriff, it's damn little."

He made the call. "Voice mail," he muttered, but then said, "Pope, it's Davis. I need you back at the office, got me? *Now.*" He slammed the phone down and shoved back in his chair.

Luke stirred. "No beeper?"

Davis's eyes slit. "No."

"Look, I know you don't like this," Monica said. "Neither do I."

"He's my man! He's worked by my side. He wouldn't—"

"Pope knew all three of the victims here in Jasper, didn't he?"

"Yeah…"

"And he was the one at the airport, the one sent to pick up Agent Kennedy?"

It would have put him right at the scene. When he'd called, had he really been checking the terminal? Or had he been driving Sam's unconscious body away?

"Yeah, you know he was the one…"

She opened one of the files she'd taken from Davis's office earlier. "And you'd already told me that he transferred back here from Gatlin, Louisiana."

Davis's Adam's apple bobbed. He seemed to shrivel, just a bit. "Not Lee. I'd know." He pointed a finger at her. "He'll be here soon, and you'll see! He's not hidin' anything. He didn't hurt those people! We need to find the real killer!"

Luke glanced at the clock. Nine-fifty-three a.m. "Maybe this will all be cleared up soon," he said.

Monica glanced back at him, the doubt clear on her beautiful face.

"Or maybe not," he murmured.

Ten forty-two a.m. Sheriff Davis was sweating. Not a trickle of sweat, but a full-on glistening forehead, beads coating his upper lip, dark patches staining his shirt.

Luke crossed his arms and glanced at Monica.

"No one knows where your deputy is." She shook her head. "The man managed to vanish awful fast."

A knock sounded on the sheriff's door. Davis's eyes widened and Luke knew hope when he saw it.

Then Vance walked in.

Hope died fast.

Vance strode stiffly into the room. He was sweating, too. Interesting.

"Sheriff." He nodded to Davis first, then shot a quick glance Luke's way, then Monica's. "You still lookin' for Lee?"

Monica nodded slowly. "Where is he?"

Vance licked his lips. "I-I don't know—"

"You two have always seemed pretty close to me," Luke pointed out. "Like good friends."

"We *are* good friends."

"Then be a friend," Monica said, "and tell me where he is so that we can clear up a bit of miscommunication."

Vance's eyes jerked to Davis. "You think it's one of us, don't ya, sheriff?"

"No," it was Monica who answered. She hadn't taken her eyes off the deputy. "That's what *I* think."

Vance turned his stare on Luke. The deputy parted his lips, then seemed to hesitate.

Luke tensed. "There something you need to say?"

His jaw flexed. "I-I saw Lee."

"When?" Monica's demand.

"About two hours ago, maybe three." He rubbed a hand over his face. "I was just coming on duty. I was...um, a little late because I had to drop a friend off at her place on the way in."

Yeah, he knew all about the guy's plans from the night before. "What happened?"

"H-he was mad—talking about you. Said you were suspecting us of the killings."

Monica's brows rose. "So much for keeping this quiet."

Right. Like she'd really wanted it quiet.

"I told him there was nothing to worry about. *I told him.*"

"Maybe there isn't anything for *you* to worry about," Luke said. He noticed the sheriff had sunk down into his chair even more. Davis wasn't a bad guy, not by any means. From what he'd seen, the guy tried his best to keep order in Jasper. Davis had never counted on a serial setting up shop in his quiet town.

No one ever counted on that.

And Luke knew that, though Davis had been fighting the idea—*on the outside, anyway*—that someone from his office could be involved in the crimes, the sheriff was starting to see the full picture. The knowledge was right there, in the pain that etched across his face.

The pieces were adding up, and everything was starting to point to the missing Lee Pope.

"Lee stormed off. I tried to stop him, but—" A shrug. "I think, uh, I figured he just needed to cool off for a while."

Or maybe he'd needed to run.

"You don't know where he was going?" Monica asked.

Vance rubbed his palms over the front of his pants. "No."

Monica raised one eyebrow. Just one. He remembered that look from their training days. One eyebrow up meant she thought the suspect was lying. "You're not trying to protect him, are you?"

"Lee hasn't done anything wrong. He's just probably sleeping off his beers somewhere. He wasn't due on shift 'til nine." Said fast. Too fast. People talked fast when they were nervous.

"Do you *really* think you know him?" Monica pressed, and her gaze was so intent on the deputy.

A grim nod. "Yeah, I do. I'd stake my life on his innocence."

Luke barely controlled a wince. Dude really needed to be careful. "Then if I were you, I'd hope good old Lee shows up for work soon."

Vance's cheeks flushed, a shade lighter than his hair. "You're lettin' the real killer get away."

Monica's gaze never wavered. "No, I'm not."

CHAPTER *Seventeen*

Be mine, Valentine. Monica squinted as she stared at the pages of data Ramirez had faxed over from the SSD.

Kyle West's mother had died on Valentine's Day. She'd been killed in a "suspicious fire" at their house.

"Suspicious, my ass," she muttered. The stove had been turned on, and accelerant was discovered in three areas of the house. That was a whole lot more than suspicious. That was clear-cut arson.

Kyle had been eleven at the time. He'd made it out. After he'd climbed through his bedroom window, he'd run to a neighbor. But his mother hadn't been so lucky. She'd gotten trapped when part of the den's ceiling fell on her.

She'd burned before help could arrive.

Monica's fingers smoothed over the grainy photo of Kyle. She died. *But you got out.*

And then went—where? To live with May? As she battled schizophrenia? She'd read the notes on May. When she'd been medicated, May would have seemed almost normal. But without her meds...

Seeing people who weren't there.

Hearing voices.

What had it been like for Kyle, living with May?

She studied the arson data again and a chill skated down her spine. *Okay, yeah, that was one hell of a coincidence.*

Valentine's Day. Fifteen years ago.

The same night that Hyde had pulled her out of that closet, and Romeo's reign had ended.

Too bad she didn't believe in coincidences.

The same night. And Romeo had been close to Gatlin, close enough for the deputies to come over and help out on the scene.

Holy hell. Monica sprang to her feet and yanked open the door. "Luke!"

He and Kenton had their heads together, staring at a computer screen. They were trying to track Lee's car.

"Luke!" Louder this time, and with a desperate edge.

His head snapped up and he focused on her.

She took a deep breath and felt all eyes on her. "We need to talk." *Alone.* There was too much tension in that office already.

He slapped Kenton on the shoulder and stalked toward her. The weight of all eyes bored down on her. So much suspicion.

Melinda walked past, gave her a slow nod. "Agent Davenport." Ice could have dripped from those words. Actually, it did. Hell, that's right. Lee had dated Melinda in high school. Had she been the bad break-up that sent him to Gatlin? That relationship would definitely explain the arctic blast.

But another hour had passed, and there had still been no word from Lee.

There wouldn't be any word. She knew that.

So the other deputies could be pissed, they could be uncooperative, but it wouldn't make a bit of difference.

Monica shut the door behind Luke. "Something you should know." The place was so small they were almost on top of each other.

He waited. Looked strong and sexy and—

I won't lose him. The case was about to go to end game. She wouldn't let it explode on her, and she would *not* risk him.

Because if she was right, the killer would be coming for her soon, and he'd try to use Luke against her.

Think like them. Yeah, that's what she was doing. She couldn't turn it off, but she could use it.

Luke was her weakness, and she couldn't afford to be weak.

Not with the killer watching.

"Kyle West's mother died the same night that Hyde brought down the Romeo killer."

A slight flaring of his eyes. "Bullshit."

"Afraid not."

He gave a soundless whistle.

"It was two counties over. Most of the deputies had been called in for backup on Romeo. The fire, um, let's just say it didn't get as much attention as it should have."

"What—"

"I'm pretty sure Kyle killed his mom." The first kill. All the signs were there. He'd started on the night that Romeo *stopped* killing. "I suspect he's been killing since then. Maybe at first, his mother's death cooled his need, and he was able to go a couple more years before he hurt anyone else…but the need would have come back." A compulsion. That's what some serials said they had.

The compulsion to kill.

"But Kyle West is dead," Luke told her, speaking slowly, thoughtfully. "He's not our guy, Monica, even if he did kill his mother."

"I want to talk to the officer who found his body." Another note she'd made. "The report I got said Kyle was killed in a wreck just outside of Mobile, Alabama."

"And what, you're thinking maybe our boy Kyle wasn't the one who died in that crash?"

Monica gave a small shrug. As elaborate as he liked to make his crimes, the way he liked to set the stage, faking a death would be nothing to him. "Anything's possible."

Luke stared at her, green eyes glittering. "That's for sure."

I won't lose him.

"So if Kyle *is* still alive, then where's Lee Pope?" He asked the question of the hour.

"That's what we've got to find out." And time was ticking away far too quickly.

His lips parted. "Wait a minute—hold up—you're not looking at *him* for the kills, are you?"

No, not at Lee. "There's no way Lee Pope is Kyle West." If West was the killer. And it was sure looking like he was. The SSD had tracked Martin's cell phone and, sure enough, it had placed him in a New Orleans hospital. Not in Gatlin. "Lee Pope grew up here, people know him. They can verify his identity."

"*Sonofabitch.*" Understanding dawned in that deep voice. The voice that could make her want. Make her yearn. "You think he's a victim?"

"Anything's possible," she told him again, because she couldn't be one hundred percent certain. Lee *wasn't* Kyle West, and if they could find out for certain who'd died in that accident near Mobile...maybe Kyle was still in the game.

And maybe Lee *was* a killer. After all, he'd been in Gatlin. He could have known Saundra. And he'd been the one at that airport when Sam's plane arrived. Lee was also the deputy who sure liked his cigars.

They were running out of time. "I need to—Luke, I really need you to trust me on this case, okay?"

"I do," he said instantly.

But it wouldn't be that easy. "I haven't always been honest with you...I haven't—I know being with me isn't easy."

He smiled then, a slow curve of his lips that made her heart race and her nipples tighten.

Not now. No time.

"Baby, I never said I wanted easy."

But she had. Pity she'd never gotten that. "I-I want to give us a chance, okay?" She was fumbling this, but she had to get the words out. There wouldn't be any more regrets for her. Not this time.

She'd be damned if she regretted anything else she did. Like she'd told Davis, there was no point looking to the past. *Just don't make the same mistakes in the future.* She wouldn't make any more mistakes with Luke.

Time to start saying just what she felt. Time to take risks and *live*. "I'm going to catch this killer, and then you and me...I want a real chance." It would be hard because *she* was hard. She wasn't used to trusting on a personal level.

Sure, she trusted the gang at SSD. She trusted them to keep her safe, to watch her back, but she'd never trusted them with her secrets.

Only Hyde. And now Luke.

"I wish I'd told you the truth years ago," she whispered. If she couldn't make it with Luke, she wouldn't make it with anyone.

His fingers brushed down her cheek and curved under her jaw. The touch heated her flesh. Just his touch, and she wanted him in the midst of hell. "The first time I saw you, I thought you were the most beautiful thing I'd ever seen."

And she'd thought he hadn't even noticed her. But then he'd crossed that room, smiled at her, and started smooth talking with that soft drawl of his.

Tempted from the first.

She rose onto her toes and kissed him. Her fingers dug into his hair, and she tasted him.

Wrong place, wrong time. Didn't matter.

Fear rode her. The case was going to explode soon, and she *didn't want to lose him*.

His tongue thrust into her mouth, and she gasped against him. That first thrust of his tongue always made her gasp as pleasure slipped through her.

Her nipples brushed his chest. Her thighs rubbed against him.

The sex during the night had been unlike anything she'd ever had before.

And she wanted more.

She'd *have* more.

Luke slowly lifted his lips away from hers. "Something you should know," he managed, voice rough.

She shook her head. No, now wasn't the time for more secrets. If he had dark deeds from his past, she wanted to hear them when they were fully alone, not there, with the chime of phones piercing the walls and the muffle of voices coming—

"For the record, hell, yeah, I'll give us a chance when this case is over, because there's no way I'm letting you get away again."

Her heart stopped.

"You're the strongest woman I've ever met," he told her. His lips were close. Full and sexy and she wanted them back on her mouth.

But she wanted him to keep talking. Because he was giving her hope. Finally, hope.

"I'd walk through hell for you, but I won't walk away from you, not again." Another kiss. Hard and fierce, and she parted her lips and took his tongue and sucked and tasted.

Lust.

Love.

Luke.

Hers. Finally, *hers.* A man who could handle her past and make her fight for a future. Her hands curled over his shoulders. Broad, strong shoulders.

The thud of approaching footsteps reached her ears. Coming closer, closer.

Right on time.

She held the kiss a moment longer. She'd savor this. Savor him, before the world tried to take him away.

When the knock came at the door, she didn't move. Not yet.

But Luke did. "Can I tell 'em to fuck off?"

If only.

"You have your backup gun with you, right?" She'd seen him take it out this morning. He hadn't worn it until Sam's disappearance, but all the agents were taking extra precautions now.

They needed to.

His brow furrowed. "Yeah, but—"

"We're going to need it." Because she knew a lie when she saw one. "Stay on guard," she whispered. "Always."

Then she left him and opened the door.

Deputy Vance Monroe stood in the doorway. He glanced over his shoulder, then back at her. "A-Agent Davenport, we need to talk."

Because he'd been lying to her.

"Come inside."

His stare darted to Luke. "Can we—can we talk alone?"

She didn't have to look at Luke to know he'd tensed. Not going to happen. "Luke's my partner on this case. Whatever you can tell me, you can tell him."

Vance's bony hands clenched into fists. "You—you'll bring him in alive, won't you?"

He knew where Lee was. She'd been certain of that. Monica had just waited for him to break. "I'll do my best."

His throat worked. "I just…*he couldn't have done it*. I'm sure it's just…"

"Where is he?" Luke asked.

"I-I can show you. You'll never find it on your own. An old hunting cabin near the river. Broken down, but Lee took me there a few times." He swallowed again and the rasp of his breath was loud and painful. "Said he liked to go out there to get away. It used to be his old man's place."

"You should have told us sooner," Monica said. "We've lost valuable time."

"I didn't want..." His hands slowly unclasped. "I *don't* want this to turn into a freak show with the media and everything, okay? I thought he'd be back. When he needs to cool off, he always goes there, but *I thought he'd be back.*"

But the hours were ticking by, and there was no sign of Lee.

Luke's gaze stayed on the deputy. "How many people know about that cabin?"

"Not many. It's far back in the woods, pretty secluded."

Perfect hiding spot.

"Just come with me," Vance entreated. "If he's there, I can bring him in. I know it, *he's my friend.*"

Now she met Luke's eyes and, after a moment, he gave a slow nod.

"All right, Deputy." She exhaled and felt the reassuring weight of her backup gun against her left ankle. "It's your show, but if he comes out armed, all bets are off."

She heard the click of his swallow and the quick utter of his prayer.

Come out easy.

What they always told the killers. But so often...

They came out fighting.

"Let me get the sheriff," she said.

But Vance shook his head. "If he did this..." The guy's skin paled even more. "If he sees the sheriff and all the deputies coming after him, I-I'm afraid of what he'll do." His voice dropped to a whisper as he said, "His old man ate his gun. I don't want him to do the same."

Kenton glared at the computer screen. The connection at this place was shit. He needed the files yesterday, and it was taking three minutes just for one page to load.

He wanted the autopsy records on Kyle West. Needed them. The sooner he could—

The light scent of lavender wrapped around him. "I've got my new phone," Monica whispered against his ear, her breath feathering over him.

Every muscle in his body tensed. *What the—*

Then she was gone.

He blinked and swiveled around. Monica was heading for the door, Dante close behind her. *Yeah, what else was new? Lucky bastard wouldn't let her get far.*

But... her phone?

The door swung closed behind her.

Hyde had brought Monica a new cell phone when he came down. The tech guys had torn apart her other one while they tried to track the Watchman.

Watchman. Fucking stupid name. Who'd come up with that brilliant tag?

He glanced back at the computer. The page had finally loaded on the screen in front of him.

But Kenton didn't really care. *I've got my new phone.* He whipped out his own cell and called SSD. Ramirez should be riding desk today, doing grunt work on the case and—

"Yo." Ramirez never bothered with ID'ing himself.

"What's special about Monica Davenport's new phone?"

"Uh, wanna run that by me again?"

He held on tight to his patience. *If Sam were in the central office, she would have already given him the info.* "I need you to check for me—find out if Monica's new phone has a tracer." A hunch. Because Monica's moves were always so precise. Why tell him about the phone? Why—

A hum of sound. Then jazzy elevator music in his ears. Oh, crap, anything but—

"Got a tracer." A hint of excitement in Jon's voice. "One of the new ones from Development. Whether her phone is on or off, we can get a lock on her and ID her exact location."

He jumped out of his chair. "Get a lock on her."

"What?"

"Get a lock on her," he repeated. "*Now.*"

Because Monica always had a reason. Always.

His gaze flew around the sheriff's office. She'd wanted to slip away from the deputies, but Monica had also wanted to make sure she could be tracked.

Sonofabitch. She'd left him a perfect trail of breadcrumbs to follow.

They tailed the deputy's cruiser through the backwoods. Over a sagging wooden bridge. Down muddied dirt roads.

As they went deeper into the woods, Luke noticed that Monica grew more tense. Not that he blamed her. Not one damn bit. This whole scene set his nerves on edge. The sooner they found Pope, the better.

Then he saw the cabin. Dark wood with a sloping porch and two small windows near the front. A line of wildflowers outside.

Wildflowers. *What the hell?*

Monica's breath came out, hard and fast. Too fast.

"Monica?"

The deputy had stopped. His brake lights flashed as he turned off the car.

"Get your gun," Monica said. "Get it and get ready."

But she'd said Lee might be the victim. Wait, shit, what—

She already had her weapon out. She didn't look at him as she said, "*It's him.*" Her stare was on the wildflowers.

Vance hopped out of his car. Paced nervously.

Luke opened his door, nice and slow. He pulled his weapon, felt the reassuring weight in his hand.

Vance squared his shoulders and marched toward the cabin. He slammed his fist on the door. "*Lee! Lee, come out!*"

No sign of Pope.

Monica climbed from the car.

Vance spun around. "I'm checking the side, he might be there. *Lee!*" He raised his voice. "Man, we've got to talk. Come on, buddy, come out!"

He disappeared. More pounding. Maybe on a second door?

Luke eyed the cabin. No lights were on inside.

"Lee's in there," Monica said, her voice pitched low. "We have to get him out." She licked her lips. "We're gonna have to move fast. As soon as you see Vance again, I need you to—"

A gunshot fired, the explosion thundering through the quiet of the woods, and Monica stumbled back.

Then she hit the ground.

Fuck!

"*No!*" Luke swung his gun toward the house. He could see the tip of a rifle, poking through a now-open window. *Bastard.* He fired. Glass shattered. He shot again, aiming for the window. The rifle was gone.

He crouched and ran for Monica. *Blood*, soaking her shirt, soaking the ground around her. But she was conscious, her eyes open as she fought to rise.

He caught her hands. "It's okay, you're gonna be all right." He yanked out his phone. "I'm getting help, baby." *Christ, her blood.*

She shook her head. "Not...Lee..."

"This is Special Agent Luke Dante, I need an ambulance—"

Her hand turned and her nails dug into his palm. "*Vance. Shoot...h-him....*"

His eyes widened, and he swung back around.

Too late.

The butt of the rifle slammed into his head.

Vance's fingers tightened around the rifle, and he smiled. *Too easy.*

Dante was out cold.

But Monica...

"*Get away from him!*" Beneath the boiling fury, he could hear the fear in her words.

"Drop the gun," he told her, "Or I kill him right now." He glanced up and saw her struggling to rise. Struggling to aim the gun at him. He'd hit her in the right shoulder. Deliberate, that. He could have hit her dead in the heart, but then how could a quick kill be fun?

The wound had her hand shaking. *Can't aim for shit, can you, bitch?*

Ah, Monica. And as a bonus, she was a bleeder. He'd realized that when Jones had shot her. So much blood, spilling all around.

And Dante, well, he didn't react so well when his lady got hit.

Exactly why I gave the bitch the first shot.

Confuse and control—the way he worked.

His finger tightened on the trigger when she didn't drop her weapon. "How 'bout I shoot him in the head? Or maybe the heart? Yeah, let's go for the heart."

Her lips trembled, and the gun slipped from her bloody fingers.

"Good girl."

He said the words slowly, letting them sink in, and he saw the way her eyes widened. *This would be so fine. Better than all the other kills.* Adrenaline spiked through his blood. He'd planned for this moment for so long. The perfect kill.

He kicked her gun away and leaned in close to her. "I know what scares you, Agent Davenport."

She tried to slam her head into his.

He laughed, then rammed the butt of the rifle into her head.

Bitch.

"I lost her." Jon's bleak voice.

Kenton's blood iced. "What the hell does that mean?"

"It means her signal just died on me—*sonofabitch!*"

But the signal shouldn't die. "I thought the damn thing worked even if the phone was off!"

"It does. It only stops if the tracking chip has been destroyed."

No. Dammit, no. "Give me the last address."

"It's not a street, man, it's in the middle of nowhere. Why is she out—"

"Coordinates." He'd find the place. "Just give me the damn coordinates." The glass doors of the sheriff's station swung open. Hyde came marching in first, followed by a pale and hunched Sam.

What? She shouldn't be there!

He scribbled down the coordinates. "Keep trying to get her signal back," he snapped, and waved for Hyde. The shit was about to hit the fan.

Hyde stopped beside him, a frown pulling his brows low. "Where's Davenport? I want an update on—"

"We've got a problem, sir." With Hyde, he'd learned it was better to get things out fast.

Hyde shook his head. "That's not what I want to hear." His eyes scanned the room. "Dante?"

They were together. He suspected that Monica actually trusted Luke more than she trusted anyone. "Davenport went in the field. She and Dante were looking for a deputy—a Lee Pope." A quick breath. "She wanted me to track her cell, and we just lost the signal."

Hyde didn't blink, but behind him Sam seemed to sway a bit.

"Last coordinates," Hyde barked.

Kenton reached for his pad. "I've got—"

"Davis!" Hyde's roar. "Get me a car and get it fucking now!"

She awoke to complete darkness. The pain hit her instantly. Throbbing in her head, radiating from her right temple. Fire in her shoulder from the bullet that had gone through flesh and muscle.

Fumbling, she reached out her hand—and slammed her palm into a wall. Her breath shuddered out. Monica turned and reached behind her. Another wall.

She judged the distance and her heart stopped.

Two by three fucking feet.

Darkness.

I know what scares you.

She shoved up to her feet. *No, no, the bastard didn't know. He didn't know her at all.*

She blocked the pain. What she'd always done.

Her hands smoothed over the walls. There had to be a door. A way in, and a way out.

Romeo had taken off the door knob. He'd sealed her in so completely.

Shit, she couldn't find a knob. Nothing but smooth wood. Nothing but—

Thump.

Thump.

Thump.

A man's groan. Pain-filled, dazed.

Luke! She didn't realize she'd screamed his name until she heard the laughter.

Her fingers flattened over the wood. If there was a knob, this would be the right height. She inched along, slowly, slowly, and after a few seconds, she felt the slight ridge. Monica traced it with her index finger. A fat square. Probably a piece of wood he'd attached over what *should* have been the hole for the knob, and he'd sanded it down for a near-perfect fit.

He'd been preparing for them.

She pressed her head against the wood—from outside she could hear rustles, shuffling, groans. God, *Luke*.

Her fist drove into that patched spot on the door. Wood shattered. Light trickled through the darkness. She knelt and squinted through that hole. She could see some kind of table with long straps dangling over its edges. A body—Luke's body.

"*Get away from him!*" she screamed. Her hand reached down to her right ankle. The holster was gone. No backup gun. Her fist shoved into the door again. Agony lanced through her knuckles. *Block it. Block it.* She kept pounding. Started kicking. She had to get to Luke.

No, she *would* get to him.

The sliver of light flickered. The laughter came again, taunting her even as it chilled her blood. "I know what scares you most." His voice carried easily to her.

Her hand slapped against the door. "Keeping me locked up isn't going to scare me, asshole! I'm not afraid of being in your damn closet!" Small spaces didn't bother her. If they had, she would have gone crazy with Romeo in those first nightmarish days. She didn't like them, but she could handle them. She could handle anything.

"Ah...Monica...I know you're not like poor lost Laura."

Couldn't save her.

"The dark doesn't bother you, either, though, at first, I did wonder about the light you liked to leave on at night."

She'd rip the door apart. It was wooden, not metal like Romeo's. She'd get out.

Before or after he killed Luke?

"Then I realized you weren't scared of the dark. You were scared of being caught off guard. No weapon, defenseless."

She always kept a weapon close. Except when she was with Luke. Then she'd just needed him.

"You didn't want to be helpless ever again, did you, Monica? Because you were helpless before. You were in that prison, listening as Romeo killed those girls, and there wasn't a thing you could do to stop him—or to save them."

She'd tried. When she'd been strapped to his table, Monica had never made a sound.

No screams.

But when she'd been in that closet, and she knew what he'd been doing to the others, she'd screamed. Screamed until she'd lost her voice. Screamed for Romeo to let her out. To let them go.

But the other girls had screamed louder. They didn't understand that he wanted *them* to be silent. Didn't understand until it was too late.

Then there was nothing but silence.

That bastard knew how to get me to scream. Pain wouldn't break me, so he used the other girls.

"I've been watching you...." came the taunting voice.

She swiped something out of her eye. Blood. Dripping down from her forehead.

"I saw your face when you found Samantha floating in that water. You were scared. *Terrified.*"

Because she'd thought another victim had died on her watch.

"Tell me," he said, and she knew he was getting off on this. Baiting her. Teasing the trapped prey. "Why did you join the FBI?"

"To put fucked-up assholes like you behind bars!"

Silence. Then, "That was the wrong answer."

"Then you tell me!" His game. Let him talk all he wanted. Monica tried to find the crevice that would mark the side of the door. Had to be there. Maybe she could pry the damn thing loose.

"You got your shiny FBI badge..." His voice came, slow and sure, "because you wanted to make up for all those girls *you* killed."

Her head pressed against the wood.

"You couldn't save them, could you? So you've been trying to make up for their deaths all these long years."

She wasn't going to answer him. That was what he'd want. The prick. Like she needed him to profile *her*.

"All these years, people talked about how good you were at catching killers, but really, you were trying to save the victims." He gave a faint chuckle. "And now you'll be a victim. You and your lover."

Her nails dug into the wood. "Let him go!"

"No." His voice grew quieter. He was leaving. She shot to her knees and strained to see through that hole. *Heading back toward the table. Back to Luke.*

Why wasn't Luke talking? Had Vance gagged him? The deputy had knocked him with the butt of the rifle, but Luke should have awakened by now—unless Vance had already started having his fun with him.

When she swallowed, she tasted fear. Once, that had been all she could taste. When she'd been trapped in the darkness, just like this.

She'd tasted fear, and she'd smelled blood.

Scream for me.

"Without him, there'd be no fear." Light glinted. Christ, he had a knife in his hands. "It has to be like before, Monica." *Romeo carved them up.* "You have to be helpless. You have to know what's happening to him, and you have to *fear*."

"I am afraid, you bastard! I'm fucking terrified! Is that what you want? I'm scared to death!" She swiped more blood away from her eyes. The cut on her forehead was streaming blood. "You don't need him. Let him go and keep me!"

"I think you care for him." Considering. "That'll make it even better. What do you think? Should I take the gag out so you can hear him scream?"

A gag. That hadn't been groaning. That had been Luke trying to talk.

"Monica!" Luke's voice.

Tears stung her eyes.

"Monica, don't worry about me, don't worry about—"

He broke off.

"Ah, that's not fair," Vance snapped, and she heard the fury in his voice. "You're supposed to scream when I cut you. *Scream!*"

Monica shoved her fist in her mouth.

Not like before. Not at all. Because Luke, damn him—he was staring at death and still trying to protect her.

"I'm gonna slice you apart, bastard. We'll see how fuckin' brave you are when I cut open your chest. You'll scream then."

"*No!*" She was the one screaming. Because she knew Vance would do it. He'd carve Luke up and keep her trapped for every moment. So she could hear it all.

Pain has a sound.

Luke would die knowing Vance had her in that closet, and he'd know that she'd be the killer's next victim.

"I know what you fear." The bastard wasn't talking to her now. His voice had lowered even more. "I know all about you, too, Luke Dante."

"Big damn deal," Luke snarled.

"Tough guy, huh?"

Silence.

He was cutting him.

"But you weren't so tough when your mom died, were you? Tell me, what was it like to watch her die in front of you?"

Her breath caught.

"Piss off." Luke's words were coming slower. Pain there. *What had Vance done to him?* That fucking knife! Covered in red now.

"Her killer, it was *her* lover, wasn't it? The guy she'd ditched your old man for. I guess the cheatin' bitch got what she deserved."

"*I'll . . . kill . . . you.*"

"No, you won't."

She found the crevice where the door would open when it swung back on its hinges. She tried to shove her fingers in that little wedge, but her nails broke. Splinters pierced her fingers. Dammit!

"You tried to stop him, 'cause you're the *hero*, right?"

Luke hissed out a low breath.

"Does Monica know?" Laughter grated in the air. "Does she know he beat the shit out of you and left you in your own vomit and blood while he killed your mother?"

No, she didn't know. Her fist pounded against the

door. "This isn't about Luke! Let him go! You've got me! You want to play your fucking games, play them with me!"

Luke. No wonder he'd always jumped to save the ladies. Even in Gatlin, with Lynn. *"Fucking makes me sick. Every time I see a guy punching on a woman."*

She tasted blood and the salt from her tears.

"When the cops came, they found you hugging her. What was it like, holding tight to a dead woman?"

A roar of fury.

"I mean, you were like six, right? That had to screw with your head. Would have turned some guys into killers—"

"Like you?" Monica yelled.

"But you..." Vance kept right on talking, too focused now on Luke. And she had to get his focus back on her. *He'll kill Luke.* "You became the boy scout, didn't you? Always got to save the day."

Monica's fingers curled around her belt. She pulled it loose, yanked it up. She grabbed the buckle, snapped it back, popping it, and tried to break it free from the leather.

"You're not gonna save the day this time, Dante. You're gonna die, and you're gonna die knowing I have *her*. I'll cut her apart, just like I'll do to you. I'll cut her, and she'll cry, and she'll beg, and she'll scream for *you*." A long sigh. "But you won't be there to save her."

The buckle broke free. Monica tossed the leather to the floor and curled her fingers around the metal.

"Just like you couldn't save your mother."

Luke's worst fear?

"I get a fucking two-for-one special!" Vance yelled

and laughter followed, the kind that told her the deputy had left the land of the sane long ago. "Now, bastard, let's see how long you last before *you* start beggin'!"

Blade hit flesh. She knew that soft noise, the unmistakeable sound as the knife dove in, then pulled out.

"Let's see!"

Her breath caught. *This was it.* If she didn't stop him, Luke would die. She pounded on the door. Pounded until her hands went numb, then choking back the fear and only letting the fury out, she yelled the words that she *knew* would get to him. Monica screamed, "Romeo let me watch!"

Silence. Breathing. Heavy. Excited.

She swiped her tongue over her lips. *Hate the taste of fear.*

Footsteps shuffled toward her. Keys jingled. *Let me out. Come on, let me out....*

Her fingers tightened around the buckle.

Light came at her. A trickle first. Then, bigger, bigger...

Vance's face popped into that light. His eyes were wild, and he wore a grin that went from ear to ear. "Just when I thought my day couldn't get better." He had a gun in his hand. One that he'd aimed right at her. "I was hoping you'd scream those magic words."

CHAPTER *Eighteen*

Luke jerked hard against the straps that held him pinned to the table. Pain burned through him. The bastard had sliced both of his arms and had driven that big-ass knife into his shoulder.

"Lee!" Monica's sharp cry.

Luke's head reared up, just a few inches because that was all he could manage. His eyes shot to the left, the right, and—there.

The other deputy was tied to a chair in the far corner. His head sagged. Blood dripped from his nose. Bruises covered him.

Because Vance liked to play.

"Don't worry about him," Vance muttered, and Luke's stare zeroed back in on the killer. Vance grabbed Monica's arm and pulled her close. He shoved the gun under her chin. "With the drugs I gave him, he doesn't even know where he is. And when I'm done, he'll eat this." The barrel jabbed into her flesh. "Just like his old man ate his weapon." A twisted smile. "Like daddy, like screwed-up son."

Blood stained Monica's face. Luke wrenched his arms, struggling to get free. *Have to help her. Can't leave Monica alone.*

Because he knew good old Vance hadn't been lying. Luke would die first, the better for Monica to watch.

Then she'd be on her own with the sick fuck. Pope couldn't help. And she'd die.

No fucking way.

With his left hand, Vance pulled out his cuffs, that stupid grin still on his face. Luke clenched his teeth. The taste of blood filled his mouth. *Kill him.*

"Let's give you a good show. Real up close..." He snapped a cuff around her left wrist. A tear leaked from Monica's eye as she stared at Luke. She didn't struggle against Vance. Just stood still and silent. "So close you'll feel the blood on your skin." The other cuff snapped around the leg of the table, the one closest to Luke's head.

She'll see me die.

He'd fucked this up. She'd told him to be on guard, but he hadn't been ready. He'd let this bastard take him down, and now Monica would pay.

I won't scream. Not in front of her. She didn't need the sound of his screams in her head. She had enough of those.

"Close your eyes," he told her. Because he didn't care what she'd seen before. She wouldn't see this. "Just close your eyes."

But she shook her head.

Beautiful Monica. The woman he'd always wanted. The only one he'd loved.

The one who'd see him die tonight.

• • •

Hyde's foot slammed the accelerator into the floorboard. Sheriff Davis sat beside him, riding shotgun in his own patrol car.

The pine trees swirled past him, and time seemed to disappear.

Sixteen years ago, he'd been driving down another dirt road. One surrounded by swaying pines.

A cabin had waited for him, with death inside.

Monica had survived once. She'd do it again.

He'd brought her out of the ashes, watched her nearly crumble over her mother's grave. He'd been by her side through the years, and he'd stood back as she grew stronger.

A miracle.

He'd gotten one before. He'd get one again.

His fingers curled around the radio. He brought the receiver up to his lips. "Go in with sirens silent. We don't want to give this bastard any notice, you got me?"

Because if he heard them coming, Luke and Monica would be dead before they ever opened the doors of the cruisers. Out in these damn boondocks, it would be hard to keep quiet.

But the killer would be focused on other things.

"Copy that."

He'd taught her how to fight. *She'd survive.*

"Can't this piece of shit go faster?" he bit out. Red dirt flew in the air around the cruiser.

Hold on. Stay alive.

"I'm sorry." Luke's lips moved silently.

Monica shook her head. He didn't have anything to be sorry for. This was on her.

Deputy Vance Monroe was good at killing. Probably because he'd been at his craft for so long.

Since he was eleven years old.

"*I love you,*" Luke told her. His eyes locked on her, and they showed no fear. Sweat beaded his face, and blood soaked his arms and chest, but fear didn't lurk in his green gaze. Not so much as a shadow.

He knew the game, too.

Way to tell Vance to piss off.

"Where do I want to start first?" Vance walked around the table. A surgical tray was on the far right side, out of Monica's reach. Vance waved his gun toward her. "Why don't you pick a spot for me? Something delicate, that will hurt like a bitch."

Monica glared back at him. *Enough.* Her turn. "How old were you?"

He blinked.

"How old were you, Kyle, when you made your first kill?"

His lips stretched. Not a smile. Not even close. "Figured that one out, did you?" He shook his head. "Guess we both like to play with names, don't we, Mary Jane?"

Luke's arms tensed, and she knew he was trying to escape the straps. But they were too tight. He wouldn't be able to get free on his own.

"I'm guessing *you* were the officer who supposedly told the sheriff's department in Gatlin that Kyle West died in that car accident?"

"Finally figured that one out, did you?" A sharp bark of laughter.

"Who really died in that car accident?" She pulled a

bit on her handcuff, testing the table. No give. "Vance Monroe?"

One shoulder lifted in a slow shrug. "It was really too fucking easy. I saw him in a bar. He looked like me. My size, my hair, my age." A shrug. "So I thought—why the hell not? And I got myself a fresh start."

And another man had died. But so what, right? In Kyle's mind, it hadn't mattered a bit. "*You* were the officer who went to see May, weren't you? *You* were the one sent to tell her about the car accident."

"She was off her meds. *Always* going off. I had darker hair, a broken nose, and a shiny uniform. When I lowered my voice, she didn't even recognize me."

"But the people in the sheriff's office *would* have recognized you, that's why you didn't tell Martin." The guy had been good. He'd done the visit to the family that would have been required, but covered his tracks well enough that he'd slipped through the cracks in the system.

A bark of laughter. "Maybe he would have. Maybe not. That prick can't find his own ass most days." His voice hardened. "You know that jerkoff thinks he can change the world. He thinks he can take a killer, get him to bare his soul, and then—*wham*—turn him into a model fucking citizen."

Was he talking about Martin and his visits with Romeo? "But that won't happen," she said, her voice soft when his was hard.

"Hell, no. Some instincts are in the blood. Nothin' will change 'em. Nothin'."

"You've got those instincts, right? Was it those

instincts that made you kill your ex-girlfriend? Those instincts made you murder Saundra?"

His eyes slit. "That bitch deserved to die! She was gonna leave me. *Me!*"

"She wasn't your first, though, was she?" From the corner of her eye, she thought she saw Lee stir. *What had Kyle given him?* She'd caught sight of loose ropes binding his hands. Ropes were so much easier to work free than handcuffs. And it looked like Kyle had kept those binds nice and light, probably because he didn't want to leave rope burns on the soon-to-be dead guy's hands.

Rope burns didn't go so well with a suicide.

Maybe he'd learned the rope lesson with Jeremy Jones.

Vance—*Kyle*—shook his head. "My first? Not even close." He put the gun down and picked up his bloody knife. "I think it's time we got down to business." He turned to shoot a quick glance at Lee—

"You killed your mother!" The belt buckle bit into her hand. "She was your first kill in that fire on Valentine's Day."

He whirled back toward her. The gloating pride vanished from his face. *All* emotion wiped away in an instant. "She deserved it."

Right, because everyone he'd killed had deserved to die.

His fingers tightened around the knife. "That bitch—she tried to kill *me*."

The last piece of the puzzle fell into place. *Kyle went after women*. They were his primary victims, and he liked to terrify them so that he could have control.

He wanted the women to be weak, powerless. Because

once, a woman had made him feel the same way. His was not instinct, more like a sick compulsion.

"She beat you." Absolute certainty had Monica's voice thickening. "It started when you were young. She'd hurt you—"

"That crazy whore kept saying the devil was in me!" Spittle flew from his mouth, and he didn't see Lee sliding free of the ropes. "She'd take her belt to me every night and tell me that she was beating him out of me!"

May had been treated for schizophrenia. Maybe her sister had suffered from similar problems. But no one had ever been there to shield her baby boy.

"She said I was evil, and that night, *that night,* she was gonna kill me!" He brought the knife over Luke's chest. Hesitated. With that hesitation, Monica knew he was seeing the past. Not the victims right in front of him, but the most important one he'd killed so long ago. "I got her instead. I hit her on the head, knocked her down, and then I poured gasoline all over her."

Accelerant had been found at the scene.

"She woke up right before I lit the first match." His eyes widened, and she knew he saw that moment with perfect clarity. "She was so scared. She begged me to help her. To get her out, but I just lit that match and watched her burn."

And he'd gotten his taste of power. Learned how heady fear could be.

He'd become a monster.

"Everybody was working on Romeo. The deputies never looked twice at me."

Because the sheriff had been there, covering his nephew's tracks? *Family.* You protected them. Maybe

Sheriff Peterson had known what Margaret was doing to her son. Maybe he'd just been good at turning a blind eye to the things he didn't want to see.

"You got away with murder." It would have satisfied him for a while. But not forever. "Did you kill May, too? Did you torch her house and trap her inside?"

He laughed at that. A low, dark laugh. "Didn't have to."

What? She'd been certain he was behind that fire.

"All I had to do was call her. When she heard my voice, she thought I was a ghost." Another laugh. "I told her to burn the house. I knew you wanted all those papers, that *shit*, she kept for years. I told her to burn it and to stay inside, to make sure the flames were bright enough."

Oh, Christ. "And she did."

His mouth hitched up. "Like I said, May was never good at taking her meds. And when she was off 'em, she'd do just about anything. Believe *anything*."

She swallowed. "How many bodies are out in that swamp?" Close to the cabins. Close to the tree that had become Saundra's grave. There could have been more. So many more.

His head cocked, and his lips stretched in a taunting grin. "You think you know me, huh? Well, *he* told me all about *you*."

"He?" But she knew.

"Romeo."

That knife was too close to Luke's chest. Luke's eyes hadn't left Kyle's face. The promise of deadly retribution glowed in those emerald depths. If she could just get him free...

"What the fuck do you know about Romeo?" Luke yelled.

But Monica stared into Kyle's eyes and finally understood the game. "Everything." The night one killer had been captured, another had been born two counties over. And coincidences, they just didn't happen.

"You had to go see him, didn't you? You read about him in the papers. His story was everywhere while your kill didn't even get a notice." It had been about pride. Some killers were desperate for their time in the light. Even boys...

"Romeo was the king." Kyle's gaze tracked down her body. "He was in every paper, on every TV show. He's a *legend*."

"Bryan Tate." It was hard to get the words out. "Guessing that was you visiting, not Romeo's lawyer." So many visits. Plenty of time to talk about death.

He leaned forward just a bit. "Tate's one of them bodies you'll find near Saundra's tree."

Bastard.

"I needed a way in. He was my ticket."

So what if another life was lost? And Romeo, oh, he would have loved the attention. He'd wanted someone who could appreciate his work. *That's one of the reasons he kept me alive. He wanted someone to see what he was doing. Someone to think he was God.* "You told him that you had the 'instinct,' right?"

A quick nod. "He didn't believe me at first. He gave me a test. Wanted to see if I was for real."

"What kind of test?"

"A guard. He wanted him dead." His gaze bored into hers. "That kill was easy enough to verify for Romeo."

And Romeo would have known he had the perfect lap-dog. "What did Romeo teach you?" Because he'd always wanted to teach, wanted someone to cross the line and be *just like him.*

His tongue swiped over his lower lip. "He said—he said I had to aim big. That I had to prove how smart I was, how good."

Fuck.

"He told me about you and that prick Hyde." A bark of laughter that held only darkness. "If it hadn't been for Romeo, I never would have found you. But he told me—he told me you'd be the perfect prey. If I could take you down, if I could break you, then the world would know how good I was. *I* would be the legend."

Romeo. Playing games so that he could finish the kill he'd lost years before. "Romeo was jerking you around."

"No, no. He said you'd tell me that." A pause. "He said you'd tell me anything to stay alive."

She glared back at him.

"Everything he told me was true. I got you in his city, I got you down here, and now...I'll break you."

"Romeo's going to rot in prison." She bared her teeth at him. He was totally focused on her now. His mistake. "Just like you will."

And she never looked away from Kyle as Lee slammed into him. The knife flew from Kyle's hand and clattered to the floor. The two men fell in a tangle of limbs and fists.

Monica snatched up the belt buckle. The knife was too far away. She'd never be able to reach it. "Hold on," she whispered to Luke, and started sawing with the buckle. If she could just get him free...

"No, *run*," Luke ordered. "*Get out! Go baby, go.*"

She wouldn't leave him.

Kyle slammed Lee's head into the floor. Once. Twice. The sickening thuds had her stomach heaving.

The strap near Luke's shoulder gave way. She leaned over him, sawing, sawing...

"What are you doin'?!" Kyle was on his feet. He swung his fist at her, driving his knuckles into her face, and Monica stumbled. "You can't save him!"

Too late. She already had.

Luke shot up, blood dripping, and plowed his fist into Kyle's stomach. The killer doubled over, groaning.

Monica's jaw burned. It popped when she opened her mouth. *Block it.* "*Luke...keys.*" They were right there, hanging from Kyle's belt.

Luke ripped the keys off and slammed his elbow into Kyle's nose. *Down, down he went.* Luke tossed her the keys. She caught them and had her cuff open in three seconds.

That was long enough for Kyle to pick his ass up off the floor but not long enough for Luke to get completely free.

Shit—weapon.

Monica scrambled around the table. The knife was right there, waiting for her. Her fingers closed around the hilt just as Kyle let out a roar of fury.

The gun. No.

She spun around. He had the gun aimed at Luke, aimed straight at his heart. His finger squeezed—

"*Watchman!*"

He hesitated, started to swing toward her.

She came up on him fast and drove the knife into his chest. As deep as she could.

His eyes widened. His lips trembled as if he would speak.

She twisted the knife, then ripped the gun from his hands.

His knees gave way, and he hit the floor hard.

Monica's breath heaved as she crouched over him. Blood trickled from his lips. His pupils were dilating, blackness spreading.

A moan bubbled in his throat.

She knew her weapon had found its mark. In that split second, there'd been no time for taking chances. She'd had to stop him, and she'd gone for the kill.

Monica yanked the knife free. Blood splattered in the air. Leaning down, she put her lips close to his ear. "Are you scared?" she whispered.

Monica felt his nod against her cheek even as she smelled death approaching.

"Good." She drew back and finally gave him a smile of her own. "Hell's waiting, asshole."

His eyes widened. A gurgle rose in his throat. He lifted his hand, bloody fingers reaching—

And went to Hell.

The hand fell back against the floor, and his breath choked away.

The door flew open behind them. "FBI! *Don't move!*" Kenton yelled.

The cavalry had arrived. Too late. She'd expected them sooner. *Bastard must have broken my cell phone, messed up the signal.*

Figured. Kyle had known all the tricks.

He'd been prepared for her.

But then, she'd prepared for him, too.

She stared into those sightless eyes. It looked like she'd been wrong. Kyle wouldn't spend the rest of his days rotting in a jail with Romeo.

Romeo would be all by himself. Just what the bastard feared. She knew his fear. Knew what scared him most. She'd learned the truth in a blood-stained room years before when the cops took her away from him and *he'd* been the one to scream—for her.

Romeo wanted someone to share his darkness. Someone who understood death and horror and fear. Someone just like him.

But he'd lost her, and he'd lost Kyle. Now he was alone.

Exactly what Romeo deserved.

Hyde shoved through the door right behind Kenton. His gun was up, steady and tight in his grasp.

The scent of blood hit him first. The stench of death.

Monica rose from the chaos. Her shirt was stained with blood, and there was a dark, purple bruise on her forehead that skimmed down the side of her face. She lifted her arms slowly, and he saw that she had a knife clenched in her right fist.

"Suspect is down," she said simply, and her voice didn't shake. Didn't so much as tremble. Rock steady and cold.

Not the girl she'd been. The woman she was.

This time, she'd taken down the killer.

And sometimes, so many times, he wished he'd let her take down the other bastard.

But then what would she have become?

And what is she now?

She dropped the knife. "Vance Monroe...he's Kyle West. He killed his mother sixteen years ago, murdered Saundra Swain, Sally Jenkins, Patty Moffet..." she swallowed, "Laura Billings, and he-he attacked Special Agent Samantha Kennedy."

What is she?

A fucking fine agent.

"*Monica.*" Dante's voice. His was boiling with emotion—fury, fear, need—the opposite of Monica.

He'd always been her opposite. Hyde had known that from the first moment he saw them together at Quantico. The two of them together were one powerful team.

When Monica heard Dante's voice, she blinked, and the ice melted away. "Luke." She spun and lunged for him.

Dante sat up on some kind of makeshift operating table. Long, thick straps held down his legs and his hips and, shit, it looked like the killer had been carving him up.

"Got an injured agent!" Hyde yelled. "Get the EMTs in here *now!*"

Two deputies lay on the floor. Vance Monroe wasn't breathing, and he had a gaping stab wound in his chest. Lee Pope's chest was rising and falling, but he looked like shit.

"Deputy down!" Kenton called.

Down, but still alive.

And his agents had survived. Hyde tried to take a deep breath but the stench of blood choked him.

Way too much blood. The EMTs needed to move their asses. Monica threw her arms around Dante. Held him tight.

Crushed her mouth to his.

Not ice.

Not anymore.

Luke pulled Monica against him. He buried his hands in her hair, and he tilted her head back.

The better to take her mouth.

Fear pumped through his blood. *Too close. Nearly lost her.*

His lips closed over hers. His blood smeared her, but he didn't care. That bastard had tried to take her away. When Kyle or Vance or who-the-hell-ever he was had gone across that table after her...

My heart stopped.

The killer had played him well. He'd been trapped, helpless to fight back, and he'd known what was coming for him.

Then *she'd* come for him. Gotten him free. Saved his ass.

And killed the serial.

His fingers tightened in her hair. She was real. She was alive. He could feel her heart pounding, racing just like his.

Safe.

Never letting go.

"Ah...Agent Dante..."

His lips pressed harder on hers.

"*Dante...*"

Hyde's voice. Probably should care that his boss saw him devouring her mouth, but he didn't give a damn.

Monica was alive. He was alive—and this was just the beginning for them.

"You have to let the EMTs look at you—both of you."

Luke pulled away from her. *Monica was hurt.*

Kyle had punched her hard, and her jaw was already swollen, darkening to match the bruises on her face and forehead.

"Do I look as bad as you?" she asked him quietly, and it took him a minute to realize the woman was joking.

"Baby, you look beautiful." To him, she always did.

"Oh, Christ," Kenton muttered from somewhere behind them. "He must have head trauma. *EMTs!*"

But Monica smiled at him.

The EMTs swarmed. "Blood loss...close the wounds...possible concussion..."

They pushed between him and Monica. Her smile dimmed and she slipped back.

He grabbed her hand. His hands were wet with blood. Didn't matter. He caught her fingers. He knew he'd never really know—not completely—what those dark times with Romeo had been like for her.

Romeo let me watch.

Had the sick fuck made her watch him hurt those women? Or had she just been playing a dangerous mind game with Kyle? A game that had worked. She'd gotten free and killed the asshole.

Either way, it wouldn't change things for him. They'd deal with her past and his, and they'd face the future.

"Stay with me," he whispered.

And she nodded.

Monica's fingers twined with Luke's as they carried him out on the stretcher. The blinding sunlight hit her first. So bright.

She'd gone into darkness before. When Hyde had come for her years before, it had been so dark.

The swirling ambulance lights were there just like before, cutting through the trees with red and yellow lights.

Deputies, so many men and women she'd never seen. Probably called in from other counties. Swarming around, racing to secure the scene.

Just like before.

And the stares...those were like before, too. The wide eyes when they saw her. The mouths that parted in surprise.

Luke's fingers tightened around hers.

Not alone. Saved someone this time.

The EMTs shoved Luke into the ambulance. His fingers broke free from hers.

She glanced back.

That place—so like the prison she'd known.

But it was just an old cabin. So small, really.

Hyde stepped outside and watched her with his hands on his hips.

There would be questions. There always were. The scene had to be secured. Reports needed to be written.

And the news crews—the vultures would be swarming soon.

"Monica?" Luke's voice.

She nodded to Hyde, then climbed into the ambulance.

"Ma'am, you should lay down. We need to check your head, your pupil response is—"

She ignored the EMT and ran her fingers down the side of Luke's face. "You sure you can handle me?" Because she knew the darkness inside her would never go away. She'd been marked too young. She'd carry that mark to the grave.

But Luke was different. *Trying to save the world.* Because of his mother. It made sense now.

She hadn't been the only one to keep secrets.

Maybe that had been part of her attraction. Luke was a hero, wanting to help, to protect.

Had he sensed what she was inside? *Lost and alone.*

His lips curved. "I'm sure."

And so was she.

"You're not getting rid of me," he told her. "Not again."

Good. Because if she lost Luke, it would tear her world apart.

The driver slammed the back doors of the ambulance. One, then the other. She leaned in close to him, remembered the smell of death and the demons from the past.

No, no more fear.

"I love you, Luke Dante," she whispered, and the sirens wailed as the ambulance lurched forward.

Hyde watched the ambulance pull away. Another EMT crew was busy hauling out Lee Pope. The deputy was coming around again, talking fast, slurring as he said, "V-Vance hit me.... H-he ... came at me ... I-I don't..."

Understand.

No, he wouldn't.

"It's okay, Lee. Everything's going to be fine." A female deputy, a small woman with tears trickling down her cheeks, hurried by his stretcher.

"Mel... what—wh-why?" The deputy's voice seemed lost.

Hyde would have to talk with Monica. He'd get her full report and find out just what the hell had gone down here.

But right now, the facts were simple. Their killer was dead. Monica had said Vance Monroe was the serial, and he believed her.

The whys—he'd deal with all of them later.

Right now, he had a scene to secure.

Sheriff Davis came out shaking his head, rubbing his eyes. Hyde's mouth tightened. "It's over, Hank."

Hank blinked and raised his chin. "H-he was the one... who told me to contact you...."

Hyde's gaze narrowed.

"After... after the second body... he said he'd read about a department in the FBI... hunted killers." He swallowed. "He mentioned your name, I—it clicked for me.... I called you."

A set-up.

The guy had probably been tracking his team for months. Studying them all and digging into their pasts. No wonder he'd been so prepared for Sam. He'd probably known what she feared long before the team came down South.

Going head to head with his agents must have been the ultimate challenge for the Watchman.

One he'd lost.

"It's over," he told Hank again. "Tell your people that their county's safe again." It would be a hard sell. Folks would feel betrayed, afraid, especially when they found out a deputy had been doing the killing.

But they'd heal. The thing about people—they always healed.

Maybe not perfectly. The scars stayed, sometimes deep inside, where you couldn't see them, but the wounds *healed*.

Monica had taught him that.

He strode inside the cabin. Crime scene techs were already there, snapping pictures of the body. Dusting for prints. Searching for DNA and every scrap of evidence they could find.

In death, Vance Monroe aka Kyle West didn't look so fierce. But then, he'd never looked particularly fierce to Hyde. Sometimes, killers could hide behind the simplest of disguises.

Like a smiling face.

Or a badge.

"Hyde, did you see this?" Kenton demanded.

Hyde glanced over his shoulder. The agent stood next to an open door. A closet. Barely big enough for a person to stand in.

"The inside of the door knob was removed, but it—it looks like someone punched through the wood that was put there."

Monica's knuckles had been bloody. Hyde smiled. "He made a mistake."

The scene had been set so well. An almost perfect match for Monica's nightmares.

A whistle from his right. "Stab wound straight to the

heart," Gerry the tech said. "Someone wasn't playing around."

No, Monica didn't play, and that had been the killer's mistake. He'd thought Monica would play his way.

But the minute he'd taken Monica, it hadn't been Kyle's game any longer.

It had been hers.

CHAPTER *Nineteen*

M onica kept her voice calm and steady as she finished recounting her version of the events that had culminated in the death of serial killer Kyle West. "After Lee Pope distracted the perpetrator," *and got his head smashed in for his efforts*, "I managed to free Agent Dante. There wasn't much time." She turned her head, barely feeling the ache in her jaw now.

It had been twenty-four hours since she'd walked out of that little cabin in the woods, but she could still see Kyle's eyes, wide open, staring at Hell. "Agent Dante punched West when he attacked again and managed to get the cuff keys away from him." A fast move that still impressed her.

"I unlocked my cuffs, managed to get the knife West had dropped, and when he came at me I had no choice but to use deadly force to defend myself and to secure the scene."

No choice.

Really?

Monica shoved the taunting voice to the back of her mind. "West planned to kill Agent Dante in front of me. I would have become his next victim, and then—"

Hyde stared at her with unblinking black eyes. "And then?"

"He would have staged the scene to make it look like Deputy Lee Pope had killed us, then eaten his own gun. I suspect West would have 'discovered' the scene the next day and taken credit for wrapping up the case."

The video equipment was recording her every word and expression, so Monica made sure she kept her face blank. Luke waited in the next room. He'd already done his interview. He'd taken his seat, recounted his capture and attack, all while covered in bandages, with stitches pulling at his flesh.

"Agent Davenport," Hyde crossed his arms and studied her. "In your professional opinion, why do you believe Kyle West killed all of those people?"

She waited a beat. "From what he told us in that cabin, his mother physically abused him as a child. He killed her when he was only eleven. An action like that, from someone at such a young age, suggests intense psychological trauma. He said she was trying to kill him—so he killed her." Monica swallowed and exhaled carefully.

"Kyle West was a very organized killer. He planned his crimes out in exacting detail." And he'd timed the kills so well: When he'd taken Sam from the airport he'd drugged her, left her tied up and unconscious in the cabin, then popped in for an appearance at the police station.

Ballsy.

Monica knew he'd gotten off on that.

Hyde glanced down at his notes, then back at her. "It

appears he specifically targeted members of the SSD. *Why?*"

This had been all she could think about since leaving the hospital. One answer came back to her, one answer based on Kyle's own words. *If it hadn't been for Romeo, I never would have found you. But he told me—he told me you'd be the perfect prey.*

Bastard. She forced her fingers to stay loose on the chair. "I believe Kyle West was in contact with the killer known as Romeo." Had to be. *Still trying to hurt me.* "I believe Romeo manipulated him and sent West on a hunt against the SSD." No, a hunt against *me*.

Now Hyde blinked. "How the hell did that bastard know about us?"

"The SSD has been making headlines recently, and when Romeo saw your name..." the name of the man who'd taken him down, "I believe he saw his opportunity for revenge." If there'd been a picture in the paper, maybe a shot of her and Hyde, he would have known her instantly.

"I plan to travel to Angola Prison to interview Romeo and confirm the suspicions that I have."

"The fuck you are." Hyde's hands slammed down on the table. "Session's over! Stop the recording—and get the hell out!"

The technician scrambled.

Monica raised her brows and stared back at Hyde.

"You're not getting near him, you understand? That piece of shit isn't going to touch you again, you're not—"

She reached for his hand. Curled her fingers over his. Tough Hyde. Hard as nails.

The closest thing to a father she'd ever had.

"He can't hurt me anymore." She was quiet.

Hyde's fingers shook.

"He's nothing now." She wouldn't fear him, not ever again. "It's time I put the past to rest."

"You don't need to see him. You don't have to go there."

"Yes, I do." Because she had to face the monster in the dark. "I want to move on. I don't want to be his prisoner anymore."

The door opened. Luke stepped inside. "Monica? What's going on? You okay?"

She gave a slow nod. "I'm fine."

"*He's* going with you." An order from Hyde.

Luke tensed. "Going where? You already working another case? You need to—"

"It's an old case," she told him. "One that I should have closed a long time ago." And she did want Luke with her.

Always.

"Davenport's got it in her head that she needs to talk with Romeo. So she can—clear up your 'suspicions' about Kyle West."

"Fuck *no*." Luke kicked the door closed behind him.

Ah, the protector. There he was again.

Not that she needed protecting.

But still, it was nice that he cared.

That Hyde cared.

She wasn't alone. Why hadn't she realized that sooner? "I'm seeing Romeo."

"*I'll* see him," Luke said, his voice dark. "It'll be my damn pleasure—"

She shook her head. "I'll be the one to talk to him." She knew he wouldn't talk to anyone else.

A muscle flexed along Luke's clenched jaw and he gritted, "Then I'll be right by your side."

She liked that idea. Monica inclined her head toward Hyde. "Guess I'll see you back in D.C."

"Count on it, Davenport." Fury there, and fear.

Not that Hyde would ever admit either, not to her. "Luke, can you, ah, give us just a minute?"

Luke's gaze darted between them, but then he eased from the room and shut the door.

"Is this going to be a problem?" she asked Hyde bluntly.

His brows shot up. "You going to see a convicted killer who would like nothing more than to screw with your mind? Hey, how could that be a problem?"

"I meant me and Luke."

He exhaled, and she knew his control was returning. *Control.* Hyde had taught her all about control and how to take it back. "You can't work in the field with him anymore, not if the two of you are going to stay together." A pause. "Are you...staying together?"

She hoped so. She wanted to be with him. "Yes." Even if being with him cost her the job. Because there were some things more important than the job.

"You and me—we've bent or broken so many rules." His teeth flashed in that tiger smile. "They didn't want you at Quantico."

She remembered. Because of her past. But Hyde had helped her.

The name change had been his idea, to give her a new start. And she'd been glad for it. Mary Jane had been through enough. She'd deserved some peace.

Monica—she deserved a future.

"You passed all those tests on your own," he said, and the faint lines around his eyes tightened just a bit. "I knew you would."

"Hyde…" She hadn't been so sure of herself.

"You've walked a thin line." He rubbed the bridge of his nose. The air conditioner clicked on above them, and a soft hum filled the room. "I worried about you.…"

His words echoed her own thoughts and had her tensing.

"Sometimes, when you go so deep into a killer's mind, it's not easy to come back out."

Monica swallowed. "I came back out." Maybe she wasn't perfect, and she knew, with brutal honesty, that she never would be. But she wasn't a cold-blooded killer.

"Yes, you did." He stood, shoving back his chair with a groan of sound. "Did I ever tell you that I used to go to Quantico to observe you?"

"What?" She rose, too, slowly. The chair rolled behind her.

"I took a risk, pushing you through the program. There were folks out there just waiting for you to crack."

She hadn't cracked.

"So I'd check in on you, every now and then. To see how you were handling the pressure."

Just fine. Or not.

"Sometimes, when I'd see you, you seemed so alone." The words were gruff. Hesitant. Hyde wasn't the hesitant kind.

Monica didn't know what to say. She cleared her throat. "I've never been big on socializing." Friendships had made her nervous.

"No." His lips rose just a bit. "But I saw you one

night... at some dive... your group was having drinks. I saw you—and Dante."

"But you never said—"

"You looked different with him. Your eyes." His hand lifted, then fell. "Not so cold."

Her breath choked out as she realized just what he'd done. "You set me up."

"You think I saved you, don't you?" he asked, confusing her. Because, yes, he'd saved her. If he hadn't come in, she would have died in that cabin. It had only been a matter of time.

"I know you did," she whispered.

"I'd been arriving too late for so long." He shook his head. "I didn't know what it was to hope anymore." He turned away from her and strolled to the door. "Be happy, Monica. I think it's finally time for you to just be happy."

Her heart squeezed. "Thank you, Keith."

He glanced over his shoulder. "Right back at you."

Her lips curved, and she had to blink, fast, because Hyde didn't like tears.

"Watch your ass with Romeo, got me? I don't want him getting any kind of hold on you again."

"He won't." Because she wasn't afraid. Not of the Watchman. Not of Romeo.

It was time Romeo started to fear her.

She came to him. After the press conferences and the newscasts, she came to him.

Her knock on his door had been so soft, but he'd known it was her.

Now she stood before him on the threshold of his room, and Luke could only stare at her.

Monica. She was so damn gorgeous she took his breath away. She'd used makeup to hide her bruises for the camera and her lips were slick with gloss, her eyes even more blue with dark shadow.

"Luke...I—" She took a deep breath. "I don't want to be away from you anymore."

He opened his arms. She stepped toward him. Pressed her body against his and *fit*.

She'd always fit.

He had stitches in both arms. His shoulder had been patched. He had bruises and cuts all over his body, and he looked like a freaking Frankenstein.

He didn't care. Neither did she.

Monica stripped him. Carefully, slowly. Her fingers fluttered over his wounds, and her lips pressed against the darkness of his bruises.

This time he knew it would be different. He let her lead him. Right then, he would have followed her anywhere.

She slipped off her dress, the dress that had driven him crazy during the press conference. A slinky little black number that had hugged her hips, cupped her breasts, and made his body ache.

When the dress fell, he swallowed when he saw the black panties and matching black bra. Small scraps of lace. She walked before him, her hips rolling, and his cock swelled even more.

"Lay down." Her sensual order. "I'll be careful. I won't hurt you."

He'd be damned if he ever hurt her.

The bed squeaked beneath him. He stretched out, unable to take his eyes off her. *What sane man would?*

Her fingers hooked under the edge of her panties. She pushed the lace down. Stepped out of her strappy shoes.

Ah, he liked those. Sexy. She could have kept those on while they—

She climbed onto the bed. Crawled over him.

So. Fucking. Sexy.

Her mouth found his, and she kissed him. Her tongue pushed inside his mouth, tasted him, licked, stroked. Then she eased back and sucked his tongue.

Luke's heels dug into the mattress. Her hand slid between their bodies. Found his cock. Ready and thick. Heavy with need. Desperate to thrust deep and hard into her.

She pumped him, worked him over and over with her tight fist and he groaned. *Fuck, no.* "I want…*in you.*" But he had to make her ready. He'd stroke her first. Find her clit. Caress that soft nub until she moaned against him and pushed her hips against his hand. He'd take her breast into his mouth. Suck her nipples. Hear her breath catch.

Monica shifted, widening her legs, straddling him, and the folds of her sex brushed over his cock.

"No, wait—"

She arched up and pushed down on him.

Luke's back teeth clenched. Ready. Wet. Tight. Hot. So good.

He tried to grab her, to slow her down. Luke didn't want to hurt her shoulder—

"No. Don't move your arms." She shook her head. Her dark locks fell around her face. "I *need* this. Let me."

He was already gone. She could do anything she wanted. As long…*ah, damn.*

Her hips rose, fell. Her sex clenched around him.

He slid his fingers between their bodies. Pressed against her clit. Plucked. Stroked.

She started to move faster.

He thrust harder. Deeper. *Inside. As deep as I can go.*

She rose onto her knees and arched down. The black lace hugged her breasts, but he could see the shadow of her nipples, stabbing out. Such pretty breasts…

Heat flushed her skin, face, chest. Her breath panted out. So did his.

The climax was coming. Her sex milked him, stroking every inch of his cock and driving him out of his *mind*.

He thrust his cock into her. Slammed balls-deep. She took him. Took everything.

Faster.

Deeper.

Harder.

Her sex convulsed around him, contracting hard, squeezing so tight. *Jesus!*

She stared right at him, her eyes blue and blind with pleasure, and she whispered, "I love you."

He exploded. Pleasure, so intense it stole his breath.

Just like she'd stolen his heart.

No light spilled from the bathroom. There was no gun under her pillow. Or his. Just the two of them, touching on the bed.

"I'm sorry about your mother," she told him, her voice husky in the darkness.

He turned toward her, feeling the pull of his stitches. He hadn't felt a thing before. "It was a long time ago." Easy words. Words most people would expect.

But he wouldn't just give her those words. He'd

tell Monica everything. "The man who killed her... he was a serial. No one knew. He'd killed three women in Texas, then one in Arkansas. He was killing them when he was with my mom. Then he killed her." She'd been so beautiful. Tall and blond, with a slow smile that he loved. She'd read him stories at night. Always tucked him in.

And she'd died right in front of him.

"My grandfather raised me. My dad was in the military. When mom died, I don't even know where he was. But my grandfather taught me how to live. How to be strong." Grandpop had helped him to channel the rage. *"Focus son, stop the ones who need stopping. Make a difference."*

He'd tried. Was still trying.

Monica's fingertips traced over his chest. "You *are* strong."

He caught her fingers, pressed them against his chest. "Did you mean it?"

A soft laugh. One he hadn't heard enough. One that sent a quiver straight to his groin and had his cock twitching. *Like once was ever enough with her.* "Yes, Luke, I think you're—"

"No." He wanted the light then so he could see her eyes. "Do you love me?" If she didn't, they'd work on that. He could give her time. He would give her anything.

Her lips feathered over his jaw. "Dante, you're the only man I've ever loved. The only one I ever will."

His heart slammed into his chest. She had to feel the desperate lurch. "Took you long enough to admit it."

That light laugh again, rubbing over his flesh. "I guess I was scared. But you know what? I'm not afraid now."

Her lips took his, and she kissed him. Deep and long and sweet.

He held her as tight as he could and knew that he'd never be letting Monica Davenport go.

Finally, he had her right where he wanted her. In his arms. In his bed.

In his heart.

When Dennis Myers was led through the heavy metal doors, Monica locked her gaze with his. He wore a bright orange prison uniform, one that made his skin appear too pale, almost stark white. His hair had receded on top and thinned out on the sides. He was too skinny, almost skeletal.

Shackles were around his wrists, linked with a thin chain to those bonds on his ankles. He shuffled toward her and a smile split his face, flashing the dimples that time hadn't changed. "My girl finally came to see me."

And Romeo sat down in front of her.

His blue eyes were bloodshot, and his perfect nose was twisted, probably broken from fights in prison.

He hadn't fared so well at Angola.

She smiled back at him. "Hello, Dennis."

His grin dimmed a bit. He'd always made her call him Romeo.

But he wasn't a Romeo anymore. He was just a man, older, thinner, trapped behind bars—where he'd stay forever.

"I knew you'd come to see me." His gaze slid over her. "Knew you couldn't stay away."

A chair screeched as Luke hauled it closer to the table.

Dennis's gaze jerked to him. "Who the hell are you?"

She caught the flash of teeth Luke bared at him. "The man who'd love to rip you apart."

Dennis shrank back against the chair a bit. "Guards, you hear that? He's threatening me. I want him out of here. I want him—"

Monica slammed her palms down on the table.

Dennis blinked.

"You're not calling the shots anymore." Her gaze bored into him. She waited a beat, then leaned toward him. She caught the heavy scent of his sweat. "You don't seem surprised I'm still alive."

His eyes narrowed to slits, and he inched forward. "Because you're mine," he whispered. "I knew he wouldn't be able to hurt you. I trained you. I *made* you."

Her stomach clenched. "But you sent Kyle after me anyway, didn't you?"

His gaze slid to Luke. Back to her. "Guess he'll be joining me, huh?"

"No. Kyle West is dead."

His nails dug into the table. "You killed him?" A laugh. "I knew, *I knew* it was in you. You wanted a taste of your own, didn't you? To see what the power was like." His head came even closer, like a snake coming for his prey. "How many? Huh? How many have you had?"

How many kills.

Monica shook her head. "I'm not like you." Simple, and all there was for her to say. "And I'm not like Kyle."

"Kyle was weak! A wanna-be! He thought he could be like me, but I had to tell him *everything!* How to build the fear, how to find the prey. He wouldn't have been able to start over as a damn deputy if I hadn't told him how to off that other bastard!"

Ah, now here we go. Romeo had always liked to talk. Made him feel important. Powerful. *Had to share his crimes.* He couldn't stand it if no one knew just how great he was.

"I had to hand feed him every damn bit of information. *He* didn't know anything. I'm the one who told him about the precious SSD, about that prick Hyde and—"

And now she had everything she needed. "That's all." She nodded to the guards. "You can take him back now." Really, he'd been so smart once. Always staying a step ahead of the cops. Maybe prison had broken his mind as well as his body.

But then, his mind had always been broken. Twisted beyond repair.

He shook his head, and his jaw dropped. "Wh-what? You're not leaving me!" He surged to his feet. Lunged forward. "I've waited for you. You're not—"

Luke punched him in the face. Bones crushed. Blood gushed from Dennis's nose.

And down he went, slamming his chin on the table.

"You boys had better move to secure him faster next time," Luke snapped to the guards.

Monica stared at the killer. He was swearing, screaming and spitting. Not the poised lover who'd lured the girls. A criminal who was lost without power over his prey.

The guards hoisted him back to his feet.

"I'll sue your ass!" he yelled at Luke. "You can't—"

"You tried to attack me." Monica shrugged and kept her voice ice cold. "You're just lucky he didn't use lethal force."

That shut him up.

"There are some things you should know, Dennis." She picked up her bag and strolled toward the door. Luke followed right behind her. She paused, then glanced back at the man who'd tried to break her. "There will be no more visitors, unless it's your attorney. Your *real* attorney who will be verified by three ID checks before he's allowed inside the premises." No more women who wanted to screw a killer. No more wanna-bes lapping up his every word.

"M-my what? Bitch, you can't—"

"I can." She gave him another smile. *Darkness. Screams. Blood.* It was all ending now.

"You've just confessed to helping Kyle West plan the abduction and attempted murders of two federal agents," Monica said. "You also colluded to help him kill a sheriff's deputy." *The real Vance Monroe.* She gave a careless shrug of her shoulders.

"That changes your game in here. You're heading for solitary, and if the DA thinks he can get a murder charge to stick on you—" One more nail in his fucking coffin— "then maybe this time, you'll get death."

He fought against the guards' hold. "*Bitch! I should have killed you! Fucking cut you apart—*"

She kept her eyes on him. "But if you'd killed me, then you would have been alone all that time, right, Dennis? No one to pay any attention to you. No one to see just what twisted hell you were wreaking."

His body trembled.

She smiled. "Guess what? You're going to be alone until you die, Dennis. All alone. Twenty-four hours a day. Just you and your cell. No, wait, you'll get out…" Her eyes flickered to the guards. "To walk, if they let you, once a day. Maybe twice if you're a real *good boy*."

He shook his head. "No, no, I won't fucking do this! You can't—"

"And if you have another trial, I don't think the judge will sentence you to more prison time. I mean, what would be the point? You'll just get death this time."

Veins bulged in his neck and on his forehead. Had he really once been handsome? Used that face to lure his victims?

"The DA will go after you only if he can get your death." She smiled, fully now. "Good-bye, Dennis."

"No, no, Mary Jane, don't leave me! You have to—"

"You'll be alone until you die," she said again because she knew the words would twist in his gut. Monica rapped on the door so the guard outside would open it for her. The door opened. She walked over the threshold with Luke at her back.

"You think you know her, Dante?" Dennis shrieked. "You think because you *fuck her* that you know her?"

She wouldn't glance back. One more door to open, and she'd be free.

"She's just like me! You hear me? Just like me! Twisted, dark and—"

"Fuck off, asshole," Luke growled and the second door opened.

Freedom.

The door closed behind her, clanging loudly, echoing, but not loudly enough to block out the sound of the killer's screams.

Dennis had always enjoyed the screams.

Monica and Luke turned in their passes. Got their weapons back. Left the prison, and walked into the light.

Blinding sunlight.

So bright it hurt.

The light could do that sometimes.

"You okay?" Luke asked her quietly.

She glanced back at the dark walls of the prison. "I'm just fine." Her hands were shaking, her knees trembling, and she thought she might vomit.

But she was outside, safe, and that bastard would die in his cell. "I'm just fine," she said again.

Luke caught her hand and brought her palm to his lips. His mouth feathered over her skin as he kissed her knuckles. "I love you."

He knew her every secret. Knew the darkness inside. And he still stood by her.

"Do you...have any doubts?" *About me*?

"Not a damn one," he said instantly.

No way would she ever lose him. Monica swallowed. "I love you, Luke." Saying it seemed so easy now. The weight of her past was gone. She'd left it in that prison with Dennis. She could be free now. She could have a life. With Luke. "You're mine, Dante." She swallowed and tried to smile. "Don't ever forget it."

"Baby, I've known it for years."

Epilogue

The call came in to the SSD two days later. Hyde listened to the voice on the line, then said, "You sure?" But he knew the warden wouldn't make a mistake, not like this.

"Dennis Myers died last night."

"How?" Because Hyde had to know how Romeo went down.

"He attacked a guard while he was on his walk out of solitary." The warden's voice sounded tired. Working Angola, that figured. "He'd never attacked a guard before." Because his prey had been girls. Weaker. So much easier to hurt.

"He got a shiv," the warden continued. "We think someone passed it to him along the cell walk, and he went after a guard named Regan Lyle. Lyle fought back, shoved Dennis against a cell door. His neck broke on impact."

A quick end. Not nearly as painful as he deserved. "Thanks, man. Appreciate the call." He hung up the phone, aware that the warden had done him a favor by calling so quickly.

Hyde turned his chair so that he could stare out the window. Myers had taken the easy way out.

Death by cop. Or, this time, by prison guard.

Hyde knew what had happened to the killer.

He'd seen Monica, and he'd snapped. Because the bastard had realized he didn't have power over her any longer.

No one would mourn for Dennis Myers, but some folks might just throw a party. The story would hit the news soon. He should tell Monica first.

He stared into that darkness just a little longer.

The Romeo Killer.

"*Playing the tough guy, Hyde?*" That taunting voice had echoed through his mind for so many years.

"*She's mine!*"

You didn't forget evil.

But you could bury it.

His gaze turned back to the desk, to the files that waited for him. So many cases.

A photo stared back up at him, a black-and-white image of a building engulfed in flames.

Some serials liked to touch their prey. They liked to use knives to make the kills intimate. Romeo had always liked to get that close, as close as a lover.

But others... some others wanted to light up the night with their crimes.

Hyde took a deep breath, and he reached for the phone.

One ring. Two. Then Monica's voice, soft but clear when she said, "Agent Davenport."

So different from the broken voice that had once haunted his dreams. *I-I'm not Katherine.*

Hyde cleared his throat. "Monica. I've got some news for you."

The monster was dead. The team was safe.

One more serial down.

His gaze lingered on that deadly fire.

The damn rest of them to go.

Lora Spade isn't interested in getting involved with anyone. But Kenton Lake isn't the kind of man who walks away from something—or someone—he wants.

———

Please turn this page for a preview of

Deadly Heat

Available in February 2011.

CHAPTER *One*

Running into a burning building probably wasn't the smartest move Kenton Lake had ever made. Then again, sadly, it wasn't his dumbest, either.

Kenton choked in a deep breath of air, already tasting the smoke, and then lifted his arm over his mouth. *Some jobs just sucked.* He went into the wall of smoke. *Ah, hell.*

His nostrils burned and heat scored his flesh but he heard the voice calling—the same voice that had lured him to the building, across the street, and into this inferno.

"H-help! Dammit—h-help me!"

His informer. Upstairs in the middle of the flames and fury.

Kenton yanked off his jacket, covered his mouth, and tried to stay as low to the floor as he could. His eyes burned and the fire and ash singed his nostrils. How the hell had this happened? He was investigating arson but he wasn't supposed to get drawn into the fire.

Part of the ceiling fell behind him.

Kenton glared up at the long row of stairs. Ten-to-one odds they'd fall away before he got to the top.

"H-help…" Weaker. He took the stairs. One. Two. Three.

And, yep, they gave way just as he reached stair number four. Kenton went down hard. The broken wood bit into his arms and legs, and the fire flew toward him.

A blast of water shot out, slamming into the flames, and someone grabbed him, yanking him up with a hand locked tight around his arm.

Kenton found himself staring right at a firefighter. He caught a smoky glimpse of narrowed eyes behind a clear shield, a thick, black helmet, a dark mask, and brown uniform—

The firefighter shoved him, obviously trying to send him toward the front of the building.

Hell, no.

More firefighters swarmed around him, battling the fire. Some struck out with axes, and some scrambled into the rooms.

Couldn't they hear the voice calling for help?

He tried to break free and jump for those stairs. There was a gap so he might make it, he might—

The firefighter who'd grabbed him before snatched him right back and gave a hard negative shake of his black helmet.

Screw that, he wasn't leaving a victim behind.

He wrenched away.

Then the firefighter slugged him. Hard. Right in his jaw. Kenton went down.

The firefighter's arms wrapped around him. Another grabbed him. Then another.

And they dragged him out of the flames.

"Idiot!"

Kenton looked up, his gaze narrowed against the smoke that still burned his eyes, and saw the firefighter—the jerk who'd slugged him—pull off his helmet and mask—

Her helmet and mask. Not a man there. No way.

Kenton swallowed and choked a bit.

He could make out her eyes better now that there wasn't a giant cloud of smoke in front of them. Gorgeous, shimmering gold, so clear and deep and—

He lowered his oxygen mask aside and leapt to his feet. "You left a man in there!"

Those golden eyes widened. Very slowly, she lifted her right hand—a fragile-looking hand that had packed a whole lot of punch—and pointed to the left where a fire-truck ladder was being lowered from the building. An older man with stooped shoulders and a soot-stained face was on the ladder. A firefighter had him in a tight grip, and the guy appeared to be coughing up a lung.

"Got him," she said sweetly, her voice a slow southern drawl that reminded him of a teammate at the Bureau.

His gaze snapped back to her, and Kenton looked now, really *looked* at her. Short blond hair, wet from sweat and the heat, molded to her head. Her face was all strong angles with a sharp, pointed chin. Wide, golden eyes. Cat eyes. Not classically pretty. Not really.

But with those full lips, those sharp-enough-to-cut-me

cheekbones and, *damn*, those eyes—sexy. *Definitely sexy.*

Her hands were on her hips now. He couldn't tell a thing about the shape of her body, not in that bulky uniform, but she was tall, just a few inches shy of his own six-foot-three.

Probably long and lean, but he usually liked them a bit softer around the edges and—

"Wanna tell me why you've got a death wish, GQ?"

GQ? He glanced down at his ruined suit. So she was funny. Or wanted to be. "I heard…" Kenton coughed and had to pause to clear his throat and breathe. "I heard…him calling for help." He wouldn't tell her the guy was his informant, not yet. That'd be on a need-to-know basis. Bedroom Eyes didn't need to know that yet.

Her eyes were impressive. They were so big that he was surprised that she'd gotten them to go so mean and small so fast.

"Firefighters fight the flames," she said. Ice could have dripped from her drawl. "Not businessmen with a hero complex."

He rubbed his jaw. It hurt but so did his ego. "You always punch out your victims? That part of *your* complex?"

She shook her head. "I only punch when the guys are dumb enough to fight help when it comes."

Ah, now that was the second time she'd insulted his intelligence. He reached into his back pocket and yanked out his wallet. The leather stuck a bit when he tried to open it, and he shoved his ID toward her. "FBI, sweetheart. I think I know how to handle a dangerous situation."

She didn't even glance down. "I think that's debatable."

A snicker came from behind him. Great. An audience. He'd forgotten all about the EMTs.

His sexy savior—with the serious attitude—turned away. "Get him checked out, Harry," she called out and marched away.

That was it?

His gaze dropped. He couldn't help it. Even in that thick garb, she had a nice sway.

"You—you assaulted an officer!" was all he could think of to say. She was heading for his informant and leaving him in her dust.

He didn't want her to go. Not yet.

Her name was on the lower back of her uniform, spelled out in big, reflective letters: L. SPADE.

She threw a vulgar gesture over her shoulder but didn't stop walking. Well, well…He didn't fight the smile that lifted his lips.

"Dude, you better stop while you're ahead," suggested the EMT. What had she called him? Harvey? Harry?

Kenton tossed the oxygen mask at him. Spade was too close to his informant. No way was she getting first crack at him. The guy was *his.*

"Hey—wait!" the EMT shouted. "You need to go to the ER, you can't just—"

Ignoring him, Kenton shoved his way through the crowd. There were gawkers lined up across the street watching the fire begin to sputter. Smoke drifted lazily into the night air, sirens wailed, and general chaos seemed to surround him.

The informant had reached the ground, and the paramedics immediately swarmed him.

"We need him taken to Langley General, stat!" Spade's voice. "Sir, sir—you're gonna be all right! You hear me? You're safe!"

The guy coughed, shuddered, and seemed to collapse in on himself. But then he broke free of the paramedics and ran right at L. Spade.

"*Sir!*"

Was she going to punch him, too?

No, a coughing fit took the man down. Then there was a pile of bodies as the paramedics got to work. When the guy appeared again, he was strapped to a gurney, twitching, shouting, and spitting.

"You're welcome." Spade sighed, running a hand through her short hair. "Must be the night for assholes," she muttered.

Kenton came up close beside her. "Guess it must be."

Her head turned toward him. Those amazing golden eyes narrowed. Huh. Kinda like fire.

But Kenton's informant was getting away. An EMT shoved the screaming man into the back of the ambulance. Great. He already knew the guy was a runner. If the fellow made it to the hospital, he'd vanish long before emergency personnel got hold of him.

"You are so full of crap." Ah, this from the sweet-tongued L. Spade.

He blinked at her. "Sorry, I'm suddenly feeling...a little woozy." He rubbed his jaw. "Could be from the blow I took. I think, I—I think I need to get to the hospital." Kenton took a step away from her, his eyes already on the ambulance.

She touched his arm. He felt the heat of that touch

right through the sleeve of his dress shirt. "What's your name, GQ?"

"Kenton. *Special Agent* Kenton Lake." So she'd noticed the connection, too, that hot zip of—

"Thanks. I needed your name because I'll be reporting your actions to your boss at the Bureau."

What? She was reporting him? She was the one who should be—

A siren screamed on. "Talk to you later, sweetheart." He broke into a run. *No, don't shut that door—* "Wait! I'm coming with you." Kenton yanked out his mangled ID again, waved it at the EMT, then jumped inside.

As the door slammed shut behind him, Kenton tossed a hard grin at the man he suspected to be Louis Jerome, informer extraordinaire. "You didn't think I'd miss our meeting, did you?"

That stopped the screaming.

"Uh, sir, you need to sit back—"

Kenton shook his head, hard, and the EMT quieted.

"Tell me what's going on, Jerome," Kenton said. "Tell me what's happening with these fires, tell me why you called—"

"N-Name's...not...Jerome." Hoarse, either from the fire or the screaming. "Larry. Larry...Powell. Don't know...who the...hell you are."

Kenton's body tensed. The words didn't sound like a lie. Those eyes didn't *look* like the guy was lying, either. And Kenton was good at finding the lies. It was a special talent he had.

Kenton reached for his phone but his pocket was empty. He must have dropped it during the fall. Dammit. He needed to run a check on this guy Larry Powell.

Because if this wasn't his informant...
Then *where's Jerome?*

He liked to watch the fire. When it danced, it was the most beautiful thing he'd ever seen. Sensual, like a lover.

The firefighters had battled his blaze with all their strength. But in the end, the fire had won—and claimed her prize.

And to make things interesting, he'd even gotten a bonus during the show. Two bonuses really. More victims.

Like the fool who'd rushed in. He hadn't counted on that. He'd underestimated the man.

But the guy had been saved. So had the addict.

Not that they mattered. They weren't really part of the game. Well, not yet.

But they'd tasted the fire tonight. They wouldn't soon forget that taste. After all, you never forgot your first.

The smoke was in the wind. When he opened his mouth, he felt it on his tongue.

She came out then. Yanking off her helmet. Pacing back and forth too quickly. *Ah, found my body.*

She understood the game. Perhaps better than anyone else. She knew what he was doing. Did she know why?

Tonight, the firefighters had lost. They hadn't searched hard enough. Hadn't responded fast enough.

The dead...was on their hands. *Her* hands.

More bodies would come. Because when you fought the fire, you learned fast that the fire fought back.

Lora Spade liked to win.

So did he.

THE DISH

Where authors give you the inside scoop!

♥ ♥ ♥ ♥ ♥ ♥ ♥ ♥ ♥ ♥ ♥ ♥ ♥ ♥ ♥ ♥

From the desk of Cynthia Eden

Dear Reader,

I like to be afraid. No, let me qualify that—I like the *thrill* that comes from being afraid, but I also like to know that I am completely 100% safe.

As a teen, I was a horror movie addict. I jumped every time a killer popped out of the darkness on-screen, and I yelled each time the foolish/brave heroine walked into the woods by herself. I loved the rush that came from watching those movies—and that same rush got to me even more intently when I read scary books. (It still gets to me!)

Fear gives you a spike of adrenaline; it makes your heart race, your breath heave; and, for the villain in my new book, DEADLY FEAR—well, *fear* makes his life worth living. The killer in this tale has an intimate connection with fear. He feels truly alive only when he can see and hear the real fear of others. So he sets out to turn his victims' worst fears into reality. Oh, yes, this guy would have scared me as a teen.

But to give him a strong adversary, I created my heroine in the form of Special Agent Monica Daven-port. Unlike the foolish/brave heroines from my past,

Monica keeps her gun close, and she doesn't let fear get to her. Instead, she gets into the killer's mind.

Getting into his mind is, after all, her job. Monica is the lead profiler for the SSD—the Serial Services Division at the FBI. Her job is to track and apprehend serial killers. Fear isn't an option for her.

But it is for me.

To learn more about DEADLY FEAR and to read an excerpt, visit my website: www.cynthiaeden.com.

Happy reading!

Cynthia Eden

♥ ♥ ♥ ♥ ♥ ♥ ♥ ♥ ♥ ♥ ♥ ♥ ♥ ♥ ♥ ♥

From the desk of Dee Davis

Dear Reader,

I read somewhere that "every character believes the story is about him." That really struck a chord with me because I've had characters hijack a book completely. In my first novel, a secondary character had too much to drink and in the course of a conversation revealed the entire plot—in Chapter 3. I took his tankard away, rewrote the scene, and lo and behold—he behaved. In my third novel, a character was supposed to have a one-line walk-on and wound up stealing the show with his dramatic death scene. So experience has taught me to always keep this in mind when I write, and I offer this same advice to any budding writers out there.

As a writer, I love all my characters equally. They're like children born from the murky depths of my imagination. But if I'm being really honest, some characters have a way of digging deeper into your heart. Tyler Hanson is one of those. Unlike some heroes and heroines I've written, who had to be dragged forcefully onto the page and compelled to reveal their secrets, Tyler sprang fully formed onto the computer screen almost from the minute I conceptualized her. She is strong, independent, and fiercely loyal. She isn't afraid of anything—except falling in love. And so I knew I was going to enjoy watching as she struggled with her growing feelings for Owen and, like all of us, the shadows that haunt her past.

One of the wonderful things about writing a series is that when the book ends, it isn't the end of the characters. They get to continue their journeys, albeit on the back burner, in future stories, and happily that means that I get to spend more time with characters like DARK DECEPTIONS's Nash and Annie and DARK DESIRES's Drake and Madeline.

And sometimes—because, after all, it's my world—I get to reintroduce someone from a previous book, someone I really hated saying good-bye to. Enter Harrison Blake. Harrison first appeared in my Last Chance series, and to date, he's gotten more mail than any other character I've ever written. So it's with great pleasure that I called on him to help Owen out in DESPERATE DEEDS. And I've got a feeling we haven't seen the last of him.

For more insight into Tyler and her romance with Owen, here are some songs I listened to while writing DESPERATE DEEDS:

"Blurry"—Puddle of Mudd

"Mad World"—Adam Lambert

"Kissed by a Rose"—Seal

I hope you're enjoying the A-Tac series. For more on the books and me, check out www.deedavis.com.

Happy Reading!

Dee Davis

♥ ♥ ♥ ♥ ♥ ♥ ♥ ♥ ♥ ♥ ♥ ♥ ♥ ♥ ♥ ♥

From the desk of Kira Morgan

Dear Reader,

I've heard that in order to write a good book, you have to take your perfectly nice characters and torture them mercilessly. Well, I'm afraid to tell you that's exactly what I've done to my poor heroine in CAPTURED BY DESIRE.

Florie Gilder is a 16th-century Scottish goldsmith's daughter with a mind of her own, a strong will, and a bright future. So what do I do with her? I confront her with an unfortunate misunderstanding, which deteriorates into a disastrous altercation, followed by a tragic accident that renders her utterly helpless. Worse, I thrust her into the path of Rane McAllister, a charming, assertive lady-killer of a huntsman who is used to getting his way, and then I leave her in his overbearing hands.

All her life, Florie has fought for respectability among her peers in the goldsmith's guild, but with a wicked twist of my pen, I upset her world and drag her down to the level of a common criminal, forcing her to claw her way back up. Knowing Florie prides herself on her independence, I strip that away from her too, leaving her completely reliant on a stranger.

Since Florie hates to be touched, Rane touches her all the time. Because she's accustomed to dining on roast capon, sweetmeats, and fine wine, Rane brings her coarse bread, hard cheese, and rough ale. Florie prefers velvet, and Rane dresses her in wool.

But I don't stop there.

Florie prefers to be alone, so naturally the hero is with her constantly. She doesn't like to be the center of attention, so I make a humiliating spectacle out of her. She's terrified of the enemy English, so they're a constant threat.

Then, when she thinks things can't get any worse, I make Florie, who has sworn on her mother's grave never to fall in love, fall in love.

Of course, I put a few thumbscrews to the hero, too.

Since Rane prefers compliant blondes, I throw him a spunky brunette. I obligate him to take care of Florie when he's supposed to be providing for starving peasants. I force him to choose between his loyalty to his lord and his love for Florie.

And because Rane is pretty much the village stud, I taunt him with women he can't have, all the while dangling the virgin Florie in front of him.

It's a cruel game, I suppose, making my characters suffer so much. But in the end, it really *does* make everyone's "happy ever after" that much happier! After all, what's pleasure without a little pain?

Enjoy!

Kira Morgan

*Want to know more about romances at
Grand Central Publishing and Forever?
Get the scoop online!*

GRAND CENTRAL PUBLISHING'S
ROMANCE HOMEPAGE

Visit us at www.hachettebookgroup.com/romance
for all the latest news, reviews, and chapter excerpts!

NEW AND UPCOMING TITLES

Each month we feature our new titles
and reader favorites.

CONTESTS AND GIVEAWAYS

We give away galleys, autographed copies,
and all kinds of fun stuff.

AUTHOR INFO

You'll find bios, articles, and links to personal
websites for all your favorite authors—and
so much more!

THE BUZZ

Sign up for our monthly romance newsletter,
and be the first to read all about it!

Luke didn't want to face
the monsters alone.
Not when he'd walk through fire
to be by her side.

"You should...go get dressed," she told him, her voice dropping and getting that husky little edge that he'd never been able to forget.

The edge that told him that she needed. Wanted. Lusted.

Just like he did.

The rain had made her shirt all but transparent. They were wet. Close.

Just as hungry for each other as they'd always been.

"You were right about me. Us. I didn't want to remember, but—" Her voice, so soft, froze him. He had to strain to make out the words.

"Remember what?" Because he'd never had a problem remembering what it was like to be with her. To touch her and taste her and see the pleasure wash over her face.

No, that hadn't been a problem. Forgetting, though, had been pure hell...

Please turn this page for
praise for Cynthia Eden...